D0369787

SERENITY

Also by Harry Kraus, M.D.

Stainless Steal Hearts
Fated Genes
Lethal Mercy
The Stain
The Chairman
Could I Have This Dance?

SERENITY

HARRY KRAUS, M.D.

Walnut Hill Community
Church Library
Bethel CT

CROSSWAY BOOKS

A DIVISION OF
GOOD NEWS PUBLISHERS
WHEATON, ILLINOIS

This is a work of imagination. None of the characters found within these pages reflect the character or intentions of any real person. Any similarity is coincidental.

Serenity

Copyright © 2002 by Harry Kraus

Published by Crossway Books
     A division of Good News Publishers
     1300 Crescent Street
     Wheaton, Illinois

All rights reserved. No part of this publication may be reproduced, stored in a retrieval system or transmitted in any form by any means, electronic, mechanical, photocopy, recording or otherwise, without the prior permission of the publisher, except as provided by USA copyright law.

Cover design: David LaPlaca

Cover photo: PictureQuest

First printing, 2002

Printed in the United States of America

Library of Congress Cataloging-in-Publication Data
Kraus, Harry Lee, 1960-
     Serenity / Harry Kraus.
          p. cm.
     ISBN 1-58134-420-1
     1. Impostors and imposture—Fiction. 2. Surgeons—Fiction. I. Title.
PS3561.R2875 S47   2002
813'.54—dc21   2002005985
                                                                       CIP

| 15 | 14 | 13 | 12 | 11 | 10 | 09 | 08 | 07 | 06 | 05 | 04 | 03 | 02 |
| 15 | 14 | 13 | 12 | 11 | 10 | 9 | 8 | 7 | 6 | 5 | 4 | 3 | 2 | 1 |

For all those on the road to serenity who,
like me, tend to forget who they are.
Take a tip from a dusty fellow-traveler:
Understanding your true identity
will shorten the journey,
quicken your steps,
and lighten your load.
Here's to the adventure!

CHAPTER
1

No one in Serenity, North Carolina, knew Adam Tyson was dead. So no one except Tilly Johnson even raised an eyebrow when he arrived in town that muggy August morning. But Tilly raised an eyebrow at every handsome man that passed her way, especially ones with impeccable dress, tall stature, and M.D. embroidered on the pocket of a long, white coat.

Adam lifted the lapels of his freshly starched coat, hoping he wouldn't arrive completely soaked from his own perspiration. He flapped the coat against the languid air. This was nothing like Southern California. No, the traffic, the wonderful climate, the night life, and the culture of funky trendsetters were a thing of the past, replaced by a single traffic light, a bowling alley, a drugstore the color of Pepto-Bismol, and a population of oystermen who wouldn't know a fashion trend from a stock quote.

He arrived thirty minutes early for his hospital orientation, time enough to acquaint himself with the coastal town. After parking in the doctors' lot, he strolled leisurely to the end of the business district, a ten-minute walk at a relaxed pace. Then he returned to pass by Bob's Exxon and the Serenity Tackle Shop, which boasted of fresh crab and shrimp and smelled of something fishy and less than fresh. There was a bank, a four-lane bowling alley, two souvenir shops, a fruit stand, a hardware store, a drugstore, the Seagull Inn, a white clapboard church with a large adjoining cemetery, and the county hospital, sitting back from the main road right next to the cemetery. *Convenient*, he thought, *if any of my patients die.*

He scolded himself for his pessimism and slowed to peer across the wrought-iron fence at the aging tombstones, monuments to crusty sailors of Serenity's past. He slipped off his white coat and wiped the sweat from his forehead. Grave markers always made him think of funerals, the graveside services that seemed to shape his destiny. He'd watched them lower Adam Tyson into the ground six months ago. It was a somber occasion as hundreds of patients came to bid him farewell, to pay homage to the surgeon's meticulous technique.

The operating room staff stood back, stayed respectfully quiet, and knew better.

Patty Bateman, an OR technician, gripped Andy's elbow as several other physicians took turns with a shovel, each saying good-bye with a scoop of dirt heaved upon the casket. "Closure," she whispered. "Everybody wants closure."

Andy squeezed her hand, now encircling his upper arm.

"Take your turn with the shovel," she prodded. "You're going to need help laying him to rest."

Andy nodded.

"How long were you with him—ten, fifteen years?"

"Eight."

Her eyes scanned the growing line of patients, some with solitary roses, others offering only a handful of the fill dirt they would drop into the fresh grave. "They will never know the truth," she said softly, inches from Andy's ear. "You kept that man out of trouble every day."

He knew she was right. Part of him wanted recognition, to shout the truth to these people who put their trust in a drug-impaired physician. But he knew he would stay quiet and preserve the dead surgeon's reputation. He had done enough damage already. He feigned a smile. "Someone had to do it."

The wail of a siren pierced the humidity and brought him back to the present in Serenity. A moment later a rescue unit passed, the pitch of the siren sliding downward as the green and white ambulance rushed toward the beachfront road. Two boys, looking no older than ten, scampered up the street behind the emergency vehicle. "Riptides," one panted. "I saw the red flags out this morning."

He watched them go, disappearing onto a side street lined with cottages, most of them second homes of people seeking solace and solitude. The siren faded, and the atmosphere for which the town was named returned.

He lifted the white coat and touched the name embroidered on the pocket: Adam Tyson, M.D. This was the realization of a dream, the fulfillment of a vow made years ago.

He checked his watch and smiled at a young lady pushing a stroller. An obvious tourist, her T-shirt was emblazoned with words lifted from a dictionary. In a dignified font, it stated, "Serenity: n. The state of calm, unruffled tranquillity." He looked toward the hospital. He certainly hoped he would find the words to be true.

Serenity was a coastal town, sitting on an island that swelled in the summer months with people in love with the beach. In the winter only the locals remained, mostly those who made their living from the sea. The hospital was the largest employer, the only one on the barrier islands on the eastern coast of North Carolina.

Adam would be their only surgeon, replacing Dr. Mark Crawford, who had drowned in a sailing accident last spring. Doc Crawford was a town saint, a medical icon whose greatness had grown since his death. Though unconfirmed, the local rumors claimed he had fallen from his boat in a drunken stupor, as there was enough alcohol onboard to keep a fraternity happy for a month.

Adam would treat minor surgical problems, an occasional case of appendicitis, and skin cancers that proliferated after a life in the sun. Serious problems, major trauma cases, and the like would be flown down to Wilmington or further inland to Greenville or Durham. He had been promised that most of these cases would be handled in the emergency room by capable physicians who would refer the patients out before Adam would need to be involved.

Like most other buildings on the island, the hospital was built on stilts. Instead of wooden ones used in the local cottages, Broward County Hospital was supported by a series of huge concrete columns. On the side closest to the ocean, a cement platform, much like those seen in parking garages in the city, led from the emergency entrance down a long circular ramp to the street level below. In the front, pedestrians had the choice of walking up the steps or taking one of two wheelchair ramps that zigzagged symmetrically to the front portico. The building was sided with large cedar shingles, giving it more the appearance of a huge country inn than a hospital.

Adam ascended the front steps, pausing as his stomach tightened and the pattern of the siren in the distance changed from a rolling wail to a short-burst staccato. He squinted toward the sound. *I thought Serenity was supposed to be a refuge for a surgeon seeking a practice free of emergencies. There aren't supposed to be sirens here.* He reminded his racing heart to listen to reason. *It's probably the unfortunate announcement of a drowning, or perhaps a cardiac arrest in a flabby tourist—a medical, but certainly not a surgical, emergency. This is Serenity, not Southern California.*

"Dr. Tyson?"

He looked up to see two women, one short, her build solid, stocky, not soft—not overly fat, but with the frame of a fireplug and a leathery complexion; not kissed but smothered by the sun's adoration. She smiled and held out her hand. "I'm Doreen. We spoke on the phone." Her grip made his hand ache.

"Adam Tyson." There. The words were out. This wasn't so hard.

"This is Beth Carlson. She's our new director of nursing. She joins our team, coming from Richmond, Virginia, where she was director of emergency services at M.C.V. I hope you don't mind if she joins our little tour."

Adam took the hand of the second woman as she offered it. "Of course not. I'm glad to meet you."

She smiled. Her hair was strawberry blonde, lifted from her neck in a french braid, knotted with clinical precision. Nurse Carlson looked like she'd stepped from a Land's End catalog—not a drop-dead, stunningly beautiful model, but a fair-complected, slender gentlewoman he could easily picture kneeling beside a child or standing by a window watering a flowering plant. Adam inhaled the delicate scent of a perfume that reminded him of fresh honeysuckle. No, he wouldn't mind her tagging along at all.

They sat for a few minutes on the expansive covered porch and sipped lemonade as Doreen expounded on the history of the County Hospital and highlighted the latest technology available within. Adam knew all of this but nodded with feigned interest as he cast secretive glances at Beth and wondered why this sharply dressed professional would choose Serenity over the big city. On more than one occasion their eyes connected for a brief moment before Adam looked away and focused on the drone of Doreen's presentation.

They progressed from the porch through the areas of patient registration to the hospital paging operator where Adam was handed a shiny black pager that he flipped on with ceremonial formality. "There," he said. "I'm officially on duty."

"Don't worry," Doreen chided. "That thing should be pretty quiet today. We haven't been admitting general surgery patients at County since Dr. Crawford retired."

They toured medical records, X-ray, and the lab and were about to take the elevator to the patient floors when a shrill, electronic chirp sounded from Adam's pager. He lifted it from his belt, holding it out as if it were hot. "Whoa," he said, forcing a chuckle. "I thought you said this thing would behave."

"Here," Doreen offered, reaching for the beeper. "Press this gray button to see the message."

He obeyed and looked at the display. "111-5000."

He held it up for Doreen, whose face tightened.

Adam could taste stomach acid. He should have had more than black coffee for breakfast. "What is it?"

"The 111 is a code for emergency. 5000 is the extension for the emergency room. Sounds like you've got business already." She shrugged and nodded with her head away from the elevators. "We might as well continue our tour in the ER and see what they want."

Beth's eyes brightened, and her pace quickened as they stepped down the pale green hallway after Doreen. With her background in trauma, she liked this kind of excitement. Adam sped up, not wanting to lag too far behind. *First days aren't supposed to start this way.*

Doreen pressed a small silver panel on the wall to activate an automatic door leading into the small emergency department, which at the moment appeared to be in chaos. A patient could be heard yelling obscenities. A young man in scrubs pushed past the trio carrying two units of blood and disappeared behind a curtain beyond a central nursing station. A phone rang unanswered. A petite woman with gray hair advanced toward a group of men and women in bathing suits. She had both hands in the air as if she was directing traffic. "You'll have to wait out there! The doctor will be out as soon as he can."

Adam peeked behind the curtain. Instantly he wished he hadn't. Six people were crouched over a chubby little boy. His skin was antique white, not vibrant but pale, very pale with thin purple lips and gums the color of Concord grapes. There was blood on the floor, the stretcher, even the wall, and blood stood stagnant in the pool of his belly button, like a blob of currant jelly smeared between rolls of white bread.

A man about Adam's same age of thirty-eight looked up. "Are you the new surgeon?"

Adam nodded, his mouth suddenly dry. "A-adam Tyson." There, he'd said it again, but not as easily this time.

The man shook his head and emitted a forced chuckle. "Heh, heh. I'm Dr. Seavers. This your first day? Heh, heh. I'm gonna need your help."

"What do you have?"

"This is a four-year-old. Victim of a shark attack. Nearly took his arm off," he said before punctuating his sentence with another chuckle. "We haven't had a shark attack in these waters since 1969, heh."

Adam found Dr. Seavers's chuckling habit far from endearing. Adam took a step forward and asked for a pair of gloves.

"Oh, I don't need you here," Dr. Seavers countered. "I'm sending this one by helicopter up to Duke." He paused. "Unless you've got an interest in doing microvascular reimplantation, heh-heh."

Adam held up his hands. "No!" He softened. "I mean, no, Duke is the proper place for a complex case like this."

Seavers pointed behind Adam. "Hear that kid screamin'? That's where I need you. Some drug-crazy kid tried to jump through a sliding glass door." He chuckled. "And the door won, heh-heh."

The gray-haired nurse pulled open the curtain, having successfully herded the beach crowd back into the waiting area.

Adam looked across the room at a young man with a large bandage on his forehead, tied in four-point restraints with an orderly the size of a moose standing guard along with several others.

The nurse held out her hand. "Dr. Tyson, I'm Karen Pebworth.

Jake over there will help you find what you need. As you can see, the doctor and I will be tied up for a little while until we get this boy in the air."

Adam looked behind the counter where a huge man was stocking a cart with supplies. He appeared to be no older than twenty and the extra-large scrub-top he wore strained against the flesh pressed beneath its drab blue surface. His head was topped with a Duke baseball cap that snapped forward as Jake nodded his salutation.

Adam lifted his hand in a weak wave and hoped Jake was as smart as he was large.

Beth Carlson stepped forward. "I'll help you. I've done ER work for ten years." She slipped off her suit jacket.

Adam looked twice. She was even prettier than he'd thought. Forget Land's End. She could model swimwear.

He walked to the cubicle that contained the writhing young man. His eyes were wide open with a look Adam had seen before: sheer terror.

Adam cleared his throat. "I'm Doctor Tyson."

The patient's head jerked around and for a long second his eyes locked with Adam's until the doctor looked away. A young girl sat on a chair next to the stretcher. She tried desperately to cling to the wild man's hand, but even with the restraints, he nearly pulled her off the chair.

"What's he been taking?" Adam questioned.

The girl looked up. "I don't know. He won't say." She looked back at the man and tried to capture his eyes, now locked on Adam. "Oh, Timmy," she cried.

Adam shook his head. "What does he usually take?"

"I don't know! I told you." She paused and looked back at Timmy. "He bought some stuff off a GI up at Camp Lejune. I'm not sure what was in it. He took it this morning. We tried to keep him at the motel, but then he got like this and jumped through the glass door."

"I'm going to need to look at his head."

"He won't let you." She pointed at the crowd around the little boy. "They already tried."

"Great," Adam muttered. He looked at Beth. "We'll just have to paralyze him and put him on a ventilator." She nodded. Then, to

Jake, he raised his voice. "Call respiratory therapy. I'm going to need to put him out just to look at his scalp."

Jake clapped two meaty hands together, and a grin broke his tough-guy façade. "Sure thing, Dr. Tyson." He turned to leave. "By the way, welcome to *Serenity*."

Adam was about to make a sarcastic reply when the patient strained against his restraints and caught Adam's eye again. "You're no doctor! You're trying to kill me! YOU'RE NO DOCTOR!"

Adam froze. His stomach seemed to flood with cold water. What did this patient know? Adam looked away as the patient resumed shouting obscenities.

Adam relaxed a notch, back to a controllable level, feeling physically weak. *Ease up. It's only a drug-induced paranoia.*

Adam hoped Beth didn't see him cringe when the patient started up again. "I want a real doctor!" He locked eyes on the surgeon like a deer in headlights.

Dr. Tyson looked away. The patient could see right through him. His charade was a failure. *Careful, don't let him scare you. It's just the drugs.*

His heart caught in his throat.

"YOU'RE NO DOCTOR! You kill your patients and put them in the freezer!"

Adam turned and looked at Beth. What was she thinking?

He took a deep breath. This wasn't what he'd signed up to do. He walked to the nursing station and touched Karen Pebworth's arm. "I need some Pavulon."

"What are you going to do?"

He smiled. "I'm going to make sure Timmy over there doesn't keep yelling bad words."

Her eyes widened. "You want him paralyzed?"

"If you can't move, you can't talk." He waited while she retrieved the syringe. He then walked back to the patient's stretcher and looked at Beth. "Let's wait a minute for the respiratory therapist. We'll have to be ready to breathe for him as soon as this is in."

"We'll need an IV."

He nodded. "Jake, hold him down. This isn't going to be fun."

Jake smiled again. "Fun? We haven't had this much fun in Serenity for months!"

Adam frowned and picked up an IV needle.

The patient squirmed and spat. His girlfriend cried. Adam thought his own heart would burst from his chest. Jake just kept smiling.

And Timmy kept right on yelling. "You're no doctor! You're trying to kill me."

Adam hurried through his work at getting an IV in the moving target. "Hold him still!"

He didn't care if the guy was off his rocker. He just wanted to make him shut up.

And the sooner the better. He lifted the syringe of clear liquid and stabbed it into an IV port. "There," he muttered. "You like drugs," he added under his breath. "Have fun with this."

CHAPTER
2

BETH CARLSON NEVER returned to her orientation. But she couldn't have been happier getting her feet wet by the immersion baptism she got in the ER. After assisting Dr. Tyson with a complex scalp repair, she took a self-guided tour through the ICU and the patient wards, spending time on each floor talking to the nurses she'd be managing. She didn't want to get lost in an administrative office. She fully intended to keep her nursing skills fresh by regularly filling in with her comrades in the trenches.

She looked at her watch. Five P.M. Her father, Isaac Williamson, would be worried. Travis, her son, would be too.

She had come to Serenity for both of them. Ike, her father, was in ailing health and since her mother died in a motor vehicle accident two years ago had become less and less able to carry on alone. Her son was adrift in a sea of adolescence without an anchor. He was full of bitterness over losing his father, and it was showing in his grades and the hours he spent on in-school suspension.

Serenity, she hoped, would be the small-town solution. It had been a year since the vacation when she and Travis played together on the beach beyond her father's cottage. It was an oasis of connection in a desert of failing communication. So when she saw an ad for director of nursing at Broward County Hospital, she jumped at the chance to combine a professional advance with an opportunity to regain a relationship with her son and father.

She started her aging Dodge Caravan and headed for home, her mind swimming with the day's happenings. She thought of the nurses

she'd met and the horrors she'd seen in the ER. A shark attack in
Serenity! She hoped Travis wasn't in the water.

Mostly she found herself musing about the new surgeon, Adam
Tyson. His technique had been meticulous, his movements fluid, and
although he seemed stressed, he never lost composure. He spoke to
the young man's mother with rare compassion, a quality she was sure
she hadn't seen in Richmond. How old was he? Probably too young
for a forty-year old widow with a fourteen-year-old son.

She sighed and turned up Ocean View Drive, the potholed,
meandering excuse for a road that ran along the beach. The road had
been washed out a half-dozen times by class five hurricanes, but the
locals seemed satisfied with a Band-Aid approach to road mainte-
nance. She looked at the horizon. It was full with dark thunderheads.
Serenity was going to get wet. Again.

She arrived home at her father's cottage to find her son immersed
in Nintendo GameCube and her father reading a novel on the back
deck. "I'm home," she called."

Travis didn't look up from his game. "What's for supper?"

She looked at the kitchen. Lunch preparations still sat out next
to the morning's cereal boxes. *Doesn't anyone do dishes in this place?* A
burner on the stove glowed orange. She flipped it off in disgust.

She walked up behind her son and stared at the screen, where a
fierce battle for Planet Earth was punctuated by explosive sounds. She
kissed the back of his head. "Hello to you too." She placed her hand
on his shoulder. "Can you pause that thing?"

He protested under his breath but obeyed after shooting an alien
spacecraft. "What?"

"I just flipped off a stove burner. Leaving it—"

"I didn't do it!"

She hesitated and lowered her voice. "Travis, I know. But leaving it on like that could be dangerous. Your grandfather could burn
the house down. You need to check up after him."

"I thought he was watching me."

"I guess you'll have to watch each other."

He grunted, and she turned her attention to her father. She
crossed the den where a plate of crumbs and an empty glass had been

pushed aside for an examination of the sports section on the coffee table.

Her father looked up from his book. "The Braves are one game back in the National League East."

She smiled. Baseball had been their link ever since she played Little League in Bridgewater, Virginia, the only girl on her team. She batted in the cleanup spot and put up with enough chauvinism from the other boys' parents to last a lifetime. "Great. So they beat Philly? Who pitched?"

"My man Glavine. Age hasn't slowed old Tommy down a bit. What's for supper?"

She sighed and sank into a cushioned wicker chair. She ignored the question and looked at the ocean before closing her eyes. "I think I could just stay right here for a few hours."

"Not a good idea. Storm will be here soon."

She opened her eyes to see her father standing, straining his eyes to the east. He looked the epitome of a crusty waterman. His hair was sparse and white, uncombed, flipping up in rebellious curls from beneath an old cap with one word embroidered on the front: *Tired*. He was wiry, with deep creases spraying from the corners of eyes made worse by his love for the sun and a disposition that burst out in a constant smile. He had been a pastor for fifty years, serving eight different churches, five of which he started from scratch. His back was bent, and he walked with a shuffling gait. He raised a spotted hand and pointed, his hand showing a hint of Parkinson's. "Gonna be a big one."

She stretched and went back to the kitchen. Obviously if she wanted to eat, it was up to her. She opened the refrigerator. The pickings were slim. She had intended on stopping at the grocery store but forgot after getting tied up at the hospital so long.

Her father followed her in and drank the last of the milk straight from the carton, spilling a little on his cheek. He still had a drop on his chin when he began to talk. "The boy won't do anything. I asked him to go fishin'. He used to like it, but now all he can do is play those stupid games."

"Didn't he play on the beach?"

Ike huffed. "He did go out for a little while. He walked down to the fishin' pier with that neighbor kid."

"Bart?"

He nodded and wiped his chin. "Yeah. I think that's his name. Wears black T-shirts and smokes."

"Hmmm." She paused and shut the pantry door. "Well, I want Travis to make friends."

"He should play with that Yarbarough kid. I hear he made the all-star team."

"Dad, Travis doesn't like baseball."

"What? He's got a great card collection and—"

"It reminds him of Barry." She turned to face him. "They played baseball every night of the summer. But he hasn't picked up his glove since his father died."

"I wish I could throw." He held up his hand and watched it tremble. "I asked Travis to go fishin'. But all he wants to do is play those stupid games."

She studied her father and nodded politely. "I need to go into town. I'll pick up a pizza at Tony's." She gave him a gentle nudge as she left the kitchen. "Don't try to cook anything while I'm gone. I'll be back with pizza in forty-five minutes." She yelled instructions for Travis to set the table and bolted for the door.

Hungry and exhausted, she groaned as the rain pelted her windshield just as she was pulling out. She lifted her car phone and dialed Tony's. *Only in town for a week and I know the number by heart. This isn't a good sign.* Suddenly she found herself on the edge of tears. The stress of a new job, a rebellious son, her loneliness in a new town, and now her worries about a father showing signs of dementia all ganged up on her at once. She didn't feel like being strong. She longed for Barry's arms to surround her and tell her everything would be all right. "Oh, God," she cried, "what am I going to do?" She sobbed for a minute, then composed herself enough to call ahead to Tony's. Sausage and mushroom pizza always soothes a good cry.

∞

Adam Tyson tried to roam the halls incognito, but even without his personalized white coat, everyone seemed to know the new surgeon.

He shed the coat after his bloody encounter with an arterial pumper during his repair of the scalp laceration in the ER. He had another at home, but if he dumped them at this pace, he was going to need a lot more.

He wasn't ready for such a quick immersion in the business. After the scalp laceration, he'd done one emergency appendectomy and an urgent leg amputation on an elderly diabetic with a life-threatening infection. This was not shaping up to be the relaxed, remove-a-mole-or-two practice that he'd anticipated. Serenity was billed to be a one-surgeon dream town. Pick what elective surgery you want to do and send the rest away; spend four days a week working and the weekends on the beach, only coming in for emergencies. Maybe it was just a bad first day. He certainly hoped so.

But he was also not ready for the across-the-board friendly reception he received from the staff. Everywhere he went it was, "So nice to meet you," "What can I get for you, doctor?" or "I'll gladly make rounds with you so you can give all the orders to me." This was definitely not the treatment he was used to, but it was something he'd enjoy.

But as nice as everyone had been to him, his thoughts continually returned to only one, Beth Carlson. She had talked little but was friendly and eager to help, even when it was clearly beyond her responsibility. He had never experienced the chemistry he heard others speaking of in relationships, but in the brief moments that his eyes had met hers, he had begun to understand. What was it he felt? Was it just due to a quickening of his heart rate or the adolescent way he couldn't think of anything to say?

He returned to the doctor's locker room outside the OR to change, still intrigued with the new nursing director. She wasn't wearing a wedding band, but he shouldn't assume she wasn't married. Many of the nurses didn't wear jewelry during clinical responsibilities. He'd make it a point to ask.

He closed his locker and straightened his tie. He would lose the tie tomorrow. No one else on staff wore one. He plodded to his car with heavy feet. He clipped the pager onto his belt, resisting the urge to fling the taskmaster against the wall. Tomorrow. He definitely hoped it would be better than today.

∞

Beth Carlson hoisted a large Tony's pizza from the counter and ran for her van, unsuccessfully dodging a large puddle beside the driver's door. She shook her wet foot and gently placed her precious cargo on the seat beside her before easing the van onto the rain-slicked street. The rain continued, heavy at times, and lightning etched the sky over the ocean. She turned the wipers on high and slowed down, thinking ahead about the dash into the house. She hadn't brought an umbrella. *I'll get soaked if I run for it. Oh well, things could be worse than being stuck in the car with a fresh, hot pizza.*

The smell from the pizza was heavenly. Suddenly the car veered to the right and the steering wheel started shaking badly. She gripped the wheel and slowly applied the brakes. To add insult to her other problems, her old van had a flat tire. The road had a narrow shoulder, so she wouldn't be able to get all the way off the road. She pulled over as far as she dared and squelched the urge to curse when she realized she was just beyond a curve, giving drivers little time to react to the obstruction. *At least they'll be going slow because of the rain. And if they hit this old bomb, I'll be forced to get something new. Maybe a midlife crisis car, a convertible . . .* She smiled and picked up her cell phone, dialing her home. A busy signal meant someone was on the phone or on-line, likely the latter. Five and ten minutes later, when she got busy signals again, she promised that she would talk to Travis about spending so much time with screen activities. If she allowed it, he could go from Nintendo to videos to computer games or be on-line for hours on end.

The rain continued, so she ate a slice of pizza. No use for everyone to eat it cold.

After two slices and another busy signal at home, and not knowing who else to call, she decided to change the tire herself. The rain, thankfully, slackened a bit; so she retrieved the jack from under the hood and lowered the tire from beneath the rear of the vehicle. *I had to be wearing a nice outfit to impress everyone the first day.* A car slowed but passed. *Hasn't anyone ever heard of being a good Samaritan?*

She wrestled the jack into position in front of the left rear tire. She was just shoving the handle into the jack when she saw the lights of an approaching car. The headlamps rounded the corner as she looked up, startled that the car seemed to be bearing down much too quickly. The car swerved and began an awkward slide. It appeared that it would just miss the back of her vehicle. She heard tires squealing against wet pavement, saw the flash of a chrome bumper and then . . . darkness.

CHAPTER
3

ADAM TYSON, M.D. dragged into the emergency room, not quite believing that he had been on duty in Serenity less than twenty-four hours. Dr. McDaniels had called. There was major trauma to deal with: a pedestrian struck by a hit-and-run driver. She was hypotensive, unconscious, with chest and abdominal injuries.

He looked up at the gaping expression of the ward clerk at the central desk.

"What?" he asked with an edge of irritation.

The young lady closed her mouth and shrugged. "You're soaking wet."

"It's raining." He squinted toward the trauma bay. "Is that my patient?"

The clerk pointed a glossy red fingernail at the chart rack. "Yep," she responded, bobbing her spiked bleached hair. "Her chart is there. Most of the labs are back."

He picked up the chart and thumbed through the lab and X-ray data, glad for something to do for a moment before approaching the curtain and the mess that waited beyond. He gripped the chart tightly, trying hard to suppress a tremor. *She's got six broken ribs on the left. She's got a pneumothorax. Must have punctured her lung with a rib fragment. Her head CT is OK. That's a relief. Her blood count is low. I wonder if this was drawn after they gave IV fluid.*

He flipped to the face sheet. Hmmm. They have her listed as Jane Doe. They must not know . . .

"Dr. Tyson!" A nurse pulled back the curtain and motioned him forward. "Her pressure's down, and we've given two liters of IV crystalloid. Do you want her to have blood?"

"What is the pressure?"

"Sixty systolic."

He shook his head. "Set up for a chest tube. After the tube, if her pressure isn't up, we'll give her blood." He paused and looked at the ward clerk. She was tapping her long red fingernails against her leather skirt. "Have you called for a chopper?"

Dr. McDaniels answered for her and came around the counter to shake Adam's hand. "We tried. It's grounded due to weather." He shook his head and frowned soberly. "Looks like you're it." He stuck out his hand. "Dr. Tyson? I'm Jeff McDaniels. I talked to you on the phone." He frowned. "Man, you're soaked!"

Adam sighed. "It's raining. Nice to meet you."

He rolled up his wet sleeves and approached the patient. At the foot of the bed he froze momentarily and steadied himself. "You know who this is, don't you?"

The nurse looked at him inquisitively.

"This is Beth Carlson, our new director of nursing." He looked at the floor. "She just started her job today."

He clenched his fists and silently vowed to think only of the work he needed to do. Dr. Tyson's number one rule: A surgeon always maintains control of his emotions.

He painted the left chest with Betadine and made a small incision in the fifth intercostal space. He inserted a chest tube and secured it with a large suture. So far, so good.

He looked at the monitor and the ventilator. The filling pressures were lower. That was good, but the blood pressure reading was still low. "Let's give blood. How much is set up?"

"She's AB negative, so the blood bank only has three units."

"Let's give the first two. And have them get more to us stat. Wilmington?"

The nurse nodded. "It's already been done. It's standard procedure on major trauma patients."

He was performing a physical exam a minute later when another physician arrived, pushing a large ultrasound unit. The female, a smiling brunette, was wearing blue jeans and a gray Duke University sweatshirt splattered with rain spots. "Dr. Tyson? I'm Dr. Morris. The ER physician asked me to come in to do an abdominal ultrasound."

"Oh, uh, sure." He moved aside. At least the radiologist appeared to know how to dress for an Outer Banks thunderstorm.

Dr. Morris ran the probe over the abdomen. "Liver looks OK. There's a lot of fluid here. Must be blood. Oh, here's the spleen. Would you look at that! Pretty nasty laceration down into the hilum."

Adam clenched his jaw, then frowned. "Let's get her stabilized and out of here to Duke University. We don't have the blood bank to deal with this."

McDaniels sighed. "A ground crew will have to come from Nags Head. That's a thirty-minute drive in good weather."

"What about the crew that brought her?"

"Left for a smoke inhalation victim down near Cape Hatteras."

A nurse squeezed a bag of packed red blood cells to hasten its delivery. Adam watched anxiously as the heart rate crept higher. After one unit the blood pressure remained low, at 70 systolic.

Adam felt a hand grip his elbow. He looked to see McDaniels's stern gaze. "You've got to operate here. You have no choice. She'll bleed out if you wait for a transfer."

His heart sank. He wasn't ready to handle major trauma on his first day. He took a deep breath. "Tell the OR to get ready. Get in a urinary catheter and another big-bore IV."

Fifteen minutes later Adam Tyson paused, scalpel in hand poised above Beth Carlson's expanding abdomen. He whispered a prayer into his mask, an act of desperation, a bargain with a God he hadn't spoken to in years.

He made quick work of getting in. He would try no fancy maneuvers to save the spleen. His only goal was to get in, remove the spleen, stop the bleeding, and get out. Splenic salvage was for experienced surgeons with the luxury of a stable patient and a large blood bank.

He worked feverishly to mobilize the crushed organ and ligate the large splenic artery and veins. In ten more minutes the spleen was in a bucket, and Adam started to close.

"Pressure's one hundred ten," the anesthesiologist reported. "Looks like the heart rate's coming down as well."

Adam felt his own pulse rate slowing. "Has she made any urine?"

"Nothing to speak of. I think we're still behind on fluids."

"Stapler."

The nurse assisted Adam in reapproximating the skin, then put on a bandage while the surgeon broke scrub and wrote the post-op orders.

Five minutes later, while seated at the Dictaphone, Adam Tyson dropped his head onto his right arm and sighed. He breathed deeply, feeling as if it was his first breath since he glided the knife over Beth's abdomen. For now he had won a small battle. But he knew there was a war to fight if she was going to make it. His patient was behind on fluid volume, anemic, and unconscious.

But alive. And for that Adam was greatly relieved.

∽

Travis Carlson stood on the back deck and looked out over the ocean. His mother should have been home long ago, and he was starving. Serenity was boring. He had few friends, no mall, and now his mother wanted him to keep an eye on Grandpa. Back in Richmond, Johnny Richards had told him how lucky Travis was, going to a summer of endless fun in the sun—vacationing babes in skimpy bathing suits— and nothing to do but surf and fish. But so far he didn't own a surfboard, and fishing didn't really interest him. Johnny was always more mouth than substance.

Travis looked back through the glass door leading to the den. His grandpa had asked him three times where his mother was. The last time he had told him she was playing golf and would be home anytime. Travis knew it was a lie, but he was tired of the question, and he knew his grandfather wouldn't remember anyway.

Now, looking at the clock, he began to wonder about the siren he had heard. Maybe his mother was in trouble. The thought chilled him in spite of the warm evening. Losing his father had been horrible. The thought that he might be an orphan frightened him even more. He couldn't stay with Grandpa for long. Where would he go? Would he have to stay in some orphanage somewhere?

He heard the phone and his grandpa's muffled voice. Maybe it was his mom.

He slid open the back door and looked at his grandfather's face. Ike's hand was at his mouth, and the color had drained from his ruddy cheeks. Something was wrong. Travis knew something bad had happened to his mom.

"What is it, Grandpa?"

The old man's hand was shaking as he laid down the phone.

"What is it?" Travis felt his own voice thickening, about to crack.

"That was the hospital. Your mom was in an accident. She's in surgery right now." He opened his arms, as if to hug Travis.

Travis didn't feel like hugging his grandfather.

Instead the old pastor dropped his hands onto the kitchen counter and began to pray. "O Father, keep Beth in Your hands."

Travis didn't feel like praying. Some good praying did when his father was sick. He prayed, and his father still died.

He interrupted his grandfather's prayer. "Come on. We've got to go."

Ike concluded with an "Amen" and grabbed his tan windbreaker. "We'll have to use my pickup."

Travis bounded down the slippery stairs with one thought on his mind. *God wouldn't dare let my mother die.* For the first time since hearing the bad news, he couldn't keep down his emotions. Tears welled in his eyes. *God can't let my mother die.* He pinched away his tears.

But that's what I thought about my dad.

CHAPTER
4

BEEP, BEEP, BEEP. The regular blipping of the heart monitor reassured Nurse Carlson that her patient was OK. Trauma patients were always such a challenge. There were ins and outs to measure, vitals to record, a ventilator to monitor . . .

Confused images clouded her mind, floating in and out of the reach of understanding. Someone squeezed her hand. *Barry? No, he's gone. Why does my head hurt? Where am I?*

She saw an image of a man's face, heard a reassuring voice. "Hold on, you're going to make it." She'd seen the face before. *Who is he?*

She strained to remember. She wanted to lift her head, to open her eyes. She started to raise up, but searing abdominal pain stopped her efforts. Her mouth was pasty. She rolled her tongue forward. There was something in her mouth. She explored it with her tongue. It was hard. The taste was terrible. She closed her mouth around the tube as the realization dawned: She was on a ventilator. She wasn't tending patients. She *was* a patient.

What happened to me? I was getting pizza. I had a flat tire. Then . . . ?

She felt a squeeze on her hand again. "Beth?" A hand on her forehead. Gentle. Warm. A finger on her eyelids, pulling them open. A bright light swinging from eye to eye. "Beth? Can you hear me?"

She strained to focus. A face. A man. Two faces. She squeezed her eyelids shut, then opened them again. The two faces merged. A man in scrubs. A man who needed to shave.

"Beth?"

There was concern in his eyes. Kindness. His forehead was wrinkled. She felt a hand in hers again. She tried to squeeze it. Was her hand obeying? Was she paralyzed?

"Easy, Beth. You don't have to crush me."

OK, my hand must be working.

"Lift up your head. If you can hold it up, I'll know you are strong enough to remove this breathing tube."

She strained to obey, fighting against the knife stabbing her in the stomach.

She heard another voice. "Dr. Tyson, here are this morning's lab reports."

The man's face disappeared. Dr. Tyson. She was remembering. The young surgeon she helped in the ER. Now he was taking care of her.

"Her hematocrit's down. Did we get any more blood from Wilmington?"

"No. Do you think she's bleeding?"

"Hard to say. I hope this is just dilutional. We've given her a lot of fluid." He paused. "She opened her eyes. I think she's coming around."

Beth could hear another voice. Her father. "Been here all night, doc?"

"'fraid so. She seems a bit more stable since her last transfusion. And we might not need to repeat her head CT after all. She just opened her eyes."

Her father's face was in front of hers. He was crying. He hadn't shaved either.

She saw Adam and felt him pulling tape away from her cheeks. "I just need to remove this tape. Then I'll get rid of this tube." The last piece was jerked free, pulling her lips forward. "There. Now cough."

She retched as the tube slid out of the back of her throat. She gasped for breath, a sharp pain sticking her in the side. She tried to talk but only moaned. Adam's gentle hand was brushing her forehead again.

"There, there, don't try to talk. You were hit by a car when you were changing a flat tire on your van. You have broken ribs and needed a splenectomy." She watched the corner of his mouth turn up. "You are one tough lady."

Her nurse adjusted a humidified oxygen face mask beneath her chin.

She coughed and ran her tongue around her dry mouth. She tried to talk but managed only a whisper. "My sausage pizza is in the van."

∞

Two hours later Beth maneuvered her hospital bed into a sitting position. "Ooooh," she groaned softly to herself before exploring her left chest with her hand for the source of the pain. Broken ribs. *This is agony. I guess you can't just put 'em in a cast to make them hold still.*

She lifted the neck of her gown and peeked before groaning again. Everything was purple. And swollen. She had gone from a B to a double D on the left. No wonder it hurt to breathe.

A knock at the door prompted her to look up and quickly gather the neck of her gown to her throat. A uniformed man entered.

The man took off his cap, revealing a head of sun-bleached blond hair. "Ms. Carlson? I'm Dan Smith, Serenity Police."

Beth didn't know Serenity was big enough for a police force.

"I'd like to ask you a few questions if you don't mind. We're looking for the person who hit you."

She slowly released her gown, pressing it flat against her chest and pulling up a sheet under her chin. "I don't remember much."

"Do you remember being hit by a car?"

She shook her head. "I only know what my father and Dr. Tyson told me. I was starting to change a tire. That's the last thing I know." She paused, studying the young man, who had a notebook open in his lap. He appeared about twenty-five and was dark, looking like he'd be at home on the beach in a lifeguard stand. "It was a hit-and-run, huh?"

"Of sorts. The driver fled the scene, but not in the car that hit you."

"What?"

"A white Cadillac was found off the opposite side of the road in the wet sand. It's registered to a Michael Cunningham of Sarasota, Florida. We think Mr. Cunningham, if that's who was indeed driving the car, stopped to help you, even apparently called 911, and then fled the scene, leaving the car stuck in the sand."

"Weird."

"Exactly." He closed the black notebook. "You don't remember being helped?"

"No. The first memory I have is waking up a few hours ago."

"Someone covered you with a blanket and pulled you out of the road to a safe spot in front of your van."

"What do you know about this Michael Cunningham?"

"Not much yet. We don't have a large police force, ma'am. We may have to get the County Sheriff's Department involved. If they want, we'll also call the state troopers. They have some detectives who will take over the investigation."

"Whoever hit me can't be far away. Did you check local hotels? The names of people renting local cottages?"

The young man made a note on his paper. "We're working on it."

She hoped she hadn't given him new ideas. They should have done this hours ago. Whoever hit her could be a long way away by now. "Are you watching the car? The owner may come back for it."

"We've got it locked away in our garage. It's ours now. Evidence."

"Why would someone leave the scene of the accident?"

"Plenty of reasons. Not many of them good."

Beth stayed quiet, hoping he would expound. He did.

"Maybe he's a married man in a car with someone he didn't want his wife to know about. Maybe a search of the car will turn up drugs or something else that will clue us in. Maybe Mr. Cunningham was intoxicated and didn't want to be caught." He shrugged. "Maybe it was a stolen car. Maybe a teenager out for a joyride. There are lots of possibilities."

He put his card on her bedside table. "If you need me, just call." He offered a smile. "I hope you feel better soon."

Beth nodded. "Thanks."

She watched him go, his muscular silhouette disappearing through the doorway into the hall. She lifted her hand to her chest, then gently lifted the sheet and her gown for another peek. *Ugh. I haven't been this heavy since I breast-fed. It will be weeks until I'm normal again.*

She looked up toward the sound of another knock on the door-frame. *Can't anyone get enough time alone to see what's injured around here?*

A short man in a three-piece suit entered. His forehead glistened with sweat, and he leaned to one side to counterbalance a large leather bag hanging from his shoulder. "Ms. Carlson? I'm Bill Youngblood. I work for Chip Dawson. Perhaps you've seen his ads on TV." The man dropped the bag on the floor and immediately deepened his voice to imitate his boss, evidently a TV commercial personality he thought she'd recognize. "Hi, I'm Chip Dawson. Have you been injured in an accident? I'm on your side to help you get the compensation you deserve."

She held up her hand. "You work for a lawyer?"

The man smiled. "Not just any lawyer. The best."

Beth dropped her jaw. "Can't you see I'm a little indisposed here?"

"Oh, I understand that, ma'am. Don't let it bother you. I'm used to working with people in the hospital. The sooner we get the documenting photographs, the more impressive your injuries will seem to a jury and—"

"Photographs?"

"For professional use only, of course. I understand you had some surgery. We'll get a shot of your scar. Juries love that. And how about big bruises? We can—"

She held up both hands. "Mr., uh . . ."

"Youngblood." He dug for a card in his jacket pocket and handed it to Beth.

"Youngblood," she repeated. "I'm not sure how you got in here, but you weren't invited."

"I told the nurse I was your brother." He smiled. He wasn't getting it.

"I don't want a lawyer. I don't want any photographs of my body. So if you'll kindly—"

"What's going on here?" Adam Tyson stood in the doorway and took a large step forward. He'd obviously overheard Beth's last sentences. "You weren't invited, and you're upsetting my patient." He smiled curtly and opened his palm toward the doorway.

"Chip, uh, Mr. Dawson is the best, ma'am. So if you need us, just call." He pointed to the card in Beth's hand. "We have a toll-free number."

The man retreated when Dr. Tyson took another step forward.

Adam Tyson shook his head. "I never expected to see that in Serenity."

Beth smiled. "Me either. How do you think he found out about me?"

"He probably listens to a police scanner. Or maybe he has a paid mole in the ER. It's hard to say."

She studied the surgeon for a moment. He had shaved and had changed out of scrubs. "You look better than you did this morning."

"Thanks." He smiled, revealing two small dimples in his cheeks. "I think."

"I'm the one who should be saying that. I never thanked you for helping me." She paused. "Thanks."

"I only did what I was forced to do. I didn't want to keep you here. I wanted to send you to a bigger hospital, a trauma center." He shook his head. "The storm got in my way."

"I'm glad. I'd much rather be here close to my family."

Adam cleared his throat. He seemed hesitant to speak. "I, uh, haven't met your husband yet. I should tell him you're OK."

"I'm not married." She looked at a window on the far wall. "My husband died a few years ago. Leukemia."

"I'm sorry. I didn't know."

She looked back and offered him a smile. "So I came to Serenity to make a new start with my son." She raised her hand and moved it in an arc around the room. "So now look. Some new start, huh?"

He sighed. "It was my first day too, remember?" He chuckled. "I had visions of losing the new nursing director on my first day. The hospital administration would have sent me back to California on the first plane available."

"Don't make me laugh. It hurts." She gripped her side. "How long do I have to keep this chest tube?"

"A day or two." He paused. "I ran into the police officer in the hall. I guess they have a mystery on their hands. Did they give you any clues as to what they know?"

"I think they're clueless. I got the feeling they don't know where to begin."

He nodded, then leaned forward and touched her shoulder gently. "You should try to rest. I'll put a sign on the door—*No lawyers*." He backed away. "I tell you what—you call me if you need anything."

"I'll do that."

The surgeon disappeared, leaving Beth with a jumble of thoughts. *He asked about my husband. Was he really wanting to talk to him . . . or just to find out about me?*

And what about Michael Cunningham? Why would whoever was driving his car hit me, then help me, then run away and leave his car?

She winced with a stabbing pain and hugged her pillow to her chest for relief. It slowly subsided, the pillow providing a cushion for her aching ribs. Unfortunately it did little to quiet her mental anguish, which seemed to race forward, stimulated by her pain, the beeping of her cardiac monitor, and her medications. *Who is Michael Cunningham? What am I missing?*

∽

That evening, at the Soundside Country Club, the staff members and administration gathered for a welcome reception for their newest member, surgeon Adam Tyson. Adam wasn't entirely comfortable with the affair, feeling more at home in an OR where he could let his hands do all the talking he needed.

He surveyed the crowd, a group of about forty, gathered in threes and fours in a two-story room with a wall of glass overlooking the sound. In the corner a string quartet played something vaguely familiar and looked very serious, much more so than the busy bartenders standing behind the long walnut counter along the opposite wall. The feel was stuffy, not what he expected from a small hospital in a town that lived off tuna and northern tourists. He swirled the champagne in his hand, the first alcohol he'd consumed since arriving in Serenity. For tonight the hospital arranged to send general surgery emergencies elsewhere. Tonight was for celebrating, and they certainly didn't want him called away when it was his arrival they were honoring.

He smiled and answered the same questions dozens of times.

"How do you like Serenity?" "Where did you train?" "I'll bet you're glad to be away from all the HMOs in Southern California, aren't you?"

And everyone seemed to know of the emergency surgery he'd done on his first day. *News in a small hospital travels faster than a barefoot Yankee crossing hot asphalt.* "Great save. Nice to have a surgeon who rises to the challenge instead of sending all the good stuff away."

The "good stuff"? I was scared to death. Give me an elective hernia and I'll show you what good stuff is.

A gray-haired fellow in a blazer slapped his back. "You're the new hero, doc. Welcome aboard!"

You really think I'm a hero?

All the compliments almost made him forget that he'd been pretty upset over the whole ordeal. Almost.

After most of the staff had consumed a drink or two, they tended to talk among themselves more, telling war stories of memorable patients, stories Adam imagined had been bantered about during similar occasions for years. Over and over and over. He listened to a bravado story here, an unbelievable feat there, nodded and smiled. After the group downed drinks three and four, the mood sobered, and they talked of insurance carriers from hell, malpractice threats, and late-night mistakes.

When they started telling lawyer jokes, Adam feigned looking for a bathroom and slipped through the double doors onto a large deck overlooking the water.

"This is what most people come to Serenity for." The voice was soft and very feminine.

He looked to see he'd been followed. She stood silhouetted by the light in the room, her dark hair accented by the illumination. She wore an emerald dress, split up the side, and she held her champagne glass with both hands. Had she been in the room the whole time?

She lifted one hand, palm down. "I'm Gerri Fiori, nurse manager of the OR."

He took her hand. "I've heard your name. Pleased to meet you."

Her hand lingered for a moment, then slowly slid from his. "You've made quite a stir, Dr. Tyson. Are you always into such grand entrances?"

He shook his head. "I'd prefer to slip in unnoticed. The grand entrance was not my design."

She kept his gaze, unflinching. She was obviously "new school." Adam doubted this woman would ever stand when a doctor entered the room, as she'd surely been trained to do.

"I hope you found my staff to your liking." Her southern charm dripped heavier than a cold glass of Coke on a summer day. When she said "staff," it sounded like two syllables.

"Very much so. They were very helpful." He broke the eye contact and looked out over the sound. They stayed quiet for a moment before he added, "Yes, I could get used to this."

She slipped closer to him, their shoulders brushing briefly as she leaned forward over a wooden railing at the deck's edge. "What would bring a handsome young surgeon to such a remote spot? Are you running from a hectic life in California?"

"What makes you think I'm running from something?"

The corner of her mouth lifted. "A hunch."

She's intimidating me, testing me to see if I'll toe the line. He locked eyes with her again. "I'm not running from anything. I'm running *to* something."

She raised her eyebrows coyly and broke his stare. "You can be a big fish in Serenity, Adam."

Bold. She uses my first name without my request.

She sipped her drink. "But there are sharks in the water who like to eat big fish."

"Sharks?"

She shrugged. "Sometimes little hospitals create little generals. Little men with little ability to swim outside their own pool. But give them a little authority, and they will try to use everyone to get what they want." She looked over her shoulder toward a group of hospital administrators at the bar.

"I'm not sure I understand."

"You will, in time. Just play your game. Your rules. I'm sure you're used to that."

Games, fish, sharks, generals. Why won't she talk to me straight? Adam decided to play along. "You like to play games."

She edged her glass toward his, clinking them together softly. "Sometimes."

"How long have you been in Serenity?"

"All my life."

"So the big-city hospitals haven't been able to lure you away?"

She shook her head and looked out over the water where the moonlight created a long, shimmering pathway to the horizon. "I love it here." She sighed, then stiffened and spoke formally, losing her alluring southern accent. "So you saved our new nursing director. Good for you."

"I guess you could say we both had a rough start."

"Worse for her than for you. When will she be on the job?"

"Beth is a tough woman. She won't miss more than a few weeks."

"Beth is it?" She swirled her glass. "I'm filling her spot until she returns."

He used her words. "Good for you."

"Have you made friends? Do you have family or friends here?"

"I'm alone. Married to my career, I guess."

"Just like me."

They looked toward the glass doors leading into the reception room. Dave Winters, the hospital CEO, was making a noisy goodbye. The door opened long enough for his boisterous salutation to Adam.

Adam watched as Gerri rolled her eyes. "Now the party will break up. No one ever leaves before Dave. Now we can go."

"Another professional game?"

"With someone who thinks he's a big fish."

She leaned forward seductively before pouring her drink into the sound. "I've got much better stuff than this at my place. Would you join me for a nightcap?"

"That's kind of you, but I really should head home. I need to get an early start in the morning, and I'm still living out of boxes."

"More reason to relax a little." She winked. "I can keep secrets, Adam. You may need a friend or two to swim in these waters."

The offer was tempting. "I've heard of the buddy system."

"Exactly."

He shook his head. "Thanks, but I'd better take a rain check."

"It's not raining."

"Are you this persistent in the OR?"

"I'm used to getting my way." She set the glass on the wooden rail. "Good night, Dr. Tyson." She pivoted and disappeared through the doors and into the crowd, leaving Adam alone.

He studied the calm waters and exhaled slowly through pursed lips. He wondered how long he could keep this up. Maybe he'd bitten off more than he could chew. It sure was nice being praised and appreciated, but he couldn't quite shake the feeling that something bad was lurking beneath the water's calm surface.

CHAPTER
5

THE FOLLOWING MORNING Travis circled the parking lot of the Serenity Tackle Shop on his bicycle waiting for Bart Gilford. After five minutes on the asphalt, he retreated to the shade on the porch, leaned against the building, and sighed. He checked his Marlboro pack. He was down to his last two. Bart had promised his brother would buy more but hadn't come through. Now Travis was reduced to meeting Bart here so they could persuade some tourist to buy them cigarettes in exchange for tips on the best fishing spots.

It really didn't take long. The first guy in, a man with a northern accent, took a five from Travis, bought him one pack of cigarettes, and kept the change. When Travis protested, he said he'd be back the following morning, and if he'd caught fish where Travis told him he would, he'd buy Travis another pack.

Travis moaned and memorized the license number on his Ford Bronco, making note of his Boston Red Sox T-shirt and shoulder-length hair. *Like I'll really report him for ripping me off.* He kicked his shoe against the curb and cussed. He knew he shouldn't. His mother had heard him talk like that one time and made him forfeit his allowance for two weeks. But it made him feel like a man.

Bart showed up ten minutes later and bummed a cigarette. "Want to go down to the pier?"

Travis shook his head. "I got some work to do."

"You gettin' paid?"

"Not that kind. Just somethin' I need to do." He explained to Bart about the mystery of the hit-and-run, then pulled out a faxed photocopy of Michael Cunningham's driver's license.

"Where'd you get this?"

"The police officer gave it to my mom. She says a man will do just about anything for a pretty girl if they ask."

Bart tossed his head back as if he understood. He took a long drag on his cigarette and adjusted his sunglasses. He was cool.

"I'm gonna show this around to a few people, see if I can come up with anyone who's seen this guy. Since he doesn't have a car, I figure he's still around here somewhere."

Bart studied the picture with all seriousness. "He's got a beard in this picture. We should try to erase it and see what he looks like."

"I could scan it onto my computer, then modify it." He slapped his friend on the back. "Good idea."

"I suppose we could put up some posters. You know, offer a reward or something like that."

"Like we have any money."

Bart laughed. "Really."

"Come on," Travis said, climbing back on his bike. "Let's start over at the Seagull Inn."

Five minutes later they walked into the lobby of the motel just in time to witness a verbal fight between a rowdy guest and the desk clerk, who Travis decided was also the owner.

A young man, unshaven and bruised, with a fresh scar with visible stitches running six inches across his forehead, pointed his index finger in the older man's face. "I'll get a lawyer! If it hadn't been a glass door, I'd be fine!"

"If you hadn't been high, you wouldn't have tried to leave without opening it!" He slapped a yellow receipt onto the counter. "The bill is five hundred and fourteen dollars, which includes a new glass door and two nights' lodging."

A second young man grabbed the first by the elbow. "Come on, Timmy. Chill out."

Timmy huffed. "I'll sue!"

The second man pulled Timmy back a step. Timmy stepped back and dropped his shoulders. "Just look at me, man! I look like a freak!" He pointed to the hotel manager again. "You'll pay for this."

Travis and Bart parted to let the tattooed duo through.

The man behind the counter composed himself, combed his

white hair with his hands, and looked up. "Oh, hi, Bart. What brings you to town?"

Bart lifted his head. "What was that all about, Mr. Crumbly?"

"Two days ago that punk was so high, he decided to jump through a glass door up on level 2. Problem was, the door was shut." The old man shook his head. "I've never seen so much blood. I called 911. He should be thanking me, not cursing me. I saved his pitiful life. He didn't even know I was there." He stared Bart down. "Don't go down that road, Bart."

Bart lifted his sunglasses. "Oh no. Not me, sir."

Mr. Crumbly paused. "How's your brother doing?"

Bart looked down. "Stan? OK, I guess. He's in a hospital over in Durham."

The man behind the counter nodded seriously.

Travis watched the interchange without speaking. He didn't know Bart had a brother in Durham.

Mr. Crumbly changed the subject. "So what's up?"

"This is Travis Carlson. He's my new neighbor. We've got something to show you."

Travis unfolded the picture. "My mother was hit by a car while she changed a tire two nights ago. The car was registered to this man. The car was left at the scene. We were hoping to find out if he showed up here."

Mr. Crumbly stroked his chin. "Nope. Can't say I've seen him. But Mildred checks in some of the night guests." He walked to the computer. "Let's see . . . what's the name on that license?"

"Cunningham."

He typed the name and hit *Enter*. "Nope. Nothing comes up."

"Thanks for checking."

"Here, let me make a copy of that. I'll keep it under the counter in case this rascal turns up."

The door opened behind them, and a man and his wife and two daughters entered.

Mr. Crumbly looked up. "Nick!"

Quickly the motel owner and the man were engaged in a bear hug. "Look at you! And these girls! Is this little Kristy?" He reached for the girl's cheek, but she dodged and gave him a playful jab to the midsection.

She looked nothing like "little Kristy" to Travis. She was blonde, like her younger sister, but this was no little girl. She was wearing shorts and a white top showing off her slender waist.

Travis found himself standing straighter and running his hand through his hopelessly curly hair. He was blond like his mother but had curls like his dad. Curls his mother loved and he hated.

He watched as the younger sister retreated behind her mother who reached for Mr. Crumbly next. "Hi, George. You haven't changed a bit."

"You can't lie." He smiled. "But thanks."

Mr. Crumbly raised his hand toward Travis and Bart. "Boys, these are my friends from Virginia. Nick and his family are here for a few months while he fills in as pastor of the beach church. Help Nick with their bags. He always comes with a load." He nodded to the lady. "Come on, Cheryl, I'll get you checked in. You've got the same rooms as last year."

The boys followed Nick outside. Travis cast a quick glance back to Kristy, who looked away, seemingly occupied with the decor of the lobby. He looked up to see a van equipped with a topside luggage compartment. In a moment Nick was standing in the opening of the sliding door and popping off the top. He passed down eight suitcases, each weighing an easy ton and a half. Travis and Bart lugged each one up the stairs to the last rooms on the second floor.

"That one's mine."

Travis turned to see Kristy pointing to a large pink suitcase sitting on the walkway outside her room. He wiped the sweat off his forehead. "Where should I put it?"

"My name's Kristy."

He nodded, his throat suddenly dry. "I'm Travis."

"You work for George?"

"Oh no. Me and Bart, uh, Bart and I just live over on the beach road." He looked away. *Good grief. She didn't ask me that.*

"Oh." She leaned out over the rail.

Travis looked for Bart. Bart was cool. He could talk to girls. Where was he?

"Do you go to the beach church? My father is the interim pastor."

"The beach church?"

She smiled and pointed across the parking lot. "That's not its real name. It's like the Serenity Community Church or chapel or something." She shrugged. "Everybody just calls it the beach church."

"I uh, well, I just moved here. We don't have a church."

"You should come. I mean, you could come. It's mostly visitors."

Kristy's little sister ran up. "We get our own room!"

Travis looked at the little girl. She would be easier to talk to. "What's your name?"

"Rachel."

"Hi, Rachel. I'm Travis. You can call me Trav. How old are you?"

It was too late. Rachel had run into her room and turned on the TV.

Kristy smiled and rolled her eyes. "We don't have a TV at home. She's seven." She looked back at him. "I'm fifteen." She lifted her shoulder-length hair and touched each of three earrings in her right ear.

"Me too," Travis lied, immediately blushing and turning away. *Why did I say that? I won't be fifteen for three months.* "I guess I should go. Do you need some help lugging that inside?"

"I can do it." She hesitated. "It's the little white chapel across from the fishing pier. Starts at nine o'clock."

"What? Oh. I might not be able to make it. I'll try." He shuffled his feet. "My mom's in the hospital."

"I'm sorry." She frowned.

Why did I tell her that? "She's going to be OK. She got hit by a car."

Travis held his breath. This conversation wasn't going like he wanted. First he lied, then he made excuses for not going to church, then he went for the sympathy factor.

"Your dad could bring you."

He twisted his nose and shook his head. "I don't have a dad. He died a few years back."

Now Kristy's hand went to her mouth. This conversation wasn't going like she wanted either. "Oh gosh, I'm really sorry, Travis."

He looked down. "Don't worry about it." He shrugged. "You couldn't know."

She hesitated. "Thanks for bringing up my suitcase."

"Hey, Romeo!" The voice belonged to Bart. What a jerk.

Travis leaned over the railing and glared at his neighbor.

"Let's go. Did you forget your little detective mission?"

He glanced back at Kristy. "I gotta go. See ya."

"Bye, Trav."

Trav. Only his mom called him that. He walked to the stairs.

"I hope you come to church sometime. Or come to the beach. We usually go just beyond the pier."

He shook his head. "OK."

He headed down the stairs, taking them in twos and threes. He was light on his feet, a butterfly. Maybe Serenity wasn't so boring after all.

His smile faded when he saw the serious look on Bart's face. "What's eatin' you?"

He pointed across the parking lot at the two older youths who had barged out of the lobby as they entered. "I think that's the kid that got my brother in trouble."

"I didn't know about him."

"My folks don't want people to know. Stan overdosed on some bad pills he got from some woman on a Harley. He'd been hangin' out with the dude with the stitches."

Travis nodded.

"It's not fair. That guy's been doing this kind of stuff for a long time, and he's out scot-free running around, and my brother is in some mental hospital."

Travis squinted toward the thin young man called Timmy as he held his head in an apparent attempt to keep it from hurting. "He sure looks like he's enjoying his freedom."

That brought a smile to his friend's lips.

"Forget about him, Bart. He's a jerk."

Bart nodded. "Yeah. Let's go catch some surf."

❧

That morning Beth awoke to a burly nurse named Brenda Miller taking vital signs. "Dr. Tyson asked me to take this out," she reported mechanically, pointing to the nasogastric tube. Then, without

off Beth's nose and gave the
nsils were being ripped from

up in her eyes. "I think that
re."

out all at once."

r blood. Finding none, she
e pulled away the sheet and
irinary catheter too."

se deflated the balloon and
s tube slipped out much eas-
exactly more pleasant.

different on this side of the
s felt this powerless. She also
o the fact that Beth was going

he nurse added. "Those naso-
gastric tubes can .... ath." She handed Beth a spit
basin and a fifty-cent red toothbrush. "I'll be back in five minutes for
your walk."

"Walk?" Beth touched her abdominal dressing and wrinkled her
forehead.

"I want you out and in the hall before Dr. Tyson makes his rounds.
I want to have a good report for him."

"What about this chest tube? I can't go very far with this."

"I'll carry the chamber for you." She smiled. "Just because you're
going to be the boss doesn't mean you're getting out of this."

*So she does know. Score one point for knowledge, but subtract two for
lack of compassion and tact. My breath stinks, huh? Why don't you just
come right out and say it?*

Sergeant Miller marched from the room as Beth searched for the
button to raise the head of her bed. Her abdomen was sore. This was
way worse than having a baby, even a C-section baby as big as Travis
was. And after a C-section, you have something good to show for it.
All she got this time was a shattered spleen.

With her head raised, she brushed her teeth and frowned at herself in the small fold-up mirror on her over-the-bed table. Her hair,

still in a french braid, was a fright, unwashed since her accident. She studied her scalp and picked at the road grime and dried blood at her hairline. Her one eye had a conjunctival hemorrhage, coloring the white part of her eye blood-red on the lower half. *Too bad it's not October. I could sit on the porch and give out Halloween candy without a costume.*

Before five minutes was up, Brenda was back. Beth was tempted to protest, but she knew the nurse was right. She needed to get up and walk. It would be good for her lungs and hasten her recovery. Brenda was from the old school. She wore a classic nursing cap over her graying hair and her ID picture clipped to her smock top. "Swing your legs over the side and grab my arm. We're going to make it to the nursing station and back."

Slowly, and with half her weight on Brenda, Beth stood. "Wait a minute. I'm dizzy."

The duo paused, then Brenda picked up the chest tube drainage system and took a step toward the door. "Let's go."

Beth's legs felt like noodles, and by two steps into the hall she could feel her hospital gown pulling apart in the back. She tried desperately to keep it together. She had nothing on under the gown, and the stupid garment parted up the rear to make it easy to put on a patient lying down. But right now the gown provided little coverage. By twenty paces, her breathing was short. They paused at the desk, and she leaned over the counter to get her breath. "This is hard work," she gasped. "I didn't realize how winded I would be from this anemia."

"Nothing good for you is fun."

Thank you, Nurse Positive Attitude.

It took ten minutes to make the trip. Ten minutes that felt like a marathon.

Beth collapsed too quickly onto her hospital bed, pain searing through her stomach like a scalpel. "Aaaahh!"

"Next time we'll make it to the elevator."

"Oh no, I'm done for the day. I feel like I've just conquered Everest."

"No pain, no gain," the so-efficient nurse responded. "I'll have the aide come help you with your hair." With that, she pivoted and disappeared from the room, leaving Beth exhausted and alone.

The nurse's aide turned out to be a Godsend. She was a nursing student, home for the summer, getting plenty of beach time and steady work as a nurse's aide. It took a full thirty minutes to shampoo and brush out Beth's hair, but Julie worked gently with each tangle and told Beth the inside scoop on all the staff on the floor.

Brenda Miller was a Serenity fixture. The only one with more experience had retired last month. Two of the night-shift nurses, Tammy and Joan, spent six hours a day training for the Outer Banks Triathlon—running, biking, and doing open-water ocean swims. John, a respiratory therapist, spent his working hours assisting patients with breathing treatments, and every break smoking unfiltered cigarettes. Everyone thought that Gerri, the OR nurse supervisor, would be the next nursing director, but, Julie gushed, she was sure Beth, whom she called Ms. Carlson, would do a better job. Gerri was a smart enough lady but dressed a little risqué for a professional and drove a Harley-Davidson.

By the time her hair was dry, Beth had a pretty good idea of the gospel according to Julie, including who to trust and who to watch out for. She was tempted to have Julie put her hair back up, but she was frankly exhausted, and Julie had started talking about her own string of boyfriends, and Beth was about worn out.

With Julie gone and the door shut, Beth let out a sigh. Just having her hair washed made her feel better. She could almost face going for another walk with Sergeant Miller. Almost. She checked the wall clock. Ten o'clock. Certainly Dr. Tyson would be around to see her soon.

She looked at herself in the mirror and wrinkled her nose. Then, straining to reach her purse from the bedside table, she retrieved a small makeup case. Nothing fancy, just the essentials. A little lipstick and eyeliner would make her feel human again.

And it won't hurt to look nice for Dr. Tyson. We are going to be professional colleagues, after all.

❧

Adam Tyson pushed open the hospital door after a quick knock. The ten-year-old boy looked up from his hospital bed. Adam winked at the boy's mother and looked at his patient. "Waazzup?"

The boy smiled. "Nuttin'. Waaazzup?"

"The nurse tells me you are eating. Would you like to get out of here?"

The patient nodded.

His mother spoke up. "When can he get the scar wet?"

"Let me look." He lifted the boy's gown to inspect the appendectomy scar. "It should be sealed enough to get in the water tomorrow."

"The ocean?"

"Sure. But watch out for the waves. A big tumble might make you sore."

"OK."

"Not exactly the way you thought you'd spend your vacation, is it, Evan?"

"Nope."

"Will you come see me next year when you come to the beach?"

The boy looked at his mom as if to say, "Why would I want to do that?"

"Hey," Dr. Tyson joked, "I'm going to get a complex if nobody wants to see me."

The mother stood. "Thanks for your help. I'm so glad you were here. They told me that if this had happened a month ago we would have had to travel inland to find a surgeon. At least this way we were able to stay in Serenity."

He smiled. It felt good to be appreciated.

He walked to the nursing station where he dictated a patient summary and wrote orders. Next he headed to the med-surg floor to check his diabetic patient who'd had an urgent leg amputation.

Again he pushed open the door after a brisk knock. "Ms. Anderson?"

The lady in the bed opened her eyes. It was the first positive reaction he'd seen since her operation. He approached slowly. "I'm Dr. Tyson. I'm the surgeon who operated on your leg." He avoided the term *amputation*, as he wasn't sure that she understood just what had happened to her. It was the first time he'd seen her coherent.

She nodded. "My daughter explained it to me." She looked down. "The nurse told me you saved my life."

"That's right."

She continued to stare at the foot of the bed. "You should have let me die."

"Don't say that. Losing your leg doesn't mean your life is over."

"Without a leg I can't take care of myself. I'll lose my apartment. My daughter has to work. My husband is dead. I'll have to go to a nursing home."

"You can get a prosthetic leg—learn to walk again. A nursing home stay can be a short time for rehabilitation, then get back to your own apartment."

Her chin started to quiver. "I used to be a dancer." She halted. "I . . . I may never walk again."

"Yes, you will. I can tell you're strong. When I first saw you, I didn't think you would survive. But you did. And you can walk again." He reached for her hand. "But it will take hard work."

She didn't speak. He moved a small box of facial tissues close enough for her to reach.

"I'll see you every day, Ms. Anderson. You'll get through this. I know you will." He retreated, closing the door softly behind him. He wrote a daily note, then orders for physical therapy and a mild tranquilizer if she needed it for anxiety or sleep.

Adam's third patient was Timmy Stevens, the young man whose scalp had been badly lacerated in a drug frenzy at a local motel. His room was empty. Adam walked to the nursing station. "Where's Mr. Stevens?"

Yolanda Peters, a ward secretary, huffed, "He left A.M.A." She held up the Against Medical Advice form. "He refused to stay until you rounded. He said the motel owner was trying to charge his credit card with a repair bill."

Adam shrugged. "Sounds reasonable to me." He picked up the patient chart. "Will he come for follow-up, let me see the sutures?"

"I doubt it. He was from out of town. Just here for a summer party, I bet."

"I wish I could get him some antibiotics. That wound was horrible. It looked like he had rolled around in the sand after getting cut."

He sighed and headed for Beth Carlson's room, tapping the door gently before pushing it open. "Knock, knock."

She looked up from a leatherbound book in her lap. Her hair was down, falling just over her shoulders. She was wearing makeup, not even looking pale.

Not bad for a hematocrit of 28.

Not bad? Who am I fooling? She's a dream even in a hospital gown.

"So the surgeons in Serenity don't have to round before 10 in the morning?"

"Sure. And we play golf and surf every day, never see any trauma patients, never deal with drug-crazed teenagers, and send every critical splenic injury to the university hospitals so we won't have to work."

She smiled. "Touché."

"How do you feel?"

She kept her voice low. "The drill sergeant made me march in the hall this morning."

"I see you've met Brenda." He pushed a chair close to her bed and sat. "I made her promise to get you mobilized today."

"She's very obedient, I'll say that."

Adam held up his head, straightened his shoulders, and imitated the older nurse. "Nothing good for you is fun."

"She said that to you too?"

He nodded. "Right after I complained about my being on call every day."

She laughed, then grabbed her side. "When can I get rid of this tube?"

He looked at the collecting chamber. "Cough."

She obeyed.

"No leak. I'll go get some supplies and get rid of it right now."

He gathered supplies and returned with Brenda. With Beth lying flat, he teased away the tape dressing holding the chest tube against her rib cage. "Oooh. That looks sore."

"Purple has always been a good color on me."

Anything would look good on you. Careful, Adam, keep your mind on the chest tube. You're here for business.

Once he had freed the tape, he snipped a small suture. "Hold your breath."

He pulled the tube with a rapid jerk and covered the site quickly to prevent air from slipping back into the chest cavity.

"You can breathe now," he coached. He winced for her, noting the tears in her eyes. "Sorry. It's best to do that fast." He reached over and wiped a tear from her cheek with the back of his hand. "You can hit me when you feel better."

Her lips turned up at the corner as Brenda left the room. "Nothing that's good for you is fun."

He paused for a moment. "Anything new on the mysterious driver of the white Cadillac?"

"No." She sighed. "I don't think Serenity is used to solving problems like this."

He nodded and backed away. "I need to get back to the office. Rest up for another round with the Sarge. I'll tell her to give you a break until this afternoon."

"Great. First I get the Pentagon Sweetheart for a nurse. Now I have to deal with the surgeon from the old school of—"

"Careful," he interrupted at the door. "I'm not that old."

She glared at him. "How old are you anyway? Old enough for me to trust?"

"Yes."

She kept her eyes locked on his. "Well?"

"Thirty-eight."

She kept quiet.

"Is that old enough?"

She picked up her book and feigned disinterest. "I'll let you know. I do prefer gray hair and experience."

He shook his head. She was definitely into head games. But he loved the playful way she bantered with him and hid her pain.

"I'll check on you this evening. When I'm older and more experienced."

He slipped away to the nursing station and wrote a daily note and orders, trying to concentrate on listing everything she needed. *She's getting under my skin. I'll have to concentrate hard to be her doctor.*

CHAPTER
6

THE FOLLOWING MORNING was moist and hot in Serenity, with predictions for the mercury approaching the upper nineties. Travis rose just as the color faded in the eastern sky, dressed in his bathing suit and an Atlanta Braves T-shirt, swiped a Pop-Tart from the cupboard, and jotted a note to his Grandpa Ike. By the time he reached the hospital, only three blocks from the house, sweat was beaded on his forehead.

He hadn't even considered going by the tackle shop to collect on yesterday morning's cigarette deal. In fact, with his mind ahead on hanging out at the beach near the pier, he'd left his smokes hidden in the bottom of his sock drawer. He was pretty sure that a girl like Kristy, with a preacher for a father, wouldn't be impressed with his adult vice.

He parked his mountain bike, a gift from his mom for his fourteenth birthday, and carefully locked it to a light pole in the employee lot. He used the employee entrance, so as not to attract the attention of hospital security. Visiting hours didn't start until 10, and he wanted to be on the beach by then. He entered the stairwell. Taking the elevator while wearing a bathing suit seemed to Travis to be another no-no, a sure way to attract unwanted attention. He bounded the stairs in twos and threes until he reached a landing between the third and the fourth floors. He was breathing hard and wondering just how much damage he'd done to his lungs since taking up smoking with Bart.

He passed a few nurses and a large breakfast cart on his way down the hall to his mother's room and looked in more than a few rooms along the way, glancing away when the hollow eyes of the patients met his. Lots of the rooms had bouquets of flowers, and for the first time he felt a stab of guilt over not thinking about that for his mother.

He stopped two doors up from his mom's room and stared at an arrangement of roses on the bedside table of an old man. They were perfect—not too showy, but elegant, just like his mom. The patient was snoring, his mouth open in a whisker-rimmed O. It would be so easy to—

"Can I help you, young man?"

Travis jerked his head up to see a woman in white. She was big-boned, not fat, and would have looked right at home on one of those wrestling shows his mom refused to let him watch. "Uh, no. My grandpa's sleepin'. No need to bother him."

She eyed him pensively and walked on.

He could feel his heart pounding a fast beat, like the music Bart's mother let him listen to. He took a deep breath and walked on toward his mom's room.

He pushed open the door. She was sitting up and was wearing makeup, a stark contrast with every other pitiful soul he'd eyed on his walk down the hall. Her Bible was open in her lap. No surprise there. It was his mother's first request for him to bring from home. She looked up. "Hi, baby. You're up early."

Baby. She'd called him that forever.

"I'm a teenager, Mom."

She pushed her lower lip into an exaggerated pout. "I'm sorry."

He approached her bed slowly, his hands bulging the pockets of his trunks. "You look better." He paused. "Almost normal."

"Is Grandpa up?"

He nodded. "He went out early. Prob'ly walking the beach."

"You could go with him."

"He takes an hour to go one mile."

She let it drop. "Heading for the beach?"

"Bart has a new surfboard. I'm supposed to meet him."

She nodded, then drifted into silence, looking toward her window. She took a deep breath and sighed. Travis knew his mom was going to say something heavy. He could tell. She always did when he interrupted her Bible reading. He tried to think of something to say. Anything to avoid the sermon his mom was sure to deliver, but his mind was blank. Suddenly his brain was like a huge library, but every book had been checked out. He couldn't retrieve an intelligent thought to save his life. He squinted and glanced around the room. Nothing.

"I know this has been tough on you. Ike told me how upset you were."

He looked down. There wasn't much to say.

"Trav, God's not going to take me away from you—"

"He took Dad!"

She halted. "We don't understand the why, honey, but we do know God still loves us."

Travis couldn't meet his mother's gaze. It sounded like a fairy tale, too good to be true. "If He's really good, you shouldn't have to cover for Him."

"Trav, I—"

"If He loves me, why did He let my dad die? And why is bad stuff always happening to us? Why did we have to move to this stinkin' little town?" He wasn't sure why he said that. It really wasn't so bad here, but something in him wanted her to suffer. He felt bad saying it but let his words hang unretracted in the silence that followed.

After a minute she changed the subject. She probably didn't have the answers or the energy to explain it. Travis doubted that anybody did. Bad things weren't supposed to happen to you once you committed your life to God. At least that's what he thought Pastor Daily said back in Richmond. He always talked about joy and victory. So much for joy. He looked down, unable to look in his mother's eyes. If she started crying, he was leaving.

Maybe God was just testing him. That was another one of Pastor Daily's explanations for bad stuff. Or maybe it was punishment for having bad thoughts about girls or smoking.

"I might get out of here in a day or two. Do you think you could set up my bed in the corner of the living room? I'm not sure I'll have the energy to climb the stairs for a few days."

He shrugged. "I guess."

She reached out and tousled his curls. "Oh, baby," she said softly, "you are going to be a heartbreaker, aren't you?"

"Mom—"

She ignored him. "I wish I had thick hair like this."

"Your hair is nice."

"Nice and flat."

But he knew she was pretty, as much as a son thinks his mom could be considered pretty. Even his friends told him so. And she was constantly being asked out . . . and turning men down. She always promised to get Travis's permission before dating. He thought she was kidding, but you could never be sure with moms.

"Be careful at the beach," she said as he pulled away.

"I will."

He retreated quickly with his head down after seeing Nurse Wrestler-in-White pass the room.

In another five minutes he was back on his bike in the summer Serenity heat. With his thoughts on a strawberry blonde named Kristy, the day was full of promise. He circled the parking lot of the Seagull Inn and squinted toward the last two rooms on the second floor. The curtains were pulled back, and the windows were dark. He made another pass around the parking lot and looked for Nick's van, but it was nowhere to be seen. He turned toward the ocean, dodging morning tourists dragging umbrellas, coolers, and well-lotioned children with towels blazoned with images from *Harry Potter*.

The pier stretched 200 feet out into the surf. Travis waved to Sammy, the man behind the bait counter at the weathered shack that sat at the pier's entrance. Sammy had a white beard and a large smile to go with his generous waist. He spoke a salty brand of southern, a language native to the Outer Banks, with single-syllable words often stretching into two, as in bayed is a place to sleep, and shortened multi-syllable words such as cap'n for captain.

"Howdy, cap'n," Sammy responded, his teeth clamping down on a fishing line to sever it beyond a knot he'd just tied. "You're up early."

Travis shrugged. "Fish biting?"

"Two boys with a New Jersey accent anchored offshore a hundred yards south of the pier are pulling 'em in right and left. Even came in to buy a second cooler."

"A guy with long hair?"

Sammy looked up.

"Was he here yesterday? Wearing a Red Sox T-shirt?"

Sammy laid down the fishing rig. "I believe he was. How'd you figur'?"

He shrugged again. "He owes me money."

Sammy let it pass. Travis was glad and slipped through the crowded tackle shop onto the pier. Midway to the end, Sammy had placed a pay-per-view standing binoculars. He put in a quarter and pointed it toward a small powerboat anchored south of the pier. *Just where I told 'em to go.*

The Yankee who sold Travis the five dollar cigarette pack was pulling in another fish. *Jerk. I'll bet he didn't show up this morning to pay me back.*

He swung the viewer to the beach and scanned the gathering crowd. After a few minutes he sighed and pointed it the other way. There, just beyond the lifeguard stand, kneeling in front of a sand castle with a small shovel in her hand, was the most beautiful girl he'd ever seen. Not that he'd really paid that much attention to them before, but this one seemed different. Not prissy like the girls back in the eighth grade in Richmond. They probably wouldn't want to get too sandy. But this girl used a shovel. Sweet.

He scanned the rest of the beach looking for Bart, then sauntered nonchalantly off the pier down to the water's edge. Bart was probably still catching z's.

Travis worked his way slowly toward Kristy and her family, paying attention to the shell fragments at his feet. He picked up a shark's tooth and kneeled to filter a handful of sand and shells through his fingers.

"Travis!"

He knew the voice by heart. He kept his gaze on the sand, wanting her to call out again.

"Trav!"

He looked up. "Oh, hi."

"What are you doing?"

"Just lookin' for shark's teeth." He handed her the one he'd found.

"Sweet."

He smiled. She even talked like he did.

"We're working on a sand castle. Want to help?"

He nodded and followed her over to her family's umbrella. He didn't want to appear too eager.

Her father edged forward and lowered the book he was reading, eyeing Travis from his curls across his lanky frame to his toes.

"Dad, you remember Travis? He carried up our luggage for Mr. Crumbly."

Travis felt suddenly self-conscious. Nick seemed to be studying Trav's shirt.

"Good to see a man with good taste."

What is he talking about? Does he know I like Kristy?

"How about that John Smoltz? Elbow surgery doesn't seem to have affected him a bit."

Whew. He's talking about my Atlanta Braves T-shirt. "Oh, uh, yes, sir. Looks like fall ball again this year." He looked over at Kristy. "You like baseball?"

"Dad takes me to see the Richmond Braves."

"Sweet!" *She even likes baseball.*

A commotion on the end of the pier caught their attention. A crowd had gathered, staring down at the boat with the guys from New Jersey.

Nick stood up and shielded his eyes. "I'll bet they caught a huge fish. That's the only time that crowd gets excited."

Rachel stood up beside her father. Her legs were generously sugared with sand. "Let's go see it."

"Why not?" Nick took his daughter by the hand.

Travis watched as Sammy dashed out onto the pier. "Somethin's up. I've never seen him leave his tackle shack."

In the distance the wail of a police siren pierced the moist air. In another minute the Serenity Police jeep slid to a stop in the sandy parking lot next to the pier. Something was definitely up.

Cheryl, Kristy's mom, called to her husband. "Nick!"

He stopped and looked back.

She shook her head. "Rachel, stay here. I'm not sure the crowd is gathering because of a fish. Why are the police here?"

Nick turned back with his youngest daughter.

Travis looked at Kristy, and she looked at her mother. "Can I go with Travis?"

Her mother frowned. "I guess."

They quickly crossed the beach and joined the throng on the pier. They couldn't see what was going on, but the murmur from the crowd indicated that the duo in the little boat had indeed pulled in something quite interesting.

A man with a brown baseball cap leaned over the rail and spit. "Jake said they snagged a body on the anchor."

"I hear they called the police from a cell phone on the boat."

Sammy pushed his way through the crowd, his face as white as his beard. When his eyes met Travis's, he placed his hand on his shoulder and turned him around. "Oh no you don't, young man. Some things are better off not seen."

"What's going on, Sammy?" Travis asked.

"The boys with the accent snagged a chain with their anchor rope. Problem was, it was tied to a couple cinder blocks and wrapped around a body."

"A body? A man?"

"Can't tell. Looks like the fish have been feedin' pretty well. How long have we been telling folks to anchor south of the pier like that?"

Travis scratched his chin. "Two, three days maybe. I've been watchin' with your binoculars so I can give tips at the tackle shop."

Sammy sighed. "I guess now we know why the fish have been so plentiful there." He walked on to the door of his bait shack with a dazed expression.

"Weird." Travis looked at Kristy. "Nothin' exciting ever happens in Serenity. But something is going on around here now. First a guy freaks and jumps through a window at Mr. Crumbly's Inn, then we have a mystery hit-and-run involving my mom, and now this." He shook his head. "A murder?"

Kristy's eyes were wide. "Unbelievable. When Mom hears this, she'll never let me out of her sight."

A moment later the crowd parted to let a young police officer and a man from the boat through. Travis looked up and recognized both men. The officer was Dan Smith, the one who had visited his mother with updates on the hit-and-run investigation. The other, the man who'd taken Travis's five dollars in exchange for one pack of cigarettes, was still wearing a Red Sox T-shirt.

The man froze, his eyes wide and his face pale. He was staring right at Travis; he seemed to be looking right through him. Travis shuffled his feet. He wanted some money back, but this wasn't the time or place to ask.

The man lifted his hand and pointed a bony finger toward Travis.

Something in Travis said, *Run*, but his shoes seemed glued to the pier.

"It was him, officer." He nodded resolutely. "I'd know that face anywhere. That's the boy I was tellin' you about."

Travis wasn't sure what he was talking about, but he knew it couldn't be good. He glanced at Kristy. Her hand was covering her mouth.

The officer nodded at Travis. "Morning, son. I'll need you to come with me."

CHAPTER
7

ADAM TYSON WORKED through his morning clinic patients in his office next to the hospital. This was what he had come to Serenity for. Thankful patients with straightforward problems who didn't want an academic explanation of their illness, just a personable, technically gifted man to do the job. And that's exactly what he was.

He saw a forty-year-old woman with gallstones, a sixty-two-year-old man with a hernia, an eighteen-year-old with a pilonidal cyst abscess, and a fifty-one-year-old woman whose sister had colon cancer and wanted a screening colonoscopy to be sure she was OK. This was the bread and butter of general surgery. He didn't want caviar. His tastes were simple. And when it came to surgery, the simpler the better. There was less chance of getting in over his head without his mentor to bail him out. Perhaps he would become more adventurous with time. The trauma on his first day had built his confidence to the point where he actually thought it was possible that one day he might really enjoy the challenge.

At one point he momentarily dropped his cover. He sat at his desk signing his charts when he thought about his slipup.

Amy Dellinger, his patient with gallstones, was desperately trying to remember the brand of birth control pills she took, and she barked to her husband, "Andy! Hand me my purse. I have the dispenser in there."

The surgeon jerked his head up at the recognition of his real name. "What?" His heart was pounding. Had he been recognized?

She began digging in a large black handbag as relief began to flood his gut. She was talking to her husband! He looked at the obedient man sitting beside the exam table. "Oh," he covered, "I thought she said, 'Adam.' That's my first name." He forced a chuckle. "Senior moment, I guess."

"Oh, doctor," the patient gushed, "you look so young. You can't be havin' those. But just wait until you hit forty. I think my body is falling apart. First I sprain my knee playing tennis. I needed a hysterectomy six weeks ago, and now this. Talk about senior moments— I think I need a real overhaul." She laughed. "Say, doc, while you're in there, could you take out anything else I don't need? I don't want to come back anytime soon."

Adam shook his head and smiled. "I think we'll just concentrate on your gallbladder, Ms. Dellinger."

"What about this?" she added, running her hand over her generous waist. "Can't you suck out about twenty pounds of this while you're there?"

It was a common request. He'd only been a surgeon for a short time, and he'd already had two similar petitions. He shook his head. "Sorry."

Andy leaned forward and patted his wife's hand. "Twenty pounds? You'd be a stick, honey."

"Better a stick than a fireplug."

His attention jarred back to the present as the phone rang. He picked it up. It was Lisa, his receptionist. "Dr. Tyson? I've got Gerri from OR on line 1. She's checking on your availability to do an add-on appendectomy."

He nodded. "OK." He paused while the call was transferred. He heard a click, then Gerri's voice.

"Hello, Adam."

Not Dr. Tyson. Adam. Boy, they were on friendly terms fast. "Yes."

"It's Gerri. How is your morning going? Will you be finished up soon? Dr. Shank from ER called over looking for you. He has a kid with appendicitis, and I can slide you into a one o'clock spot if you bring your handsome self this way."

Handsome? Adam took a deep breath. Her voice was so feminine. Like silk. He remembered his welcome reception and her emerald dress with the long slit up the side.

"Adam?"

"I'm here. Just finishing up some paperwork. I can be there in ten minutes."

"Great. Can I tell Dr. Shank to expect you?"

"Sure."

She paused. "Listen . . . I'm putting together a little dinner party at my place to introduce you to a few of the OR staff. Would you be free for dinner Friday at 7?"

He smiled to himself. Being a real surgeon had its advantages. "I'd love to."

"Wonderful. I'll give you directions when I see you this afternoon."

"OK." He looked up at the diploma on the wall. Adam Tyson was never this good.

"Stop by my office. It's just outside the double doors beside the recovery room. We'll share a cup of coffee."

Share a cup? Everything she says sounds so . . . inviting. Yellow flags were up. She was just too friendly.

He cleared his throat, shrugging off his uneasiness. *I guess it comes with the territory. Bright, young surgeon. Single. A promise of riches.*

"I'll stop by."

∞

Timmy shoved a Budweiser can into the sand, stood up for a better look at the boat beside the pier, and muttered a curse. His buddy, Keith Lasorda, repeated his words, a little too loudly for a family beach. "You idiot! Why did you drop it *there?*"

Timmy cringed. That made his scalp hurt. And the sunburn across his stitches didn't help. "Hey," he countered, whispering, "you try carrying a two hundred pound stiff in a kayak. I'm lucky I made it beyond the breakers before capsizing."

"That dude is going to be mad. You told him you'd dropped it way offshore."

"I dropped it offshore all right. I couldn't help it. He had it chained to cinder blocks to make it sink. Once they fell overboard, I couldn't keep the kayak upright." Timmy shrugged. "I figured it would be gone in a few days."

"You idiot."

"What's he going to do? Ask for his money back? He never wanted to see me again."

"We'd better get out of town."

Timmy huffed. "Some vacation town this turned out to be." He touched his scalp lightly, exploring the long row of nylon stitches. "Who's going to take these out if we leave before my appointment with the doctor?"

"My sister's a nurse." Keith smiled. "Or I can do it. I watched the doc take out the stitches on my brother's knee. Nothin' to it."

Timmy cursed his friend. "The cops are here. Let's get out of this creepy town."

Keith picked up a cooler, laughing in a mocking voice. "Serenity. A place to relax."

Timmy cursed and shuffled his feet through the sand, leaving two beer cans and a snakelike trail on the beach behind him.

∽

Beth never thought she would pray that she would pass gas.

Such a common thing, and rude, something Beth never gave a second thought to, except to scold Travis for being ill-mannered around her. She had grown up with sisters and was unprepared for the volume or frequency of raspberries that her husband or her son seemed capable of.

While growing up, Beth and her sisters had experienced an occasional dainty feminine excuse for the rare mistaken public gas displacement. But now Beth was forced to think about it, even hoped for it. Prayed for it. Anything to get rid of her post-operative bloat and back to her slender outline she'd worked so hard to maintain.

She wanted something to eat, but no, flatulence needed to occur first. Doctor's orders, she was told. And so she strained, as much as her fresh sutured abdomen could take. And walked. And walked. And rolled from side to side. Anything to stimulate the crude noise she'd been so properly trained to avoid.

But this morning the vulgarity occurred, and Beth whispered, "Hallelujah."

A smile curved her full lips as she punched the nursing call button. "Bring me some oatmeal," she grunted. "Code green accomplished."

She basked in a moment of private afterglow before a knock interrupted her commemoration. "Ms. Carlson?"

Beth looked up to see her door swing open and a sharply dressed member of the Serenity Police enter. The man appeared to be in his young thirties, a bodybuilder no doubt, with a pressed blue uniform and shoes so polished she imagined you could comb your hair in the reflection.

"Deputy Monroe, Serenity Police."

She nodded.

"I've got an update on Michael Cunningham."

She adjusted her hospital bed, raising the head. "I'm all ears."

"I've been in contact with the Sarasota Police Department. It seems Mr. Cunningham hasn't been seen for two months. He rented an apartment two blocks from a hospital where he worked, and he told someone he was moving to California, but left no forwarding address. We ran checks on all the common utility accounts, but he hasn't surfaced in California either. He hasn't used a common credit card since May. Either this guy is dead or he's trying awful hard to be invisible."

"What about the car? Any clues there?"

"The car's clean. Records in the glove box indicate meticulous attention to upkeep. Last service was in Sarasota in April, a routine oil change."

"Any sightings around here?"

He shook his head. "My guess is someone else was driving his car."

"Why?"

He shrugged. "Just a hunch."

"What's next?"

"Unless we find him soon, I'll need to make a trip to Sarasota. Do a little snooping."

"Serenity Police force will send you?"

"Sure. We have a fund for just such investigations. Of course we rarely use it, but this is our case, and it's our job to follow it through."

She scratched her chin and sampled the air drifting from beneath her sheets. She studied the officer. Apparently he wasn't appreciating the green cloud. She cringed and tried to bring the conversation to a hasty conclusion before he fainted. "Well, thanks for your work." She picked up her Bible, signaling an end to the encounter.

He retreated a few steps. Either he was done or she had smoked him out. "I'll let you know if we come up with anything else."

She waited until the door closed before she lifted the sheet and began fanning furiously.

Ah, glorious relief!

Travis had never been in a police vehicle before. This one was definitely cool, with video and audio surveillance equipment, radar, spotlights, and radio. But his enthusiasm was dampened by the humiliation of being escorted into the jeep in front of Kristy like he was a common criminal. At least they didn't put him in the back. As he sat in the passenger seat, he cast a longing glance in her direction, hoping she wouldn't run to her father and report his apparent delinquency.

Dan Smith steadied his clipboard on his knee. "Why did you tell him to fish in that exact location?"

"I'd seen boats in that area the day before. They were pulling in fish right and left." He shrugged. "The tourists are always askin' the locals for tips. So I told him. That's all."

"You traded this information for cigarettes?"

Travis cringed. He had hoped the Yankee wouldn't have shared that tidbit of information about their interaction. He looked down at his sandy shoes. "Yes, sir," he said politely. No use lying about it. As long as he could keep that juicy morsel from Kristy and his mom, he'd be happy.

"Are you twenty-one?"

Travis knew he was ribbing him to make a point. "Not until next month, sir."

The officer looked up from his clipboard. "Very funny."

"Yes, sir." He watched as Kristy turned and stepped onto the beach. "Can I go now?"

"I'll need your address."

Travis recited it.

"Your mother is Beth! I thought I'd seen you before."

He nodded. "Do me a favor. Could you skip the part about the cigarettes if you talk to my mom?"

"Maybe."

Travis sighed. "Maybe?"

"Promise to quit?"

He nodded solemnly. "Deal."

Travis heard the clicking noise as the door lock disengaged. "Thank you, sir," he said. He opened the door and sighed.

Kristy was a hundred yards down the beach, and not looking back.

She probably thinks I dumped that body. He looked down as he imagined the conversation she'd have with her father, the pastor.

He kicked his shoe against the parking lot and decided to look for Bart. Maybe he could get his mind off the girl if he tried hanging ten from a surfboard.

CHAPTER
8

By Friday afternoon Travis had wrestled his mother's queen-sized mattress and bed-frame down the stairs and rearranged the living room around it. Now she would only need to get up the front steps, the equivalent of one story, to get safely into their stilted cottage.

The hospital's administration had made it abundantly clear: No coming to work until she was fully recuperated. So all she had to do for the next three weeks was lounge on the deck and soak up the sun. She'd told Travis that if she could just get him away from his Nintendo and her father out fishing, she might just enjoy the solitude, maybe read a Gayle Roper mystery or two.

Her father drove her home in her own Caravan, complete with a new left rear tire. She walked slowly to the house holding Travis's arm. It seemed only yesterday that she'd carried him into their home, a helpless, dependent infant, and now he was supporting her, coaxing her the whole way.

"Easy, Mom. Watch the bush. OK. Take a step up. Now lean on me and rest."

She climbed two steps, then panted and held onto her son's arm. "You're getting so tan. You must have given up your game system."

He smiled. "Not completely, but the surf has been good this week." He paused. "Up one more step."

"You're worse than the sarge I had for a nurse."

"I think I saw her. Does she look like she could beat Hulk Hogan?"

"That's the one. Meaner than a snake," she puffed. "But the best nurse I've ever seen. She could motivate a cat into swimming laps in a pool."

Five minutes later she entered the den, where a bouquet of fresh flowers with a *Welcome Home* sign sat on the coffee table. Her bed was next to the wall, the couch was pushed aside, and the only remaining furniture was a big stuffed leather recliner, right in front of the TV. "Where to?" asked Travis. "Chair or bed?"

"Chair."

They were barely settled when a voice called through the still-open front door. "Ms. Carlson?"

"In here," she called weakly.

A man walked in. It was Dan Smith, Serenity Police. "Hi, Travis," he said, nodding and removing his hat. He looked at Beth and nodded again. "Ma'am."

"Please don't call me that. I'm not old enough for you to call me ma'am."

"I call every lady ma'am, ma'am. Everyone older than me, that is."

"Careful," she snarled.

"Yes, ma'am," he said, wincing immediately. "Old habits die hard."

"Yes, sir," she mimicked. "Do you have news about Michael Cunningham?"

He sat down on the edge of her bed. "Maybe. I'm not sure."

Travis plopped down on the couch.

"I'm sure Travis told you about the body that was pulled up the other day down at the pier."

She nodded.

"We still don't have a positive ID, but a few interesting things have turned up."

"Interesting things?" Travis responded.

"The body was in bad shape. We couldn't even tell the sex."

Grandpa Ike cleared his throat and shifted in his place on the sofa. Travis groaned. "You mean—"

"Don't make me explain. Suffice it to say that certain positive identifying features were nibbled away."

Beth sighed. "Gross."

"Anyway, we think it was a male. The hair was relatively short, and the only clothing was a shirt with a single engraved gold cuff link on one arm."

"Engraved?"

He nodded. "M.C."

"Michael Cunningham," Beth whispered immediately. "It has to be."

"I'm not so sure. It's going to take the state lab a few weeks to process the body and do a complete autopsy."

"But have you had any unsolved murders in Serenity?"

He shook his head. "There's never been a murder in the town in recorded history."

"Anyone missing?"

"Only a handful of people presumed drowned. And most of them were witnessed in boating accidents or riptides." He paused, apparently interested in cleaning the dirt from beneath a fingernail. "But bodies don't last long in the ocean. Scavenger fish reduce 'em to bone fragments within a few days."

Travis leaned forward. "It makes sense. The car along the road is registered to Michael Cunningham, but he is nowhere to be found. A few days later a body turns up wearing cuff links engraved M.C. Who else could it be?"

"We aren't closing any doors at this point. We need to wait for the autopsy. And I'll tell the state lab about our suspicions. They may be able to find Cunningham's dental records for comparison."

"Any more word about the search for information in Florida?"

"Not yet. Greg Monroe, the other officer in our department, is getting ready to go down next week. We needed to arrange for someone from the county sheriff's department to cover his shifts while he's away."

Beth nodded. Nothing seemed to happen fast enough to satisfy her curiosity.

But then again, nothing about the pace of life in Serenity hinted at anything close to serene.

She watched the officer let himself out, and Travis helped her into a more comfortable position with her feet elevated.

Home at last.

CHAPTER
9

THAT EVENING AT A few minutes past 7, Adam Tyson pulled into the oceanfront home of Gerri Fiori, the OR nursing director. There was only one vehicle in the driveway, a Ford Explorer. *Hmmm. Everyone must be fashionably late.*

He parked his Dodge Dakota pickup and carried the freshly cut flower arrangement to the door. Gerri answered his knock. She was wearing a simple and very short black dress. Her dark hair glistened with blonde highlights and was cut just above her silver earrings, which were small dolphins jumping over a half-moon. The dress was low cut, making Adam force his eyes away to look over her lovely home. She seemed to appreciate the difficulty he was having.

"First one here?" he asked timidly.

She threw up her hands after placing the flowers in a vase. "Would you believe Donna Snyder backed out on me at the last minute? She said her son was in the championship game in a local Little League competition and he'd never forgive her if she missed." She huffed. "The nerve!"

She continued, "And Deb Parrish was called out of town because her mother is ill."

"That's too bad."

"So I called David Winters, the hospital CEO, thinking I can't have this be a total waste of an evening for you, but he and his wife have gone to Atlanta for the weekend." She held out her hands, palms up. "So I guess it's just us." She smiled. "I hope you like shrimp scampi. We've got enough to feed an army."

"I love seafood."

She took a step toward the kitchen. The main level of the house followed an open plan, with a living room and dining area together flowing right into the kitchen, separated by cabinets to set apart the food preparation area. "Well, I had hoped you'd have some company while I finished dinner." She gestured toward a large couch with a green floral print. "Make yourself at home."

With that, she retreated toward the kitchen. "Wine?" she called back. "I'm drinking white, but I have a selection."

"I'd better pass. You never know what might happen in the ER in Serenity."

A minute later she reappeared, carrying two glasses. She handed him a goblet. "One glass of wine won't hurt," she added before retreating again.

From where he stood, he only had to stoop slightly to look under the overhanging cabinets to see where she worked. He sipped at his wine slowly and promised himself he'd stop at half a glass. He surveyed the room. The decorating theme was nautical, with seascapes and lighthouses predominating. He looked for personal pictures, clues to Gerri's private life, but saw none. Her books were a smattering of popular fiction, with self-help, management, and eastern mysticism topping her nonfiction titles. The largest book by far was a coffee table reference volume lying by itself on a footstool in front of a leather recliner. It was easily two inches thick and appeared to be the ultimate encyclopedia of Harley-Davidson motorcycles. He hoisted the volume after setting down his glass. He raised his voice. "Don't tell me you ride."

She leaned out over the counter beneath the overhanging cabinets. "Every chance I get."

He shook his head, amazed. He couldn't quite picture this slender woman straddling a powerful v-twin, wearing a black half-helmet and a pair of leathers. His next thought was out of his mouth before he could check it. "I suppose you have a tattoo as well."

She pressed the top of her little black party dress to her chest. "It's not something I can show you on our first date."

So now it's a date. I thought this was an introduction to the OR staff. The staff that conveniently deserted me.

He forced a chuckle but couldn't stop his imagination from try-

ing to envision such a work of skin art. He returned to scanning the
room. It was tastefully decorated in a casual style he liked, a mixed
breed of casual-beach-American-modern. The family room opened
onto a screened-in porch that contained a second seating area with
an overhanging ceiling fan. He slid open a glass door and stepped into
the evening air. The ocean breeze carried the scent of the sea, and
the sky over the water was just beginning to change color. He turned
at the sound of her voice.

"The sunrise is beautiful from this porch. The sunset is prettier
from the deck of my bedroom on the third floor. You can see the
sound from there." She held her wine glass with both hands and
leaned her head to one side against the door-frame. "I spend more
time on my decks than anywhere else."

He stared out over the ocean. "I can see why."

"So how is our new nursing director?"

"Better. Discharged today."

"Discharged?" She paused, her tone of voice suddenly cool. "I'll
have to fix her a casserole."

He didn't reply.

"She lives just four houses down. Her father has a place right on
the beach." She pointed. "Right over there, where she can keep an
eye on me."

"I'm a little surprised that you didn't want her job."

She kept her head against the door-frame, appearing relaxed
enough to be off-guard. "I did want it," she replied. "But I'm afraid
I've done too good a job in my present position. Mr. Winters, our
beloved CEO, can't seem to do without me running the OR." She
sipped her wine. "I told him I wanted the job. He gave me more
money to stay in mine instead."

She spoke again after draining her glass. "I'll need only a few
more minutes, then we can eat."

"Can I help?"

She shrugged. "You can supervise."

He followed her black dress into the kitchen. It certainly wasn't
designed for warmth.

She sautéed the shrimp in a mixture of butter, garlic, and wine.
The aroma was heavenly. A ten-inch TV was on, mounted under a

kitchen cabinet. He hadn't paid attention to the advertisement until Gerri raised a polished fingernail at the screen and quoted the Domino's pizza jingle at the mischievous mascot. "Bad Andy. Good pizza."

His breath caught in his throat at the recognition of his real name. He quickly chided himself. *Careful, Andy. It's only a pizza ad.*

She served heaping portions of steaming pasta bathed in scampi with jumbo shrimp. There was fresh broccoli, salad, and hot garlic bread slathered with melted butter. Since it was just the two of them, they carried their plates to the deck to look at the ocean.

While they ate, Gerri prodded. Where was he from? Where did he grow up? Why did he leave California? Why leave a practice in mid-career?

He shifted in his seat and tried to appear comfortable at her inquisition. His *modus operandi* had been to take only Adam Tyson's credentials, education, and boards. The rest of his life was his own. His upbringing, his family, his likes and dislikes were authentic Andy. That way he would always remember what he said. The second part of his plan was the area where he seemed to be letting down his guard. He had planned to never socialize outside the hospital with professional colleagues. Sooner or later, if he allowed himself too close, someone would see a discrepancy. But tonight was not supposed to be an intimate dinner with Gerri, so he wouldn't blame himself for that. He couldn't very well just excuse himself when the other guests declined the invitation.

Gerri reached for her glass, her dress edging higher. She made no effort to anchor it in place. Adam took a deep breath and tried to concentrate on his scampi. When she crossed her legs, Adam looked away and stabbed a shrimp.

He turned the table and began his own inquiry. Family? In Georgia. Marriages? One. The only good thing to come of that was her Harley. Children? Never wanted them. School? University of North Carolina. Tar Heels basketball was only one of two things that would ever make her miss a meal. The other? "I can't tell you on our first date."

The dating reference again. Did she really view this as a date? The dress edged north again. He cleared his throat and studied the carpet. Caution lights flashed for Adam big-time. *Either this wine is getting to her or she knows exactly what she's doing.*

He tried unsuccessfully to concentrate. "The scampi is wonderful."

She only smiled and slowly teased the tail from a shrimp between her lips.

He stayed another hour, sipping coffee and having a small slice of peach pie, an item Gerri had purchased from a bakery north of Serenity. He stood, wanting to make a polite exit before the black dress made rational thought impossible. "I really should check on my patients."

He made a hasty retreat, thanking her for her willingness to feed him in spite of the impoliteness of the rest of her invited guests. She made an obligated protest at his departure and stood silhouetted in the doorway as he descended the stairs to his pickup.

Once seated with his seatbelt on, he adjusted his rearview mirror to look at his hair. His mind returned to the little black dress. "Bad Andy," he whispered to himself. "Bad Andy."

∞

Gerri watched him disappear before meandering back to her kitchen where she poured herself another glass of wine and cut a second piece of pie. Her first, consumed in front of her guest, had been so small.

She plopped onto her recliner and punched number 2 on her phone, speed-dialing David Winters, the hospital CEO.

"Hello. Dave Winters."

"It's me."

"Alone so soon?"

"Surgeons eat fast."

"Any luck?"

"He's as naive as Crawford, but better."

"Better in what way?"

"The nurses say he's faster, more efficient."

"Good. It will be believable when we post such high numbers."

"Really. I think this is going to work."

"So finally you admit that I made the right decision."

"Maybe. But I worry about his past. I still think you should have checked him out personally."

"Linda looked at his application—"

"She's a secretary, Dave. She doesn't know medicine."

"He passed the Credentials Committee," he huffed.

"They rubber-stamped him just like they do anyone with a license and a current board certification."

"Why are you so down on Tyson?"

"I'm not down on him. It's just that maybe he seems . . . well, too good. I still think you were too quick to hire the first guy who was willing to come."

"He's going to work out fine, Gerri. Stop worrying. You were as anxious as I was to get back in business."

She swirled the wine in her glass. "I hope you're right."

"Trust me. It will work. So the nurses say he's better than Crawford."

"Anyone would be better than that saint."

"And that's exactly why we hired Tyson. He's no saint, that's for sure. And he doesn't have the family attachments like Crawford did. I thought Crawford's wife was going to blow up when the media reported he'd been drinking."

"But Reba just let it go."

"She didn't seem to have the energy to defend him after all."

She sipped her wine and smiled. "I wore the little black dress."

"I wish I was there."

"Tyson had a hard time keeping his eyes on the shrimp."

"Anyone with a functioning Y chromosome wouldn't have noticed the shrimp with you in that dress." He sighed.

She enjoyed the power she held over men. Let them see a little skin, and you might as well completely sever them from their frontal lobes. All that's left is a brain stem. Pure animal responses.

Dave cleared his throat. It was a nervous habit that annoyed her. She could pick him out of a crowded room just listening for that sound. "I guess you heard about the body."

"You think it's our man?"

"Who else would it be?" he huffed. "Just wait until I see that punk again. He told me no one would ever find it."

"He was a druggie. He probably lied about access to a boat."

"What's done is done. They'll never link him to us anyway."

"I wish there was another way."

"We couldn't leave him in the freezer forever."

"But it sure was convenient that the hospital remodeled the kitchen when they did." She tapped her glass against her teeth. "I just wish he would have gone away. I didn't want him dead."

"We never chose to make it this way. He had cancer, you know. He wasn't going to be around long anyway."

"So I heard."

"No one could have known he would die from one punch."

"Murder is murder, Dave."

"It was an accident. We've been through this."

She swirled the liquid in the glass, then drained it. "So when will the billing start with Tyson?"

"We need to let him get established for a while. Insurance companies won't believe it if he's that busy right away." He cleared his throat again. "We'll be up to Crawford's level in six months. In the meantime, keep an eye on Tyson. I want to know what's up with him."

"My pleasure. He's cute."

"Careful, sweetheart. Don't enjoy your assignment too much."

"I won't. So are you coming over or not?"

"Still have on the black dress?"

She giggled. "Of course."

"I'm on my way."

She hung up the phone and shook her head. *What is it with that Y chromosome anyway?*

❧

Greg Monroe, Serenity Police deputy, sorted through the file on his table. Unlike the other deputy on the police force, he was in his early thirties, but he shared an enthusiasm for police work, bodybuilding, and carbohydrates. He was taller than his partner, had his uniforms laundered with extra starch, and polished his shoes once a week whether they needed it or not. He brushed the crumbs from his protein powerbar off the desk. "Say, Dan, what do you make of the fact that our only real suspicion for an ID of the body is the same as the owner of the car that ran into Beth Carlson?"

Dan shrugged. "So?"

"So her son seemed to know where the body was. At least he pointed out the spot to the man who snagged it."

"Are you suggesting that Travis had something to do with the body being where it was?"

"Or that he witnessed it being dumped there."

"Doesn't seem likely." Dan filled the coffeemaker with water. It was 4 in the afternoon, but he had the night shift.

"But didn't they train us not to believe in coincidences? So why would the son of the woman injured know the location of the body of the man who hit her?"

"Faulty assumptions. First, we don't know that he knew the location of the body. All he knew was that the fish were feeding there—"

"Yeah, on Michael Cunningham's body."

"Not necessarily on Michael Cunningham's body. That's your second assumption. We don't have a positive ID yet."

"Can you think of another missing person with the initials M.C.?"

Dan shook his head. "Not offhand, but—"

"But nothing. I'm keepin' an eye on the kid. He may not be telling us everything."

"You just want to keep an eye on his mom."

"Professional duty," he said, laughing and twisting the wedding band on his left hand. "I don't think she's keeping her son reined in."

"He seems like an honest enough kid."

"He's been lying to his mother about smoking. Maybe he's lying to us to cover for himself." He paused. "I'll bet the next call we get about that kid is another OxyContin overdose."

"You think he's a druggie? He's a little young."

"I've seen it before. How many OxyContin overdoses have we seen in the last few months?"

Dan shrugged. "Three or four."

"And all teenagers. And one was the boy who lives on the same street as this punk."

"Bart?"

"No. His older brother, Stan."

Dan held up his hands. "OK, I'll keep an open mind."

Greg shut the file. "I'm out of here. I hope Serenity's quiet for you tonight."

Dan mumbled. "Right."

∞

Beth Carlson disrobed and took her first real shower since her accident. The warm, soft water seemed to wash away not only the dirt and grime, but the fear she'd had that had plagued her since her accident—that she'd made a horrible mistake in bringing Travis here, and the hit-and-run was sure proof. She shampooed once, then repeated the process, amazed that she was still able to scrub old blood from her scalp. She was anemic, she knew that. Only a little exertion made her short of breath. But every day was better than the day before. She wanted to be back on the job in two more weeks. Dave Winters, the hospital administrator, wasn't pushing her. Gerri Fiori, the head nurse in the OR, had generously agreed to stay on as interim nursing director. The only thing pushing Beth Carlson to recover quickly was Beth Carlson.

She ran her towel and then her hand over her left breast, the side of her injury, and explored the large bruise. The swelling was receding, but a pecan-sized knot was still present in the tail of the breast, near her left armpit. *Probably just a hematoma, a collection of blood from the accident.*

She thought about her own mother, who battled for years against breast cancer, and a twinge of doubt called from the edges of her mind.

Don't be stupid, Beth. You get a lump in the breast after being hit by a car. It's trauma. Not the big C. Stop being paranoid.

She stood in front of the mirror and raised her hands over her head. Slowly, so as not to stretch her broken ribs. A small dimple formed over the lump when she raised her arms. Just scar tissue. She smiled. *I'll check it again in a couple weeks. It will be gone.*

She dried her hair and was just slipping into her pajamas when she heard the doorbell. She called to her son. "Travis, could you get that?"

She put on a modest robe and towel-dried her hair before brushing it out. As she brushed, she listened from a crack in the bathroom door. It was Adam Tyson, who had heard she lived close by and stopped in to see how she was getting along. He brought a basket of fruit and muffins for breakfast. This man was too much. How thoughtful!

She looked around the bathroom. The supplies were limited. She didn't even have her makeup down here yet. Travis had moved her bed down, but a fourteen-year-old boy couldn't be counted upon to know everything a woman would need. She fluffed her hair with her hands and shrugged at the image in the mirror. *Oh well, he'll have to settle for clean instead of made up.*

She pushed open the door and walked slowly to her recliner. "Dr. Tyson, how nice of you to stop in."

He stood politely by the door wearing a casual print shirt and a pair of pressed khaki pants. "You look great."

Ike slapped the surgeon on the shoulder. "We owe a debt of thanks to you, doc."

"Don't just stand there by the door. Come in." She gestured to the couch. "I'm afraid it's a bit crowded in here. I had Trav move my bed down until I feel up to doing the stairs."

"On one condition." He raised an index finger. "You call me Adam. You can call me Dr. Tyson in front of the staff at the hospital, but when it's just us, call me by my first name."

She tested it. "Adam," she said quietly. "I suppose I'll agree to that."

He sat on the couch after assisting Beth into her recliner. Ike sat on the bed. Travis took the muffins to his mother and then on to the kitchen.

"Thanks for the fruit, doc," Ike said.

"Adam."

Ike snapped his fingers. "Adam," he repeated.

The surgeon looked at Beth. "How was your day?" He paused. "You really are looking great."

Right. No makeup. My hair is wet. And I look like a grandmother wrapped up in this old terry cloth bathrobe. She joked, "Oh, I feel like a beauty queen."

"Believe me. As far as patients go, you get a 10."

"Most of your patients are Medicare."

He frowned. "Got me there."

Ike leaned forward. "So." He lifted his right hand, palm up. "Who are you anyway?"

Adam's head snapped up.

Beth cringed. She knew what her father was after.

Adam's voice was quiet. "Who am I?"

Ike smiled. "Don't be alarmed. I spent my career getting to know people. Everybody finds their identity somehow. Some people by their careers, others by their abilities. It just occurred to me that you saved my daughter's life, and I don't really know anything about you."

"I, well, I'm a general surgeon." He shrugged. "College and medical training at UCLA."

Ike nodded. "That's what you do. But who are you? What defines you?"

Beth was used to this line of questioning coming from her father, the retired pastor. He loved to challenge men to find their identity outside of their own accomplishments. She just prayed that Adam wouldn't be put off. Ike had a direct approach to everyone. He wouldn't have been intimidated by the President of the United States.

"Adam Tyson," he said quietly. "Who am I?" He studied his hands for a moment before turning the tables. "Who are you?"

Ike smiled. "Fair enough. I'm Ike Williamson, beloved child of God. I've come to understand His love for me independent of anything I do. If I define myself this way, I can always feel good about who I am. If I define myself any other way, say by my occupation, then I only feel good if my performance is up to my expectations."

Beth reached over and touched her father's arm. "Dad, Adam just got here. He didn't ask for a sermon on identity."

Adam shook his head. "It's OK. I appreciate a man who knows what he thinks. What was your job, Ike?"

Ike smiled.

Beth answered for him. "He was a pastor. Big surprise there, huh?"

The old man chuckled. "I'm sure it's no surprise. I've talked to hundreds of men just like you, Adam. We get our self-image from our jobs." He shook his head. "But when that's gone, what's left?"

Adam nodded. "Something to think about, that's for sure."

"How about you, Adam? Do you have a relationship with God?"

Beth looked down. She knew the discussion was important but found herself cringing inside, hoping that Adam wouldn't think they were some sort of religious fanatics. Her father was nothing if not direct.

Adam ran a hand through his short, dark hair. "I—I guess I wouldn't put it that way." He paused. "At one point I would have said, 'Sure.' I went to church. I was confident back then."

He halted. Ike stayed quiet. He knew Adam would say more when he was ready.

He did. "I even had dreams of being a missionary surgeon, working in Africa or Asia in a mission hospital." He shook his head. "That was a long time ago."

Beth wanted to speak before her father, the pit bull, had a chance to bite again. "Are you comfortable with this, Adam? Can you tell us what happened to your dream?"

He nodded. "It's OK. I just haven't talked about this for a long time." He looked toward the back deck and the darkness beyond. "I don't really know. Slowly I lost my zeal in a series of disappointments. I lost faith in a God who cared anything about me."

"Medical training challenges a lot of people," Ike added.

"That was part of it, I guess." He reached for a small framed photograph on an end table beside the couch. It was a picture of Travis in a Little League uniform. The picture was a few years old. Obviously he wanted to change the subject. He looked at Travis. "You?"

Travis nodded.

"Do you play? I love baseball. I pitched at Fresno State."

"What about UCLA?" Travis questioned.

Adam looked down at the picture. "Uh, oh, I transferred there to finish up, but I didn't play baseball there." He set the picture down and rubbed his shoulder. "I'd love to throw with you. It's been a long time for me. Do you still play?"

Travis shook his head. "Not since I was ten."

Beth smiled. "You were very good, Trav. Too young to give it up."

"I can give you some tips."

Travis frowned. "I don't know. Our yard isn't big enough to hit a baseball."

"How about I rummage through my boxes? I'm sure I can find my old glove." He pointed with his head to the beach. "We can make a pitcher's mound on the sand, step off the distance to home plate. We can have a regular baseball clinic."

"I haven't played for a long time."

"Neither have I, Travis. It would sure be fun for me."

"Tell you what. I haven't played baseball for a long time. You haven't been to church for a long time. You go to church with me, and I'll play baseball with you."

Beth's jaw dropped. She couldn't believe what was coming out of her son's mouth. This was the child she practically dragged to church every Sunday of his life. And now he and her father were ganging up on poor Adam to sanctify him in one visit. "Travis," she scolded, "we haven't even been to church yet ourselves. We can't just—"

"I want to go to the beach church."

"And what's wrong with First Presbyterian? I've been going there since—"

Beth silenced her father with "the look." "If the boy actually wants to go to a church, I'll be the last to get in his way."

Travis stuck his chest out. "Hey, I've wanted to go to church before. It's just that, well . . ." His voice trailed off.

"Enough of the saint act, Trav. You've protested every weekend for years." Beth shook her head. "So what is it with you two? Adam is nice enough to bring me a basket of goodies, and you guys gang up on him like some evangelism project!"

Adam leaned forward and touched her arm. "Easy, Beth, I haven't felt like a project. I can see how sincerely Ike believes what he's telling me. And as for this guy," he added, pointing at Travis's chest, "I like baseball enough to make a trade. I'll go to church with you if you'll be my throwing partner."

Travis smiled and held out his hand. "Deal."

Ike laughed. "OK."

Beth shook her head. She was suspicious. Travis wanted to go to the beach church? What did he know about that?

She studied her son for a moment. When she'd left for pizza last week, he was a grumpy, negative teen who spent hours in front of the TV playing video games. Now he spent his days playing with friends on the beach, fixed up the den for her recovery, bought her flowers, and invited Adam to church. The boy looked like her son. Even sounded like her son. She smiled at the thought.

Aliens must have taken over my son's body.

∞

That night Adam walked alone on the beach, the moon and its reflection his only light. He'd never met a family quite like Beth and her father and son.

Why had he felt compelled to visit anyway? He knew the answer. Because the highlight of every day since he'd come here was the time he spent with Beth.

He'd have to reevaluate his commitment to keeping his distance with his fellow professionals. Gerri was a snake. Lovely, and so apparently interested and available, but his guard was up. Why did she come on so strong?

But what would be wrong with enjoying a little of what she was offering? He shuffled along, kicking up the sand. No, he decided. Caution flags were up. He'd better drive slow around Gerri.

His thoughts returned to Beth. She was so sweet, so pretty, and . . . what was it about her? He couldn't pinpoint it beyond the fact that she just seemed so comfortable and confident with who she was, even in hard times. Quiet strength. That was it. She was a woman of quiet strength, and that attracted him more than anyone ever had.

And what about Ike? What was up with him? He'd known a few preachers in his life. Plastic ones interested in milking people for their money in the name of God. He remembered his conversation with Ike. As beautiful as Beth was, her father was equally as real and committed to what he believed. He could sense Beth's irritation at her father's abrupt manner. She told Adam so in so many words when he told her good-bye not thirty minutes ago. She'd walked him to the door and apologized over and over for her family's attack.

But strangely enough, he told her, he felt the exact opposite. He felt valued. He could tell Ike was really interested in him. "Don't be upset," Adam said, touching her shoulder. "It's really OK. I had an interesting chat."

"Thanks for paying attention to Trav." She paused and looked down. "He and his father used to play baseball nonstop. If he plays with you, it will be the first time since his father died."

"I didn't know," he said. "I wouldn't have pressed him."

"It was fine," she reassured. "Besides, he's the one who made the deal." She looked up, and their eyes met. Adam was captured by her simple beauty. To kiss her would have spoiled the intimacy of the moment. This was something more than physical. He looked in her eyes for a moment, unflinching. *She can see right through me. I'll never be able to hide from this woman.*

Now, on the beach, the memory of her eyes haunted him. He felt both revulsion and fear. *She'll find out who I really am!* He also felt the enticement and possibility of love. *I've never wanted to know someone so deeply.*

His thoughts returned to Ike and his direct questioning. His identity was a charade. If he pulled this off, he should go to Broadway.

The question haunted him as he stared up at the moon and its reflection on the pounding surf. *Who am I?*

CHAPTER
10

BETH'S FIRST NIGHT at home was far from restful. She hadn't realized how much she depended on the nurses to help with the little things. Getting to the bathroom with a nurse was one thing, but asking her father or Travis to help with such duties seemed another altogether. She took Percocet to help with her pain before retiring at 10, but awoke feeling groggy and disoriented by midnight. She stirred, not awake, not asleep. She rose thinking the pain in her abdomen was a full bladder. She was in her old house in Richmond and couldn't seem to find the bathroom that had always been by the kitchen.

Some smart-aleck had moved the bathroom. Or did he just move the door? Beth backtracked into the living room—her bedroom—and started out again. The kitchen seemed to be in the right place, so the bathroom needed to be there too. Maybe the pain in her abdomen wasn't just a full bladder. She'd been reading in the *Richmond Times Dispatch* about a recent shooting in a local emergency room. It must have been her. She was the victim. In fact, maybe the gunman moved her bathroom.

"Mom, what are you doing?" Travis had turned on the kitchen light.

"Don't turn on the light," she yelled, "he'll get you too."

Travis obeyed, snapping off the light. "Who?"

"Travis, I've been shot!"

"Mom?"

The kitchen started coming into focus, illuminated by the moonlight coming through the window. Travis slowly turned up the dimmer switch on the light over the kitchen table. The refrigerator was stark white, not bisque like hers in Richmond. *Wait a minute! This isn't Richmond.* She sniffed and fought back tears. "Travis, where am I?"

"Mom, you're in Serenity. We moved into Grandpa Ike's."

She gripped her stomach, feeling a row of skin staples running up and down next to her navel.

"Mom?"

"I'll be OK, Travis. I—I just—" She rubbed her eyes. "Good grief, Travis, I'm not taking any more of that Percocet. I was back in Richmond, trying to find the bathroom. But a man shot me in the gut and remodeled our kitchen."

Travis raised his voice. "Mom?"

She sighed and rested her forehead on her hands, leaning over the counter. "I'll be all right."

"W-want some water? Aspirin?"

She listened to the quiver in his voice and studied his face for a moment in the dimness. He was a boy on the verge of manhood, trying to be brave, choking back his fear. His hand covered his mouth.

"No, honey," she responded. "I just want some sleep."

She took his arm, and he escorted her to her recliner. "My knight in shining armor."

"I miss Dad."

She eased into the chair. Slowing down was the worst part, sending knives into her stomach. "Oh." She took a deep breath. "I do too, baby."

Travis sat on the bed and stared at his mother. "Do you like Dr. Tyson?"

"He's a good surgeon."

"That's not what I asked."

"Do you mean, do I like him, like do I like him like a boyfriend?" He shrugged and looked at the floor. "Something like that."

"He's very nice. He's kind and considerate. He's very handsome."

"He likes baseball."

"Yes," she said quietly.

"Why haven't you had any boyfriends?"

She sighed. "It's late, Trav."

"Why?"

"I've met some men who are interested in me, Trav, but they aren't the type of men I want."

"It's because of me, isn't it? What man wouldn't want you? You're pretty! It's because of me. They don't want the baggage."

"Baggage? I've never considered you baggage! And anyone who would think of you that way isn't welcome in my life." She longed to hold him in her arms like a child, but she hesitated, knowing he was growing up . . . and away. Middle schooler. Young man. One minute secure, challenging a surgeon to go to church; insecure the next, afraid he was the reason she hadn't been dating.

"Trav," she said, reaching for his arm, "modern-day men only want me because I'm pretty. They want more than I can give them without a marriage license. And that's the reason I don't get dates, not because of you. Do you understand?"

He sighed. "Yeah."

She squeezed his arm, prompting him to look up. "Do you like Dr. Tyson?"

He tried not to crack a smile. "He's a good surgeon," he mimicked.

She laughed. "Go to bed."

"Are you staying up?"

"For a while. I want to let this Percocet wear off before trying to sleep again."

He stood and kissed her forehead. "Night."

"Hit the light switch on your way. I'll just rest in the chair."

She sat in the room alone, her only light the moon spilling through the windows. The old clock on the stone mantel ticked loudly, something she'd never appreciated before experiencing this room in the night silence.

She thought about Adam Tyson. She was intrigued at the idea of a relationship but told herself to beware of a schoolgirl crush just because he'd intervened in her life in a crisis. And she didn't think he was a Christian. That was definitely important to her. And she was smart enough to know dating was no place for evangelism.

But still, he seemed so mysterious. Why would a successful young surgeon come to a small town mid-career? Midlife crisis? *Is he running from something?* Beth took a deep breath. *Am I?*

And why is a successful man, a man so buff, as Travis would say, single? Is he just married to medicine? Could I ever compete with a mistress so demanding?

Is he interested in me? Or just worried that his first case might have complications? Does he think I'm special? Or does he treat all of his patients with such tenderness?

After a half hour she pried herself out of the recliner and plodded mechanically to the bathroom. Then she slipped out the back door onto the deck to listen to the ocean, eventually finding sleep while lying on a padded wicker couch.

She awoke to the pounding surf, opening her eyes to see an orange ball just inches above the ocean horizon. This was her favorite time of day. The tourists were sleeping off the alcohol from the night before. The beach was inhabited only by nature and a few morning joggers. She could think. And pray.

In silence and solitude she had nothing to lean upon except God Himself. She prayed for Travis. For Ike. For her new job.

And for the wonderful Adam Tyson.

❧

Sunday morning in Serenity saw new tourists settling in after hectic Saturday afternoons spent unpacking. The early risers strolled lazily along the beach, picking up shark's teeth and colorful shell finds, watching the sunrise and dreaming of a life without cell phones and paging systems. The new day began with a hint of cooler weather. This brought out the joggers in force and gave Adam Tyson a moment's pause as he headed out the door for rounds at the hospital. Maybe he should consider getting a little exercise today.

He saw his inpatients in less than an hour, ate a shrimp and cheese omelette in the hospital cafeteria, and hung out in the ER talking to Natalie, the young ward clerk with six earrings, spiked bleached-blonde hair, and a tight leather skirt. As he leaned on the counter, laughing at her stories of last night's adventures, he found himself wondering if she had any other body piercings. She tapped the counter with her polished nails, the ones that used to be bright red but now were striped blue and orange. "Two more kids from an

Ecstasy party were in last night. I don't know what these kids nowa-days are thinking."

He studied her with a moment of wonder. She couldn't be more than twenty-five herself. But to hear her talk, she was already sepa-rated from the new generation and their problems. He nodded. "Amazing."

He surveyed the cubicles and the washable marker board where the patients were listed. The problems were mundane. Sore throats, cough, sunburn, and ear aches predominated. Nothing for the on-call surgeon. He walked out into the cool morning and checked his watch. It was still before 9.

He thought about Travis and his mother. He'd made a deal with Travis. It would be so nice to have the day to himself. A chance to unwind, maybe arrange the books in his study, take a walk on the beach, maybe go canoeing on the sound—but a deal was a deal. He sighed and headed for the white clapboard church building across from Serenity's fishing pier. He didn't feel like going to church, but then again, maybe Beth would be there. Just seeing her would be worth enduring an hour of propaganda.

He stepped into the foyer of the little church, a cramped area with a pine floor and a table complete with an open guest book and paper bulletins, the kind with a picture of a deer drinking from a mountain stream on the front. *Things haven't changed since the last time I attended church. Fifteen, twenty years ago?*

He scanned the guest book. People from Virginia, Maryland, North Carolina, and Pennsylvania were represented. He declined the written offer to sign up and slipped into the back of the auditorium. Immediately Adam felt out of sorts. This was a place for families. People with a common bond he no longer shared. He sat in the back row and pretended to be absorbed in the bulletin as he glanced around for Travis.

He hadn't shown. Adam took a deep breath and was about to slip out when an economy-sized woman and her equally large husband scooted into the bench beside him, walking sideways, their bellies dusting the back of the bench in front of them. The woman smiled and held out her hand.

It was cool and meaty, and she let her palm lie limp in his, without a squeeze. It was the kind of wimpy handshake that made Adam feel like wiping his hand on his trousers. "Clara Eavers. This is my husband, Fred. We've been coming to the beach church every summer vacation we've taken for years."

He forced a smile. "Andy Tyson." He caught himself after it was too late.

Fred leaned forward. His handshake was far from wimpy. He gripped Adam's hand and smiled, revealing a quarter-inch gap between his front teeth. "Nice to meet you, Andy." Fred released his death-grip, and Adam rubbed his hand, wondering if he needed an orthopedic consult.

Adam slid over. Some piano music had started, a hymn he remembered from childhood. A pleasant young woman at the front played the black and white keys without the benefit of any sheet music.

What am I doing here? Travis didn't even show. Beth isn't here to impress. I don't really need this crutch anymore. He looked around at the faces in the crowd. *Am I the only one who isn't immediately joyous at the playing of this music?*

He was conscious of a dull pain in the pit of his gut. His heart rate quickened, and he wished someone would turn on the large overhead fan above him. *I'm a hypocrite. I only came to see Beth.*

The front of the church had a small wooden railing and an upholstered kneeling bench, similar to the one he'd known as a teenager in Southern California. Perhaps the knife in his abdomen had something to do with the picture it brought to mind: kneeling, praying fervently, making a commitment to missionary service as a doctor. His excitement of carrying the Gospel and medicine to a needy foreign land.

He shook his head, wanting to forget. *You didn't keep Your end of the bargain, God. I was willing, but You let me down.*

The room felt close. He was about to slip out when Travis Carlson walked in the back door and grinned. They made eye contact, and Travis walked around the bench to come in from the other side. There was no way in past the super-sized duo next to Adam. Travis scooted over to sit beside him.

"I can't believe you came." Travis beamed.

Adam shrugged. "I guess I'm a little desperate for a baseball work-out." He looked over his shoulder, hoping that Beth was going to come, but quickly chastised himself for thinking she would get out so quickly after surgery.

Travis quieted down while a man in front introduced himself as Nick Thomas. The congregation stood for two hymns, sat, stood again for a prayer and an offering, then sat for a sermon.

Adam shifted in his seat, feeling like a cat in a mouse costume at a mouse reunion.

Nick Thomas appeared to be in his late thirties, with dark curly hair and a broad chest. He looked like a boxer, with a nose slightly misshapen from too many fights. He spoke in plain language, not the King James English Adam had been used to growing up.

Adam watched Travis out of the corner of his eye. Travis strained his head to the left, intent on something, or someone, up front. Adam leaned his own head to see around a man in front of him. *So that's it. A young lady with blonde hair sitting next to her mother and younger sister on the front row. Could this be why Travis was anxious to come to church without his mother?*

"There's been a murder in Serenity." Nick set his Bible on the podium and stepped aside to be closer to his audience. "A tragedy in a place of tranquillity. A ripple in a calm sea." He opened his Bible and read from Genesis, the story of Adam and Eve, of sin in a garden paradise. Of relationship owned and lost. Of glory and intimacy with God, and failure and separation.

Adam knew the story. He'd heard it before. But now he just wanted the service to be over. He'd fulfilled his part of the deal. Why did he want to play baseball with Travis anyway? Did he just want to get close to Beth?

Nick talked on about the solution for sin, of Christ's sacrifice, a way for intimacy with God restored. "It all comes down to faith . . ." The preacher's voice droned on as Adam's mind drifted.

These people have no idea. They are holding blindly to promises. Just like I did once. It's not all roses. God will let you down.

He endured for another twenty minutes, stood for another song, and was anxious for escape after a benediction. He looked at Travis. "You owe me, buddy."

Travis nodded, his eyes narrow. "I'm pretty rusty at baseball."

"Me too."

He was about to say more, even make plans to come by the Carlson cottage, but Travis slipped off on a beeline course to the front of the church. Adam's suspicions were confirmed when he heard the girl's excited voice. "Travis! You came!"

He eyed the teenager for a moment before walking out the back of the church, dodging women herding small children and men talking about fishing or the body that was found in the water off the pier. He even heard the rumor that it was the owner of the white Cadillac, the driver of the hit-and-run vehicle. He kept his mouth shut and edged around a line of people waiting to shake the preacher's hand.

Once outside, he looked at the sky, blue and full of promise. But the service left him feeling less than encouraged. It seemed to remind him of a happier time in his life, a time when he was able to trust, a time that had been long buried beneath the disappointments of growing up. He looked over his shoulder at Nick, a large smile breaking across his face as he hugged an elderly woman wearing a white dress to match her hair.

It's good for you, Nick. And good for grandma there. But those of us who have seen the real world have learned to rely on something a bit more practical—getting ahead by good old-fashioned hard work.

He pushed away the next thought, a stab of conviction at the fraud he'd become—*getting ahead by good old-fashioned deception.*

He squinted at the sun. *Oh well, who's the wiser? Nobody's been hurt. And I'm finally able to put my skills to work to help people who really need me. What's so bad about that? I thought church was supposed to make you feel good. So why do I feel so guilty?*

He knocked some sand from the top of his loafers and walked across the parking lot to his pickup.

"Nice to meet you, Andy," a shrill voice called from across the lot.

He glanced over at Fred and Clara Eavers, on their way to a seafood buffet, no doubt. He waved. *I should have given her my card. She's sure to have a gallbladder attack sooner or later.*

He sat alone in his truck. *What is it about these people? Are they really as happy as they seem? Or are they in some glorious state of denial of the realities of life?*

He started his truck struck by the fact that in this new town he had nothing to do and nowhere to go. No close friends to visit and no hobbies to keep him occupied.

Why did I think that all the respect I'd get as a surgeon would be enough to keep me afloat?

∾

The following day Greg Monroe, Serenity Police, rented a car in Sarasota, Florida, to investigate Michael Cunningham. Cunningham's last address was an apartment in North Sarasota, a place he hadn't been to for two months. That much he'd been able to tell by phone. To get more, he needed to follow up some leads face to face. The manager at the apartment complex was marginally helpful, said Cunningham was a quiet renter who'd only been there three months and only had a six-month lease. He was employed as a physician's assistant with a general surgery group, Bay Surgical Associates, and always paid his rent on time.

A criminal background check revealed nothing. A financial search showed no outstanding debts. His parents, Ned and Margaret Cunningham, were dead. He had no siblings. It was time to talk to his former employer.

The four partners at Bay Surgical Associates couldn't be reached. They were tending to emergencies in the hospital or were operating. But Greg was able to interview an office nurse, a straightforward woman of about fifty, dressed in a purple scrub top and white pants.

"No one here knew him too well," she began. "He was only with us for three months."

"Where was he before that?" Greg asked as he looked around the sparsely decorated professional office where he'd been escorted for the interview.

"Another surgical group in Tampa Bay—Suncoast Surgical Group, I believe."

Greg made notes. "Where'd he go from here?"

"Said he was heading back to California. I got the feeling that his old boss gave him a lot more independence than our surgeons. He always talked as if he knew more than his bosses. That didn't make him a favorite."

"Was he good?"

She nodded. "A few of our surgeons were intimidated by everything he knew."

"Any reason to think someone would want to kill him?"

"Is he dead? I thought you just said you were investigating a missing person."

"I did. But in the time we've been searching for him, a body has surfaced. We haven't gotten an ID on the body, but it's a possibility."

She ran her hand through her short, gray hair and sighed. "I hope he's all right. He always treated me nice."

"Back to my speculation. Any reason to think anyone would want to kill him?"

She sat on the edge of an examining table and seemed to be studying a diploma on the wall. "He wasn't well liked because of his knowledge, but no one around here wanted to get rid of him. Our docs didn't fire him. He quit suddenly, stating he wanted to get back to the West Coast." She paused as her hand went to her chin.

"How long did he work in Tampa Bay?"

"Not long. He'd only been there two months or so. But he worked for a real control freak up there. The surgeons up there didn't let the poor guy even take out stitches without supervision. I got the feeling that he could put them in better than most. He couldn't stand that environment, and he told me as much."

"And before that—any idea where he was from?"

"Like I said, Southern California somewhere." She scratched her chin. "That's all I know." Her eyes brightened as though she'd remembered something. "Except . . ."

"Except what?"

"I remember him giving a talk at our local high school on drug abuse. It was a real passion for him. Evidently someone he'd worked for in the past had real problems, and it destroyed his career. He would tell the story in an assembly. Really made the kids think."

Greg sighed. Nice information, but nothing really to get too excited about.

A female cleared her throat from the doorway. Greg looked up to see another nurse, dressed in a white uniform. She was young and very tall, perhaps six feet, and had short, brown hair. "Brenda told me you were back here talking about Mike. I went to that assembly at Sarasota High. He tells quite a story. Evidently Mike turned in his former employer, a surgeon in California. He says it was the most difficult thing he's ever done, but he was convinced it was the only way to get the guy any help."

"A surgeon?"

She nodded. "But he cut his own throat. In turning the guy in, he lost his own job."

Greg reached out his hand. "Thanks for the information, Ms.—"

"Andrews."

"Greg Monroe, Serenity Police."

He stared at his notes. "What happened to the surgeon?"

"Lost his license. Had to go into a rehab program."

"Do you remember his name?"

"He didn't give it. Just told the story to help the kids see how harmful drug abuse can be."

"Hmmm." He looked back at the older nurse. "A motive?" He paused. "Anyone around here having problems with drugs? Something like that would make him want to look for a job elsewhere."

The nurses looked at each other and laughed. "Not these guys. No way," they said.

"So it's back to Southern California, huh? Any idea where? Did he have his resumé forwarded anywhere?"

Nurse Andrews shook her head. "Nope."

"This makes little sense. He left no forwarding address with the Post Office, he hasn't used a major credit card since May, and no one has seen him either. He hasn't applied for a new driver's license or registration. His Cadillac was found in Serenity, North Carolina, with the Florida tags and registration."

The older nurse shifted on the examining table. "Why?"

"It seems he wanted to disappear."

"Disappear? Why?"

"Various reasons. Bad marriage. Bad debts. A desire for a new start. Or . . ."

"Or what?"

"Was he afraid of something? Afraid of someone? Maybe he needed to disappear to protect himself." He pulled his cards from his pocket. "If you think of anything else or hear anything from him, let me know." He handed one to each.

They nodded and escorted him through a back exit to avoid the busy waiting room.

He walked to his rental car.

This guy just vanished. But why?

∞

Beth was resting on the wicker couch on the back deck when the doorbell sounded. "Pop? Can you get that?"

Ike responded and opened the front door. She could hear voices, a man's and a woman's, but didn't recognize either. Perhaps some friends of her dad's.

A minute later she looked up to see a man and a woman and their teenage daughter carrying a large casserole dish and a basket of peaches.

Ike raised his hand to the little group as Beth gathered her robe at her neck and sat up. "This is Nick and Cheryl Thomas and their daughter—" Ike stopped suddenly as his cheeks reddened.

"Kristy," Cheryl prompted.

Ike nodded and smiled, a gesture that Beth recognized as a cover-up for his real frustration. He used to be so good at names. He was so good at remembering church visitors and calling them by name on the street. "Nate is the summer pastor at the beach church."

Nick looked down and let the slip-up pass.

Beth smiled. "What a nice surprise. Dad, why don't you take that casserole to the kitchen?"

Nick leaned forward and shook her hand. "Hi, we've heard so much about you. So sorry about your accident."

"Heard about me, why—" The startled look on her face must have prompted him to explain.

"Travis was in church on Sunday and ate dinner with us after-wards. He told us all about his family." He looked at Ike who was just arriving back from the kitchen. "He seems awfully proud of his grandpa. He tells you started many new church congregations."

Beth couldn't keep her eyes from widening. She looked at her father and mouthed, *Travis?*

"I didn't know he was at your house for dinner." She shook her head. "That rascal. He's been keeping a few secrets around here and—"

Kristy interrupted. "Is he home?"

Beth studied the beautiful young woman for a second before the light came on. *Of course. He's suddenly interested in going to church. Without me. Suddenly proud of his grandfather, to impress her father, the pastor!*

"Travis," Kristy repeated. "Is he around?"

She nodded. "He's upstairs. First door on the left. At the computer."

Cheryl spoke up. "He's such a polite young man."

Beth bit her tongue. "Of course." She paused, processing the new Travis. "Please, have a seat."

Nick had a kind face. Not drop-dead handsome but OK with dark curls and a nose that seemed too flat, a face you could look at for thirty minutes on a Sunday morning without being distracted by overwhelming beauty or homeliness. He folded his hands. "How have you been doing?"

She didn't know them well enough to complain of post-op constipation or explain the Percocet nightmares, so she settled for "slow but sure."

Cheryl was blonde, like her daughter, with a figure suited for an aerobics instructor. *Like mother, like daughter. No wonder Travis is smitten. I should have seen it. He hasn't been talking about Bart lately.* The pastor's wife shook her head. "We were amazed by the story of your hit-and-run. And Travis tells us the police are hot on the trail, and that perhaps the body found near the pier was the owner of the car?"

She could imagine Travis embellishing the story a little, enjoying a rare bit of attention from an adult who didn't want a homework assignment. She smiled pleasantly. "It's been quite an introduction to Serenity."

"We've been coming here for years and have never heard of something like this," Nick explained. "And to think Travis was responsible for the fishermen finding the body. He sure was chagrined when the police wanted to talk to—"

Beth held up her hand. "Time out. What? Travis was responsible for what?" *Just what kind of tall tale has Travis been spinning this time?*

"Travis told the men the spot where the fishing was hot. They went where he told them and snagged the stiff."

Cheryl frowned. "Don't call it that. It was someone's body."

Nick blushed. Beth didn't imagine too many things could bring color to his cheeks.

"He never told me that detail. He only told me that the body was pulled up by the fishermen."

"I hope I didn't betray him, " Nick responded. "The police questioned him about why he told the men to fish there. Maybe he was concerned about what you'd think." He shrugged. "As I understand it, he just directed them to the place he saw others catching fish the day before." He paused and looked at his hands. "I guess the fish were feeding on . . ." He looked at Cheryl before continuing. ". . . the body."

The image of a fish feeding frenzy floated in Beth's mind and, judging by the silence, probably in everyone else's too. She broke the silence. "Travis enjoyed the church service. Even invited a guest, my surgeon, Dr. Tyson."

"So we heard. Didn't get to meet him though. I think he sneaked out while I was talking to the other visitors." He looked at Ike. "Where do you attend?"

"First Presbyterian."

Nick nodded. "Of course. We at the beach church have a ministry mainly to the tourists."

Ike and Nick traded war stories, while Cheryl gave Beth some instructions for reheating the chicken and broccoli casserole she'd brought. "Travis loved it. Ate it on Sunday."

Beth just shook her head. She'd been trying for fourteen years to get Travis to eat broccoli without success, and Cheryl did it with one casserole.

They stood and excused themselves, promising to visit again soon, not wanting to wear out their welcome. They called for Kristy, who wanted to stay and finish a neat on-line game.

Cheryl looked at Beth for approval. Beth smiled and whispered, "Sure. I'll have Travis escort her back in an hour."

The couple disappeared, leaving Beth contemplating the new influence in Travis's life.

She slowly laid back down on the wicker couch and listened to the rhythm of the surf.

So it wasn't an alien that took over my son's life. It was a little woman named Kristy.

CHAPTER
11

THAT EVENING, AFTER SUPPER, Travis and Ike rinsed the dishes while Beth supervised from a kitchen bar-stool. "Above the microwave." She pointed. "In the drawer by the dishwasher." She paused. "Under the sink. Boy," she sighed, "you'd think you two had never put away dishes before."

"I managed just fine without you for a long time, thank you very much," snapped Ike. "You must have rearranged everything."

She stared at her father and shook her head. *You are so articulate one moment, challenging Adam to think about his identity, and now you can't remember where you've always kept the cheese grater.* She kept her thoughts to herself. "Rearranging kitchens comes naturally to me."

"Hmmpph."

A sharp knock at the front door interrupted their banter.

"I'll get it," offered Trav.

"Oh no you don't," Beth scolded. "You're not done with those dishes. If anyone needs us, they can wait for me."

She scooted off the stool and slowly made her way to the door. She opened it to see Adam Tyson holding a bouquet of fresh-cut flowers, wearing shorts, a T-shirt, and a baseball cap.

He smiled. "Can Travis come out to play?"

She smiled back. "You brought Travis flowers? I'm worried about you, doctor."

"The flowers are for you. I know how left out women can feel when their men go out and play."

She shook her head.

"Aren't you going to ask me in?"

Travis came out of the kitchen holding a dish towel. "Hey, Dr. Tyson."

"Hey, Trav. I've got something to show you."

Travis wrinkled his nose. "Flowers? For me?"

Adam sighed and handed the flowers to Beth. "Remember how you said you didn't have yard space to hit a baseball?"

"Yeah," he said, looking between his mother and Adam toward the driveway. "What's that?"

"That," he said proudly, "is what I came to show you."

He pushed open the door to reveal his Dakota truck in the driveway. In the back was a strange-looking contraption made of metal tubing and net. It stood the height of an adult man, and a baseball was suspended from the top crossbar by a bungee cord.

"Just what kind of machine is that?" Beth questioned.

"It's for solo batting practice. I used one in college. It's awesome." Travis's eyes were wide.

"Here," Adam said, handing the flowers to Beth. "Come on, Trav. I'll show you how it works."

"Sweet!"

The two men scampered down the steps and lifted the apparatus from the back of the truck, setting it in the driveway. She wanted to join them but didn't feel up to doing stairs just yet. Instead she closed the door and watched from a window. Adam selected two bats from a large canvas bag and took a batting stance in the yard. Travis mimicked his movements, and Adam nodded, then reached out and adjusted the boy's arm, raising his elbow a few inches. She couldn't hear them speak but watched as Adam instructed Trav step by step. Eventually they stepped toward the hitting practice machine, and Adam took a swing. She heard a solid thud as his bat impacted the ball, sending it into the net. Travis was next. Adam watched his swing and offered advice, pointing first to the ball, then the bat, then to Travis's arm and eye and back to the ball.

Travis hit the ball again. And again. After ten hits Adam sat on the tailgate of his truck and shouted, "Attaboy."

She walked back into the kitchen and pulled out a brownie mix. "Come on, Pop. Help me make some dessert for Travis and his friend."

They baked brownies, Ike went off for some alone time, and Beth was pouring lemonade just as the two baseball players stomped up the stairs forty-five minutes later. Sweat poured off Travis's face. "Mom, that thing's awesome! I bet I could hit the ball over the two-hundred-foot fence down at Ruritan Park easy."

Adam nodded. "He's got natural talent. Just needs a little groomin', that's all."

Travis beamed. "Dr. Tyson had the lowest ERA for any pitcher in his conference. He even got invited to training camp with the Rockies."

She handed Adam a glass of lemonade. "I'm impressed." She watched him nearly drain the glass with one lift of his hand. "So why aren't you playing baseball?"

He hesitated.

Uh oh. Sore subject.

"I wanted to do something else. I wanted to go into medicine so bad, I left training camp after being drafted."

Travis was incredulous and just young enough to ask, "Why would anyone do that?"

"I thought that's what God wanted me to do."

Travis looked down. "Oh." How could anyone argue with that?

Beth remembered what he'd said a few days before and nodded. "The missionary plan, right?"

He drained his glass and rattled the ice.

That was something Barry used to do. Something she scolded him for continuously.

"I guess," he responded.

The subject seemed sticky, a swamp too unyielding to wade through. "I baked brownies."

Travis grabbed some dessert plates and pried out the first steam-ing square. He started to take it to the table to sit when his mother caught his eye and nodded her head toward their guest. "Oh," he moaned. "Here," he said, handing the brownie to Adam.

They ate quietly for a moment. "I'll leave the Solohitter with you, if you'll use it."

"OK." Travis acted more interested in his brownie.

Beth knew it was an act, an attempt not to act too excited, which might not be "cool." Being cool is the ultimate goal of the typical fourteen-year-old male.

"We still need to work on your pitching." He smiled as Beth slid another hunk of baked brownie onto his plate. "I'll see if I can find my old catcher's mitt. I think I have a video or two on mechanics too. I can bring them over . . ." He looked at Beth before continuing. ". . . if that's OK."

"It's OK with me." She tousled her son's curls. "OK with you, sport? You haven't played ball for a long time."

"I've been thinking about it since my deal with Dr. Tyson. I think Dad would be glad if I played again. For a while I couldn't do it because it made me think of him, but . . ." His voice weakened. "I think he'd like me to."

Adam nodded his head. "I think you're right."

After Travis inhaled a third brownie, he headed for his room, leaving Beth alone with Adam.

"Thanks," Beth said softly. "He hasn't played baseball since his father died."

"I hope I didn't make him too uncomfortable with—"

"No," she interrupted. "It's fine. Travis needs this."

They sat silently together. Beth listened to the sounds of the surf drifting through the screened-in porch.

"So how are you doing? Recovery on track?"

"It's funny," she said reflectively. "For the first time in my life I've found myself on the other side of the stethoscope. I take so much for granted when I'm well. Now I'm thankful for a few uninterrupted hours of sleep, a shower where I can face the water without wincing, a bowel movement, a—"

He held up his hand. "I get the picture. I get the picture."

"Come on, surgeon. Surely you're not shy when it comes to talking about bowel function."

"I only talk about that stuff at work."

She laughed. Laughing still hurt. She gripped her stomach. "Oh."

"I take a lot for granted too." He looked into her eyes. "When you move to a new town, you're thankful for having a few friends to talk to." His eyes drifted toward the ocean. "I've enjoyed talking to you, getting to know you and Trav. I'm just sorry it had to be this way."

"All things work together for good."

"I used to think that way."

"And now?"

He rolled his lower lip inward and bit down on it with straight, white teeth. "I guess I've had a few doses of reality."

"God never promises a life without pain, Adam. He only promises to be there with His children in the pain. He didn't spare His own Son from suffering, did He?"

He shook his head.

"What changed, Adam?"

He stiffened. The wall was going back up.

"It was a long time ago. People change, see things differently, that's all."

Beth took a stab in the dark. "Ever been married? A handsome surgeon like you?"

"No. Close once."

"What happened?"

He took a deep breath. "I loved a girl in Southern California. She introduced me to her church, her way of looking at the world." He shook his head. "Jesus. Love. Sharing. Community."

"Your missionary dream?"

"Born in a gospel mission church with a beach ministry in Southern California."

"What happened to the girl?"

"We were going to take Jesus to the world. You know, medicine and the Bible." He chuckled. "It seems naive now." He halted. "Sylvia ran off with a friend of ours who made it into medical school." He looked up. "I mean before me."

"Stupid move." Her words were out before she could stop them.

"I'm not so sure." He paused. "What about you? Married once?"

She nodded. "Just once. To my college sweetheart. Married for sixteen years before he died."

"I'm sorry. That's got to be tough."

"All things work together for good."

"How can you say that? How can it be good for a young mother to be without the man she loves? How can it be good that Travis is without a father?"

"I didn't say it was good. I said it eventually works together for good. At least that's the promise for God's children. I like to think of our suffering as the knotted side of the tapestry. We are going through all of these tough times. From our perspective it all looks like confusion and knots. But from above, from God's perspective, well, it all works into something beautiful."

He looked at his hands. "I don't know, Beth. I wish I believed the way you do. You seem to have such a simple faith, a trust that allows you to rest in bad circumstances."

"I didn't act that way when Barry died. I almost fell apart. If I hadn't had Travis to look after, I don't think I could have forced myself to endure." She took a deep breath. "But eventually I began to understand that God's love toward me had never changed. The bad things in my life weren't evidence that He didn't love me anymore. When I was a young Christian, I spent a lot of time trying to earn God's favor. Then when I lost my husband, I thought my faith must have let God down. It took a long time for me to realize that God's love for me was never based on me or my performance. It is unconditional. I didn't have to work for it in the first place. Once I understood that, I viewed the bad stuff that happened to me differently. It was no longer evidence of my own failure, of God withdrawing His love. It was God's love that allowed me to go through suffering."

"I have a hard time believing in a God who loves without conditions. It doesn't make sense." He blew his breath out in a low whistle. "Does everyone who comes over to play with Travis get into these deep discussions with you?"

"No one can play with Travis unless they talk to his mom. It's a Carlson rule."

"I see." He stood up. "Feel like looking at the ocean?" He held out his hand. She took it and allowed him to assist her up. His hands were soft but strong.

"The sun should be setting soon. Too bad we can't see the sound from here."

They walked, Beth holding Adam's arm, out onto the deck where Ike sat reading a biography of Abe Lincoln. He pointed to the water. "Moon's out. Look at that reflection, would you?"

Adam nodded. The moon was a copper coin. "Awesome."

His beeper sounded. "Uh-oh," he responded, looking at his beeper. "ER calls."

Ike chuckled. "Hopefully not another hit-and-run."

"I could go a lifetime without that experience again. Say, any word on your man? Have they found Michael Cunningham?"

Beth shook her head. "Nope. The man's disappeared. Dust. A rumor."

"Hmmm." He scratched his head and patted Beth's arm. "I'd better answer this."

She let him go with a little squeeze of his biceps before a lingering release. *He may be a surgeon, but he still has a pitcher's arm.*

He came back a few minutes later and excused himself. A vacationing child with appendicitis. "Guess I'd better go."

She walked him to the door. "Thanks for asking Trav to play." She hesitated. "And for talking to his mom."

He nodded and brushed her chin with his hand before turning away. "I'll teach you to hit when you recover."

"Are you going in like that?"

He looked down at his shorts and held up his hands. "This is a small town. The kid will probably be in a bathing suit. I'll have to change into scrubs anyway."

He had a point.

"See you."

Beth sighed. *Father, bring him back to You.*

And bring him back to me.

∾

The following day, a breathless Greg Monroe swung open the front door of the little Serenity Police Department building. "Chief!"

Dan stood in the hall holding a cup of coffee. "Chief's over at the Inn eating breakfast with the boys." He sipped his coffee. "How was Florida? Did you find our boy?"

Dan was curious. Greg was melodramatic. "Just be patient, lifeguard boy."

Dan frowned and inspected the tan on his arms. "Hey, when I was a kid I was twice this dark. You're just jealous." He slapped his friend's gut with the back of his hand.

Greg puffed out his chest. "And you're dreamin'. Now sit down. I want to give you my findings in order of discovery." He followed Dan into their small office.

Dan rolled his eyes. "OK. Just tell me what's so important."

"I'll get to that," Greg said, lifting the lid to a box of donuts. "I went to Mr. Cunningham's last employer and found out he'd only been there for three months. I found out he was a model physician's assistant, except for his arrogance, and the nurses I talked to thought it was justified. The guy's so brilliant, he intimidated the surgeons he was working for. Anyway, I find out the guy's a real star citizen as well. He had a bad experience with a former employer who became a drug addict. He goes out to schools to tell his story in assemblies to warn kids about drug abuse."

Dan ran his fingers through his blond bangs. "OK, he's a good guy in Florida. What's he doing here? Vacation?"

"I don't think so. Just listen. I follow this guy's trail up to Tampa Bay, where he used to work before moving to Sarasota. It sounds like he worked for a real jerk there. The guy wouldn't let Cunningham do half of what he was trained to do. So Cunningham only stayed with him for two months."

"Did you find him? Is he still in Florida?"

"Stop interrupting. I didn't find him, OK?" Greg huffed. "Listen, the story gets better. He left Sarasota telling the nurses at the office that he was moving back to California. But he didn't ask for any recommendations for a new job, and he didn't leave a forwarding address. The Post Office doesn't have anything either. As far as they know, he hasn't asked for a Post Office box anywhere else."

"That's it? We still don't have any leads, do we?" He put his feet on his desk.

"Just listen! In Tampa Bay he worked for a group of surgeons who hired him straight from a job in California, the job he lost because he turned in the surgeon he worked for for doing drugs. His boss had his license suspended and was forced to go into rehab. The office manager in Tampa was great. She showed me his employee file and everything. His former boss wouldn't give him a recommendation, even though he'd worked for him for nearly fifteen years. She said she had a clear memory of a call she'd made to his former boss. She said he wouldn't give her the time of day. Evidently he voiced a lot of hostility about Cunningham. In fact, she couldn't believe it when I told her Cunningham was going back to California. He'd complained to her that his old boss had made it impossible for him to find work in his hometown."

"So how do we know this guy isn't back working in California? It's a big state."

"He might be, but if he is, he's being awfully quiet. He isn't using any major credit cards, he hasn't requested phone service, and he doesn't have an account with any utility company."

"So we still don't have any leads. Does he have any bank accounts in Sarasota?"

"His landlady told me where he banked. They told me he withdrew all his money in May. Cash. Five thousand in savings."

"So why did he come here? And if he did, why did someone off him and dump him by our fishing pier?"

"Assuming the body belongs to him."

"What else do we have?"

"One more piece of evidence in this crazy story. I may have found out why he came to Serenity."

Dan waited. "Well?"

"I think he came to see Adam Tyson."

"The surgeon? What makes you think that?"

Greg lifted a donut from a box on the desk. "Adam Tyson was his boss in Southern California."

CHAPTER
12

SAMUEL HARRIS HAD been Serenity's Chief of Police for ten months. He took over when the town council fired Bud Dyerlie for taking a bribe. Nothing exciting ever happened in Serenity. A few college partyers got drunk every summer, and some of the kids that couldn't afford to go to Mexico or Fort Lauderdale for spring break stopped on the Outer Banks and got arrested for public nudity. Nothing was ever reported stolen, except Bill Jenkins's Jet-Ski, and even then they found out his son had beached it on a sandbar and was too afraid to tell.

But all of that changed two months ago. Since then there had been four drug arrests, all teenage kids taking OxyContin, a powerful oral narcotic that had become a fixture in the party scene. And in the past two weeks Serenity had seen real action. A hit-and-run and now a submerged body chained to cinder blocks just up from the fishing pier provided the department with some real challenges.

The mayor, Joe Atwell, was a retired banker from Durham. He had a ruddy complexion and a nose too rosy for a teetotaler. He weighed fifty pounds too much and had a weakness for Cuban cigars and saltwater taffy.

Chief Harris liked Joe about as much as a steak-and-potatoes man likes brussels sprout casserole. Harris took the head honcho position in the police department at Serenity to get away from the hassles of running a larger department in Wilmington. Samuel ate breakfast with Joe once a week and kept him abreast of town trouble.

Sam was eating his normal fare—grapefruit and oatmeal—the breakfast of a sixty-year-old who looked fifty and acted forty. He tried not to watch as Joe dropped another tablespoon of butter onto his grits and splashed on the Tabasco.

Joe slurped his coffee. "How do you know the body means there was a murder? It could have been a suicide, right?"

"Not likely. Most people don't commit suicide by forced self-drowning. Besides, to get that far from the pier, he would have needed a boat, and we haven't found one adrift."

"Good point."

Sam knew there were rumors about the body's identity, and he had his own suspicions, but he wouldn't let Joe in on any of his investigation unless he was sure it was soon to be public knowledge. They hadn't told the media about the cuff link with the initials M.C. and certainly hadn't told them they thought it might be the same person who owned the car involved in the hit-and-run. Sam had a gut-level dislike for the media, having dealt with too many copycat criminals in Wilmington after media hype about weird crimes. So now his *modus operandi* remained secretive, revealing only what he was convinced would help them solve a crime.

He was anxious to confront Adam Tyson. Greg and Dan wanted to do it yesterday, but he made them confirm the history of the suspension of Tyson's license for a drug violation before rushing in. Besides, this was his department, and if there were any big fish to catch, he wanted to be the one holding the pole. He planned to corner him at the hospital later in the morning. But for now he had to humor the mayor who wanted to play cops and robbers.

He had checked the California State Board of Medicine for Tyson's records. It was on the Internet, public knowledge. His license was suspended for irregular narcotics-prescribing practices. If Greg and Dan were correct, Adam Tyson might have been the reason for Michael Cunningham's visit. Coincidence? Unlikely. Perhaps Tyson had invited his former employee to Serenity. Perhaps Cunningham came to do Tyson harm. Or could Tyson have been setting Cunningham up just to ambush him? And what did the hit-and-run have to do with it? He needed answers, and he knew the person to talk to wasn't eating breakfast across from him.

"How are Amy and the kids?" the mayor asked.

Good. Once he starts asking about the kids, he's getting ready to leave.

I could tell him my wife went to Mars and he wouldn't care. He never listens to my answers anyway. "Amy won the lottery. Scott was drafted by the Baltimore Ravens. Kevin got a scholarship to Harvard."

Joe chased the last of his grits around the plate with a biscuit. "Harvard?"

He listened? Sam smiled. "In my dreams."

Joe drained his coffee mug and stood. "Town council on Thursday. The guys will probably want an update on police activity."

Sam nodded. *Busybody council.* "Later, Joe."

He watched as Joe bumped his way through the breakfast crowd and disappeared through the front entrance. Sam signed the bill and headed for his jeep. Something smelled fishy in Serenity, and it was time to go fishing.

He drove under the speed limit up the meandering road next to the ocean, backing up a line of tourists too afraid to pass. When he arrived at the hospital, he radioed Greg with his location and walked up the stairs to the hospital's main lobby.

The smell of antiseptic hit him as soon as he pushed through the revolving front door. It was an odor he'd long associated with pain. It was the smell of bike wrecks and stitches, of fellow police officers injured in the line of duty, the smell he associated with the birth and death of his first grandchild who died of meningitis at age three.

He forced the memories away and tried to focus on a game plan. Surprise was the element that Sam depended on. The surgeon was most likely to give important information in the first visit, before he had a chance to formulate a defense.

Chief Harris followed the signs to the operating rooms and stood momentarily outside a double automatic door labeled, *Do not enter.* It was a sign he would ignore. His badge gave him the right to dismiss the instructions.

He pushed a small metal plate on the wall to activate the doors, which opened into a short hallway leading to a central nursing station. Behind a counter, at a computer console, a young woman in scrubs stared at the screen in front of her. Another woman with her hair covered by a blue stretchy cap was writing on a big white board with an erasable marker. The cap reminded Sam of the ones you might see if you ventured into a restaurant kitchen, ugly but functional. *But it would be hard to make this woman ugly,* Sam thought. He walked close enough to read her name on her ID badge before speaking. Gerri Fiori was beautiful. If he ever needed intensive care, this was the nurse he wanted.

"I'm Samuel Harris, Serenity PD."

The nurse looked up from her writing. "May I help you?"

"I'm looking for a surgeon, Dr. Adam Tyson. Perhaps you can direct me to him."

"He's operating in room 1," she said, pointing the red marker toward another set of double doors. "But you can't go back there. It's a sterile environment."

Sam frowned. Of course. What was he thinking? That he could just interrupt a surgeon for a few questions while his patient lay anesthetized with some body cavity open to the air? He looked at the doors, contemplating his options.

"You can have a seat in the waiting area. It's just to the left beyond the main OR entrance." The woman took a step toward him and stood unflinching while tapping the marker against the palm of her other hand. Her posture said, "Don't mess with me."

"How long will he be?"

She looked at a clock on the wall. "Dr. Tyson is doing a hernia repair. He's very fast. I don't think he'll be much more than twenty minutes."

Sam nodded. "Please inform the doctor that he needs to talk to me as soon as he is finished."

He walked back to the waiting room and contemplated the magazines on a small table. It was either *Redbook, Cosmopolitan,* or *Field and Stream.* He had twenty minutes to learn to flatten his stomach, learn about sex after sixty, or find out how to stalk a moose. Having reached a silver age, he was tempted by the sex but opted for the moose. He couldn't be seen reading *Cosmopolitan* in public.

He picked up the tattered magazine, which was ten months out of date, and looked at the faces of the others in the room. A elderly man stared at Sam with empty eyes. He had so many wrinkles, Sam couldn't tell if he was worried or just old. A middle-aged woman ignored him, apparently absorbed in a paperback romance. A young lady sat with a toddler on her lap, trying to interest the youngster in

a small stuffed animal. She too gazed at Sam with the eyes of someone expecting bad news. Unfortunately, he had delivered too much
of that in his career as an officer of the law.

He settled into a chair and had just begun learning the five secrets
to bagging a prize moose when Dr. Tyson entered.

"Mrs. Smallwood?"

The young mother looked up. "Yes?"

He reached for her hand. "Your husband is going to be just fine.
Everything went great."

"Thank you," she responded. "When can I see him?"

"After an hour in recovery, he'll be taken back to the ambulatory
surgery waiting area. You can join him there."

Sam stood and stepped toward the surgeon. Their eyes met, and
the surgeon sighed. "You wanted to talk to me?"

"Yes."

Tyson retreated, not offering his hand. "We can talk in the physicians' lounge."

Sam followed him out and entered a doorway to the right of the
OR entrance. The room appeared to be more of a locker room than
a comfortable hangout. Lockers lined one wall, a bench bolted to the
floor in front of them. An old TV sat on a table in the corner, and a
red flowered couch, looking like a yard-sale treasure, had been pushed
against the wall opposite the lockers.

"I'm Sam Harris, Serenity Chief of Police."

Tyson took his hand, offering a firm shake. "Adam Tyson."

"I know. Have a seat," Sam responded, motioning to the couch.
"I need to ask you a few questions. Mind if I tape our conversation?"

The surgeon shrugged and plopped onto the old couch. "Mind
telling me what this is all about?"

Sam sat on a wooden desk chair and leaned forward. "Oh, I bet
you know what this is about, doctor. I want to know about Michael
Cunningham." He flipped on a small pocket-size recorder.

"Do I need an attorney?"

"Have you done anything wrong?"

Tyson sighed. "No."

"I want to know why you haven't come forward. Why didn't you
tell us you knew Michael Cunningham?"

Tyson shifted in his seat. "Look, I don't know anything about where he is. I knew Mr. Cunningham, but all that is past. I have no idea what the man was doing in town."

His response brought a smile to Sam's face. "No idea, huh? Do you mind telling me why you've kept your relationship with Cunningham a secret?"

"There is no secret here. No one ever asked me the question."

"Why didn't you bring it up? What do you have to hide, Dr. Tyson?"

The surgeon dropped his eyes to the floor and hesitated. "Look, I—well, I—"

Sam let him stew.

"I came to Serenity to make a new start. My intentions were to leave California, to leave Cunningham and all the problems he caused in the past." He paused. "I guess you know all about the drug allegations."

The information he wanted. Sam nodded and tried not to widen his smile. "Why don't you fill me in for the record?"

Tyson sighed again. "I employed Mr. Cunningham for a long, long time. He was the best assistant I ever worked with. Very good with his hands. But he had a moral chip on his shoulder. He made some allegations to the State Board of Medicine. I had to endure a peer review. They recommended a suspension of my license and a drug rehab program." He shook his head. "It didn't matter that the allegations were false. The accusations stuck. My practice was ruined." He picked at nonexistent dirt beneath his fingernails. "I came to Serenity to start again."

"Why didn't you tell us this before?"

"Drug accusations aren't exactly the type of thing I wanted to be known for here. I figured if no one asked, I wasn't going to tell. Cunningham found new work in Florida. I decided if no one tracked his life back to mine, I wouldn't go there on my own."

"What was Mr. Cunningham doing in Serenity?"

Tyson continued to stare at the floor. He answered in a monotone. "I don't know."

"Do you think I could believe that it is merely coincidence that you and Mr. Cunningham show up in the same small town across the country from where you used to work together?"

"Believe what you want. I have nothing to do with Michael Cunningham anymore."

"Did he contact you? Tell you he was coming to town?"

"No."

"Give me something here, Dr. Tyson. Why do you think he showed up in Serenity? Was he looking for you?"

"I don't know."

"Take a guess."

"I don't have one."

Sam tapped his pen on his knee, frustrated by Tyson's lack of cooperation, or knowledge. The surgeon appeared sincere, but it seemed unlikely that Tyson wouldn't know anything about his former employee. "Where is he now?"

"I don't know. I don't keep up with him."

"Is he dead?"

"How would I know?"

Sam decided to press him. "What about the body that was found out by the pier? Know anything about that? Could that be the body of Michael Cunningham?"

"How would I know?"

"We're going to know soon enough, doctor. The autopsy and identification information should be available soon."

Tyson stayed quiet, his eyes fixed on the floor.

"If this is Cunningham's body, you're going to have some questions to answer."

"I have nothing to say."

"You'll have some explaining to do."

Tyson lifted his head. "Maybe Cunningham committed suicide. Maybe he looked me up and decided to do himself in while he was close to me to make me look guilty one more time." He shuddered. "I don't know."

"That makes no sense. What does he have against you?"

"Nothing. I've done nothing to him."

"Why would he do such a thing?"

"I don't know," he responded, raising his voice. "Cunningham is a self-righteous jerk. He felt obligated to report his suspicions about me, even when he realized that ruining my career would leave him without a job. If you ask me, he's a frustrated man with a righteous persecution complex. Why he would come to Serenity is beyond me."

Sam slouched and folded his hands. Tyson wasn't giving him anything useful. He seemed evasive. His explanation about not wanting the community to know about his past seemed reasonable, but not coming forth with the information about his past with Cunningham certainly made him look guilty.

Tyson's demeanor changed. "Look," he pleaded, "no one in Serenity knows about this. I came here for a new start. I really don't want these false accusations ruining my chances to make a successful beginning here." His eyes met Sam's. "Can I trust you to keep this quiet? If you leak this, I might as well move again."

"If you cooperate with me, I'll keep this quiet."

"I am cooperating," he said with exasperation.

Sam stood and glared at the surgeon, who slumped forward with his head in his hands. "We'll talk again. I'll keep this news about your drug problem quiet, if you come forward with anything helpful."

"I don't have a drug problem."

"I'm not the one who suspended your California license, Dr. Tyson."

He looked up, his eyes clear. "No, you didn't. Perhaps you would have been a bit more fair."

Sam stepped to the door. "I'll be watching you, Tyson. Step out of line in Serenity, and everyone will know about your colorful past."

∞

That evening Beth Carlson felt good enough to prepare a simple supper of grilled cheese sandwiches and tomato soup. Getting up and doing light work made her feel useful. She certainly wasn't used to sitting around all day doing nothing. Working made her feel almost human. Almost. She needed a shower and makeup before rejoining the human race.

As she showered, her hand explored the lump in her left breast. It was still there, though the surrounding swelling was receding, and the whole chest wall bruise was mellowing to yellow. She toweled off and stood in front of the mirror, raising her hands above her head to complete her self-exam. She frowned. There was a faint dimple over the lump in her breast. Not a good sign.

It's probably just resolving scar tissue, drawing the skin inward. I shouldn't be afraid. Cancer doesn't occur because of an accident. This is from my trauma, pure and simple.

Her mental gymnastics helped a little. She put on eyeliner, and lipstick helped even more. By the time she kissed a Kleenex, she was thinking of pouring a glass of lemonade and taking a slow stroll on the sand.

The doorbell sounded just as she walked back into the living room. She looked through the front window and smiled. Her surgeon was becoming a regular visitor.

She opened the door. He was holding fresh flowers. As usual.

"Do you own stock in a florist shop or something?"

He looked at the bouquet. "I just thought Travis would like these."

"You can't lie with a straight face."

He handed her the flowers. "I just thought they'd brighten your day."

"You were right. Will you come in, or are you just delivering?"

His face sobered momentarily. "I'd like to come in. I'd like to talk to you."

Her curiosity was pricked. Her intuition said something was up. "Sure."

"Feel up to a slow stroll on the beach?"

"I think so." She raised her voice. "Pop, I'm going out for a walk by the ocean."

She heard him grunt a response as she looked at Adam. "Travis is trying to teach Ike the basics of Internet travel."

"Uh oh. I'd like to see that."

"Trust me, you wouldn't. Travis keeps saying, 'Just double click. Use the mouse.' I think it's best to slip out before he raises his voice again."

He followed her to the back deck and slowly down the steps onto the sand.

"Look," he said, his voice quiet, "I need to tell you some things.

Some things are going to get out about me, and I wanted to talk to you first."

She studied his face. Concern and fear registered there. "Sure."

"I . . . well, I've found myself more and more concerned about what you think of me. I know we started out briefly as professional colleagues, and then as I treated you as my patient, but . . ." He halted. "I guess you know that I don't bring flowers to all my patients." He looked toward the surf. Was he afraid of her response? "I find myself thinking about you, wanting to visit with you, seeing you more as a treasured friend than a patient."

She slipped her hand into the crook of his arm. "Me too."

He looked at her, his eyes open, searching. "You are going to hear things about me . . . I wanted you to hear me first." He paused. "I am not a drug abuser. There were accusations where I used to work. One of my employees thought I had a problem. He reported his suspicions. Things snowballed. I had to sit before a board of medicine review panel. They suspended my medical license and recommended rehab. I complied, but my practice was ruined. I came to Serenity for a new start."

"Why did they suspend your license? If you were innocent, couldn't you fight it?"

"The police were never involved. I suspect if they had any evidence, they would have been. As it was, there were only accusations and suspicions. And there is no appeal process with the board. Either I comply and get my license back, or refuse and get another job."

"Why are you telling me this now?"

"The police have been investigating Michael Cunningham."

"I don't understand. What does this have to do with—"

"Beth, Michael Cunningham was my physician's assistant. He was the employee who reported his suspicions."

"The man who owned the white Cadillac?"

"The same."

"Why didn't you say something? Why keep this a secret?"

"The administration knew about the State Board of Medicine panel but agreed to give me work anyway, in light of my other qualifications. But I knew that if someone dug deep enough, they might find out about Mr. Cunningham being my employee. And if they found that out, the news about the drug problems would be next. My career would be in jeopardy again. I couldn't let that happen."

"But I thought you lived in California. Michael Cunningham is from Florida."

"He moved there after losing his job with me."

"Is he mad at you?"

"I don't think so. He only has himself to blame for losing his job. When he reported me, I lost my job; so I could no longer employ him."

They made little steps along the water's edge, watching the orange tint in the sky intensify as the day's end approached.

"I know it sounds unreasonable, but I need to know you'll believe me. I don't care that much what others think about this. I don't want it getting out that I have a sordid past, but as long as I know that you believe the truth, I think I'll be OK."

Beth shook her head. "I'm flattered you care about what I think. And you have to know that I've appreciated you beyond our doctor-patient relationship. You've been a great friend to me, and to Travis. But this . . ." Her voice trailed off. "I don't know what to think. I don't believe you would lie to me, but . . . well, why wait to tell me about Michael Cunningham until you were forced? It seems a little shady somehow."

"I wanted to forget Michael Cunningham. I came here to start over. I hoped no one would ever link him to me again. All I can say is, I am not using drugs. I never have. And I didn't want to bring up my employment of Cunningham because I knew this would come out and make people wonder about me again."

"Why would Cunningham be in Serenity? Was he here to see you?"

"I don't know."

"I guess you know about the body they found near the pier. If that turns out to be Cunningham, you are going to be a suspect."

"The police chief has already talked with me. I think he's suspicious of me. I'm afraid. I've never been in this kind of trouble before."

"Look at me, Adam. Look into my eyes. Tell me the truth. Did you have anything to do with Cunningham being in town? Were you trying to get even with him? Are you really innocent of drug charges?"

He took her hands, staring into her eyes unflinchingly. "I am not a drug user, Beth. And I didn't invite Cunningham to Serenity. And I certainly am not out to get him. And I didn't kill him. Beth, I promise."

She was satisfied. He was telling the truth.

And she liked the fact that he was so concerned about what she felt about him. It was a comfortable feeling. It felt right, like an old shoe.

But something was amiss. Michael Cunningham's visit to Serenity, if he was driving his car at all, had to have something to do with Adam Tyson. The odds were too great against it being a random event.

She pulled his arm closer to her side as they walked along leaving marks in the wet sand. "I believe you, Adam. I don't think you'd lie to me."

"I don't want to hurt you. That's the last thing I want."

They walked along in silence for a minute until she verbalized the question that hung in her mind like a thick fog. "So what was Michael Cunningham doing in the same town as you?"

CHAPTER
13

SAM HARRIS SHOVED the preliminary autopsy report to the corner of his desk and called to Dan Smith, "A couple things still don't add up. The autopsy age estimate is fifty-five to sixty-five. They say they haven't seen dental fillings like his since the thirties. And I'm not sure what to make of all the tissue damage. They say there is more soft tissue destruction than can be accounted for on the basis of simple drowning. They say it looks like the body was frozen."

"Frozen?"

"That's what the report says."

"Anyone in Serenity have a freezer big enough for a body?"

"I suppose lots of people do. You could put a body in that extra freezer I have in my garage."

Dan raised his eyebrows. "Well, well."

"Oh, shut up."

Dan cleared his throat. "What do they say about the cause of death?"

"It wasn't drowning. The body was long dead before being sunk in the ocean. Likely it was related to a blunt blow to the head. They report a small fracture on the top of his skull."

"OK, let me put this together. He gets killed by a blow to the head. Then the killer stores him in the freezer until disposing of him in the ocean. Doesn't make much sense."

"Nothing about murder does." Sam flipped a page on the medical examiner's report. "It says the victim had cancer. A cancer of the colon that had spread to his brain. They saw bleeding around the tumor in his head."

"He died of cancer?"

"No, it still looks like a homicide. They are hypothesizing that a blow to the head caused the bleeding around the tumor and subsequent death."

"Anything new on Tyson?"

"His record is clean as a whistle. Not even a malpractice suit. And every doc in California has a few of them. Nothing up until his license was suspended."

"But he never had a motive until now."

"True." Sam cleaned his fingernails with a pocketknife. "Why don't you snoop around his place. See if he has a big freezer."

Dan nodded. "I'll do it before my patrol this afternoon." He stood and cleared his throat. "Say, boss, I know how you are about the media, but how about throwing them a little bone here? This freezer theory is just weird enough that releasing some of the autopsy data might stimulate a helpful memory somewhere."

Sam muttered, "That means I'll have to share the autopsy with the mayor." He looked up from his nails. "OK. I'll call Joel Bedford over at *The Outer Banks Daily*. He's always been pretty fair."

"Mind if I drop by the hospital? I'd like our friend the doctor to see a man in uniform every day or so just to let him know we're around."

"Let him see you. Let him know we're watching."

"Exactly. What if the body isn't Cunningham after all?"

"I'll still swear the doctor's involved. Why else would his employee show up in this town? And if something weird hadn't gone down, why haven't we found Cunningham? Why did he flee the scene? Or did he not flee the scene? Did Tyson have something to do with that? Could he have been running from Tyson, not the accident?"

"Hmmm. Hadn't thought of that." Dan scratched his chin.

"That's why I'm the chief."

Dan smiled. "I'm off to watch the doctor. He's bound to make a mistake eventually."

Sam huffed. "And we'll be there when it happens."

∞

Two days later, with Beth threatening to go stir-crazy, Ike agreed to let her ride along to go grocery shopping. "I'll sit in the car, for crying out loud," she said, protesting her father's insistence that she take it easy and let him and Travis take care of the household.

So she sat, windows rolled up and air-conditioner blasting, in the Food Lion parking lot listening to Point of Grace on the radio.

She watched people with interest—tourists with armloads of food for their weekly rentals, children with inflatable ocean rafts, and the locals with gray hair and leathery tans. In the far edge of the lot, a large truck caught her eye. On the side, a Broward County Hospital emblem was emblazoned in red and blue, and a short line of women stood outside the back of the truck. What was this, a parking lot medical supply sale?

She had given Ike a list of twenty-two items, so she calculated at least a thirty-minute wait as her father shopped his way through the list. The last time he'd gone to pick up a carton of milk, he'd returned with a fishing magazine and a half-gallon of his favorite ice cream, and no milk. This time she wrote everything down and handed him a pencil so he could cross each item off the list as he found them. *If he gets any more forgetful it won't be safe to let him out alone.*

She looked again at the truck across the parking lot and reached over and shut off the car. She slowly made her way across the hot pavement until she recognized the truck as a mobile mammogram unit. The program was sponsored by her own hospital. All you needed to provide was the name of a physician to send the report to. She looked at her watch and bit her lower lip.

My X-ray is bound to be abnormal because of the giant bruise on my chest. But if it's normal, I'll sure feel better. She weighed her options and joined the line behind two other women. She gave her name and insurance data to an intake secretary and in a few minutes was handed a gown and was asked to disrobe in a small changing area. She obeyed and waited another minute until the mammogram tech called her name.

"Ms. Carlson?"

Beth stuck her head out from behind the curtain. "Here."

"Follow me," the cheery, youthful blonde said, leading the way to the X-ray unit.

Beth followed.

"You'll need to disrobe from the waist up and—" She halted in midsentence when she looked at Beth's chest. "Whoa! What happened?"

"I got hit by a car."

The tech shook her head. "I'm not sure I should do a mammogram now. You're still swollen. This is just for screening."

"Look, I'm already under a surgeon's care. What harm can it do to take a look?" Beth held her place.

The tech sighed. "I'll at least need to report what I see on the request." She held up a form. "Any family history of breast problems?"

"My mother had breast cancer."

"Do you do self-breast exams? We have some literature for instruction."

"I do. I can feel a lump over here." She lifted her hand to the upper outer portion of her breast.

"Please stand over here." She moved the unit close to Beth. "The compression is not going to feel good. Especially with that bruise."

That was an understatement. As the tech flattened Beth's breast between the plates, tears welled up in Beth's eyes. She bit her lip to keep from crying out.

"Hold your breath. I'll try to do this fast."

After two views, Beth was convinced she would pass out. This was not a good idea.

"Would you like to sit down? How about a sip of water?"

Beth steadied herself against the wall. "I'll be OK. Just give me a minute before we do the other side. The worst part is over."

Ten minutes later, her exam completed, she maneuvered between the parked cars over to her vehicle. She slouched in the passenger's seat and started the engine, desperate for air-conditioning to beat the humid heat.

I hope Adam isn't upset with me for using his name to get a mammogram. She groaned and shifted in her seat. *I never thought an X-ray could be so intolerable. It will take me a week to recover.*

Her hand went to the throbbing pain under her blouse. Anything to buy a little peace of mind.

∞

The warm summer evening had Andy thinking baseball. Even with the garage door open, sweat poured from his forehead. He hoisted another cardboard box onto a card table and yanked the tape in half with a pop. He had an old catcher's mitt from his high school days in here somewhere, and he was determined to find it so he could play with Travis.

He sighed and wiped his forehead with the back of his hand. Since his encounter with the Chief of Police, his emotions had ranged from angry to confused. He had only wanted to use Adam Tyson's name, his degrees and credentials to land a great job as a surgeon. He hadn't anticipated all the baggage that had come with it. Now he faced the suspicions of the police, and the potential of ruining his career and jeopardizing the trust of a beautiful woman all because of the history of Tyson's prior drug use. He'd wanted to keep his own past, his own personality, likes and dislikes, and only changed his name to get a job. But now the surgeon's past had surfaced like an ominous whale looming in the fog. He was in a rowboat looking at the rising silhouette and wondering when his dream would be smashed beyond recognition.

He could ride it out for a few weeks, see how things played out. If worse came to worse, he could always disappear, perhaps resurface later in a new town, get a new job, and begin again.

If it weren't for Beth Carlson.

How had he let her get under his skin so fast? He hadn't come to Serenity to fall in love. Yes, he dreamed that maybe someday, far in the future, when he was established as a surgeon and life had settled down, he would find a special woman, someone he could trust with his deepest secret.

If it wasn't for Beth, I could leave now, before the police dig too deep.

He watched the sweat drip onto the floor. Sweat from the heat and from the anxiety his deception promoted. He had never intended to lie to the law. He planned to be himself in everything and Adam Tyson only in name and credentials. But now, in an attempt to explain away Adam's past, the lies had begun. Would they grow and gather speed before he could gain control again?

He sighed. Worst of all he had begun to lie to Beth.

He looked up as a white Jeep Cherokee with a blue police insignia on the side slowed to a stop in his driveway. *What is the deal with these guys? First I see 'em in the hospital, then behind me on the road, and now here.*

Dan Smith lowered the window. "Evening, doc. Hot one, ain't it?"

Adam nodded and watched the officer climb slowly from his truck and stride up his driveway. He paused at the entrance to the double-car garage and poked at a box with the tip of his foot. "Need some help unpacking?"

"No thanks."

Dan leaned against a large freezer and rubbed his hand across the top. "What's a bachelor need an extra freezer for?"

Adam shrugged. "I don't like to shop. I buy enough frozen dinners and pizza to last a long time."

"Mind if I take a look?"

Adam opened another box. "Help yourself."

The surgeon looked for his catcher's mitt and listened to Dan's rambling.

"Ooooh, ice cream fan. I love this Ben and Jerry's. This pizza—is it really as good as delivery?"

"Huh, oh . . . it's OK." Adam shoved the box away and popped the tape on another one. "I'm not too picky."

Adam took a step toward the officer as Dan sized the freezer up against his own body. "Do you mind telling me why you've taken such a sudden interest in frozen foods?"

Dan smiled widely. "Worried?"

"About what? Is Healthy Choice about to stop making spicy beef stroganoff?"

The officer didn't see the humor in Adam's comments.

Adam continued, "I don't get this. You guys are watching me like I've got something to hide. I'm just a surgeon in a small town trying to do my part. Why should I be worried?"

"Don't play games with us, Tyson. Michael Cunningham was your PA. He comes to town and is involved in a hit-and-run. He's disappeared, and you hold out on us about your relationship. Somethin's up, doc, and I want to know what it is."

Adam lifted an old basketball from a box. He was getting closer. He pushed away a Fresno State pennant and smiled. His old catcher's mitt had been found. He slipped it onto his left hand and pounded it with his fist, raising a small cloud of dust. He inhaled. "Ah, the smell of the infield never quite comes out of these babies."

"Don't change the subject."

"Hey, if I remember correctly, I was searching for this glove before you came in, uninvited. I've got nothing to hide, except a past with Michael Cunningham I'd rather forget. I've put that life behind me. I've come to make a new start." He slammed his fist into the glove again and stared at the young policeman. "I'm sure the chief shared that fact with you. I didn't come forward because I didn't want the accusations that Cunningham brought into my life to torture me a second time."

"You should have come forward. You should have known we would find out about this."

"Why should you? Cunningham worked for at least two other sur geons after me. How am I to know what he's up to?" He paused. "You never answered my question. Why are you interested in my diet?"

"I'm not," he responded, stepping away from the freezer and step- ping over a box and out of the garage.

Adam lifted his eyes to follow Dan's who squinted toward the sig- nature rumble of a Harley-Davidson. A woman in tight black leathers cruised to a stop between the officer and his jeep. Gerri Fiori pulled off her black half-helmet. "Come for a visit, Dan?" She flashed Adam a smile. "Or did you come for a curbside surgical consult? Hemorrhoids bothering you again, Dan?"

He stepped back and stuttered, "I—I . . . uh . . . no."

She looked at Adam. "Wanna play catch?"

He held up his glove. "It's the one I used in high school." He hes- itated. "A good fiber supplement and a long soak in a hot tub should help, Dan. I'll drop some samples by your office."

He glared at Gerri. "I could sue you for a break in confidentiality."

"It's not a confidentiality issue if I heard you complain to Sam over at the Inn." She let her fingers drift across each of three silver earrings. "Why, Dan, did I see you in the OR?"

He looked away. "Never mind." He pointed an index finger toward Adam's chest. "I'm watching you, Tyson."

Adam took a deep breath as Dan climbed into his jeep.

Gerri waited until he left to push her kickstand down and swing her leg over the bike. "Don't let him worry you. Dan is like a kid play-ing dress-up in that uniform."

"You know him?"

"Since he was a little kid playing cops and robbers. Seems to me he's never grown up. Was he bothering you?"

"No." He didn't want to talk about it.

"What, just helping you unpack?" She hesitated. "Hey, I know they've been talking to you. I saw Sam the other day at the hos-pital." She hung her helmet on the handlebar. "I just wanted to make sure you're OK. Any trouble the hospital can help you with? We have some good attorneys on our side if you need some assis-tance."

"Thanks, but no thanks. I'm not in trouble." He set aside his glove and dusted off his Fresno State pennant. "At least not yet."

"Then why—"

"Because Michael Cunningham, the owner of the white Caddy who struck Beth Carlson, used to work for me in Southern California. He was my PA. The police seem to think I have something to do with him disappearing. Like either I know where he is or what he was doing in town. Good ole Dan there wanted to look in my freezer. I have no idea what they're after."

"Your freezer?" She shrugged. "Maybe he's hungry."

"Funny."

She lifted the lid and pulled out a frozen dinner, sesame seed chicken and rice. "You eat this stuff?"

"Every chance I get. It's fast. And easy to clean up."

She let the lid drop. "Let's go out." She walked over to her bike. "You need to vary your diet."

"Hey, you didn't look around long in there. I've got plenty of variety."

"Come on. I'll drive."

He looked at his clothes. "I'm a mess. I've been unpacking."

"So change your shirt. We'll go to the Crab Pot. It's casual."

He kicked a box with his shoe. He wasn't busy. He didn't have a good reason to refuse. "What if I get paged?"

"So I'll take you to the hospital."

He changed his shirt and, in spite of his better judgment, climbed onto the back of the Harley-Davidson, gingerly holding onto the back of the seat.

"Put your arms around me."

It wasn't a request. She eased off the clutch and twisted the throttle. Adam tightened his grip around her rock-hard abs to keep from falling off.

If Gerri wanted him to hold her tight, she was getting what she wanted. He leaned forward until their bodies moved as one through the curves along the oceanfront highway, first leaning left, then right, then left again.

"Don't fight me," she coaxed loudly. "Lean into my body so you can sense my direction."

He complied. He wanted to live. She opened the throttle.

He suspected Gerri was used to getting what she wanted.

He held on as she rounded another gentle curve, wondering what it would be like to be loaded onto a backboard if they crashed. Helmets may prevent head injuries, but they never keep you from breaking your neck.

Gerri reached back and touched his leg, encouraging him to be even closer.

What is it with this woman? Is she really interested in me?

Or just keeping tabs on me like the rest of Serenity?

∾

The next morning, Anna Barrymore sipped coffee and studied the morning paper, *The Outer Banks Daily*. Her work as a shipping clerk at the Island Hammock Company didn't start until second shift. She liked that because it offered her the chance to enjoy a leisurely beginning to the day. Not that anything had been leisurely about her life in the past few weeks. Her son, Kyle, had the notorious distinction of being the first known Serenity shark attack victim in more than a decade and had nearly lost his right arm in the process. Three surgeries in six days at Duke University Hospital, daily home-health nursing visits, and an extensive plan for Kyle's physical therapy had left Anna's life fraying at the edges, a barely recognizable silhouette of her former routine. Since Kyle's discharge he'd had frequent nightmares and a visit with a child psychologist for whom Kyle drew pictures of sharks. Her family had been upended, Anna's old-shoe comfortable routines displaced. She added a generous dollop of vanilla creamer to the steaming mug and sighed. Morning coffee with the paper and the backdrop of the rhythmic surf offered the promise of comfort, a pattern she loved. Things would be normal again soon.

She opened to the local page and contemplated the debate on building a new bridge to the mainland to offer relief to the weekend tourist traffic congestion. The red flags had been up a record number of days in July, indicating unsafe surf conditions with riptides. Harrison Ford had been spotted in a local restaurant. The shrimping industry was experiencing a banner year.

The news was predictable. A nice change for a family who had experienced one of life's curveballs. She turned the page and looked closer at a picture of Serenity's fishing pier, an interview with local police, and a headline she'd been waiting for. "Body Found Shows Evidence of Foul Play." She read with interest, ignoring her coffee. Finally someone was reporting something about the body pulled from the Atlantic by the tourist fishermen. She'd heard the local rumors, even talked to a member of the police force, but everyone was either ignorant or tight-lipped.

The article brought up an interesting theory. The autopsy revealed evidence that the body had been frozen after death. The police theorized that someone had stored the body in a freezer unit before dumping it in the sea. They hoped this hypothesis might prompt locals to come forward with other possible evidence.

She slid back her chair and listened for Kyle. All was quiet. She stood and pulled back the worn curtains over her kitchen sink as a vague memory floated at the corners of her mind. She turned on the water and began scrubbing at the frying pan left by her husband, Gene. An omelette fanatic, he'd agreed to cut back to two per week. She picked at a stubborn spot, evidence that this morning's variety contained green peppers.

A frozen body.

Images of Kyle's recent trauma floated in and out of her consciousness. The shrill scream forever etched on a mother's memory. The color of blood in the water. The ambulance ride and the emergency room at Broward County Hospital. The horrible events of

Kyle's accident would be difficult for time to scrub away. The memory tapes played back the moments following their arrival in the local emergency room. It was a busy place, a repository for some of life's down-and-outers. A drug abuser shouted obscenities at a surgeon who'd arrived to help. She snapped off the spigot. Something clicked.

What was it the young man yelled?

"You kill your patients and put them in a freezer!"

A freezer?

She'd dismissed the screaming patient to pay attention to her son. But now his words seemed to warrant evaluation, like a pebble in her shoe. Something wasn't right and needed attention.

A freezer?

She dried her hands and leaned over the table, studying the story she'd just read. The body found in the Atlantic was suspected of having been frozen.

An odd coincidence?

The paranoia of a mind fried with party drugs?

Or evidence worth reporting?

She picked up the phone. It wouldn't be the last time she looked like a fool. Once she'd called the police to report a prowler who turned out to be a raccoon in her trash can. And once she'd called 911 when her son Kyle had his tongue stuck in a pop bottle thirty seconds before he pulled his tongue out with a raspberry noise and grinned.

No, this was too weird to ignore.

She looked at the sticker on the back of the phone and dialed the number of the Serenity Police.

CHAPTER
14

ADAM TYSON'S EYES widened as he recognized the name on the mammogram report. He reread the findings with growing concern. "Architectual distortion. Stellate lesion with microcalcifications. Highly suspicious for malignancy. Biopsy and surgical consultation recommended."

Left side. The side of her trauma. This could all be from bleeding within the breast from the accident.

But I could never justify sitting on a report like this. She needs a biopsy.

His thoughts turned to an examination of her beauty. She'd become a wonderful new friend. And there was no denying his strong attraction to her.

How can I ever examine her with any kind of objectivity? A tender, meticulous, detailed probing of her skin . . .

He shook his head and muttered, "Get a grip. She's a patient."

He picked up the phone and dialed her number, one he'd easily committed to memory from his calls to check on her progress.

Ike answered. "Hello."

"Ike, it's Adam Tyson."

"Who? Who are you?" It was a friendly routine Ike had initiated to remind Adam to think of his identity.

"I'm a surgeon. Surely you've heard of me by now."

"That's your occupation. But who are you?"

"I get your point, Ike." He didn't want to go a full round with him this time. "May I speak to Beth?"

The old man chuckled. "Sure."

After a brief wait, the charming sound of her voice rewarded him. "How's my favorite washed-up baseball player?"

"I didn't realize you were a fan."

"You've never seen my card collection."

"Invite me over."

She giggled. "Is that why you called? To manipulate me into inviting you over?"

"I could always ask Travis to do it."

"He has to ask my permission."

He lifted the X-ray report and paused. "Say, Beth, you didn't tell me you were getting a mammogram."

"I was bored waiting for Ike at the grocery store parking lot. There was a mobile screening campaign going on. I just did it to kill time. Did I pass?"

"Not really."

A moment of uncomfortable silence followed.

"Your left side is far from normal."

"I didn't need a mammogram to tell me that. I'm just about ready to wear normal clothes again. It's good I like fall colors."

"Very funny." He hesitated. "Look, you're going to have to have this checked out. Do you have a family doctor or gynecologist?"

"You're my doctor."

"But I'm also a friend."

"I trust you. You saved my life, didn't you? I can't imagine anyone more caring."

His heart quickened. She was going to force him to do this, wasn't she? He took a deep breath and nodded. He could do this. He would just view it as a professional obligation. Divorce his emotions. It would be business only. Just a part of the job. Just because she was the most beautiful woman he'd ever laid eyes on . . .

"Adam?"

"I—I'll get my secretary to give you an appointment. You're going to need an examination and a needle test. It's probably just related to your accident, but we need to be sure."

"I trust you."

He sighed. "OK."

"Does this mean you didn't really call to get invited over?"

"Well . . ."

"Travis is using the hitting machine every day. Besides wanting to spend his summer up near the pier, it's all he wants to do."

"I was fourteen once. I understand."

"Will you join us for dinner? I'd like to see you again."

He heard a clicking noise, like she was tapping the phone with a fingernail.

"And Ike likes you too. Don't be put off by his questions. It's just his way of making you think."

"I thought he'd forgotten who I was for a second. I wasn't sure he was playing around."

He heard Beth sigh. "Well, I hope he was trying to make you think and not covering up for his forgetfulness." She paused. "So will you come?"

"Tonight?"

"Why not? Six-thirty?"

"Deal."

He smiled and said good-bye.

He replaced the phone in its cradle.

Beth Carlson was the best woman in the world.

∞

Beth hung up the phone and slipped her right hand beneath her blouse. She was still sore from the mammogram, the test that was supposed to relieve, not intensify her fears.

"What did the doctor want? Don't tell me he's just checking up on his favorite patient again. I've heard that line before."

"Dad, it was business this time." She looked away. "I had a mammogram done."

She heard him suck in his breath, a subtle but recognizable indicator that Ike was nervous.

"Adam says I need to get something checked out."

Ike was motionless. "Do it then. Don't wait around. Your mother always ignored—"

"I'm not ignoring anything, Dad. But don't worry. It's probably all related to this tremendous bruise."

Ike's hands trembled slightly before he clasped them together. To keep them from shaking? He looked pale.

"Dad, we don't even have a diagnosis yet."

"I can't help but think of your mother."

"Dad, it's probably nothing."

"Your mother always ignored her symptoms. She couldn't even believe it when Dr. Lareau told her she had cancer. She went running all over the country for second and third opinions, trying to find a doctor that would tell her what she wanted to hear." His voice cracked. "I can't help but wonder . . . if she would have just gotten help sooner—"

"Dad—"

"She had a good surgeon ready to do the surgery." He shook his head. "But she had to delay. She had to ask another doctor. And another."

"She was afraid."

"It might not have spread if she'd have listened and had the surgery when—"

Beth gripped his hand. "We've been over this before."

He squeezed back. There were tears in his eyes. "Cancer has to be treated right away." His head bobbed rhythmically. "Right away."

"Dad! Settle down. I don't have cancer."

His eyes were distant, staring through her.

Beth's heart quickened. Her father, the rock, was dissolving into insecurity.

"Daddy?"

He shook his head.

"God is sovereign. You've told me that a hundred times."

Ike's eyes lit up. As suddenly as he had panicked, he was back. He cleared his throat. "A thousand, more likely." He maneuvered his way past the bed in the family room and sat on the couch. "I've been a Christian more than fifty years. When do you think I'll begin to respond to pain like one?"

She walked to his side and placed her hand on his shoulder. "You're the most godly man I know."

"You don't know many men, do you?"

"Enough." She hesitated, looking on as her father leaned forward and gripped his head with both hands. "Are you feeling OK?"

He nodded slowly. "Sure."

She didn't believe it, but she didn't have time to worry about her father. She had to prepare for her dinner guest. "What would you like for supper? I invited Adam."

"He calls to give you bad news and you invite him for dinner?"

"It just worked out that way."

Her father picked up the biography of Abraham Lincoln that he'd been reading. "Do you really like him?"

She stopped and looked across the kitchen counter. "He's nice. He has a good job. He gets along with Travis."

"That's not what I asked. Besides, there are other considerations."

She didn't want to talk to her father about Adam right now. She knew what he was going to say. Be careful. He's struggling with his faith. If he has any at all. "Daddy, I am just being a friend. He's new in town. He needs—"

"I've seen him look at you."

"You sound like a mother."

"Men can have intuition too."

She rolled her eyes, knowing he couldn't see. *What is it with him? One minute he's near panic, the next he's back to giving me advice.*

"I just want you to be careful."

Beth mouthed the last two words with him. It was the one predictable phrase that had come out of his mouth every time she dated as a teenager.

It was the only downside of having the godliest man she knew as a father.

∞

That evening, armed with a fresh warrant from the magistrate, Greg Monroe leaned over the counter in the medical records department toward the young blonde secretary. "Evening, ma'am," he said, tipping his head forward.

The woman looked up from a desk cluttered with a hundred charts. Her eyes widened at the first sight of the uniform. Her back straightened. "May I help you?"

Officer Monroe identified himself and offered a thin smile. "I need to see some medical records." He handed her a slip of paper. "I need the emergency room census from this date."

She wasn't as naive as she looked. And maybe not as innocent. She pushed a rebellious strand of sun-bleached hair away from her blue eyes. "Medical records are confidential. I'll need to see the magistrate's approval."

He nodded again and produced the paper.

She studied it and pushed back her chair. She was wearing shorts, probably because things were more relaxed on evening shift. "I'm not sure how to do this. If you had medical record numbers, I could pull the charts, but I'll have to talk to my supervisor." She laid the request on the counter. "She works during the day. Can you come back tomorrow?"

"Could you call her? It's important."

She shrugged. "It's Deana's bowling night."

"Call her at the alley."

She smiled. "You don't give up easily, do you?" She picked up the phone and cradled it against her shoulder while tapping on the computer keyboard in front of her.

Greg watched as she talked and typed. In ten minutes she retrieved the list he'd requested. Twenty-seven patients had been seen on the same day as the Barrymore child, the shark victim. He circled three male possibilities and pushed it back across the counter at the secretary. He squinted at her nametag. Georgeanne Summers. *I'll bet your daddy wanted a boy.* "Can you pull these charts?"

She stood and disappeared into a maze of shelving. After a few minutes Georgeanne was back with the folders. "Here," she offered, laying the charts on the counter. "You aren't allowed to remove them from this room. You can use the desk over there." She pointed to a series of cubicles along the wall. Each one had a dictating machine for completing medical summaries.

"Thanks." He lifted the folders, each one a thin record with only a few pages of information. He inspected the records while standing, preferring the vantage point of the counter, so he could glance periodically at the gorgeous Georgeanne.

He found the one he wanted immediately and began recording

the data in a small leather book. Timothy Stevens, Baltimore, Maryland. He recognized the name. If he had his facts straight, Mr. Stevens would be due back in county court on drug charges made during an arrest after he damaged a glass door at the Seagull Inn.

He copied the facts with precision, glancing periodically at Georgeanne, who diverted her eyes down to her work each time he looked her way. Body language for attraction. He smiled the next time she looked up. "Is there a number where I can reach you?" He cleared his throat. "I might have some questions about the medical records."

She handed him a business card.

"Police work isn't 9 to 5. What if I need to reach you after hours?"

She didn't flinch. "Nice try, Officer Monroe. You can leave a message at work." She pushed a chart rack toward the shelving maze. "I don't date married men."

Touché. His right hand instinctively reached for his wedding band as he retreated to the door.

Evidently he hadn't been the only investigator in the room.

∽

That night after the sun submerged itself in the ocean and the orange sky faded to black, Beth stood at the sink and stared at her reflection in the window. The evening had been wonderful. Adam and Travis had to be forced away from the Solohitter, where Adam convinced her son to alter his batting stance. After supper they had made an absolute mess of the living-room floor, where they sorted and re-sorted Adam's aging baseball card collection. They quizzed each other, and Beth, on baseball trivia and laughed when she offered "Babe Ruth" as the answer to every single question. She'd watched Adam indiscreetly during her father's lengthy prayer and smiled when he appeared to be honestly praying himself. Maybe there was hope for him yet.

Her hand went instinctively to her chest as she paused from drying the dishes.

"It worries you, doesn't it?"

She looked at her father who sat at the dining table across the counter. She nodded.

"How do you feel about having Adam taking care of you?"

She looked away at the dishes. "What do you mean?"

"You know what I mean. He's a friend. A good friend. How do you feel about letting him see—"

"Daddy, it's just business for him. He's a professional. He—"

"He's a man, Beth. Don't think he isn't human. And you're a beautiful, young lady. I've seen the way he looks at you. Don't tell me it's all business."

She sighed. "Everyone I talk to says he's an artist in the operating room. Every stitch is precise. Every knot is even."

"I didn't ask you if he was qualified. I knew that from the way he pulled you through the accident." He paused. "I asked you how you feel. Can you treat it like a professional encounter?"

"Daddy, I—" She halted and took a deep breath. "I think I can." She looked at her father. Leave it to him to drive straight to the heart of an issue. Just like he did with Adam every time he saw him. "Who are you really? What defines you? When will you surrender to the One who is relentless in His loving pursuit?"

Ike stayed quiet, sipping coffee from a mug emblazoned with the image of a sailfish.

"What do you think I should do?"

He appeared to be studying his coffee. "I think your options are limited. He's the only surgeon on the Outer Banks. Picking another doctor would chance delaying a diagnosis." He shook his head slowly. "Your mother put off going to the doctor for six months after she found a lump. I keep thinking that if she'd only have gotten treatment sooner, maybe things would have turned out differently."

"OK, pastor, how many times have I heard you tell people they can't live by the 'if-onlys'?"

He smiled. "How does Adam feel about this? Have you asked him?"

"Not really. But surgeons are proud, Daddy. His ego will make it hard for him not to treat me if he thinks I trust him to help."

"When is your appointment?"

"Adam said he'd work me in tomorrow morning. That way he can get the slides made and read by the pathologist before the weekend."

Ike set down his mug and clasped his trembling hands together. "Good. He needs to be quick."

She nodded. "I think he's as anxious as I am."

"Can he be objective?"

"He's a professional."

"So you've already reminded me." He stood and handed her his empty mug, still warm from its contents. "Just get the test done. It's the quickest option available. Then we'll decide together about the next step, OK?"

She nodded. "I'm a big girl, Daddy."

"But I'm still your father."

She put down the drying towel and stepped into her father's open arms. He was old but strong.

And she suspected she might need a hug to make it through tomorrow.

∞

Adam Tyson walked to the end of the wooden-slat sidewalk before slipping off his shoes and plunging his feet into the still-warm sand. He continued onto the beach, pausing briefly beside a sand dune to pick up a worn shell. He rubbed its smooth surface as he walked, trying to sort out the jumble of thoughts in his mind.

Beth Carlson had messed up his tidy plans. He was ready to carry on a professional charade because he deserved the respect. He was good at what he did. He was needed here, after all. But he wasn't so sure about love.

He hadn't planned on this.

Beth was so open, so trusting . . . so vulnerable.

He was skilled in the profession. So what if he didn't have the paper credentials? He had the hands, the mind. These were God-given. He had an obligation to use them to help others, didn't he?

His rationalization fell flat when he thought of deceiving Beth. Honesty was the foundation for any successful relationship.

She made him feel so alive. How long had it been since he'd opened his heart to love?

Could he possibly trust her with his secret?

His fingers explored the ridged surface of the shell in his hand.

He walked for a few minutes more before sitting down in an abandoned lawn chair facing the surf. Things were rapidly spinning toward an inevitable breakdown in his complicated charade. Beth would certainly reject him if she knew.

Adam sighed and heaved the shell toward the surf, glistening in the moonlight. But more important than what Beth thought, he was starting to think about God again. Did He care about all this? Is it possible that Jesus was as reckless in His love toward him as Ike proclaimed? Or did unconditional love exist only in fairy tales?

Ike's questions probed his mind with increasing intensity. *Who am I?*

Can I admit the truth to Beth?

Can I admit the truth to myself?

Being honest with himself was something he'd avoided successfully for a long time.

There was too much at stake. He had worked hard for the success he had. Getting close to Beth would certainly mean giving up his dream. The prospect of love enticed him, but Beth liked him as she thought he was. Certainly she would reject him if she knew the truth.

He scooped up a handful of sand and let it begin to sift slowly through his fingers. His grip was loosening. Honesty would mean losing Beth, but a real relationship couldn't be successful without it. And honesty would mean a loss of his profession, everything he had dreamed of since college.

It wasn't worth the risk. He would have to maintain appropriate distance or lose everything.

He could end up in jail.

Or worse.

Beth would hate him too.

CHAPTER
15

THE NEXT MORNING Beth studied the faces of four other people sitting in Adam Tyson's small waiting room. A middle-aged woman flipped through a *Cosmopolitan* with a speed reflecting either her inability to read or her anxiety. Beth wondered what she was here for. Perhaps she had a lump and was worried too. Maybe she had gallstones or a mole hidden somewhere beneath her flowered dress. Why had she dressed up so, just to see the surgeon?

Beth looked away to a window and remembered how she too had spent extra time selecting makeup and clothing she wasn't even sure Adam would see.

A second woman sat hemmed in by a walker in front of her chair, the white bandage on her lower leg spotted with green drainage. Everything about her spoke of fatigue, a life of pleasure and spontaneity long past. Beth had selected a chair far away from the woman's walker. She imagined whatever was living in the green drainage would certainly be ready to jump to a welcome host that brushed by unsuspecting.

A teenage boy slouched beside his mother, his head tilted back, his eyes and ears closed to his mother's constant jabber. His silence did not slow her comments about everything and anything she thought about as she sat hidden behind the day's newspaper.

After a few minutes Beth was ushered into an exam room and handed a paper with a hole in the center, a poncho of sorts, certainly not designed for modesty or warmth. The nurse, a young brunette Beth judged to be under thirty, was too pretty to be working for Adam. Beth was sure he hadn't mentioned her when he talked about his office staff. "You'll have to take off your blouse and put this over your head."

Beth took the paper obediently.

"I'll be back to get your weight and blood pressure."

Beth undressed, slipped the paper half-gown over her head, and climbed onto the center examining table.

A few moments later, instead of the nurse, Adam appeared after a gentle knock. He looked at her chart. "Hello, Ms. Carlson."

Beth smiled. He was going to be totally professional. She could do this. She lifted her hand. "Dr. Tyson."

He pulled out a foot extension on the table and instructed her to lie down. He asked about her pain, her exercise tolerance, her bowel function, and her wound. "Any drainage? Soreness? Redness?"

He lifted the paper covering, sliding it up a few inches to examine her abdominal scar. He nodded, apparently pleased with his work.

Of course there was the other matter of her concern. Adam made a note in the chart in his hand and then launched into a series of questions about her breast lump.

"Pain? Nipple discharge? Family history? Age at first menstrual period? Age at first pregnancy? Miscarriages or abortions? Use of hormones?"

Then, without additional commentary, he nodded again. "I'll get Tonya."

Not the nurse, or even my nurse, but Tonya. *Careful, Adam. We're being professional here, remember?*

A minute passed, and Beth had time to remember what it was like taking her mother to the surgeon's office for breast exams. Dr. Lareau had always taken such good care of her. And of course, Dr. Laureau's nurse, Bonnie, was sweeter than honey and on the safe side of fifty.

She had wanted to thank Adam for the wonderful evening last night, for paying such good attention to Travis. But here in the office Adam seemed to be completely absorbed into the Dr. Tyson role. Probably for the best. Beth sighed and tapped her fingers on the exam table.

When Adam came back, he stood on her right, and Tonya on her left. Tonya lifted the paper to expose Beth so the exam could begin.

"I know the concern is about the left, but I need to start over here on the right to get an idea of what the normal side is like." When he said, "normal," he framed the comment in quotation marks traced in the air with his fingers.

His exam was thorough and gentle and involved feeling deeply under her arm for enlarged lymph nodes. Her mind spun from wondering if she'd remembered deodorant to being self-conscious over her own perspiration to an article she'd read recently in a women's magazine about breast exams in surgeon's offices. The number one complaint registered by women after an exam by a male surgeon was, "He didn't spend enough time doing the breast examination." The second most common complaint was, "He spent too much time doing the breast examination."

Beth studied his eyes, hoping he wouldn't look at her face. She tried to discern his thoughts. No luck. Surgeons wear a poker face during breast examinations. At least good ones do.

She watched him as he began the exam of the left breast. His fingers slowed to measure the lump, which he carefully moved beneath his hand. He wanted to see if it was fixed to the chest wall. He palpated her armpit, and glanced almost imperceptibly at Tonya, who raised her eyebrows in a question. He nodded, and she stepped away and began gathering supplies, the result of the silent communication between them, working like an old married couple.

"I'll have to do a needle test," he said. "It's probably just a hematoma from the car wreck. A blood collection," he added, as if she wasn't a nurse. "But I want to be safe."

Beth clenched her teeth and nodded. "I want to be sure."

He swabbed the skin with an iodine solution and warned her of the bee sting to come.

The prick wasn't bad, the needle's probing tip searching in and out only for a brief moment before he removed it and instructed her to hold gentle pressure with a white gauze.

Adam and Tonya worked to make the slides and preserve them in a solution to take to the pathologist.

Tonya spoke next. "Would you like to come in to discuss the results, or should Dr. Tyson call you at home?"

"Can you stop by the house?"

Beth watched as Tonya exchanged glances with Adam. She

sensed immediately that she'd crossed some invisible line, a barrier patients are not allowed to penetrate. Stopping by was something that friends did. Surgeons don't just "stop by the house" anymore. This was business. Adam, Dr. Tyson rather, would prefer to keep this exchange purely professional. His upper lip tightened. Was she perceiving something new? Was he afraid of what he'd felt? Was the mammogram that concerning? Was he withdrawing from her as her friend? Maybe she'd been wrong to think they could relate on two levels. Was he pulling away from her or just following through with his commitment to be completely professional?

He cleared his throat and straightened the lapel on his starched white coat. "I'll give you a call after I talk with the pathologist. I have a few cases this afternoon, so it may be tomorrow."

The alarm must have registered on her face.

"I'll try to get Dr. Patterson to look at the slides today," he added before leaving her in the room with Tonya, the young, I-know-your-needs-without-you-saying-a-word super-nurse.

Beth looked up as Tonya placed her hand gently on her forearm and said softly, "Don't think anything of it. I know ya'll are friends. But Adam told me he wanted to keep this visit completely on a professional level."

Beth's blood boiled. *Adam! You call him Adam? What happened to your professionalism?* The thought of Adam warning this nurse that he wanted to keep things professional revolted her. *As if he thought I was going to try to take the visit to a personal level or something? So Adam warned her so she could help keep me in line?* Her own thoughts speared her with condemnation as she remembered asking Adam to drop by the house. Her emotions swung on a pendulum from anger to embarrassment. Her face reddened.

She wanted to be alone, but Miss Clinical needed to take her blood pressure. Beth steamed as the pretty office assistant evaluated and recorded the vitals. *My pressure must be 1,000 over 500 if it reflects how I really feel.*

Tonya flashed a smile of white, even teeth. Beth couldn't return an honest smile. *She probably suffered through a horrible adolescence of dental torture and orthodontic nightmares. At least I hope so.* The thought enabled Beth to manufacture a little grin.

The nurse spoke. "Show this card to Jolene in the front office."

After dressing, Beth left through the front office. Jolene was prettier than Tonya, a near-twin to Lisa, the young receptionist who'd signed Beth in earlier in the morning. Hadn't anyone ever heard of ugly office help? Certainly the patients wouldn't feel so bad about themselves if the staff weren't so perfect.

She exited into the sunshine of a hot North Carolina morning. Everything about the atmosphere suggested slowing down. And Beth sensed the message to her own soul. She moved slowly to her van, opening the door and struggling into the driver's seat before leaning over the steering wheel and trying to suppress the urge to cry.

She shut the door and lifted a worn pocket Bible that lay on the seat beside her. It was her father's. He would never be far from a copy of the Scriptures. On this, her first driving outing since her accident, she should have been rejoicing in her regained freedom. Instead she found herself in a turmoil of fear, jealousy, and embarrassment.

Adam was just doing what he needed to do. I'm the one who put him in this awkward spot. What must he be feeling? Is he angry at me for pushing him to relate to me on two levels at the same time? Or is it easy for him to treat me on a purely professional level? Maybe he isn't even tempted by other thoughts when he touches me with his white coat on.

Is it only in my mind? No, I'm sure I've felt his admiration before. And being married for as long as I was taught me a few things about how men think. This whole thing may have been a real test for Adam.

But a surgeon would never admit it.

The pride is too ingrained.

She nodded her head as another realization hit. *It's pride that keeps Adam from turning back to God. As long as he can find satisfaction in self, he'll never decide to find satisfaction in God.*

She turned the ignition and began to pray. Ironically, it wasn't for her own health, even in the presence of such a potentially serious threat. Instead she prayed for the surgeon, the man Dr. Adam Tyson.

❧

Sam Harris, the Serenity Police chief, retrieved the fax from the state medical examiner's office and studied it while sipping his third cup of black coffee. "Monroe? Smith?"

The officers approached the chief's office. Greg knocked on the door-frame. "Yo, boss, what's up?"

"Time for a new hypothesis, boys. The dental records show the body pulled from the ocean couldn't be Michael Cunningham. Cunningham had a partial plate this body didn't have."

Greg pulled a donut from an open box on the chief's desk and brushed the white powder from his blue tie. "I think we need to let the newspaper know a little more information about the body."

"You just want to talk to Linda Johnson again," Dan responded, watching Greg devour the donut in two bites.

Sam tapped his hand against the desktop. "Easy, Dan, he may have a point."

Dan scoffed. "What? You would give the media information?"

"Only when letting the public know might help my investigation." He shrugged. "We're at a dead-end. We thought we knew the identity of the body. Releasing details about the body didn't serve a purpose then. It might now."

"You're the boss."

"Any luck finding Timmy Stevens?"

"I found his mother. She says she hasn't seen him for a month."

"Any prior arrests?"

"Three. All drug possession."

"Any other contacts?"

Greg nodded. "A guy named Keith Lasorda shared a room with Timmy at the Seagull Inn. His phone was disconnected last week."

"They're supposed to be in county court next month to face drug possession charges."

The trio was silent. They knew the suspects weren't likely to show.

The chief broke the silence. "Talk to Linda. Tell her about the cuff link found on the body. Tell her the ID doesn't match Michael Cunningham. We've got two mysteries on our hands—the missing hit-and-run driver and a corpse."

"Maybe someone will know the identity of the cuff link."

Sam sighed. "Anything on our new doctor?"

"No," Dan responded. "But he knows I'm watching."

"That's what I want. Let him see you. The pressure is bound to get to him."

"I don't know, chief. I've seen this guy's work schedule. He doesn't slow down too often. He's been cool so far."

"Just keep it up. What's he do after work?"

"He doesn't have many hangouts. Doesn't drink. Stays at home and eats microwave meals."

Greg pushed another donut into his mouth and talked through the mouthful. "The only place he goes is to visit a beachfront cottage owned by Isaac Williamson."

Sam shook his head. "Don't know him."

"I think he's seeing his daughter, Elizabeth Carlson."

"Carlson? Mother of the kid who clued the boys in on where to fish?"

"The same."

Sam Harris stood, wiped the powdered sugar from the corner of his desk, and frowned. "Eat over the trash can, would you?"

Greg picked up his third donut, lifted a trash can under his chin, and mumbled, "Sure."

"There are too many coincidences here. The guy who used to employ Michael Cunningham is visiting the very person that Cunningham ran over?"

Greg turned a wooden chair around and sat in it, facing the back of the chair. He leaned forward and confessed, "I don't get it."

"Why is the doctor visiting her?"

Dan spoke up. "She's a looker. I talked to her in the hospital. My guess is the new doctor is making house calls to make sure she is OK." He laughed sarcastically.

"The lady is new in town too. She's the new director of nursing at the hospital," Greg reported.

Sam paced around his desk, weaving a path between Dan and Greg, pausing to pick up a donut crumb and toss it into the trash can. "These two newcomers have been in the center of trouble ever since their arrival in Serenity."

Greg patted his gut. "And so far we've got more questions than answers."

"Monitor the newcomers. And talk to the newspaper. Sooner or later something's gotta break around Serenity."

⚉

Bill Patterson, M.D., ran his fingers through his long beard and squinted into the microscope. "Look at these cells, Adam." He paused, moving the slide. "And these here. They are very immature, angry."

Adam nodded and pulled his head back from the two-headed teaching microscope, his stomach gripped in a tight knot. *Cancer. Beth Carlson has breast cancer.*

"You say she has a history of trauma?"

"She was hit by a car. I was almost sure this was just a hematoma from the blunt trauma."

"That would explain all of the blood in the background." He adjusted the slide again. "But here's another cluster of duct cells, very bizarre nuclei. Yep, this is cancer all right. No doubt about it."

"Her mother had it," Adam mumbled, stepping back from the scope. His mind was dizzy with the implications. *Can I trust myself to do her surgery? She deserves an experienced cancer surgeon.*

I'd trust myself to operate on another woman with breast cancer. But Beth Carlson?

His distress must have shown. The pathologist looked up. "Hey, are you OK?"

"Huh? Oh, sure." Adam looked away. "It's just that this patient happens to be a friend, that's all."

"I see." Dr. Patterson set the slide in a tray for storage. "Well, don't let your emotions get in the way. This patient needs surgery, and that means she needs an objective surgeon who won't let her tears get in the way of treatment."

Adam swallowed hard. The pathologist was right. He walked away without another word, trying to figure out how he would break the news to Beth.

Maybe this was the warning he needed. He had allowed his heart to become entangled. Now he would have to divorce his emotions in order to do the right thing for Beth. He could be her surgeon or her friend. And as her friend he'd have to be honest, and honesty would threaten everything he'd worked so hard to obtain.

But what good is a life without love?

His shoulders were stooped as he walked down the long hospital corridor.

I had love once. And it slipped away because I wasn't good enough.

Certainly love will come my way again once I have respect, money, and prestige.

But how will I explain that to Beth?

His beeper sounded, interrupting his thoughts. He looked at the number. Emergency room. Probably a kid on vacation with belly pain. *At least I can put off calling Beth for a little while.*

CHAPTER
16

REBA CRAWFORD STILL used her finest china for her breakfast coffee, even when she ate alone, which was most of the time since her husband died last spring. She had reached a certain station in life, and drinking from a common mug just didn't fit her self-image anymore.

Since Mark died, her life had become a series of routines. Breakfast coffee with the morning paper, the Outer Banks' pathetic excuse for a newspaper, a walk along the beach, an hour in the flower garden, an hour with a novel, lunch on the deck alone, an afternoon siesta, reading the mail and a review of her stock portfolio and the *Wall Street Journal*, the evening news, another hour with a novel, a late supper, and bedtime.

Now she looked through the paper, immediately drawn to an article about the autopsy findings on the body recovered close to the fishing pier.

MEDICAL EXAMINER RAISES
QUESTIONS OF BODY'S IDENTITY

A medical examiner's report was released yesterday afternoon by the Serenity Police. The body, a male discovered by fishermen just off the Serenity Fishing Pier, was suspected to be the missing Michael Cunningham, but this has been disproven by careful examination of his dental records. When asked why the police had assumed the identity, Chief of Police Harris pointed out two facts. "One, Michael Cunningham has been missing since his car was found at the scene of a recent hit-and-run, and two, a cuff link engraved with the initials M.C. were recovered from the shirt found on the body."

Reba gasped as she read and reread the article. Her husband, town surgeon Mark Crawford, had owned a set of engraved cuff links.

She stood and began to pace. This made little sense. Her husband's sailboat was found a good thirty miles from Serenity's fishing pier. But his body had never been found.

Could this be my husband?

She looked back at the article, which detailed that the man had died from a wound to the head. Murder?

This is silly. Everyone loved my husband. He was the pride of Serenity.

She tried to reason away her anxiety, but the fact remained. Her husband's body had never been recovered, not an unusual occurrence with a deepwater ocean drowning.

She couldn't shake the gnawing feeling that the body might be her husband's.

She walked to her bedroom. It was time to dress for the day.

And time to talk with Sam Harris, Serenity Chief of Police.

∞

Beth busied herself with light housework, dusting, and doing dishes, anything to keep her mind off her own health. Adam hadn't called or stopped by the night before, something Beth knew she shouldn't expect but still hoped for. She had wanted the breast lump to disappear, for Adam to come by and play baseball with Travis, to sip coffee with her on the deck and talk about his journey of faith. But he hadn't come by, and her last interaction with him had been professional and distant, underscoring the schizophrenia of their relationship. Was it friend to friend, doctor to patient, the business relationship of coworkers, or the lingering possibility of lovers?

The phone rang, and instinctively Beth's hand slipped to her left breast. She moved slowly to the phone. "Hello."

"Beth?"

She recognized Adam's voice immediately. "Hi, Adam. I was hoping you'd call."

He cleared his throat. "The results of your needle test are back." He paused.

Beth's throat was dry. She couldn't speak.

"It's positive, Beth."

"P-positive? It's cancer?"

"Yes. It's cancer."

She steadied herself against the kitchen counter. "Now what?"

"I'll need to see you in the office. We need to do a few tests. Make sure you understand your options."

Beth nodded numbly. She knew her options. She had been through this with her mother.

She was young. She wanted to marry again. She wouldn't accept having her breast removed unless it was a last resort.

"Shall I have my office staff call you with an appointment?"

"Sure." She hesitated. "Can you come by the house? Maybe we could talk?"

He seemed to hesitate. "Things have been pretty crazy here at the hospital. I'll see."

"I understand," she mumbled before setting down the phone. She lifted her fingers to comb her bangs, already anticipating the need for chemotherapy and the inevitable loss of her hair.

She heard Travis coming down the stairs. She quickly dabbed her eyes with her sleeve and turned away to the window. She would have to be strong for him. Losing his father had been horrible. Fearing the loss of his mother would be devastating.

"Mom?"

She steadied her voice and answered, a little more loudly than she'd planned, "Yes?"

"Who was it? Was it Dr. Tyson? Did they find an answer?"

She couldn't lie. She had to be strong. But suddenly, to say the word was impossible. In fact, speaking seemed impossible. She nodded quickly, trying to keep her chin from quivering.

"Mom?"

Her silence was the answer.

"It's cancer, isn't it?"

She nodded and edged forward, thinking that perhaps he would need a hug. She knew she did.

But Travis couldn't hold back the tears. Her fourteen-year-old son was one minute a man, one minute a child, and at this moment his reversion to immaturity was marked by a cry that ripped into his mother's soul. "God is always letting me down!" He spun to avoid

Beth's grasp and ran through the front room, exiting the house with a slam that knocked a family photograph off the front wall.

Beth followed him with a pace hampered by her recent surgery. She looked at the picture and its broken glass. It was one of her, Barry, and Travis, taken at Barry's last Christmas.

How fitting, she thought as she picked up the pieces. *This family is falling apart.*

What will ever bring healing to our brokenness?

∽

Sam Harris looked at the men's watch that Reba Crawford had given him.

"I had the watch and the cuff links engraved at the same shop over in Durham. Just show me the cuff link. I'm sure I'll be able to identify it."

Sam pushed back from his desk. "Your sailboat was found halfway to Ocracoke. There's no way it could have sailed all that way if Mark had fallen off the boat up here."

"It said in the paper that the autopsy showed evidence of an attack, murder. Maybe my husband wasn't on that boat. Ever think of that?"

"We consider everything. Including the fact that your husband had a few drinks on the boat with our hospital administrator before setting sail."

"My husband didn't drink. I told you that when you did the original investigation of his death."

"But what about all the alcohol on the boat?"

"Someone hid it there."

"Ever heard of a closet drinker, Mrs. Crawford? Perhaps your husband had secrets. The alcohol wasn't out in plain sight. Perhaps he kept it hidden from you. Did he like to sail alone?"

"You know he did. We went over all this when he disappeared. It was his sanctuary, his place of peace. When he was on his sailboat, he could lay aside the stressors of his life in surgery."

"Perhaps he drank alone. Without you."

"Impossible. He always preached against it to his patients."

"Look, Mrs. Crawford, Dave Winters, one of the administrators, met with your husband on the boat, had a few drinks with him before he set sail. We've got an eyewitness." He sighed deeply. "Look, I'm not out to destroy your husband's reputation, but I have to look at this objectively."

"Show me the cuff link. If it's his, you can have them test the body for alcohol. That will prove I'm telling the truth."

"Mrs. Crawford, there's no doubt in my mind that you believe you are telling the truth, but we have to face facts here. Your husband was—"

She raised her voice. "He didn't drink!" She pointed her finger at his chest. "He was on call all the time. Drinking would have put his patients at risk. That's not the kind of man or surgeon he was."

"Please, Mrs. Crawford, lower your voice. Have a seat," he said, gesturing toward a wooden chair.

She bit her lip and dusted white powder off the chair before sitting down.

He kept his voice low. "I didn't want to tell you this. And I've kept all of this from the media. Dave Winters went to confront your husband about that very fact on the night he disappeared. There was concern that he was drinking on the job."

"What?" she huffed, "Well, I never—"

The sheriff folded his hands and leaned forward with a patronizing air. "Look, I'm sorry to be the one to tell this to you. I wanted to protect your husband's image. But I've got eyewitnesses. Gerri Fiori, the nurse manager of the OR, raised concerns—"

"They are lying!"

"Why would they lie?"

The question stumped her. "I don't know. But I do know my Mark. He was a godly man. If people are saying those things, they're unfounded."

With that, she slapped her knee. "I want to see the cuff link."

The sheriff shook his head and stood. "Follow me."

They walked into a back room, where he unlocked a file cabinet and pulled out a box with a number on top. He retrieved the cuff link and held it up to the light.

"He never dressed up when he went on his boat. He always wore an old sweatshirt and jeans."

"So it's not his then?" He shrugged. "I had my doubts. He didn't disappear anywhere around here."

Reba Crawford took the cuff link in her fist and clenched it tightly before starting to cry. "Oh, it's his all right. You've found my husband."

She couldn't be consoled. "And he was murdered right here in Serenity."

∞

That night, after the sun had set and Travis retreated silently to his room, Beth watched Ike as he mused over another chapter in the life of Abraham Lincoln.

Ike scratched his chin. It was something he often did if he had something to say.

"What is it, Daddy?"

"It says that Abraham Lincoln talked to Harriet Beecher Stowe."

Beth frowned. He had told her all about this earlier in the day.

"You know, the lady who wrote *Uncle Tom's Cabin*."

How can you remember the name of an old novel, but not that you told me this two hours ago? She sighed. "I know about the novel. And about what the President told her." She hesitated. "Daddy, I need to go out for a little."

He folded his book after carefully placing a worn bookmark in the center. She wasn't sure why he used it. He seemed to just pick up the book and reread what he'd been over the day before. "You think if you go to Adam's house, he'll tell you the diagnosis?"

She shook her head. She approached him slowly and sat next to him on the couch. She put her hand on his. "Dr. Tyson already called."

Ike's head begin to shake. "No." He touched his forehead. "You didn't tell me this before, did you?"

"No."

That seemed to comfort him. He nodded and squeezed her hand, confident he was in control. "Good."

"Actually, it's not good, Daddy. It's cancer."

"It can be treated. That's what the doctors told your mother." His hand went to his mouth. "You need to do whatever he tells you. Just get it treated right away."

"OK."

Ike lowered his hand to hers again and nodded. "He's a good surgeon. He saved your life."

"I'll be fine. I know I'm in good hands."

"God's hands, honey."

She nodded. The moment rang with irony for Beth. She was the one with cancer, yet she was concerned for her father's well-being. And even though he was giving advice, she understood he spoke from a platform of insecurity, a fear that she would end up like her mother. She accepted his counsel without question in order to reassure him, not vice versa.

She searched his eyes, watching for a flicker of the old confidence that had shone so brightly. They were eyes made compassionate by a lifetime of service to others. But now they were dimming. The fire that could burn right through Beth as a young woman was now only an occasional spark during a conversation about issues dear to his soul.

She stood up slowly, aware that she still couldn't move too fast without her abdominal incision reminding her to ease up. "I need to go out."

"You're going to him, aren't you? You think he can comfort you more than your dear old dad?"

Beth took a deep breath. "Of course not."

He waved his hand at her. "Go ahead. Tell him you want the surgery right away."

"Dad, I need to talk to him." She hesitated. "About other stuff."

Ike squinted and mumbled, "Other stuff."

"He's been acting so distant. I need to know what's in his head."

"Maybe he's having a hard time playing the dual role of doctor and friend."

"Maybe so." She stepped slowly toward the door. "It won't hurt to ask."

Ike's eyes twinkled. "I'll wait up for you."

"I won't be gone long."

She used her minivan and drove slowly past Adam's place to see if she could discern signs of life. *He mentioned things were hectic, so maybe he's still at the hospital.*

His car was in the driveway, his garage door open. A single window was aglow with light. She parked and ascended his front steps and rang the doorbell.

After a brief wait the door opened. Adam's hair was uncombed, his shirttail out. He still had on his work clothing, except he had traded his shoes for a pair of pale blue flip-flops. "Beth!"

"I hope I'm not interfering with anything. I was hoping we could talk."

He shrugged. "Come on in. I was just finishing dinner."

"It smells good."

"Microwave sirloin tips over pasta."

She looked around the spotless room, witness to a surgeon delighted with order. She sat on a flowered couch, easing down slowly.

"Still having pain?"

"Not much. Going from standing to sitting and back up again mostly."

"What's up?"

"Adam, you know what's up."

"You want to talk about your diagnosis? Maybe we should talk about this at the office." He shifted in his seat, a cushioned leather recliner.

"I don't want to talk in the office. And I'm not here to talk about my cancer. I know all about breast cancer. I saw my mom go through it." She leaned forward. "I want to talk about us. And about you. How you feel."

"How I feel? You are the one facing a crisis."

"Adam, today when I saw you in the office, you treated me like a stranger."

"I was being your surgeon. I wasn't there to be a friend."

"Well, maybe I didn't like it. Maybe I wanted to feel like I was special to you." She sighed and looked at her hands. "Maybe I shouldn't have put you up to this. Maybe I shouldn't have asked you to be my surgeon and my friend. Is this something you can handle?"

"I thought so. But I decided that in the office I would concentrate solely on being a surgeon. I might be able to play both roles, but not at the same time."

"But how can you do that? How can you divorce your feeling about me and treat me like anyone else?"

"I'm sorry, Beth. Maybe I stepped over the line. I never should have started acting this way. It's never a good idea for a doctor to fall for his patient."

"Is that what's happening, Adam? Are you falling for me?"

He pulled away from her gaze and walked to a glass door overlooking his deck. "Beth, I don't want to hurt you. I'm . . . well, I'm having trouble sorting things out. I've been concentrating so hard on my surgeon role, I guess I haven't really gotten my feelings figured out. Your father has made me think about who I really am." He looked back at her, his eyes searching her face for a sign of understanding. "Look, Beth, I—well, I—I just want what is best for you. Maybe you should go to another surgeon." He still didn't meet her eyes. "What if something went wrong?"

"I know you're the best around. If something goes wrong, that's just part of the risk. I know that. The question is, can you play both roles? Can you be my surgeon and my friend? I'm not sure I'm willing to give up our relationship."

Adam started to pace. He rubbed his hand through his already disheveled hair. "I'm a capable surgeon, Beth, but you are going to be the director of nursing."

"And also a friend. Adam, what's going on? Just a few nights ago we walked beside the surf and you told me you were concerned about what I thought about you. Now it's apparent that I have a huge health problem, and you act like we just met." She stood to face him. "It's true I need a surgeon, but I need a friend right now."

"You are special to me. I think you know that. But . . ." He hesitated.

"But . . ." she prompted.

"You don't really know me, Beth." He looked away. "I'm not sure I even know who I am anymore."

"Adam," she responded, reaching for his arm, "most people live their lives not truly understanding who they are. Even most Christians live their lives with little understanding that they are really loved by God. They are so consumed with the outward things that define them that they never come to grips with the largest reality of all."

"I don't know anyone like you. Everyone I know puts on a false front. Nobody in medicine is allowed to get emotionally tied to a patient for fear of being led by passion instead of science."

"Medicine needs a compassionate face."

"Surgeons aren't very good at letting down their guard."

Beth sat back down. "I had a part in a play once. It was a one-act play by Thornton Wilder called *The Angel That Troubled the Waters*."

He looked back at her, not speaking. He sat across from her in his leather chair.

She continued, "Remember the story in the Bible where an angel comes and troubles the water at the pool of Bethesda? The first person into the water after the water is troubled will be healed. Wilder's play tells the story of a physician who goes to the pool for healing of his depression." She smiled. "I played the part of the angel."

"I could have guessed." He gave the first hint of a smile.

"After I stirred the waters, the physician tried to get in, but I told him the healing was not for him." She shifted in her seat. "Help me up. I think I can still remember my lines."

He pulled her to her feet, and she backed into the center of the room. She paused and closed her eyes, bringing the high-school memory up to the present. She lifted her hand, open palm up, extended toward Adam. "Without your wounds where would your power be? It is your melancholy that makes your low voice tremble into the hearts of men and women. The very angels themselves cannot persuade the wretched and blundering children on earth as can one human being broken on the wheels of living. In Love's service, only wounded soldiers can serve. Physician, draw back."

Adam clapped and assisted her onto the couch again. "So tell me what you are trying to say."

"Only that we spend so much time working on false identities, the false images we allow others to see. We dare not face our brokenness for fear others will reject us. But it is only in embracing our own sin that we lay claim to grace. And we will never help another if we hide from our own humanity."

"But we in medicine try not to let our humanity get in the way. Emotion is messy, interfering with objective decision-making."

"But only in embracing our frailty will we ever be able to be truly compassionate."

"Why are you telling me this?"

"Because I want you to be real with me. Don't play games with me. Adam, I see so much good in you. I believe you really care about people. You're friendly, confident, and you've been wonderful with Travis. You're an excellent surgeon, but . . ."

"There's always a but."

"But you could be so much better if you learn to be human yourself."

"Are you accusing me of hiding behind a false front?"

"Only to the extent that we all do it."

He walked around the room, apparently contemplating their conversation. When he spoke, he turned the conversation to her health. "I'd like you to see another surgeon. Maybe I will agree to do your surgery, but I want another surgeon to agree on a plan of action. Do you know anyone else you respect?"

"Only back in Richmond. I know quite a few surgeons at the Medical College of Virginia where I worked."

"Pick one. I'll send them your data. You can take your mammogram and let them give you advice."

She attempted a smile. "Will you remain my friend? I'm not sure I like the either/or arrangement."

"You ask a lot of questions." He took a deep breath. "How do you feel?"

"I'm getting stronger."

He shook his head. "I don't mean as a patient. How do you feel about me? This honesty stuff has to go both ways. Are you falling for your doctor?"

"You didn't answer me when I asked you the same question."

He raised his eyebrows. "You noticed."

She studied him for a moment before struggling to her feet for a final time. She stepped toward him and leaned forward, planting a kiss on his forehead. "You are a special man, Adam. Come to understand the meaning of this: You are beloved of God. Until you love yourself, you'll never let another love you, and you'll never really love anyone else."

She walked to the door. "I'll see Dr. Warren Harper in Richmond for a second opinion. I'll call your office with his fax number in the morning." She opened the door and looked as Adam touched the location of her kiss with his fingers. He didn't look up but sat transfixed in thought.

She walked into the night air and looked at the stars.

Abba, she prayed silently, *help him to understand the love You have for him.*

CHAPTER
17

THREE DAYS LATER Jim Manning sipped coffee in the Broward County Hospital cafeteria and scanned *The Outer Banks Daily*. He had envisioned that life in the FBI would be a bit more glamorous, but a three-year stint working on fraud and Medicare abuse convinced him that boredom was a cornerstone of this assignment.

He had started looking at some suspicious billing practices involving a Dr. Mark Crawford six months before, until the disappearance of the suspect stalled his investigation. But yesterday his superiors asked him to take a second look at the quiet town of Serenity. It seemed the body of Dr. Crawford had been identified, and the medical examiner suspected foul play. And if there's one thing he had learned in his years with the feds, it was that coincidences just don't happen. If two suspicious activities take place in one small town, there has to be a link.

But reviewing the hospital's records revealed only that the Broward County Hospital must have the busiest general surgery department in North Carolina. The hospital administrators willingly opened the patient charts for inspection and explained that they had advertised for Medicare patients in northern states for elective surgery to be performed in a vacation setting. What better place to recover from your hernia or gallbladder surgery than on the white beaches of North Carolina?

It all sounded nice. But the numbers didn't add up. Dr. Crawford's tax returns showed only a modest income, a take-home pay of just over one hundred thousand dollars. It was a comfortable income, to be sure, but certainly not the income of someone billing Medicare for over eight hundred procedures a year. Had Dr. Crawford lied about his income, or were the billings being done without his knowledge?

Interviewing Dave Winters, a hospital administrator, only raised the agent's suspicions further. Either Winters was very stupid and actually believed the astronomical number of cases the OR claimed to do, or he was in on the fraud from the get-go. Jim believed the latter. Proving it would be another matter entirely.

This was what Jim had been waiting for. This was more than just a paper chase. Something in Serenity hinted at a deeper evil. He stroked his neatly clipped brown crew cut and peered over his paper just enough to catch the eye of Gerri Fiori, the OR nursing supervisor. He had interviewed her the day before, looking for the paperwork confirmation of all the reported cases. She had been cooperative. Too cooperative in Jim's book, and he wanted her to see him hanging around just to make her nervous. If this was fraud, the hospital was doing a bang-up job of making it look legit.

He checked his watch and decided to head down to the beach. He wanted to talk to Reba Crawford, the deceased surgeon's widow, and it was almost time for her morning walk.

He changed in the back of his van, abandoning his Rockport casuals for bare feet and his standard khakis for a pair of faded blue-jean shorts. With a Serenity T-shirt, he looked the part of a tourist. At thirty-one, all he needed was a few children to fit right in with the beach crowd. But his job had taken precedence over that.

Jim wasn't undercover, but he was far from bound to a suit and tie. Most of the time he wore a sport coat merely to hide his gun holster. Not that he needed it while investigating Medicare fraud, but it was one of the last links that still helped him identify himself as an agent of the law.

He slid his Glock handgun under the driver's seat and drove to the fishing pier. If he knew Reba Crawford, she would be passing this way, pumping her arms in an exaggerated fashion typical of power walking. He walked onto the pier, which was already speckled with fishermen. He put a quarter in a pair of stationary binoculars and began to survey the beach. The college crowd had yet to rise, but that didn't upset him. The young mothers were already out in abundance, and Jim allowed himself the luxury of examining a few of them as they chased their toddlers back from the surf. After ten minutes he spotted Reba Crawford, her arms pumping wildly and her white hair graced by a canary yellow sun-visor.

"Gotcha," he whispered to himself, backing away from the binoculars. He jogged to catch up with her just beyond the pier. He called out, "Ms. Crawford."

She turned but did not slow down, casting a glance in his direction with apparent surprise. "Do I know you?"

Jim settled into the rhythm of her stride beside her. "I'm Jim Manning." He paused. "FBI."

Her eyes narrowed. Evidently he didn't look the part.

He pulled out his ID. "Here. It's legit. I want to talk to you about your husband."

She stopped in her tracks and pulled the picture ID closer, lifting and dropping her eyes to compare him with his photo. She handed it back to him. "What do you want?"

He lifted his palm in a gesture down the beach. "We can keep walking if you like. But perhaps at a slower pace." He smiled.

She resumed her walk. "Did Sam Harris call you in? He doesn't seem to have a clue."

"No, ma'am. I'm investigating Medicare fraud." He paused. She showed no hint of a reaction. Maybe her husband kept her in the dark. "We were contacted by Medicare administrators when several patients reported mistakes on their Medicare bills."

No reaction. She started pumping her arms again and eased into a quicker pace.

"It seems some people are reporting having received Medicare statements reflecting payments for operations they never had. Once we examined the data, it looked as if Serenity, Broward County Hospital in particular, may be involved." He sped up to keep pace. "The surgeries in question were billed under your husband's Medicare number."

She jerked her head around. Finally a reaction. "What are you suggesting? My husband was as straight as an arrow."

"I'm not making any suggestions at this point. I'm just looking at the facts and trying to see how they all fit."

She shook her head. "My husband was a gem of a man. Too honest, if you ask me. He made me save every single receipt from Amazon for the books I bought off the Internet, so I could report them on my state taxes." She paused. "None of my friends do that."

"Maybe your husband was being used. An innocent bystander so to speak. Did he ever express any concerns like that?"

"Never. He didn't talk business with me. He hated business."

"Who managed his billing?"

"I don't know. The hospital, I guess."

"Did you ever suspect he made more money than he let on?"

This time Reba stopped. With her hands on her hips, she glared at him. "Perhaps you didn't hear me the last time, Mr. Manning. My husband was as close to a saint as a man can be. I endured the town gossip after they found his boat. People said he was drinking." She forced a chuckle. "That's a slander to his Christian name. Mark never touched alcohol, not even when we were away from Serenity on vacation. And if you suggest he was stealin' from the government, you can take your suspicions elsewhere. This conversation is over. My husband's memory is all I have, young man. And I'll expect you to respect it."

He took a step back. If this was an act, it was worth an Oscar. "I— well, . . . yes, ma'am."

She resumed her power walk. He watched a young woman applying sun oil, then jogged to catch up.

"Look, Ms. Crawford, someone could have been using your husband without his knowledge. Did he ever raise any questions to you?"

"Never. But Mark was a quiet man. Serenity was just the town for him. Not too busy, giving him the quiet life he sought, away from the pace of the city."

"How often did he operate?"

"Mondays and Tuesdays," she answered. "That way if his patients had to stay in the hospital, he almost always had them cleared out by the weekend, so he could go sailing." She smiled for the first time. "If he had to choose between that boat and me, I'm not sure I'd have won."

Jim nodded his head. "My father was the same way. Except for him it was his '72 Corvette."

He ran the numbers in his head. There was no way Crawford

could have done the number of cases he was billing if he only operated on Mondays and Tuesdays.

They walked along in silence until they reached the back of the Crawford home, a modest two-story house with natural wood siding and a large deck overlooking the Atlantic.

Nothing about the place set it apart from the houses on either side. Certainly nothing reeked of wealth. His face must have betrayed him. "My husband could have made more if he practiced in Durham or Jacksonville, but he chose lifestyle over money, as you can see."

Jim looked at the driveway, which contained only an aging green Buick.

"Any reason to believe someone would want to kill your husband?"

Ms. Crawford looked out toward the ocean. "My husband had no enemies."

"Any malpractice suits? Anyone angry with him?"

"No one. Everyone in Serenity respected him."

"Certainly you've come up with your own theories about his death, since Mr. Harris told you what the medical examiner thought."

She took off her visor and wiped the perspiration from her forehead. "I suspect someone mugged him, thought he would be easy to rob. Maybe someone from another boat came up while he was sailing." Her eyes met Jim's. "The police found alcohol on his boat. Someone must have planted it there to make it look like he was drunk." She shook her head. "It didn't fool me."

"The medical examiner mentioned the fact that it appeared his body had been frozen. What do you make of that?"

"I have no idea. Only that it means he didn't fall straight into the ocean. Someone stored him somewhere for a while." Her eyes teared, and her voice began to thicken.

"I'm sorry, Ms. Crawford. It sounds like he was a wonderful man."

She bit her lower lip and nodded. "Do you believe in prayer, Mr. Manning?"

The question struck him as odd. "Well, I, er . . . I guess so. I—"

"My husband was a praying man. He prayed every day that his life would make a difference. He prayed for every single patient, Mr.

Manning. He said that did more good for them than anything he could do with a scalpel."

Jim nodded without speaking, knowing he couldn't shut off the widow's memories.

"He was a wonderful man," she said, reaching for a tissue to dab her eyes. "Prayer for him was so natural. He used to sit at the kitchen table and pull up an empty chair beside him just to help him focus, to see in faith that Jesus was sitting right beside him. Then he would talk to Him like an old friend and tell Him about his patients and ask for help."

Jim cleared his throat softly. He shifted uncomfortably, feeling like he was peering in a window at something so intimate, he ought to look away.

"Maybe you should ask God for help, Mr. Manning. Help to find out who did this to my husband."

He nodded, feeling like a hypocrite as she repeated with a sob, "Find out who killed my husband."

∾

Two hours later Jim Manning was dressed again in casual business attire and sat in an uncomfortable wooden chair in the Chief of Police's office. Local officials were always so put off by the FBI. They acted as if someone were honing in on their turf, stealing the glory, skimming the pot for the cream. Sam Harris was no different. He leaned forward and stabbed an unlit cigar toward Jim's chest. "What I want to know is why you didn't let us know you thought there was a problem in Serenity."

"I told you before, Sam," Jim said, using his first name just to put the officer off. "Medicare fraud is not a local issue. It's a federal issue, and the crimes are of no interest to you."

"If it happens in my town, it's of interest to me," he huffed. "How long has this been going on?"

"We don't know. We are understaffed just like everyone else. We looked at Dr. Crawford about six months ago, and I was packing my bags to come down here when we got the word that he'd died. Without our main suspect, and with so many other cases to look into, we shifted our focus elsewhere."

Harris lit the cigar. "So why come back now?"

"Because we heard that Crawford had been murdered. It makes it more likely that the foul play was related to the fraud we were investigating." He shrugged. "The stakes are higher. Even the government is more interested in murder than a few million dollars."

Harris leaned back and put his feet on his desk. "So what do you want from me?"

"We're just looking for cooperation. We want to know your theories. Any suspects?"

"A few. We've had our share of druggies using our town as a party location. Maybe they thought the good doctor would be an easy score."

"So you thought it might be a random hit?"

"Maybe. But you never told us about the fraud investigation, remember?"

Touché. "You said, 'a few.' Anyone else you're looking at?"

"The new surgeon, Adam Tyson. Something about this guy just doesn't add up. I suppose you know about our hit-and-run case?"

"Just what you've released to the media. Michael Cunningham used to work for Tyson. Then his car is found at the scene of a local hit-and-run in the very town where his boss now works. And it seems no one can find Cunningham." He opened a small notebook. "You think Tyson killed Crawford?"

"Maybe."

"What's your evidence?"

"I'm not sure I can put everything together, but weird things keep happening around this guy. First his former PA disappears. Then a body turns up, and the medical examiner says it looks like the body was frozen, and I have the testimony of a witness that says she heard someone accusing the new doctor of killing his patients and putting them in a freezer."

"Weirdness doesn't always translate into evidence."

"True enough. But weirdness raises yellow flags. And that's where I start digging."

Manning started a hypothesis. "Suppose you're right, and suppose I'm right, and the murder has something to do with bilking the government out of a lot of money."

"Maybe Tyson knew about the hustle and wanted in on the action."

"So he knocks the town doctor off so he can take his practice and get in on the goods?"

"But Cunningham, his former PA, knows what Tyson is going to do and wants in on the action himself."

"Or threatens to expose Tyson's drug problems if he won't let him in on it?"

"And Tyson is forced to kill him too."

Jim scratched his head. "Only one problem with our neat theory," he added. "We don't have any evidence."

"Have you seen evidence of improper billing by Tyson?"

"Not yet. But he hasn't been here in practice long enough."

"So how do you connect the hit-and-run?"

"I can't. I suspect it is random. Something unplanned happened that threatened to expose some other crime. Cunningham must have been doing something he didn't want someone to know about or he wouldn't have left the scene."

"He ought to be afraid."

Manning leaned forward. "Who? Tyson? Why?"

"If he's innocent, he should be concerned that the doctor he replaced was actually murdered."

"So what's your plan?"

Harris's eyes narrowed, as if he was suspicious of the feds taking over. "I'm keeping my eyes open. And I've got a line out trolling for a few witnesses who may know more about the new doctor."

Jim nodded his head. "Maybe I'll talk to him. See if I can get anything."

"Be my guest. But turnabout is fair play. If I share my theories with you, you need to tell me what you find."

The agent stood up and shook the police officer's hand. "Deal. Maybe together we can find out just what's not so serene about Serenity."

∞

Adam Tyson was a jumble of contrasting emotions. He was repelled by the thought of the honesty required in a relationship with Beth, but drawn at the same time by her openness, her personality, and her looks. He was proud and confident of his surgical skills, but horrified that he might have to apply them again to Beth Carlson, and this time not just operate on a colleague, but on someone he was deeply attracted to. One hour he was committed to professional distance, to success in his career, the pursuit of a life married to surgery and the rewards inherent there. The next hour he found himself dreaming of a life with Beth, of the warmth of her skin against his own. But all of his fantasies ended in the same fear: *I'd be out on my own if she knew me as I really am*. And so he would commit himself again to the avoidance of relationships and the conquest of professional greatness.

But in a weakened moment his loneliness surfaced, and his reservations vanished. He called to see if she would accept a dinner date.

And two nights later he found himself across the table from the most beautiful woman he could imagine, sipping a glass of wine and enjoying the view of the setting sun.

Beth seemed disinterested in her salad. "I'm heading to Richmond on Monday."

"To see a surgeon at M.C.V.?"

She nodded. "It's funny, but I'm not even nervous."

"You're a strong woman."

"It's not that, Adam. I know I'm not in control. I think God is orchestrating everything. I've even started looking at my accident differently."

"How so?"

"Just think about it. If I hadn't been in the accident, I wouldn't have found my cancer. Without the bruise, I wouldn't have paid any attention. Maybe until it was too late."

Adam wasn't so sure about her reasoning. In his book the cancer and the accidents were bummers, both reasons to doubt God, not love Him. Before he could object, she added, "And who knows? Without my accident, I might not have become your friend."

He looked away, trying to understand. "But if God is orchestrating everything, why would He let you suffer so much? First you lose your husband. Then your accident, now cancer." He shook his head. "How you sit there in quiet peace saying God is in control is beyond me. If He had orchestrated those things for me, I think I'd be angry. Certainly not thankful."

"If you understood Him, you wouldn't say that."

"And you understand Him?"

She smiled. "Of course not completely. But I know Him well enough to trust His motives. Something happens to me that seems bad, but He allows it, knowing something good will come of it. I don't have to understand it to trust Him."

"How can you be so sure?"

"I'm not always so confident, Adam. I have my moments of doubt. But sometimes trusting is a choice. That's the way it is in any relationship, I guess."

Adam looked through the window at the sun dropping into the sound. He didn't really want to talk about trust and relationships. He felt like such a fraud.

After a moment he changed the subject. "How's Trav?"

She smiled again. "He's working on his hitting. I think he's anxious to show you."

He nodded. "What about your diagnosis? How's he dealing with that?"

Her face fell. "Not so good. He feels God is betraying him, taking his mother just like He took his father. He's afraid God won't answer his prayers."

"I can understand that."

"He's pretty fragile. One minute he acts like such a man. The next, he's screaming like a toddler."

He lifted his wine glass. "Sounds like a few surgeons I know."

She smiled, then looked away at the orange reflection of the sun in the sound. "Ike's not doing much better."

"Ike? He's a rock."

"A rock at times, as confident as ever." She shook her head. "But there are times he seems so forgetful and insecure. I think this whole deal with my cancer bothers him more than he is letting on."

"How so?"

"He's always pushing me to get it treated as fast as I can. He's not happy you want me to see another surgeon."

Adam set his glass down. "But I want you to get a fresh, objective—"

She raised her hand. "I understand why you want it. Daddy's just thinking of my mother. She ran from doctor to doctor seeking opinions about her treatment. He thinks the delays may have given the cancer a chance to spread."

"How long a time are you talking about?"

"Six, maybe eight weeks max."

"It's not likely that made any difference."

"I know that. But try telling that to Ike." She shrugged. "I think he's on the verge of losing it sometimes. He's getting so forgetful. And several times when we've talked about my cancer, he acted like he was about to panic."

"Put yourself in his shoes. He's lost his wife. Now he probably realizes his mind isn't working as well as it used to, but that's not the end of the world 'cause you're here to take care of things." He held up his index finger. "But what if he were to lose you too? That possibility probably scares him to death."

They looked up as their food was delivered. Scallops alfredo, crab cakes with red pepper sauce, steamed vegetables, and peanut butter pie.

While they ate, and later on the ride home, Adam steered clear of deep conversation, preferring to explore Beth's childhood and college days. He was just starting to dream of kissing her good night as he came to his own driveway. There, with lights on and engine running, sat a gray Chevy van.

"Expecting company?" Beth asked.

He pulled in behind the van. "No."

"You're blocking him in." There was alarm in her voice.

"He can still get around. Regardless, he's trespassing. I want to know who it is." He stepped out of his truck.

He walked up to meet a young man of medium build, with a short brown crew cut, wearing a sport coat and an open-collar shirt.

"Can I help you?"

"I'm looking for Adam Tyson."

"Who's looking?"

The man reached in his coat pocket and flashed a badge. "Jim Manning, FBI."

Adam sighed and nodded. "You've found him." He followed the man's gaze beyond his right shoulder. Beth was walking toward the van.

"I'd like to ask you some questions, if that's OK."

Adam shrugged. "Sure."

The man looked tentative and cast a second glance at Beth.

"You can ask whatever you want in front of her." He held up his hand to Beth and made introductions.

Beth put her arms around her own waist. "Can't we do this inside?"

"Sure," Adam responded.

Adam helped her up the steps as Jim followed. Once inside, Adam asked to see the man's ID again. He inspected it more closely and handed it back to Jim. "What can I do for you?"

They sat in the den, with Adam and Beth on the couch and Jim on a leather chair. "I've been investigating Medicare fraud and abuse."

Adam shifted in his seat, aware of a vague heartburn starting behind his sternum as the man paused, his eyes fixed on Adam's face.

"We have some good evidence that your hospital and your predecessor, Dr. Crawford, may have been involved in fraudulent billing practices."

"I'm afraid I wouldn't know anything about that. I never met Dr. Crawford. But everything I hear about him would make me question what you're telling me. He was a straight shooter from everything I've heard."

"You never met him?"

Adam looked at Beth and raised his eyebrows. This guy must be hard of hearing. "Never met him. He died a few months before I came to town."

"Were you aware they just found his body?"

Adam leaned forward. "No."

"Do you read the paper?"

"Sometimes I pick up the *Washington Post*. I haven't gotten used to the small-town paper yet."

"The body pulled from the ocean near the pier—that was him."

Beth gasped. "That was Dr. Crawford?"

"Exactly."

"But he disappeared months ago. How do you explain that?"

"Maybe he died months ago and was just disposed of recently."

Adam watched Beth wrinkle her nose. It was a distasteful thought. "Why would I know anything about this man?"

"You took his job. Perhaps you stepped in to fill large shoes."

"I think I'm up to it."

"How many cases do you think you'll do this year?"

Adam shrugged. "Two, three hundred maybe. It's a nice town. Not too busy. Mostly just tourists and a few retirees."

Jim Manning put his hands behind his head in an exaggerated display of relaxation. "Would you believe Dr. Crawford did just over eight hundred Medicare cases alone last year?"

Adam dropped his jaw. "No way. Eight hundred! He must have been working night and day."

"If he really did the cases."

Beth touched Adam's arm. "We should be able to access the OR log. I'll call Gerri Fiori tomorrow. She will know."

"I've already spoken to Ms. Fiori." He paused and looked at Adam. "She speaks highly of you."

Adam watched Jim's eyes studying Beth's reaction before the agent continued, "All the paperwork is in order. And it all corresponds to the patient records I've examined."

Beth rotated her right hand palm up. "So where's the problem?"

"We've had a number of seniors notifying us of bills they received for operations never performed."

"So why didn't you bust Dr. Crawford?"

"We were about to do that when he disappeared. For months, until his body reappeared, we just figured he staged his drowning and went to the Caribbean. With so many other problems in the Medicare system, we didn't have the manpower to look for him. So we went fishing elsewhere. But when his body turned up this week, my bosses felt it might deserve another look. Perhaps Crawford wasn't working alone. Perhaps someone offed him when he wanted to squeal."

Beth pulled Adam's hand onto her lap, cupping it in her own. "You can't think that Adam had anything to do with Dr. Crawford's death. He never even knew the man. He's the most compassionate—"

Jim raised his hand. "No one's accusing anyone of anything, Ms. uh—"

"Carlson," she filled in.

"We're just trying to collect the facts. Sooner or later something will turn up, and we'll piece all of this together."

He stood up and handed Adam a card. "Just give me a call if you have anything to report. Call the cell phone number. It will ring no matter where I am."

Adam stood, along with Beth, who still clutched his arm.

Jim excused himself, and Adam and Beth stood in the doorway to make sure the agent could get around Adam's Dakota.

Adam took a deep breath. *Just how much do the feds know about me? Is he just yanking my chain, hoping I'll sing?* The whole thing felt like a threat. It gnawed on him and felt very, very bad.

Beth squeezed his hand, the one she had kept cradled in her own since defending him to the agent. He relaxed as he felt her fingers holding him tight.

And that felt very, very good.

CHAPTER
18

TRAVIS CARLSON HAD put up a teenage-size protest about having to go to Richmond, Virginia, to accompany his mother to see a surgeon. That is, until he found out that Cheryl Thomas had volunteered to drive, and Kristy was likely to pal along. When he found that out, he put up a perfunctory whine, went to the mirror to check his hair, and then began to collect the things he wanted for the trip. Early the next morning, ten minutes before it was time to go, Travis was up, showered, and dressed with all his traveling supplies gathered next to the door.

The Thomas van arrived right on time and Travis remembered unloading the top luggage rack with Bart the day he'd met Kristy at the Seagull Inn. He watched the van from the window. He mustn't appear too anxious. Being cool meant keeping women from thinking you were too easy. He walked away from the window and sat at the kitchen table, where he removed a Pop-Tart from its foil wrapper. It was his favorite, cinnamon. The bell rang. He ignored it and let his mother welcome Cheryl and Kristy. He listened to the small talk while pretending to be more interested in his food.

Kristy came in.

"Oh, hi," he said.

"Hi." She was wearing a white top embroidered with small pink flowers and jeans that had faded to sky blue. She was perfect.

"Want some breakfast?"

She wrinkled her freckled nose. "I don't usually eat so early."

"Me neither. But my mom bought these." He pushed the box toward her.

She studied the box before picking up a foil package and sniffing it. "Where's the toaster?"

He pointed. They ate in silence before Travis's mom called for him to help her carry a small cooler to the van. She had packed some sodas and snacks. Kristy tagged along.

"I brought some dc talk CDs and my CD player," she said.

"Sweet." He placed the cooler between the front seats. "It was nice of you to come along."

"I wanted to support your mom." The edges of her mouth hinted at a smile.

He nodded. It wasn't exactly the response he wanted. But the hint of a smile was nice.

"Do you play chess? I have a magnetic set we can use."

"My dad likes it. But he's too competitive. He won't let me win."

"You could probably beat me. I play my grandpa, but he's getting so he doesn't see ahead too well, and he makes dumb moves."

She nodded, then lowered her voice. "Did you hear about the body they pulled out of the ocean? It was a surgeon who worked at the hospital."

"That's what my mom told me."

"Have you talked to Dr. Tyson? Is he scared?"

"Scared? What for?"

"Because someone killed the last surgeon who worked here. That's pretty spooky."

"What, like someone just murders doctors?"

"I guess that doesn't make sense, does it?"

"Not really." They laughed together, then jumped into the van to join their mothers.

It was a bummer having his mother right in front of him. It was bad enough he had to think of things to talk about, but worse having his mother listening from the front seat. Fortunately, Kristy talked all about her friends, her school back home, and her plans to go to college. Travis talked about the Atlanta Braves and his old neighborhood in Richmond.

They played chess. Travis won, but he had a suspicion that Kristy planned the whole thing. She left her queen wide-open right before

Travis thought for sure she would be putting him in checkmate. All
she said was, "Oops!" before giggling and punching his arm.

They stopped once for gas and once at a Burger King for breakfast. They could have stopped fifty times for all Travis cared. Right
now nothing seemed better than stretching out a trip where he was
confined in a vehicle with Kristy Thomas. Besides, at the other end
of the trip a hospital was waiting, and he wasn't looking forward to
the tense wait to see a surgeon.

For several stretches he listened to her CDs and pretended to
stare out the windows, but glanced secretly at her from the corner of
his eye. She seemed so outgoing and confident; but then, why
shouldn't she be? With her blonde hair and smile, he was sure she
could get anything she wanted.

They arrived at the Medical College of Virginia hospital just before
10 A.M. and parked in the visitors parking deck. It was only a few minutes before they were entering the Cancer Center. There they took an
elevator to the third floor to check in and wait to see Dr. Harper.

Then the duo and their mothers sat in stuffed vinyl chairs and
waited. The cheery conversation from the trip up was over. Everyone
had one thing on their minds and didn't feel like talking. Pamphlets
on coping with cancer were scattered on a coffee table. Travis felt like
gathering them all up and throwing them down the hall. This just
wasn't right.

He picked up a *Sports Illustrated* and sighed. Widowed mothers
weren't supposed to get breast cancer.

Maybe Dr. Tyson was wrong. He was just a country doc. Maybe
he'd made a mistake.

Travis sunk a little lower in his seat. He knew Dr. Adam Tyson.
He knew he was the best around, maybe even better than these university doctors.

And if Dr. Tyson was right, their life might never be the same.

∽

Beth fidgeted with a *Good Housekeeping* magazine and glanced around
the crowded waiting room. Two of the women were obviously wearing wigs. Probably undergoing chemotherapy for breast cancer.

After what seemed to be an hour, the receptionist called her name. She grabbed the folder with her mammograms and squeezed Cheryl's hand.

Cheryl held on. "Should I come with you?"

Beth shook her head. "I'll be OK."

She walked behind a nurse in white down a brightly lit hallway. The nurse opened the door to the exam room, instructed Beth on removal of her clothes, and handed her a skimpy paper top. Beth handed the nurse her X-rays. "Dr. Harper will want to look at these."

Soon Beth sat shivering on the exam table in the middle of the room. After ten minutes Dr. Warren Harper entered. She'd known him for years, having seen him in the emergency department where she used to work. He had a reputation for compassion and for treating surgery as art. In the OR he was said to have the touch of Michelangelo's brush. He smiled when he saw her. "Beth, I'd thought you'd moved away."

"I have." She reached out her hand and took his, immediately noticing its smooth texture. "I'm just back for a second opinion."

The blond-haired man unbuttoned his white coat and sat on a padded stool. "I've examined your mammograms. Tell me how all this began."

Beth started with the hit-and-run and the large bruise and swelling that followed. "When the swelling went down, I noticed a lump. Here," she said, motioning under her white paper top.

"I treated your mother, a wonderful woman."

"Yes," Beth responded, surprised by the sudden tightening of her own voice. Her mom had been gone for several years, but the familiarity of being in the same office again brought freshness to the memories and tears to the verge of eruption.

Dr. Harper ran through the list of necessary questions. Nipple discharge? Tenderness or pain? Prior biopsies? Obstetrical history? Abortions or miscarriages? Any other family members with cancer of any kind?

His nurse joined him for the exam. Her breast was still sore from the accident and her last needle aspiration. She winced as his hands explored the mass.

Carefully he probed deep into her armpits and above her collar bones, searching for evidence of lymph node spread.

His expression was stone. Never once did he even raise an eyebrow or the corner of his mouth.

"Things seem rather straightforward in my mind." He paused. "Do you trust your current surgeon?"

"Of course. He is very good. I trust him completely. He insisted on this opinion, not me."

"I see. I have no reason to doubt the pathologist's reading. Your mammogram and exam are completely consistent with carcinoma." He sat on the stool again. "At your age, I would recommend a lumpectomy and a sentinel lymph node biopsy to see if you need an axillary dissection. You'll need radiation. Is it available in your hospital?"

"Not in Serenity. But I can travel over to Greenville or to Durham."

He nodded slowly.

She hesitated. "Can you predict the outcome?"

He gave a standard answer. "It will be based on a complete evaluation of the tumor once it is out. And on whether the cancer has had a chance to spread to the lymph nodes."

Of course, Beth already knew the answer. But she desperately wanted someone to say with an authoritative voice, "You're going to be fine. Just a little surgery and radiation and you can get on with your life." But no one would say it. No one could say it without more information. She knew that. But it didn't stop her mind from wanting a rock to cling to.

For the same reason she gave the same evasive answers to her own son when he asked for reassurances. As a mom, she wanted to abandon truth for the sake of soothing his fears. But as a nurse, she required the facts, proof on which to base the words of wisdom she dispensed.

She had abandoned reason when dealing with her husband's cancer, giving Travis the comfort he wanted, the reassurances that everything would be OK. But her words had come to haunt her now, and her assurances, the white lies told in the hope against hope that the unlikely would be true, felt like a betrayal to her son, a wedge in a relationship based on truth and trust. That relationship with Travis was the very reason she'd sought healing and renewal in Serenity.

But what a joke that had become. Serenity, the town that

promised peace, that held out the hope of a new start, had provided nothing but new challenges and mystery. Her accident delayed fulfillment of her anticipation of a new job. And now her cancer threatened to unravel the already worn fabric of her family. Her father was forgetful. Her son was bitter. And she had let herself fall in love with a man whose Christian faith was infantile, if present at all.

Perhaps that was the biggest problem of all. She had given reason the backseat and let emotion pull her deeper into dangerous waters. Was her attraction to Adam all about the damsel in distress falling for the white knight who saved her? But hadn't God placed him in her life and used him to save her after her accident? Adam was so strong, so good with Travis, so gentle . . . But did he share the faith that defined her? Could she risk a love relationship with a man who might not be able to share the most intimate longings of her heart, her love for Christ? But wouldn't turning away from him now threaten the seed of faith she saw beginning to sprout within him? And wouldn't turning away risk a loss of such a wonderful love that they had just begun to explore? Didn't she feel her heart quicken every time she heard his voice? And didn't she recognize the brightening of his eyes every time he saw her?

"Dr. Adam Tyson!"

Beth looked up as Dr. Harper spoke the name she'd come to cherish.

"Boy, that's a weird coincidence," he added, shaking his head. "It says on this sheet that Dr. Adam Tyson referred you."

Beth was confused. "He did."

"I trained with an Adam Tyson." He paused. "There must be more than one."

She smiled. "I'm not sure the world is ready for two Adam Tysons."

He chuckled. "Boy, that's for sure. But it is a weird coincidence."

"How can you be so sure he's not the same man you trained with?"

"It couldn't be. We trained out west." He paused. "UCLA."

She straightened and smoothed the front of her paper gown. "So did this one."

"That is odd."

"It's probably the same guy. Did you know he moved to North Carolina?"

"It's not the same one."

"How can you be sure? Have you kept in touch since college?"

He shook his head slowly and touched the side of his head. "No."

He stepped back to a counter and set down her chart. "But it isn't the same man." He took a deep breath. "The surgeon I knew had problems with drugs. He needed some shoulder surgery, then got addicted to painkillers." He paused. "His license was suspended."

"Adam's problems with drugs are a thing of the past. He moved to Serenity to get a fresh start."

"It isn't the same man."

"It has to be. How many Dr. Tysons who trained at UCLA, became surgeons, and had their medical licenses suspended due to problems with drugs could there be?"

"It's just a weird coincidence, I'm sure."

Now Beth was getting annoyed. Dr. Harper was denying the obvious. "Why?"

He paused and looked down. "He was a personal friend. He died of an overdose. I attended his funeral in Los Angeles six months ago."

CHAPTER
19

IT WAS MID-MORNING at the C. U. Surfin' Shop in Serenity when owner Rick Chico slapped the newspaper on the counter and yelled to his partner, Marvin Underwood, "Where'd you put the lost and found box?" He hated to ask, because Marvin always accused him of not knowing where things were.

But this seemed important. He could have sworn that the cuff link he'd found on one of their ocean kayak rentals had initials on it.

"Look under the cash register," Marvin yelled back. "The shoebox."

Rick lifted his eighty-dollar sunglasses to the top of his curly black hair and pulled out a box big enough for Marvin's size 13 Nike basketball shoes. As he rummaged through the box, he hummed along with the beach music that Marvin played for the customers.

In a minute key rings, a wallet without identification, two pairs of sunglasses, a tube of sunscreen, a yellow bikini top, a Nintendo Gameboy, three T-shirts, and a gold cuff link were scattered across the countertop. "Here it is!"

Marvin walked in scratching his armpit. "Here what is?"

"An engraved cuff link." Rick held it up to the light. "M.C."

"What?"

"I read in the paper that the body they found in the ocean by the pier was wearing a shirt with a cuff link engraved with the initials M.C." He smiled. "Just like this one."

"I'd better tell the cops. It might be a clue."

"What do you think? Maybe someone rented one of our kayaks to dump the body?"

"Possibly. When did you find it? Do you remember who rented it?"

"A few weeks ago. It was some dude from up north. I remember because I saw it in the floor of the boat when he turned it in. I asked him if it was his, and he said no."

"Maybe someone else left it."

"No way. I check each one of those kayaks. I'd have seen it. I remember this 'cause the guy didn't seem like a cuff link kind of guy. He was young. He had long hair and wore a baseball cap."

"Check our records. See if you can find his name. Then I'll call the police."

"I'll call the police. I'm the one who found the cuff link. I should be the one to—"

"All right already," Marvin said, retreating behind the counter into the back room. "It's not like there's a reward or anything."

Rick hoped he was wrong. But even if there wasn't, he didn't want Marv stealing the show. That's what he did the last time they had one of their kayaks stolen. Rick had found it and everything. But Marv was the one to call the police and act like he was the one to notice the problem.

Rick started paging back through their rental receipts. After a few minutes he had it. "There," he whispered. "An overnight rental to Timmy Stevens." He squinted at himself in the mirror next to the sunglasses. *I wonder if they'll want my picture for the paper?*

And to think I might have made a rental to a murderer.

He shoved the piece of jewelry into his pocket. "Marv, could you watch the counter for a few minutes? I need to do a little errand." He opened the front glass door, which was painted with their logo *C. U. Surfin' Shop.* He loved that name. He'd come up with it himself. In addition to sounding like "see you surfin'," it stood for Chico and Underwood Surfin' Shop.

As he left, Marvin was answering the phone, "C. U. Surfin'. How can I help you?"

Rick nodded his head. This cuff link thing was going to be good for business. Free publicity didn't happen every day in Serenity. Now everyone would hear of their shop.

Gerri Fiori slipped into Dave Winters's office and shut the door. He looked up, surprised. "Thanks for knocking."

"Since when do I have to knock?"

He nodded. "What's up?"

She lowered her voice. "You know what's up. You read the paper. They know the body was Crawford's." She paced around the spacious office, weaving a path from window to window, dodging a coffee table with a Chinese vase in the center.

"It can't be linked to us."

"The police will ask questions. And that FBI guy is still hanging around."

"The guy was drunk and fell off his boat. End of story."

"His boat was found near Ocracoke, Dave."

"Ocean currents do strange things."

"There were cinder blocks chained to the guy's ankles."

Dave looked down at his desktop. "Oh." He paused. "They still won't be able to link it to us. The guy never saw me. I called from a phone booth from the fishing pier." He chuckled. "I told him I was a doctor, a surgeon, and that I needed him to dispose of a cadaver."

"A cadaver."

"He *was* a cadaver. That part wasn't a lie."

"Why would a doctor do that?"

"I told him that OSHA was giving us trouble about disposing biologicals, that we were going to have to pay a thousand dollars to a mortuary to cremate the body. I just wanted the body dumped in the ocean where no one would find it."

"There's only one surgeon in Serenity. We don't want Tyson under suspicion."

"The police won't pin it on Tyson just because of a druggie's confession."

"We need Tyson to stay with the program. His reputation as a surgeon in this town is impeccable. I want it to stay that way."

"Stay away from him."

She sat on his desk. "Tyson?"

"Yes."

She smiled. "I thought you wanted me to keep an eye on him."

"That was only to see if he would work out. So far he hasn't shown any interest in the billing end of his business. He's too busy operating. He likes it that way. He cuts, we bill—what could be better?"

"Maybe we should let him inside."

"No way. If he finds out, he'll run. Just like Crawford."

"We still have his past. He doesn't want the community to know about his past."

"And I want to keep that card in our hand. We'll play it only if we have to."

"If he threatens to expose us?"

"Exactly."

"He won't. I'll see to it."

"Stay away from him. You enjoy watching him too much."

"Are you jealous?"

Winters pinched her chin in his hand.

It hurt, and Gerri tried to pull away, but he forced her face forward into his. She accepted his passionate kiss without enthusiasm.

"Just remember what your little life was like before I came along." His grip lessened, and he stroked her cheek with the back of his index finger. "Let's go to New York for a show this weekend. It's time for us to get away, just the two of us."

Fear mixed with desire within her. Gerri loved him before he started lavishing her with the spoils of their plan. He'd never resorted to force before. She felt her throat tightening.

He kissed her again. More tenderly this time. She responded, but only by not trying to pull away. "Come on. It will be fun."

She nodded without speaking, hoping her eyes would not betray her with tears. "What will you tell your wife?"

"Hospital business. She won't want to go. She hates the city."

She pushed him away and whirled around to face the door. "I'll check my calendar," she said with feigned nonchalance. "I'll let you know."

She walked to the door, pausing only when she heard his voice behind her. "Don't worry about Crawford. Just lay low and this will all blow over."

Adam Tyson had a difficult time concentrating on his morning hospital rounds. He only had five inpatients, but it seemed every time he sat down to write a progress note, his mind drifted to the FBI agent Jim Manning. *Why was he questioning me? How much does he know? Was he just baiting me? Or is he really just trying to find out information about Dr. Crawford?*

On rounds, he casually questioned the nurses about Dr. Crawford and listened to the gossip mill at the nursing station.

"He was a good man and a good surgeon. He wouldn't have harmed a fly."

"He must have had a double life."

"He took out my gallbladder. He was so gentle. I can't believe he was a drunk."

"He lost that little girl last year. What was her name? Her father was so angry. I'll bet he killed Dr. Crawford for revenge."

"No one gets fed to the sharks unless they're swimming in the wrong pool."

"He went to my church. I know he didn't drink."

"I saw his wife in the grocery store. She thinks her husband may have saved someone the Mafia wanted to die."

"Mafia? In Serenity? You're crazy."

"Well, someone killed him. But who?"

"The pro-abortionists probably did it because he spoke at that pro-life rally last year."

"I think you're crazy."

"What do you think, Dr. Tyson? How's it feel to take over the job of someone who was murdered?"

Adam didn't like the feeling at all. In the first place, he'd come here because he thought this would be a quiet place to practice simple, straightforward surgery with little supervision and little hassle. But now other questions were assaulting him. Should he be afraid, knowing his predecessor came to such a violent end?

And perhaps more importantly, was he at risk for a similar demise? Were there people whom Dr. Crawford had angered and with whom Adam also was interacting?

He wrote a note, then examined a patient with bowel obstruction. The patient, a man with six previous abdominal operations, most certainly had a bowel blockage on the basis of scars from his previous surgeries. Fortunately, he had begun to open up, and a seventh surgery would likely be avoided. Adam asked him questions and tried to concentrate on the answers, but found himself repeating the questions, much to the patient's dismay.

"I told ya, doc. I moved my bowels this morning."

Adam nodded sheepishly. "I'll let you have some liquids to drink. If you're not sick to your stomach, of course."

"Doc, I told ya I'm not sick anymore. Are you havin' trouble hearin' me?"

"Uh, no. Of course not," he said, retreating to the door. "I'll leave the orders with the nurses."

Adam walked into the hall shaking his head. He had never been so afraid of being exposed. With all this attention by the law, some clue somewhere was bound to come up and his party would be ended.

And what would that do to his relationship with Beth Carlson?

But a lasting relationship will require honesty. And she couldn't love me if she really knew who I am.

She'd be gone, in search of another man as certain as the grass is green.

And who would I be then? Without a job, what will define me? Without the love of a woman like Beth . . .

Could I ever be happy just being me?

"Dr. Tyson."

The words invaded the fog. "Huh, yes?"

The nurse was standing only five feet away, acting as if she'd repeated his name over and over. Her hands were on her hips, and her voice was loud. "The ER's been looking for you. Is your beeper working?"

He touched the pager clipped to his belt. The button on the side was shifted to the *Off* position. *Oops. I forgot to turn it on this morning.* "As far as I know," he fudged. "I'll get the operator to test it." He turned to leave, wondering what the ER had in store. "Thanks," he said, glancing over his shoulder to see the nurse shaking her head.

I'd better get my mind on this job or I won't have a reputation to worry about losing.

⬿

Travis wasn't sure he'd ever understand women. But then his dad used to always say that no man should ever try. His mom had gone in to see the doctor acting so brave, but came out acting strange. Not afraid, really, just quiet, with her mouth held in the same position she held it in when they played Jeopardy and she wasn't sure she knew the answer. He asked her what the doctor had said, and all she would report was, "The same thing that Adam said."

To Travis, that seemed like good news. It meant Dr. Tyson was right, and his mom should be able to trust him to be her surgeon. At least that's what he thought. He wasn't sure why she wanted to come up here in the first place. It wasn't like Dr. Tyson wasn't trustworthy or anything. After all, he had saved her life once. The only difference, as far as Travis could tell, was that his mother had started to like him. Really like him.

And somehow he knew that's what all this was about. The far-off look in his mother's eyes must have to do with her relationship with Dr. Tyson. Adam liked him well enough, but he knew his mother would struggle with a bigger question. She had told Travis a thousand times that when he started to date, he should only date Christian girls, but now he saw his mom falling for a man who knew less about God than she did.

He wasn't sure what was in his mother's mind. Maybe she was hung up on being both Dr. Tyson's girlfriend and patient at the same time. He'd heard his grandpa and her talking about it. And he'd also heard his grandpa warning her about seeing a man who didn't share the same thoughts about God.

Travis glanced over at Kristy. Talk about hard to understand. Kristy was talkative and smiling one minute and shy and quiet the next, claiming she wanted to rest and needed a blanket to cover up. She took a full five minutes fluffing and spreading out the silly old comforter that her mother kept folded behind the seat. She'd even lifted it up so it spread out on Travis's leg.

"There," she said, leaning her head back and closing her eyes.

He looked at the old blanket and was about to shove it off when he glanced at Kristy again. Her eyes locked with his and squinted.

Whatever else she was saying, he wasn't sure, but he got one message loud and clear. He wasn't supposed to mess with the blanket that she'd arranged with such care.

He wasn't cold. After all, it was summertime. What did he need with a blanket?

It was then he felt a nudge on his left hand. A shiver shot through him. It was just a quick brushing of skin, Kristy's hand against his. He couldn't afford a look in her direction. Certainly it had been an accident. Against his better judgment, he shot a quick glance her way, pretending to look at the cars behind their van. Her eyes were closed.

It had to be an accident. She was just stretching before taking a nap.

He felt her hand brush his again. He froze, unable to move, not wanting to move, wanting her to accidentally touch him again.

He edged his hand in her direction, hidden by the blanket.

She nudged him again, this time only her little finger. But this time there was a tickle, an obvious show of purposeful movement. She wasn't asleep.

He turned his hand palm up, aware that his heart might beat out of his chest if she stroked him again. Her hand was warm, her index finger against his palm, tracing a pattern of circles on his hand. He closed his hand around hers and looked at his mom.

His secret pleasure was hidden from her view.

Kristy wiggled her fingers around until they slipped gently into place, each digit interlaced with his.

She was good at this.

His heart was pounding. His palm was beginning to sweat.

But there was no way he'd let go of her now.

It sure was nice of Kristy to need a nap and a blanket.

CHAPTER
20

DAN AND GREG sat around a wooden table at the home of Chief Sam Harris. "We've got a chance to do a little real detective work here, boys. But it's going to take going the extra mile."

Greg stretched and sipped the sweetened tea Sam's wife had made. "So you're telling me that Crawford's other cuff link was found on a kayak rented by Timmy Stevens, the same one who busted the glass door over at the Seagull Inn?"

"Exactly. And the same one who accused Dr. Tyson of killing his patients and putting them in a freezer."

Dan tapped his knee. "I'm not following you. How does this fit?"

"I'm not sure," Sam responded. "But my hunch is that Tyson had a body to get rid of, and Stevens was the one to do it. But maybe he didn't know who it was. Maybe he thought it was one of the doctor's patients or something. Anyway, when he needed surgery to fix up his scalp wound and saw Tyson, he freaked out, knowing what Tyson had done to the body he'd had Stevens dispose of."

"I don't know about this, chief," Dan said, glancing at his watch. "How does all this play into the hit-and-run?"

"Maybe it doesn't."

"But you said yourself that we need to look for connections. How often do we have even one crime in this boring little town? And now to have two in such a short period, we ought to think about it anyway."

"What are you thinking of?"

"Just suppose they are related. Suppose Michael Cunningham and Adam Tyson are in on killing Mark Crawford."

Sam folded his arms across his chest. "What's the motive?"

"A new job? Maybe they needed a new place to start practice. A small town where they could abuse drugs together and no one would know."

"Why would they kill him just for his job? Why not just get a new job somewhere else?"

Dan shook his head. "That's what we need to figure out. Maybe Doc Crawford was getting in their way somehow. Maybe he knew something. Knew too much."

Sam Harris started to pace. He opened the refrigerator and popped a Budweiser, handing one to Dan, leaving Greg with his tea. "Sorry," he offered. "You're on duty." He sighed after taking a long swig. "One thing's for certain. We'll never be certain of Dr. Tyson's involvement in all this unless we find out more information."

Greg pushed back his chair. "That means we have to find Timmy Stevens."

Dan cleared his throat. "That would be key."

"I want one of you to go to Baltimore. That's the city listed on his ER record. See what you can find out. Chase down his mother. Maybe he's talked to her since we last asked."

Greg spoke up. "I got to go to Sarasota looking for Cunningham. Let Dan go to Baltimore."

Sam nodded. "Fair enough. Make sure Stevens knows we'll help him cut a deal. I can get the drug and property damage charges reduced if he helps us find out who killed Dr. Crawford."

"Sweet."

Sam laughed. "Whatever."

∞

The following day Beth sat on the examining table in Dr. Tyson's office back in Serenity. Even though Tonya, Adam's young, perfect nurse, insisted that Beth exchange her clothes for a gown, Beth had refused. She'd come with half a mind to blast Adam, one moment convinced he wasn't who he said he was, and the next moment convincing herself of the likelihood that there must be two Adam Tysons. After all, it really wasn't an uncommon name. There might be hundreds of them in the U.S. Was this a mere coincidence? It seemed crazy, but in the fog of her desire for Adam as a man, she desperately wanted to believe he wouldn't deceive her.

Adam opened the door carrying Beth's office chart. "Hi."

"Hello."

"How was your trip to Richmond?" He sat down. "I haven't gotten back a written consultation."

"It was fine, Adam. Dr. Harper feels exactly as you do. I need a lumpectomy and a sentinel lymph node biopsy."

He nodded. "I see." He paused. "Still want me to operate?"

"Everyone around here says you're the best." She hesitated. "And I know you care about me."

"That's right," he said softly. "Which might make it hard if you have problems."

"I won't blame you, if that's what you're worried about. I know there are risks."

He seemed to be staring at a spot in front of his stool, which he rolled slowly back and forth.

"Dr. Harper said a weird thing. He said he knew you from medical school."

Adam jerked his head upright and squinted. "Maybe a mistake. Harper?"

"Warren Harper. UCLA."

Was she mistaken, or was the color draining from Adam's face? She stayed quiet.

"It was a long time ago. What did he say?"

"Not much."

"I don't remember him."

The silence hung uncomfortably between them.

"Shall I put you on the schedule?"

She sighed and nodded.

"Beth—"

Her eyes met his.

"I'm not sure I'm the one to do this. I—"

"No," she interrupted. "I know you can do this. I'm not just listening to my heart, Adam. I've talked to the nurses in the OR. They've told me how meticulous you are."

"But—"

She raised her hand. "Look, I don't want to delay this. It has been torture for my father just following your advice to get a second opinion. He is fixated on moving forward without delays." She shook her head slowly. "I'm afraid it would send him over the edge if I told him I needed to start over with another surgeon."

He seemed to be studying the tops of his shoes. Then he lifted his eyes to meet hers. "Beth, personal feelings might make this difficult." He seemed to hesitate. "I didn't come here looking for love, but—"

She teased him with formality. "Have you found it, Dr. Tyson?"

He reached for her hand. "What if something happens to you?"

"I know you are the best around." The corner of her mouth turned up. "And I know that you believe that too."

"You know me better than I thought." He returned her smile.

"But you didn't answer my question, Dr. Tyson. Have you found love?"

He squeezed the hand he still held. "I hope so."

Sun broke in on her cloudy day. Even in light of the reason she sat in a surgeon's office, her heart brightened at the words he spoke. But what of her concern for his faith? And what of her fears that Dr. Harper had raised?

She tightened her grip on his hand. Hadn't God placed this man in her life? Her heart so yearned to return the love he was offering. She had to give him the benefit of the doubt. She couldn't voice her reply, but for now the touch was enough.

She made a willful choice to believe. In her heart, blinded as it was by love, she could not choose to do otherwise. Dr. Harper knew another Dr. Tyson, not her Adam, not this man so full of knowledge and compassion. She watched his chest rise in a deep sigh. Perhaps he too was afraid. "Don't be afraid for me, Adam. I know you'll do your best. And God will be taking care of me."

"You never seem to doubt."

"I trust you, too, Adam. God has placed you in my path." She sniffed. "And me in yours. Who else but you would treat me with such tenderness?"

Her eyes studied his. He could not seem to speak. His eyes were moist. Beth heard Tonya in the hall outside the room.

Would they be discovered, holding hands, tearfully sharing their hearts?

Adam had heard her too. He slowly released her hand, seemingly about to say something important, but stopping with only her name as a knock sounded on the door. "Beth—"

Tonya intruded, catching Adam's eye.

"Schedule Ms. Carlson for surgery as soon as possible."

"Your first case tomorrow, the Davis baby with a hernia, has a cold. Anesthesia just called to cancel."

He looked at Beth with the question. "Shall we proceed tomorrow?"

She nodded.

It was set.

Tomorrow it would be.

✎

That night, long after his office staff had departed, Adam Tyson pulled a book from the shelves behind his desk. He wanted to refresh his memory about sentinel lymph node sampling.

With the book open, he flipped to the chapter highlighting the procedure and stared at the pages. But the words blurred, and his heart sank. The stakes had never been higher. Could he really follow through?

The phone rang. He looked over at the blinking light. It was his private line, the one known only to a select few. He picked it up.

"Adam? I was hoping to catch you." Beth's voice penetrated his turmoil.

"Hi." He squeezed his hand into a fist to keep it from shaking. "I'm just finishing up some desk work."

"Ready for tomorrow?"

"Sure." He hesitated. "Having second thoughts?"

"Not me. I didn't call to tell you I was backing out. I called to tell you something else."

His throat was dry. "OK."

"I've thought about you a lot since we've been hurled together."

He chuckled nervously. "Is that how you describe it?"

She continued, "I don't have much experience with relationships with men. Since my husband died, it seems everyone who showed any interest in me either backed away because of Travis or came on too strong in areas I wasn't comfortable with."

He stayed quiet, aware that his heart was racing.

"Some men that I thought would be good fathers, churchgoers who had the right resumés, couldn't get their minds out of the bedroom. But you . . . How can I say this and not sound wrong?" She hesitated.

"What, Beth, what is it?"

"You . . . well, you're not what I was looking for in a man. I wanted a strong Christian to lead me and Travis. I wanted a man who could share the most important thing in my life."

"I believe in God, Beth."

"But it's not the same as knowing Him, Adam. It's close, and yet it's a world away."

"I can change. I—"

"Please listen, Adam. I don't want to hurt you. In many ways you've been a knight in shining armor to me. It's strange, but I have this memory of seeing your face as I drifted off into unconsciousness at my accident. It's like you were holding me, calling my name. That image used to haunt me. But as I've grown in my relationship with you, it's an image I cherish."

"I was there when you awoke."

"Yes, maybe it's that image that I store in my heart. But as much as I know God put you in my path, I'd be less than honest if I didn't tell you how I've struggled. No, you don't have the Christian resumé I've been searching for, but my heart is drawn to you like no other man since Barry. No one has been so good with Travis. No one has treated me with such respect." She paused. "I left you hanging this afternoon. I asked you if you'd found love." Her voice thickened. "You said, 'I hope so.'" She sniffed. "You don't know how hard it was for me not to take you in my arms and tell you how you had, how my heart bursts to pour my love out upon you, to promise to give you my all . . ."

He lowered his head into his hand and listened for the "but" to come.

She began to sob. "But I can't give my love to you and know I'm pleasing God. I know it must sound horrible to you, but I love Him first. I want to love you, Adam, but I need to get out of your way. If we are to be together, it will have to come on God's terms, not mine."

His head was spinning. Oh, what a fool he'd been. God's terms? "Wh-what do you mean?"

"It means that we can't be right together. Not now. It may come in His time, but not now."

"You want to love me?"

"Yes," she sobbed. "But I can't." He heard a door close as if she were walking out onto her deck. He pictured her looking out toward the ocean. "I'm making a choice, Adam. A tough choice."

"Where does that leave me?"

"A friend. A great friend, Adam. I want to keep seeing you. Travis would be heartbroken if he thought you were going to disappear." She sniffed again. "I think even Ike would miss his theological banter with you."

He wanted to scream. His world seemed a shade darker, his heart cool. He wasn't sure he could do this. Only a friend?

Tomorrow she would put her life in his hands. Why did she need to get so brutally honest now?

Tomorrow he would be her surgeon. Could he also be her friend? Only a friend?

He didn't know how to respond. "I'd miss them too," he mumbled. He stared at the receiver for a moment before adding, "Get to bed early tonight. You've got a full day ahead of you tomorrow."

He laid down the receiver and dropped his head to the desk.

He stayed that way for a few minutes, allowing the hard wood to indent his skin until his forehead burned with pain. It was time for inventory. He looked at the book he'd shoved aside, open to a page describing axillary sentinel lymph node biopsy. He hurled the book against the far wall and dropped his head into his hands, whispering to himself, "She'd never want to love me if she knew who I really am."

He walked to the small bathroom off his office and washed his face. As he dried his face with some paper towels, he looked in the mirror at the sagging image in front of him. He talked to himself in bitter tones. "Did you really think you could fool them all if you can't even fool yourself? Who are you? Adam? Andy?" He threw the wadded towels into the trash in disgust. "Beth will never love you, Adam. She cannot love a fraud."

He looked at his hands. Adam's hands. And he remembered a phrase from the Bible he'd heard at his cousin's wedding, something about love rejoicing in the truth. His life was a lie. He'd tried to become a man he could love, a man others would respect and admire, but he found he couldn't escape the man he'd always been. He'd built a complicated falsehood based on his surgical knowledge, an identity for others to envy, to admire. But love? Love rejoices in the truth.

Will I ever be able to love myself as I am?

Will Beth?

I love you just as you are. The thought came from nowhere. An aberration of a mind under stress. Adam turned the thought over in his mind. It was the concept that Ike must have told him a hundred times. But he expected it from Ike. What else would a gentle, old pastor say?

He looked at his hands. Andy's hands. And he remembered feeling inadequate. He remembered the rejection of a medical school. He remembered the loss of his parents' love and the loss of a woman's love. He was never good enough.

I love you just as you are.

Adam shook his head. *There is no such thing as unconditional love. It's a stupid concept of fairy tales and the happy endings of storybooks.*

Next he walked to the diplomas and certificates hanging on the wall above his desk. It was Adam Tyson's ego wall, a testimony of hard work, a witness to his image and status. He started with the medical school diploma. He lifted it from its resting place and hurled it through the air into the wall, sending broken frame and glass bouncing to the floor. He picked up a framed certificate indicating his status as a fellow in the American College of Surgeons. "Fake!" he screamed, throwing it to the floor. The framed diploma of his board certification took flight from his hand next, adding to the crash and clatter of his erupting emotions. "Fraud!" he wailed. One by one each framed diploma, award, and certificate that fed the false ego he'd cherished as his own, the life that he'd told himself was his by right, the honors he deserved, were trashed in a broken heap in the middle of the floor.

But his anger had not yet found full release. He seized the edge of the desk and flipped it forward, spilling the charts on its surface onto the carpet. The surgical texts were next, falling with a heavy thud as he pulled the bookshelf forward onto the upturned desk. He hoisted the heaviest book, the latest yellow surgical textbook, into his hand.

"Good-bye, Adam," he said before heaving it through the plate-glass window into the bushes below. A shrill alarm erupted. He'd triggered the security system.

The shrieking sound pierced the night.

The police would be coming soon.

It was time to disappear. Andy picked up his white coat, then shook his head and tossed it on top of the mess he'd created. It was a snow-covered mountain of broken dreams and desire.

Andy laughed at the thought before running from the back door and into the night.

CHAPTER

21

IT HAD TAKEN Dan Smith less than twenty-four hours to find Timmy Stevens. Dan was in the living room of a small row house with Timmy's mother, who was dutifully proclaiming her ignorance of Timmy's whereabouts when a friend of Timmy's pounded on the door-frame.

He opened the screen-door. "Hey, Ms. Stevens," he said, glancing at the woman and Dan where they sat on the couch. "I'll let myself in. I'm just here to see Timmy."

She began to stand. "Uh, Timmy's—"

Her words drifted as the young man shouted, "Timmy!"

Dan heard footsteps in the back of the house and rose to investigate. When he arrived in the kitchen, Timmy was quietly opening the back door. Dan raised his voice. "Hold it right there," he said, jumping forward and slamming the door. "Timmy Stevens?"

The boy nodded.

"Dan Smith, Serenity Police," he said, holding out his badge.

Timmy raised his hands. "Hey, I'm going to pay for the door, man. I told that dude I was good for it. I—"

"I'm not here to talk about the Seagull Inn," Dan responded.

Just then Timmy's mother entered. "Timmy! I didn't know you were here."

"Been here all day," he muttered.

"The boy's just so quiet, I lose track of him." She smiled, showing too many yellowing teeth, and walked out the back door.

The second youth followed Mrs. Stevens out the back door. Dan sat at the kitchen table, a shaky linoleum model with red trim and four metal legs. "I want to talk to you about Dr. Mark Crawford."

Timmy didn't flinch. "Who?"

"We have evidence that links you to him, or should I say, to his body."

"I'm not following you, man."

"I think you helped dispose of his body. Dumped him in the ocean near the Serenity Fishing Pier."

Now Timmy flinched. He pushed his chair away from the table and shook his head. "I don't know anything about any body."

Dan leaned forward. "Look, Timmy, I've been authorized by our Chief of Police to assure you we can work a deal. You're facing some pretty serious charges in Broward County. Possession of drugs, destruction of private property—"

"What's that got to do with all of this?"

"Cooperate with us in this investigation, help us nail a murderer, and we'll see to it that you get a light sentence. Keep quiet, and we'll keep you on our short list of murder suspects. Now—"

"Wait a minute, dude! I didn't kill anybody. I swear. You can ask my buddy. He was with me the whole week."

"Tell me what happened. I can help you. I'll make sure things work out for you."

Timmy looked away to the door. Dan let him look. If he tried to run, Dan was sure he could catch him. He watched as the youth picked a pimple on his shoulder.

"I was just getting rid of a body. Nobody was murdered or anything. You got it wrong. It was a cadver, er, a cadaver or something."

"A cadaver?"

"Yeah, you know, one of those bodies that doctors dissect for practice."

"Why were you disposing of it?"

"Some dude called me one day while I was hanging out at the fishing pier."

"Called you?"

"Yeah, real secretive like. I never even saw him. This guy who owns the pier comes out and says that someone was on the phone for me. I didn't think anyone knew where I was, so I asked him about it. He just shrugged his shoulders and said someone wanted to speak to the guy with long hair and the Boston Red Sox T-shirt.

When I answered, the guy talked real spooky, like he could see me or something."

"What'd he say?"

"He said he needed someone to dispose of a cadaver. He said he worked at the hospital and needed to dispose of an old body. When I questioned him, he said OSHA regulations were driving him crazy, and they were going to have to pay a mortician a thousand dollars to cremate the body. He said he'd pay me two hundred dollars to dump it in the ocean, to get rid of the problem for him. I thought about it. I'd spent more money that week than I'd anticipated."

"You partied pretty heavy, didn't you?"

He lifted his eyes. It looked like he was still partying too heavy.

"I like to party."

"Did you do it?"

"I picked up the body the next night from an old walk-in freezer in the hospital. It was right where the dude said it would be."

"Did it look like a cadaver?"

"Never seen one."

"Did it have clothes on?"

"I didn't know then. It was wrapped in red plastic bags labeled hazard or something like that. But I could tell it was a body." He held up his hands. "About my height and weight."

"What did you do next?"

"I took the body to the beach. My buddy was supposed to have a boat, but he didn't show; so I rented a kayak and paddled it out myself. I had tied a cinder block to the body to make it sink. But I capsized in the surf and almost lost the body. The red bags came off. I tried to haul him back in, but I only managed to pull his pants off. Since I couldn't get him out any further, I figured as long as he was on the bottom, the fish would just have to eat him right where he was." He paused and smiled. "And true to form, the doctor left two hundred dollars in the freezer for me the next night."

"The doctor?"

"Yeah."

"Did you ever meet him?"

"No."

"Did he identify himself by name?"

"I don't think so. But I know who it was. He said he was a surgeon. And Serenity only has one." He touched his scalp. "That hack knocked me out and sewed me up."

"How do you know it was him who asked you to dump the body?"

"It has to be. After the body rolled off the kayak and I got a glimpse of it, I started kinda freakin' out about it. I realized it didn't have any dissection that I could see, so I figured the guy was just covering up for bad medicine. I figured I was just disposing of some unfortunate patient."

"That makes no sense."

"That's what you think. But when I cut my head and they told me they'd called a surgeon, I started to worry that it was the same guy I talked to. When I accused him of putting his patients in a freezer, he shut me up with a dose of medicine that knocked me flat. I could think and feel everything, but I couldn't move. I couldn't breathe. It was horrifying. He put a tube in my throat to force air into my lungs to keep me alive while he stitched up my head. I felt every stitch. The guy was killing me. I think he knew I was on to him and was a threat. They put me in a hospital room, but I left before he could see me the next day. There was no way I was going to let that guy touch me again."

"Adam Tyson."

"Huh?"

"Dr. Adam Tyson. That's the surgeon's name. We've had our suspicions about him for a long time."

"Yeah," he said slowly. "Tyson. That's it. He's the one. I'm sure."

"Would you give us an official statement about this?"

"You say I can get off the charges against me?"

"I'll even get someone to pay for the door you damaged."

"Deal."

Dan shook his head and held out his hand. "Sweet."

∞

Andy stopped his truck in Beth's driveway and slowly opened the driver's door. He was a defeated man, but somehow free. He knew the charade was over. Whatever Beth would think of him, at least he felt the liberty of being himself.

She answered his knock, opened the door slowly, and stepped onto the front deck, radiant in the moonlight. She wore only a nightgown and a long flannel robe. "Adam?"

"We need to talk."

"Are you upset about my phone call? Have I confused you that bad?"

He shook his head. "No."

"Come in," she said, motioning to the house. "The night is cool."

He looked around. A lamp by her lounge chair provided soft light. A Bible was open on the table by her chair.

"Ike is in bed. He gets up early, retires early." She nodded to the stairs. "Trav is playing on the computer." Her hand went to her mouth. "You're not here to tell me you won't do my surgery, are you? Ike was so glad to hear that you were not going to put it off any longer." She shook her head. "Please don't tell me that. I'm convinced the man has Alzheimer's or something. He's on an emotional seesaw, one minute stable, the next . . . Well, I don't think I could stand to tell him—"

Andy silenced her with an uplifted hand, walked to the table, and picked up the Bible.

Beth's jaw dropped. "Adam, what's this about?"

"It's not what you think."

"If you think I'll just change my mind about us because you read the Bible, well . . . it's not that simple."

"I'm not here to change your mind about being more than my friend." He motioned to the chair. "Sit down."

She sat on the lounge chair across from where he positioned himself on the couch. "Help me find something," he said, holding the book with two hands.

She nodded silently.

"I went to a wedding. My cousin's. The priest read a passage about love. Something about love rejoicing in truth."

"Look in the New Testament. The book of First Corinthians, about three-fourths of the way to the back."

He thumbed his way through. "Psalms, Matthew, Mark." He flipped some more.

"Keep going."

"Romans."

"Slow down. Next book. First Corinthians 13."

He started reading, his voice broken and thick. He didn't stop when he passed the phrase, "rejoices with the truth." Instead, he read the entire chapter.

He hung his head. "I'm a phony, Beth."

"A phony?"

"I'm not the man I pretend to be. I pretend to be a strong, confident, smart physician, a compassionate surgeon, a man with answers and a healing touch."

"You are all those things, Adam."

"No." He shook his head. "That's what I'm pretending to be. You don't know me, Beth. You don't want to love me. You want to love who I'm pretending to be."

"Adam, we all put up fronts. You have to come across as confident, compassionate, even when you don't feel it. That's what your patients need. That doesn't make you a phony."

"With me it's more than a front. But promise me you'll give me a chance to explain. Promise me that."

"Adam, what's this all about?"

"Will you let me explain?"

"Of course."

"Promise me you'll not leave me until you understand. Until I have a chance to tell you my side."

She sighed. "I promise."

He pointed to the Bible. "That verse about love—'love rejoices with the truth.' That's what this is all about, Beth. I didn't come to this town to fall in love. I came here to start out a new life as a surgeon. It was a fresh start. My old life was left behind."

"I know about the drugs, Adam. I don't care about that."

"It's not the drugs, Beth. I never took drugs."

"But you lost your license. The board—"

He held up his hand. "Listen. I can explain it all. Adam Tyson took drugs. Adam Tyson lost his license. But that's not me. I came here for a new start. I wanted to make a new name for myself, be the surgeon I knew I could be, doing essentially what I'd been doing for the last decade, but without the admiration and respect that I thought

I needed. I wanted to be looked up to, to be respected. I wanted to be calling the shots, not taking the orders. I was tired of bailing out the surgeon and not getting the credit." He hesitated.

Beth leaned forward and squinted. She wasn't understanding.

He went on, "But then you came along. And I found myself drawn to you. I wanted to be with you, and you responded. You liked me. You respected me, wanted to be with me." He hung his head. "At least with who I pretended to be. I was thrilled. I was—I am in love with you."

"Oh, Adam, we talked about this. I want—"

He lifted his eyes from the floor and captured hers with a look. She stopped short, knowing only that he demanded her silence, her attention.

"But love cannot be based upon a lie. I didn't love myself. I was never good enough for my father. I was never good enough for my fiancée. I was never good enough for me."

"Adam, we're all unlovely. We're all in a helpless state."

"No," he responded, "I'm not speaking of that. I decided I would change. I would be the one whom people looked to for help." He dropped his face again. "I would be the one that women would admire." He paused. "But then you came along. And love requires honesty, an open look at who I really am."

"We all want respect, don't we? We all want to be admired. What's wrong with that?"

"I lived for it. I created a false identity just to boost my flagging ego."

Beth leaned back in her chair and clutched at the neck of her robe. "You're talking in circles, Adam. I'm not following you."

"You don't know who I am."

"OK," she said with a sigh. "Tell me."

"I'm Michael Cunningham."

CHAPTER
22

MICHAEL ANDREW CUNNINGHAM. I go by my middle name.
My friends call me Andy."

Beth shook her head slowly. "What?" Her hand went to her
mouth. "Michael Cunningham?"

"That's right. I was Adam Tyson's PA."

She was incredulous. She felt her face redden with anger. "You
lied to me!" She stood up too suddenly and felt stabbing pain in her
abdomen. She began slowly backing away, staring at the man she
thought she knew, the man who only hours ago she confessed to
wanting to love. "I can't believe you," she huffed. "No," she said in
disgust, "I can't believe I trusted you. I thought you were so wonderful, but you . . . I mean your car . . . the white Cadillac—"

He hung his head. "I'm the one who hit you, Beth. I'm the
driver of the white Cadillac."

She didn't want to believe it. "You drive a truck."

"I have, er, had two vehicles, a truck and a Cadillac. But since I'd
only just been in town a few days, no one realized the car was mine."

Her mind blurred. "But you—you operated on me. You saved my
life. But . . . you're not a surgeon at all!" She picked up a small brass
lighthouse that sat on an end table and clenched it in her fist. She
drew it back, ready to heave it at Andy.

He held up his hands. "Beth, wait!"

She took a deep breath and slowly let her arm relax. The idea of
his deception infuriated her. She hoisted the object up and down in
her hand and squelched the urge to scream. "Uggghh! I can't believe
what I'm hearing!"

Andy lowered his hands and stared at the floor in front of him, looking very much a broken man, but also an easy target for the light-house she gripped so tightly. She slammed the little object into her other hand while she counted to five under her breath. "You jerk," she mumbled, setting the lighthouse down. "You'd better just leave." She pointed to the door.

"Beth, no."

Her hand began to tremble, still pointing. "The door is right there."

"Let me explain."

She shook her head, feeling anger one moment and embarrass-ment the next. She looked at Adam. His eyes were pleading. She slowly placed her hand at her side. "I can't believe I was so stupid. How could you have done this to me?"

"I didn't come to town to hurt you, Beth."

"Oh, you just decided to waltz into Serenity and pretend to be a surgeon? Didn't you think that you might hurt someone in the process?" This time she pointed at him. Her voice thickened. "And don't you think I mean patients." She started to cry.

"Beth, don't cry. I came to explain. I came to be honest."

She inhaled sharply, rhythmically, like a child trying in vain to stop crying. The gasps for breath sent spasms of pain through her abdomen. She pressed her hands against her surgical scar and eased herself into the lounge chair again. She wasn't sure she wanted to hear what he had to say. But he didn't seem to be leaving, and she couldn't exactly throw him out. She sighed, her breath catching again in a sob. She held up her hands. "So explain."

"The memory you have of seeing my face is true. I was at the scene, Beth. I called the 911 operator. I didn't want to leave you." He paused. "I didn't know what to do. I stayed with you as long as I could, until I saw the flashing lights of the rescue squad and then—"

"What? You left me?"

"I didn't want to leave! But I didn't want to be discovered either. I knew I'd need to show my license or my car registration." He hung his head. "You were breathing. You had a strong pulse. I wasn't leav-ing you to die."

"But you left me alone!"

"Yes, I left you alone, but only for a few moments." He shook his head. "It was the wrong thing to do, OK? I know that."

"So how did you end up being my hero?"

"At the last moment I ran to a sand dune beside the road and laid down where I wouldn't be seen. I watched to make sure you were taken care of. Then I hoofed it through the rain back to the hospital to meet you."

Beth sat with her mouth agape, leaning forward, staring at the man she thought she knew.

"Beth, I'm sorry. It was an accident. I left the hospital late. It was dark and rainy. I rounded the corner and didn't see your van until the last second. I tried to stop, but my car skidded on the slick road." He pinched his eyes closed at the memory. "And then I saw you."

"You?"

He nodded slowly.

"But you were such a skilled surgeon."

"I still am."

"But you're a fake."

He nodded silently.

"How could you think you could pull this off? How—"

"I worked across from Adam Tyson for years. He taught me everything. Most doctors take five or six years of residency to become qualified to do surgery. I had eight years with Tyson and a few with another surgeon before him. Tyson was a patient teacher, very skilled, and delicate in his technique."

"I—I can't believe this!"

"Beth, it's true. Dr. Tyson let me do more and more. At first I learned to close up at the end of an operation. Later he let me open and close and assist as he did the operations. Then, about two years ago, he was in an accident himself. He needed shoulder surgery. He got addicted to pain pills. I was the first to suspect it. During long operations he would become irritated, sweaty. Sometimes he would even scrub out, leaving me alone to operate in his absence." Andy squinted. "That's when I first realized I could do this on my own. He had taught me so well, I knew I could help people without him."

"He lost his license?"

"Not completely. He was forced to take drug rehabilitation." He shook his head. "I'm the one who reported him to the board. It was one of the most difficult things I've ever done. He went to rehab, but he was never the same. After his second round of rehabilitation, his wife left. Then he died of an overdose."

"Suicide?"

He shrugged. "Maybe. I tried starting out again, working for other surgical groups. I left California because everyone there loved Adam Tyson. In a way, even though he was the one abusing drugs, it seemed they blamed me for turning him in. I moved to Florida, but it was never the same. The surgeons there never gave me the independence Dr. Tyson had. I watched them make mistakes that I could have prevented. And they hated it when I pointed out easier ways to do things. That's when I realized how good Dr. Tyson had been, and how well he had taught me."

"So you just decided to operate yourself."

"Beth, I knew I could do it. I was good at it. Better than the surgeons I was hired to assist." Andy looked at his hands.

"But you're a fake!"

He repeated her words slowly. "I'm . . . a . . . . fake."

"I can't believe this," she huffed. "Why? Why did you do this? How did you think you could get away with it?"

"I know it was a dumb thing to do. But I knew I could do it. I'm a good surgeon. I'm just not board-certified."

"You took responsibility for people's lives."

"I know. I didn't do it cavalierly." He stood up and drew his fingers through his blond hair. "I know it doesn't justify it, but I talked myself into believing I deserved this. For as long as I can remember, I wanted to be a surgeon. It was true that at one time I wanted to be a missionary surgeon—"

"What, so everything you told me wasn't a lie?"

He shook his head. "Only my name. Only my credentials. I really did play baseball. I tried to get into medical school. My fiancée and I dreamed of being missionaries together." He started to pace. "I got rejected from medical school. I became bitter. My girlfriend left. She married someone who got into medical school."

Beth sighed. "So why tell me this now?"

"I finally had everything I'd dreamed of. I had a great job, respect, the ability to do surgery independently. I had satisfied patients. I had everything . . . except love."

Beth sat there with her mouth open.

"You probably hate me for this. But I finally realized that love meant being honest. And I was willing to give everything up just for a chance at that."

She shook her head. "Does anyone else know what you've done?"

"No." He paused. "Only you."

"So now what? What will you do?"

"I'm not sure. I'll need to talk to the hospital administration. They'll report me to the police."

She put her hand to her mouth. "You'll go to jail."

"Probably." He hung his head. "I've really fouled up. The feds and the state will want me for insurance fraud. The locals will want me for your hit-and-run."

"It was an accident."

"It was an accident until I left the scene. Now it's a crime." He sighed. "I'm sorry, Beth. I'm so sorry."

She stood and walked to the glass back door. "Don't do anything sudden, Adam . . . er, Andy. You'd better get an attorney to help handle this. Maybe they can work out a better deal with the authorities if you come forward on your own."

"Maybe. I don't know anyone here."

She turned and faced him. "Are you telling me this because you were afraid I was on to you? That Dr. Harper had tipped me off and your little game was coming to an end?"

He shook his head. "No. Believe me, Beth, my intentions weren't to have to go around lying all the time. I just wanted to be me, but with a new name and the job I'd always wanted to do." He put his hand on her arm, but she pulled away. "When you told me about what Dr. Harper said, I told you the truth. I didn't remember him. I didn't know him. The real Adam Tyson did." He stepped toward her again. "I could tell you wanted to believe me, even more than I wanted to believe in myself. Seeing that only helped convince me that I couldn't keep lying to you this way. Falling in love with you became the only thing that mattered."

He inched closer, but she backed away. "Beth, I'm still the same man."

She put up her hand, stopping his progress. "But you lied. You—your life was such a lie." She locked eyes with his. "I don't know you."

"Beth, I'm sorry. I never wanted it to be this way."

She shook her head. "You'd better leave."

He started to protest, but the fear in her eyes made the words catch in his throat.

"Just leave!"

He walked to the door, pausing at the door to say, "I'm sorry" again. She looked away, unable to respond, and listened as the door closed before she let the tears begin. She cried, muffling her sobs in the sleeve of her flannel robe.

She looked back at the couch where the Bible still lay open to 1 Corinthians 13. *He says he loves me.* She looked at the verses that Andy had read just minutes before. "Love bears all things," she whispered. "Believes all things, hopes all things, endures all things."

What am I to do now?

❧

As he closed the door, Andy felt as if he were shutting out his last chance for happiness. The darkness of the night enveloped him. He paused on the front deck, leaning his back against the door. He could hear Beth sobbing inside.

Her cries were arrows in his chest, each one finding its mark in the depths of his heart.

"O God," he whispered, "what have I done?"

He descended the front steps in silence, pausing only once to look back at the house. He could imagine the reactions of Ike and Travis to the news of his charade.

He drove home in sadness over the mess he'd created, but lightened by the fact that he wasn't going to have to hide behind a lie any longer. He would make a confession to the hospital tomorrow. Or maybe Beth was right and he should find a good attorney.

When he pulled into his driveway, Greg Monroe was waiting, sitting in a Serenity Police jeep with the engine running.

Beth didn't waste any time calling the police about me.

He stepped out of his truck. Confession time. Might as well get this over with.

The door to the police jeep opened slowly, and Officer Monroe stepped out. "Evening, Dr. Tyson."

Andy's guard was up. If Beth had called him, why was he calling him "doctor"? He nodded. "Evening."

"I'm afraid there's been some trouble."

Andy was ready to face the music. "I can explain everything."

"You know about the vandalism?"

"What?"

Greg squinted. "The vandalism. Someone trashed your office."

"Oh, that." He nodded. "I know."

"You've seen it?"

Andy chuckled. "You might say that."

"Any idea who might have done this? Anyone around Serenity have a score to settle with you?"

Only a lovely lady with a broken heart.

"Dr. Tyson?"

Andy looked back. "Oh, sorry."

"Any idea who might have vandalized your office?"

He nodded. "Yes. You don't need to worry about it. I'll pay for the damages."

"If you know who did it, you may be able to get them to pay—"

Andy held up his hand. "I said I'll take care of it."

"But this is against the law. You shouldn't drop the charges. You—"

"Don't worry about it. I know the person who did it."

"Who?"

Andy dropped his eyes. "Me."

❧

The next morning Sam Harris was in the office early. Dan had called the night before with the information supplied by their key witness, Timmy Stevens. It was just the break he'd been looking for. A chance to break a big case in Serenity didn't happen every day. Now all he had to do was get to the magistrate and get a warrant to arrest Dr. Adam Tyson.

It all fit together so neatly with what Jim Manning had told him about his suspicions about big-time insurance fraud going on in Serenity. Dr. Tyson killed Dr. Crawford to get in on the action. Or perhaps somehow Tyson found out and confronted Crawford, and things got ugly, out of hand. It didn't really matter to Sam. All that mattered to him was that he had a witness that claimed Tyson hired him to ditch a body, the body of Dr. Mark Crawford. That, with the probable cause of wanting Crawford's job, was enough to get a warrant.

It was all falling together like the pieces of a puzzle, right down to the damage he'd seen last night at Dr. Tyson's clinic. The guy must have a violent temper to have done all that damage to his own office.

He checked his watch and sipped black coffee. He hadn't been able to sleep last night. He was keyed up about the investigation. He couldn't wait to see Tyson's face when he arrested him. He leaned back in his chair. The best thing was that the doctor was playing it so cool and confident that he wasn't at risk of running.

Sam wanted the media to know about this one. He'd give the full story to the reporters himself. This would be a regional story for sure. Doctors always get attention like that. And then everyone would see what a wonderful job the Serenity Police Chief was doing as well.

He checked his watch again. The magistrate would be in her office soon. He pulled his feet from his desktop and allowed them to slap onto the floor. He needed to go over to the county courthouse to get the arrest warrant, and then on to the hospital where he would present Dr. Tyson with the surprise of his devious little life.

∽

Andy Cunningham spent the night in fitful turning, finally rising at 4 to face the gloom that would certainly confront him for the foreseeable future. He washed, dressed, and walked to the kitchen when he noticed that a familiar low-level feeling of caution and regret were gone. His honesty with Beth had lightened his step, removing an unseen weight that he had ignored too long. He knew the future held hardship, but there was something refreshing about walking forward in the openness that he'd initiated the night before.

His father had been a recovering alcoholic and swore to Andy over and over that step five in the recovery process was the most important: "confessing to myself and another the exact nature of my misdeeds." But wasn't there another part that he was missing? Confession to God or a higher power is part and parcel of the program.

Andy looked out the window to the darkness beyond, seeing only his own reflection. "God," he whispered, "I feel like such a hypocrite, praying when I'm not sure I even believe. But Beth and Ike keep telling me You love me. If You're who they say, then I guess You know how desperately I'd like to believe that right now."

His voice broke. Tears started to form. "I've been running from You. Running from myself. It seems stupid to be coming to You now, when I'm in so much trouble. I don't deserve Your help." He pinched his eyelids shut. "But I don't know where to turn. I need help. I'm afraid. Help me do the right thing."

He stood in the silence for a long time, hoping for an audible voice, something to convince him that the words Ike had spoken about his true identity as someone loved by God could possibly be true. But he heard nothing, becoming conscious only of the faint buzzing of his refrigerator and his own breathing.

Just asking made him feel better. But maybe that was just a placebo—he wasn't sure. For once he wished he could find the faith that seemed to come so naturally to Beth. Her talk of God's sovereignty seemed to give her the strength to accept even the hurtful things in life with reckless hope.

He made coffee, doubling the amount called for on the side of the blue can. This wasn't a morning for weak java.

He sipped coffee and made plans. He would go by the operating rooms and cancel his cases. Beth Carlson was to be his first case, so he wouldn't have to worry about her showing up. Hopefully he could have the staff get ahold of the other patients before they left the comfort of their homes.

Then he would go and talk to the administration, making a full confession of his true identity. After that, he wasn't sure what life would hold. Police investigation? Public humiliation?

He sipped his coffee and sighed. It didn't seem to matter. The load of pretending to be what he wasn't was gone.

At 7:30 he poured a cup for the road and drove a mile to the hospital. He parked in the doctors' lot, promising himself that it would be the last time. He dropped by the OR, walking by the desk and seeing the face of Gerri Fiori brighten.

"It's about time you showed up. Dr. Tracey is about to take your first case into the operating room."

"My first case?" He tried not to look shocked. "Beth Carlson?"

Gerri nodded. "Sure. You know we like to start by 7:30. Go get changed. Your patient came in at 5 for her radioactive injection in preparation for the sentinel lymph node mapping."

Andy walked toward the men's dressing area in a mental fog. *Beth showed up for her surgery?*

He changed into scrubs and stumbled down the hall to OR 2, where Beth was just being wheeled into the room.

"Beth!"

She looked over as he grabbed the railing of the stretcher, halting its forward progress. "Dr. Tyson," she responded.

He lowered his voice. "What are you doing here?"

"I've come for my surgery, of course."

"But—" He halted. "After last night I thought—" He stopped again and looked at the nurse who was still standing with her hands on the railing of Beth's stretcher. "Could you excuse us for a minute? I'd like to speak privately to Be—uh, my patient."

The nurse nodded and retreated into the operating room as Andy pushed the stretcher back into the hall where they could be alone.

"Are you out of your mind? Or did I just dream that I told you the truth about me last night?"

Her eyes and a barely perceptible shake of her head arrested his sentence. "I have breast cancer. I need a surgeon. If I had other options right now, I would take them," she said quietly. "I was all set to tell my father everything this morning, but I could see he just couldn't take waiting any longer."

"But—"

"I need you to do your best. I know you are capable." She sighed and looked away. "I know you care about me."

He placed his hand upon hers.

She pulled away. "Look," she said, "I realize it took guts to be honest with me." She locked her eyes on his and added, "Finally."

"Beth, I came in to resign, to tell the administrators what I did."

"Please, not just yet."

"But Beth, I—"

She held up her hand. "Maybe being honest proves you to be more trustworthy." She took a deep breath. "Ike is very fragile right now. His fears seem irrational. I worry this may be the start of Alzheimer's or something. I just didn't have the heart to tell him I wasn't having surgery today."

"You know who I really am and you want me to operate?"

"Last night you read to me from 1 Corinthians 13. You said you were in love with me. Is that true?"

"Yes."

"Well then, you have meticulous technique, you have the knowledge, and . . ." Her voice became even softer.

He leaned forward to hear.

". . . you say you love me. So who else would offer me the same care and tenderness?"

"Beth, this isn't rational. This is the very reason we questioned whether I was the one to be operating. I'll be tempted to think with my heart instead of my head."

The door to the operating room pushed open. The anesthesiologist, Dr. Sarah Tracey, stood with her hands in the air. "I've got a full day ahead of me, and Dr. Klim may need to bump the schedule for a C-section. Are we going to get on with it?"

Andy looked back at Beth, who nodded.

"Do your best. That's all I can ask."

"OK," he responded numbly. He stepped back as the nurses wheeled Beth into the room and positioned her on the table. He watched as Dr. Tracey induced the anesthesia. He shook his head and quickly donned a mask. It was time to wash his hands. His patient was waiting.

He scrubbed his hands, lathering and rubbing each finger with the sponge side and the bristle side of the sterile scrub brush. As he washed, he tried to collect his thoughts, to make sense of this new development, the unlikely fact that Beth Carlson knew everything about him and still willingly laid her life in his hands. He mentally ran through the steps of the operation. He'd helped Adam Tyson do this very thing dozens of times.

Then, in a horrible moment, a grim thought rose from somewhere in the recesses of his mind. Beth was the only one who knew his true identity. Without her, he could resume his life as a surgeon in this town, and no one would be the wiser. Adam Tyson, M.D. would live on, operating, relishing in the healing brought by the skill of his hands. It would be so easy—a slip of the knife as the dissection neared the axillary artery, or a sudden puncture through the breast into the chest to collapse a lung. He closed his eyes and fought the urge to vomit into his mask. After a moment the sensation passed, and he entered the operating room, his hands held high, with the water dripping from his elbows.

He stood back, gowned and gloved, watching the iodine prep of the operative field. He squared the field off with sterile blue towels and draped a large sterile sheet exposing only his patient's breast and left arm.

He palpated the firm mass and asked for the blue dye that would serve to help him find the sentinel lymph nodes, the first nodes to drain the cancer in the breast. He slowly injected three cc's of dye above and below the cancer. He massaged the tissue gently for five minutes, trying to focus on the technical challenges ahead.

"Scalpel." He held out his hand.

He laid the knife on her flesh, gripping it too tightly and exhibiting a fine tremor. *Not too deep, Andy. Slowly, just through the dermis. Then use the cautery.*

He touched the tip of the cautery to a bleeder just under the skin, sending smoke and the familiar acrid smell through his mask and into his nostrils.

He pinched his eyelids shut momentarily.

He heard a female whisper, "Are you OK?"

He glanced up into the eyes of his assistant and nodded. "Sure. Let's do it."

Andy walked from the recovery room to the waiting room to find Ike reading the Bible and Travis sitting next to Kristy playing chess on a portable magnetic game set. He held out his hand as Ike struggled to his feet. He took a deep breath. "I'm all done."

"How is she?"

"Great. Everything went smoothly."

The anxiety on Ike's face broke into a broad grin. "I'm not surprised. I awoke last night just after midnight and found Beth still sitting up. She was pretty upset. But after we prayed, she seemed to be enveloped in such peace." He nodded. "She has a lot of faith in you, doc."

"She has faith in God, Ike. I don't need to tell you about that."

"I think she was worried about you, more than the surgery itself. I think she worried that she had put you in a tough place, making you play the role of surgeon and boyfriend like she has."

Andy's head jerked back. *Boyfriend? Is that how Beth describes me? Or is that the perception of an old man with early dementia?*

Andy saw Ike's face fall again. Andy looked over at Travis and Kristy, who held her hand up to her mouth. He followed their eyes to the doorway of the waiting room. There, blocking the doorway, was the entire threesome making up the Serenity Police force. Their eyes were locked on Andy.

"I hope we're not interfering, Dr. Tyson."

He took a step away from Ike and shook his head. "We were just finishing."

The presence of the police stunned him as much as Beth's showing up for her surgery had ninety minutes before. *Beth must have told them about me.*

"Excellent. Maybe you could come with us."

"Whatever you have to say to me, you can say in front of my friends here. I have nothing to hide."

"Suit yourself." He nodded. "Please hold out your hands."

He obeyed, but Ike protested, "You mind telling us what this is about, Sam?"

Sam Harris chuckled. "Why sure, Ike. Dr. Tyson here is under arrest."

"Under arrest?" Ike took a step forward.

Andy nodded. "I'll explain everything later, Ike. I told it all to Beth last night."

Ike persisted. "Under arrest for what?"

"Murder."

Andy's jaw dropped. "Wh-what? That's not what this is about!"

"The murder of Dr. Mark Crawford."

Andy's mind whirled. He felt the handcuffs snap around his wrists and was vaguely aware that the police chief was reading him his rights. Then he stumbled forward as Dan Smith grabbed him by the elbow.

"You're going to jail for a long, long time, doc."

Sam stabbed a finger in his chest. "You're going to regret coming to Serenity, boy."

CHAPTER
23

WITH SOME PERSISTENT persuasion, Adam convinced Samuel Harris to let him stop back at the recovery room to write orders to care for his patient, Beth Carlson. With Sam in front of him, and Dan holding his elbow, Adam walked, head down, into post-op. The nurse looked up and, not seeing Adam, spoke up. "You're not allowed in here," she said, pointing toward the door. At that moment her eyes met Dr. Tyson's. "Dr. Tyson . . . Oh! . . . . Well, I—"

He forced a smile. "They're OK. They're with me."

He walked to the counter and lifted his hands to reveal the cuffs. "Can you take these off for a moment so I can write my orders?"

The chief was unmoving. "Try."

Adam brought his hands to his chest and lifted a pen from the front of his scrub-shirt. Silently he endured the stares of the nurses, aware of their hushed whispers behind cupped hands.

He looked at the head nurse. "Could you notify the rest of my patients that I'll be unavailable for surgery? They can contact my office for further instructions."

The nurse leaned forward and spoke quietly. "Are you all right?"

"A misunderstanding, I assure you."

Just then he felt the grip tighten around his biceps, a vice pushing toward the bone. "*You* misunderstood, Dr. Tyson. Thought you'd get away with knocking off Serenity's finest surgeon?"

The nurses gasped.

He shook his head but didn't respond, knowing it would only stimulate a fresh rebuttal from the police.

A few feet away Beth Carlson was waking from anesthesia. She squinted bleary-eyed in their direction. "Hey, officer," she yelled, "it was an accident. He didn't mean to hit me! I'm not pressssing ccch-hhargesss," she slurred.

"You hit her?" Dan yanked up on his arm again.

Adam felt himself being shoved toward the door.

"Let's move, doctor," Sam ordered.

"Nooo!" Beth screamed. "He's innocent. He saved my life. Don't take him away!"

A recovery room nurse restrained Beth's arm. "Easy, Ms. Carlson. You're delirious."

"I'm fine," she yelled, her voice trailing behind him. "He's innocent!"

Dan leaned close to Adam's ear and gripped Adam's arm tighter. "What's up with her, doc? What else have you done?"

Adam winced at the warmth of the officer's breath on his cheek, a smell of fast-food burgers. "I can explain everything. You guys are making a mistake here."

Sam smacked his clipboard. "The magistrate didn't think so."

Adam plodded mechanically toward the front of the hospital. It seemed his escorts made no attempt to steer clear of crowds in the hospital's lobby, choosing instead to head straight through two small gatherings, snapping in a loud manner, "Coming through! Move away!"

A wave of murmuring and gasps of shock followed the trio on the path from the OR to the hospital's exit. Each hushed comment with his name found a mark in Adam's chest. This was humiliation at its worst.

Outside the front entrance, a half-dozen reporters with video cameras were waiting. As they passed, Adam observed Samuel Harris standing a little taller. He was enjoying this. Adam looked straight at the cameras, choosing to stay quiet rather than respond to the volley of questions lobbed at him by the reporters.

He bent forward as Dan shoved him into the back of the police cruiser. He careened over awkwardly without his hands to stabilize his body in a sitting position. He struggled back upright and listened as the door slammed with a heavy thud.

Adam looked back into the flashes from the reporters' cameras and took inventory. *I'm a fraud. I've lost my career and probably my chances for a future with Beth. I'm suspected of a murder I didn't commit. I'm going to go to prison for practicing medicine without a license. I'm guilty of a hit-and-run. And now my mistakes are going to be paraded out in public by the media. But . . .*

Andy shook his head in wonder. There was freedom in being honest. And Beth Carlson had trusted him, even knowing everything about him. The possibility of unconditional love was alive, shown to him in clear terms by the most wonderful woman in the world.

He thought back to his morning prayer for help. *Is this what I get for praying?*

He took a deep breath. The charade was over. What he needed now was an attorney. He knew he'd better not break the news of his deceit on his own.

So for now Andy Cunningham continued his life as Adam Tyson and chuckled at the thought of informing the police that the man they thought was guilty of murder had been dead for six months.

They took him to the local police station, a small building made of painted cinder blocks, lacking the stilts present on most coastal buildings. When he refused to answer any questions without an attorney, they shoved him into a locked, windowless room with a single table and a wooden chair. He didn't know anyone to call. They would assign him a public defender and assured him he could see him later in the day.

And so for the next three hours Andy waited. And waited. He was offered no food or water, no access to a phone, and heard no noise except for occasional footsteps in the hall outside, each one raising his expectations as they grew in volume, then dashing his hopes when the footfalls faded in passing.

For the first time that he could remember, he wanted only to be himself. And for the first time since college, he had started to believe that the words Beth Carlson had shared just might be true. He took a deep breath. The nagging anxiety that had dogged him since he'd started his charade was gone.

I love you not because of who you are, but because of who I am.

Andy looked up. The thought had been his own . . . or had it?

Beth had put her trust in him in spite of his confession. No one had ever given him a reason to believe in unconditional acceptance, unconditional love. Until now. And that fact, coupled with the words he'd heard over and over from Beth and Ike, made him consider the possibility that he'd been wrong. Maybe there was unconditional love. And maybe Beth was showing him a little glimpse of the type of acceptance that comes from the heart of God, acceptance not based on performance or a balance of the scales in his favor.

"Can it be true?" he whispered. "Is this what You've been trying to show me all along? That it's not just a fairy tale? It just might be the truth? You love me like I am?"

The bare walls offered no answer. He heard no audible voice. Yet somehow he knew he was at a crossroad. He had hit bottom. And maybe the sovereign God of the universe whom Beth believed in had orchestrated it all to make him look up . . . to make him believe.

God loves me? He loves me. He stared at his trembling hands. The thought, so powerful and clear in his mind, was accompanied by the memory of a verse learned years ago in Sunday school in California. "For God so loved the world that he gave his only Son, that whoever believes in him should not perish but have eternal life." The idea that God loved him just as he was flooded his mind with peace. And there, sitting alone in silence, in a police station in Serenity, he believed. There were no fireworks, no chorus singing "Just As I Am." There was only a sudden realization that his heart was somehow different, changed. Doubt in a God who loves beyond reason was replaced with faith that he was accepted.

He came to Serenity to find a new identity, and now, through his tears, he began to understand who he really was, loved independent of position or skill, valued simply because Jesus had died to give him life.

He slowly whispered the name of the One he had so often cursed, now the name that brought real serenity to his harried soul. "Jesus . . . Jesus . . . Jesus," he whispered, watching his tears drip to the linoleum floor beneath him. "Forgive me, Father," he asked. "I've been so messed up." He paused, aware of a deepening calm. Somehow he understood. He was forgiven even before he asked.

He thought of his pride, the deceit of the last weeks. He thought of the bitterness that had grown against God since his rejection from medical school, the dashing of his career dreams. He sucked his breath in irregular, quick sobs. These were tears of joy, the realization that nothing mattered now except that he was loved, deeply and unconditionally. Now he could face the consequences of his actions, knowing with confidence that he would never be alone again.

He had attended church before. He had even been swept up in his own agenda to be a missionary . . . but he hadn't really believed.

He wiped his eyes with the back of his hand and studied a small spot on his scrub-pants. Blood. Beth's blood, shed during her morning surgery. He reached for it instinctively, not caring about the precautions to avoid blood contact that health professionals follow with religious conviction. This blood was different, precious to him, the blood of the woman he loved. He traced the perimeter of the stiff red-brown stain with his index finger. Could she ever give herself to love a man so filled with fault?

He touched the stain gently, almost reverently, and nodded his head in a silent resolution. Relationships could not fulfill him. A job could not fulfill him. He had come to tranquillity, an understanding that God alone was the source of satisfaction.

He did not pray for deliverance from his situation but only whispered the name of his Savior in quiet thankfulness.

"Jesus . . . Jesus."

He looked up as the door swung open. Samuel Harris stood with a second man, a portly gentleman of about fifty. He wore blue jeans and a golf shirt one size too small for his potbellied stature. His eyes were clear, sparkling above a dimpled smile and one too many chins. Harris shook his head. "I don't think your tears will help you now, doc."

"It's not what you think. I finally understood something I've been missing for a long time."

He felt their eyes on him, examining him, from his wet eyes to his wrinkled bloody scrubs. They said nothing, waiting for an apparent explanation.

"I, well . . . I know that God loves me," he sniffed.

"Religion ain't gonna help you now, partner," Harris huffed. "I've seen it before. Handcuff religion." He elbowed the man with the blue golf shirt. "Cuff 'em and they're suddenly sorry for their sins."

Andy knew better than to try to explain what had just taken place. He wasn't even sure he *could* explain it. And he was sure the chief would just use it as an excuse to ridicule him further.

The chief escorted the other man through the door. "This is your attorney, Alton J. Bell. He will represent you in the case the state is preparing against you. Now maybe you can unzip your lips and talk." He stepped back and shut the door and bolted it noisily.

Mr. Bell held out his hand.

Andy stood and took it, receiving a strong squeeze from this gentle-appearing man.

"Alton Bell," he said with a bass voice. "Everyone calls me Al."

"Michael Andrew Cunningham," he said, watching the man's reaction. "Everybody calls me Andy."

"What?"

"Sit down. I'll explain." The two looked at the only chair in the room. "You take it," Andy said. "I suspect you'll want to take notes."

"I don't understand. I came to meet Adam Tyson."

"I know," he said, settling into a sitting position on the edge of the table. "It's a long story."

"I've got all evening."

Andy took a deep breath, wondering where to begin. "Where do I start?"

Al popped the latch on an old leather briefcase and pulled out a yellow legal pad. "How about the beginning?"

"I always wanted to be a surgeon," Andy said reflectively. "I thought there was never anything else that could possibly bring me a full life." He paused, noticing a slight tremor in his hand. "That is, until today."

∞

Elizabeth Winters had been married for twenty-two years, and happily married for sixteen. But things had changed in the last few years. Dave, her husband, was making money. Lots of money. And while the money didn't satisfy her need for companionship, it went a long way toward buying her the house and status she'd always known she deserved. But with the money, Dave had grown distant and rarely affectionate, and his hours at work slowly overtook everything at home. Was there another woman? Her suspicions changed from rumor to substantiated fact when her good friend in Medical Records spilled the beans about her husband's relationship with an OR nursing supervisor.

Her reaction to the affair had been sad indifference. She hardly cared to fight for the man for whom she'd ceased to care, and as long as he seemed content to stay and bring home lots of money, she didn't want to throw him out either. He seemed content with the public image of a happy family man. She seemed content with the money. Why not let him carry on with a woman half his age?

But the summer found Dave Winters on edge, snapping at Liz, drinking himself to sleep most nights, and working an overbearing schedule. Tonight he arrived home two hours after dinner and went straight to his study, where he pored over his financial records and sipped Caribbean rum.

When the phone rang, Liz picked it up in the bedroom but paused to swallow the diet soda in her mouth before speaking. In that short moment her husband picked up in the study and answered before she could speak.

"Hello."

"Dave, we need to talk." The voice was soft and feminine, but not sweet. Urgent and laced with pressure.

Her husband hesitated, probably closing the study door. His voice was hushed. "Gerri, what's the matter?"

"You know what's the matter," she huffed. "You know the police arrested Tyson."

Liz listened as her husband's breath blew into the mouthpiece. She heard ice rattling against glass before he spoke. "I know."

"But this can't stick. He's no dummy. He'll have an alibi. Sooner or later the police are going to figure this out."

"Harris? I wouldn't worry about him."

Liz covered the phone with her hand and held her breath, then turned down the TV in the bedroom. *Gerri Fiori? She's our daughter's age!*

"Dave, what about that FBI agent? He's asking all the right questions. I think Crawford must have tipped him off before he accused us."

"Not likely. He was under investigation too, you know."

"I don't like this. I want to leave." She paused. "Why can't we just head for the islands like we planned? Things are getting way too hot around here."

"If we give it a few more months, we will be up to speed with Tyson's billing. We'll make twice what we did last year."

"Not if Tyson's in prison. We'll have to recruit yet another surgeon. Why'd you have to frame him?"

"It was an impulsive decision. I hadn't planned on it, but the kid was asking questions. I never really thought they'd track him down."

"Well, they did track the kid down, and now they think Tyson killed Crawford."

"Better him than us."

"I want to leave. We've got enough to live on. Why wait for more?"

"We are just getting started, Gerri. I talked to a guy in Durham yesterday. The university there is a wide open avenue for the OxyContin."

"It won't matter if we're in prison."

"You worry too much."

"And you're letting success make you careless. I'm leaving." Liz heard a tapping sound as if Gerri clicked her polished nails on the phone. "With or without you."

"Where will you go?"

"The Caribbean. Island to island. No one will trace me there."

"Gerri, I—"

"You said you were ready to make a move. You said you loved me."

"Gerri, I—" He paused.

"Come with me. We'll take your new yacht. We'll catch lobster every day and skinny-dip after drinking margaritas on the deck at sunset. We'll dive for old silver coins, read murder mysteries, and sleep in the hammock in the afternoon." More tapping sounds. Gerri's voice turned even more whispery, dripping with seduction. "When we tire of lobster, we'll fish. We'll eat conch and shrimp and buy citrus at the markets. Remember the bananas in Jamaica?"

Liz felt her cheeks redden. When had Dave ever been to Jamaica?

Dave's voice softened. "Yes."

"The FBI is closing in, honey. This Manning guy isn't going away."

"Maybe the bumbling Serenity Police will keep him misinformed."

"Dave, I'm serious. It's time to make our move."

"You would leave without me?"

"Yes. I wouldn't want to, but yes." She hesitated. "I'm afraid to stay."

"OK, OK," he whispered.

"Let's leave now. I'll meet you at the dock. Most of my stuff is there already."

"I need a little time. I'll need to straighten some things at the office, go to the bank."

"When can you be ready?"

"I'll need to tell Liz my plans. I'm sure she knows it's coming."

Now I do, sugar daddy.

"When, baby?"

"Let's leave at midnight tomorrow."

"I'll write my resignation."

"I love you."

"Until tomorrow."

Liz waited until she heard the phone line click before hanging up the phone. *Just what were they talking about? OxyContin? Dr. Crawford?*

Her husband was in trouble. All she needed was a scandal and her public image would be lost. And if Dave left her, the money would stop.

So he was leaving town tomorrow?

She'd see about that.

CHAPTER
24

THE NEXT MORNING Travis dutifully picked up a tall Kenyan coffee laced with French vanilla creamer for his mom and bought the morning paper. What he read on the front page made him hurry his pace, spilling precious drops of coffee through the small opening in the safety cap. He dropped his bike in the driveway without bothering with the kickstand and ran up the front steps. The rumor his mother had heard yesterday at the hospital was true!

"Mom! Mom!"

He tore through the foyer into the kitchen where his mother sat on a bar-stool. She wore her long robe, and her hair was uncombed. "Quiet down, Trav. Your grandpa is still asleep." She rubbed her eyes with her right hand. Moving the left irritated the incision under her arm.

"Mom, you don't understand!" He plopped the paper on the counter in front of her.

"Where's my coffee?"

She sniffed the brew and popped off the cap. "Did you use the French vanilla creamer?"

He sighed. "Two little containers, just like always."

She ruffled his curls. "You're going to make some woman very happy someday."

"Mom, would you just look at the paper?"

She sipped her coffee. "Ummmm."

He watched as her eyes focused on the top story headline. Her eyes widened.

LOCAL SURGEON ARRESTED FOR MURDER

"What?"

They read the story together. The article was generously sprin-
kled with quotes from Serenity Chief of Police Samuel Harris, who
had personally made the arrest. The article claimed a key witness that
linked Adam Tyson to the body of Mark Crawford.

Travis smacked the paper. "You told me they arrested him for your
hit-and-run."

"That's what I thought. I figured he must have confessed." She
pinched the bridge of her nose. "I saw the police, but everything was
a bit cloudy. I was still in the recovery room. No one in the hospital
seemed to know what was going on, only that Adam, er, Andy had
been taken away in handcuffs."

"Why doesn't he just tell them who he is? He couldn't have murdered Dr. Crawford. He was in Florida."

His mom looked at the paper again and moaned. "I can't believe
this. Everything has gotten so messed up."

"Mr. Harris is crazy! Adam is innocent. He wouldn't kill
someone."

"Calm down, Trav. Mr. Harris isn't the brightest man I've ever
met, but he must have his reasons."

"I'm going down there! I'm going to talk to Mr. Harris."

"You'll do no such thing! It's not like your word is going to carry
a lot of weight down there. What Andy needs right now is a good
lawyer." She hesitated. "And our prayers." She pushed the paper
back and lifted her right arm to her chest. "Oooh. I think I stretched
something."

Travis hadn't even been thinking about his mother's surgery. He
felt a stab of guilt. "Oh, how do you feel? Are you in much pain?"

"Not much," she said, moving her left arm slowly. "As long as I
don't move too fast."

"When do you get the biopsy report?"

"Not for a week. Something about the radioactive tracer that was
injected for the lymph node biopsy. They have to wait before processing it."

She gently touched his arm. "If the lymph nodes are positive, it
will mean more surgery and chemotherapy."

He felt his stomach tighten. "Like dad?"

She nodded. "Not exactly."

He tried to smile. "At least your head has a nice shape if you go bald. Dad's had that flat spot."

His mother smiled. "I think he knew every bald joke in the book."

"How many bald guys does it take to screw in a lightbulb?"

"Don't get started."

He hesitated. "Dad would like the beach." He looked toward the back deck. "I miss him."

"Me too."

Travis plodded to the stove and opened the cabinet above it, selecting his standard sugar cereal. It was also his father's favorite: Cap'n Crunch. He selected a small mixing bowl that held easily double the amount of cereal a soup bowl could hold.

He poured the cereal and watched his mother's eyes roll. "What?" he protested. "Those wimpy bowls don't hold enough."

He quietly munched his breakfast. "Do you think you and Ad—uh, Andy will ever get together?"

"Get together?"

He didn't look up. "Get married."

"Married?"

"Yeah, you know, rings, a white dress, vows."

"Very funny." She swirled her coffee. "He's been wonderful to you. But there are issues."

He chewed without looking up. "Issues?"

"He lied to us, Trav. That's not exactly the kind of man we need."

"But he confessed, didn't he? You're always tellin' me that if I own up to something I did, you wouldn't mind so much."

"Not as much as if you didn't own up."

"He owned up, Mom."

Beth sighed. "You know what we need, Trav. A godly man, one who follows Christ." She set down her coffee. "Someone who isn't in jail."

"Mom!"

She smiled and slipped off her stool.

"What are we going to do about Andy?"

"Pray, Travis. That's all I want you to do. You will not go to the police." She picked up the paper. "Is that understood?"

"I guess—"

"Travis!"

"Yes, ma'am."

❧

Al Bell started his day with black Colombian coffee and a sincere prayer for wisdom. The case he'd been assigned was a complicated one. His client was guilty, but not of the crimes suspected. But getting him off the assortment of other misdeeds would take a legal manipulation of a monumental order. Carefully he weighed the facts on the yellow legal pad in front of him. Certainly it would help that the police had jumped the gun and accused him of murder. But he was guilty of hit-and-run, practicing medicine without a license, and insurance and Medicare fraud for billing under Tyson's unique Medicare provider number.

On the other hand, there had been no complaints from his patients, and Al was sure he could gather positive testimony from people Andy had treated. But that wouldn't go far enough to convince a judge to go easy. He needed something more.

And so he poured another cup of coffee and prayed some more. For Al, prayer was more than a stab-in-the-dark desperation. And it wasn't an afterthought or a last resort. For Al, who had been raised in a Southern Baptist church by a strong father with a smile as large as his spankings were firm, praying was the only way to start the day. Sure, he'd gotten away from the narrow path while he was in college, but his faith had been challenged and grown during law school when he found himself in the minority and on the defensive end of his faith.

"Help me know how to lead Mr. Cunningham," he prayed. "Give me insight and wisdom. And strengthen the bud of faith that has started to blossom in his life."

He straightened with a start. An idea was taking shape. What knowledge could Andy Cunningham have that could be of use to any of his accusers?

What if Andy could help deliver the real perpetrators of the drug trade and insurance fraud that were so likely to be tied up with the murder of Dr. Crawford?

The idea intrigued him. But it was so unlikely. But what if . . .

He walked to his bedroom, shed his wrinkled pajamas, and showered before putting on a three-piece suit. Today he might need to look like a real attorney.

He checked his watch and placed a call to Joe Smuland, a private investigator, the best and perhaps the only one on the Outer Banks.

"I need a favor," he said hurriedly into the phone. "I've got a client in some major trouble, and I think you might be able to help."

Al imagined Joe chewing slowly on the end of a stubby cigar, his feet propped up on an old desk. "You're calling early."

"I need help, Joe."

"I need coffee."

"You need to stop drinkin.'"

"That's beside the point. What's up, Al?"

"I need to find an FBI agent who's been looking into some Medicare fraud at Broward County Hospital."

"The feds are here? Is your client the doctor?"

"What do you know about it?"

"Just what I read in *The Outer Banks Daily*. Sounds like he's in some serious doo-doo."

Al wrinkled his nose at Joe's choice of words. "Whatever. Can you help?"

"How's the FBI going to help?"

Al was reluctant to spill his plan to the investigator. The fewer the people in on his plan, the better. "Let's just say I hope we can pay him a favor."

"What's his name?"

"Jim Manning."

"Where's he staying?"

"If I knew that, I wouldn't be calling you, would I?"

"I can find him. Then what?"

"Have him call me." He thought about Joe's priorities. "Today."

"In a rush, are we?"

"Let's just say my client has a secret or two that won't keep long."

"I'll see if I can work you in."

"Joe, I need more assurance than that."

"He'll call you within the hour. Will that do?"

Al took a deep breath. "That will do."

"You still owe me for the Mac job."

"I had Susan mail you a check weeks ago."

"Better talk to your staff. Maybe someone's skimmin' your profits."

"Very funny." He looked at his watch again. "I'll talk to you later."

"Later."

Click.

Al shook his head and set down his phone. Joe needed a lesson or two in etiquette, but his connections were unbelievable.

Al walked to the front hall, where he looked in the mirror to straighten his tie. It was time to get to lawyering.

∾

Jim Manning sighed with frustration. His only chance to break a big case seemed to be slipping through his fingers. That very morning, while eating breakfast at the Broward County Hospital cafeteria, he'd talked with Liz Winters about her husband Dave, who Jim was sure had something to do with setting up the Medicare fraud. It was then he learned that two of his suspects were getting ready to flee. But Liz couldn't tell him anything more. All she knew was that Jim was making Gerri Fiori awfully nervous, and she was sure her husband was involved with her in making a large amount of money.

Jim sipped hot coffee and made a few notes on a paper napkin. Liz was light on facts, heavy on suspicion. She'd overheard Gerri Fiori tell her husband she was afraid the police would figure out Mark Crawford's real killer. That didn't exactly make her or Dave Winters the guilty party, but why would an innocent bystander worry? And Dave Winters said he wanted to stay to get Dr. Tyson's billing up to speed. And in addition he mentioned a wide-open opportunity for OxyContin.

So not only was Manning on the verge of cracking a Medicare fraud case, but somehow the local drug problem and murder were lurking closely in the shadows. But where was the light to expose it all? And now Liz informed him that her husband was about to leave for a new life in the Caribbean.

He looked up to see the very couple he'd been thinking about. Dave Winters wore a three-piece suit and a big smile and Gerri Fiori on his arm. Evidently the secrecy about their relationship was over. Jim watched silently as they went through the line for their selections. They looked more like a couple on their honeymoon than serious hospital employees.

He checked his watch. "Great," he muttered into his steaming coffee. "These guys are fleeing the country in less than fifteen hours, and I have nothing but a handful of suspicions."

A few minutes later Dave Winters passed Jim's table, all smiles, slowing to rub salt in an already open wound. "Still hanging out looking for trouble, Mr. Manning?"

"It's the best breakfast spot in town, Mr. Winters," he said, meeting Winters's eyes. "I hear you're resigning your position."

"News travels fast."

"What are you running from?"

Winters smiled as Gerri approached. His eyes were hungry and drifted slowly over his new girlfriend. "I'm not running from anything." He lowered his voice. "Unless you count a dead-end relationship to a bitter woman."

"So what's the deal then? You think the Caribbean will offer new opportunities for OxyContin traffic?"

He studied Winters's response. There was a slight squinting of the eyes, a sure indication of surprise. And a hint that the next thing he spoke would be a lie. Winters forced a chuckle. "You are in left field."

"Am I?"

Gerri touched Winters's arm. "Let's go."

Jim took another stab, this one further into the dark. "And what about Dr. Crawford? Was he in left field when he threatened to expose your little fraud?"

Another twitch at the corner of Winters's eyes. And a tightening of his lips. But no verbal response.

Perhaps Manning had struck a mark. He decided to push Winters again. "Did you think you could silence him and get away with it?"

This time Gerri Fiori spoke up. "Just what are you implying? The police arrested his killer yesterday." She put her hand on her hip. "Or don't you read the paper?"

"Dr. Tyson hasn't been tried and found guilty. Other possibilities exist."

Winters rolled his eyes. "My eggs are getting cold," he said, stepping away from Jim's table.

Gerri smiled. "Do you have a business card, Mr. Manning? I'll send you a postcard."

"You do that." *It will make it easier for me to track you.* He handed her his card.

She accepted it without speaking and turned to follow Winters. "Ms. Fiori?"

She cast a glance over her shoulders without speaking.

"The problem with running away is that we can never escape ourselves."

She huffed and turned away again.

Jim nodded to himself. He could tell from their reactions that he was near the mark. He studied his napkin. He was missing something. He needed evidence.

And time was running out.

Why did everyone else in the department seem to be able to reel in the big cases, and he continued year after year following paper trails?

He looked up as an elderly couple bowed their heads in silence before eating their breakfast.

Maybe that's what I need.

Maybe it's time to pray. I suppose it couldn't hurt.

But it's been so long, I'm not sure I remember how.

He thought about his elementary school and Sunday school days. He sorted through "Now I lay me down to sleep" and the only phrase from the Lord's Prayer he could remember, "Give us this day our daily bread." *It's no use. God probably wouldn't recognize my voice after all these years.*

Just then he remembered what Reba Crawford had tearfully told him about her husband, how he had sat at the kitchen table next to an empty chair and prayed like he was talking to an old friend. He was just desperate enough to try. He looked around the room self-consciously. He slid back the chair next to him to accommodate an invisible listener. He raised his napkin to cover his mouth and whispered, "God, I need Your help. I need a break."

He closed his eyes and tried to concentrate, to discern any new thoughts about his case. Nothing. Nothing except a bright white image that came from rubbing his eyelids too hard with his fingers. This was crazy, the stuff of the pious elderly without a real life to live.

He felt a flush of embarrassment. What was he doing? He was an officer of the law, not a weak old man crying out for help.

He picked up his coffee, which had rapidly cooled to lukewarm. He was about to go for a refill when a sharply dressed man in a gray suit approached the table.

"Mr. Manning?"

Jim nodded without speaking.

The economy-sized man lifted his hand. "I'm Al Bell. I represent Adam Tyson. I think we might have an opportunity to help each other."

Jim lifted his eyebrows and looked at the chair, already pulled out to receive his visitor. "Have a seat," he said. "What's on your mind?"

∞

Two hours later, with the beginnings of a plan roughed in, agent Jim Manning sat across the desk from attorney Al Bell.

Jim stood and began to pace around the paneled office. The office wasn't plush, but certainly not neglected. A portrait of Thomas Jefferson hung behind Al's oak desk. A Persian rug covered a wooden floor. "I just had a thought."

"Are you OK? You look pale."

"I—I'm OK. Did it ever occur to you that your client might be lying to get out of trouble?"

"He's not exactly getting out of trouble."

"True, but hit-and-run and fraud carries a lot less time than murder."

"He couldn't have hatched such a scheme on his own."

"I've heard of stranger things. Psychopaths who lie through their teeth without even a hint of guilt."

Al held up his hand. "Chill out, Jim. I checked out his story with the city of Los Angeles. Adam Tyson, M.D. is dead and buried. I even pulled up an old newspaper obituary on the Internet." He handed a page to Jim.

"Well, I'll be." He chuckled. "This is all pretty scary, you know? You go to a guy with a serious illness and lie down under his knife, and all the while the guy's a total fraud, never even been to medical school."

"True enough. But I spent two hours last night on the phone, calling patients he told me could serve as references." He shrugged. "His patients think he walks on water. Even Beth Carlson. He basically saved her life."

"Yeah, right after he almost killed her."

"True enough, but that was an accident."

"OK, OK, let's say you convinced me. But it's going to take a lot more than a copy of an obituary to convince Samuel Harris he's arrested the wrong man."

"Here," he said, plopping a folder in front of Jim on his desk. "Andy gave me the keys to his home and told me where to find these."

Jim sorted through the papers. Al had arranged a driver's license, a birth certificate, a physician's assistant license, and a Social Security card as well as several old hospital IDs with Michael Andrew Cunningham's picture. "This doesn't look much like him."

"Take away the beard and you've got our man." He opened a college yearbook. "Look at this. Here's Andy playing baseball." He turned a few pages. "Here's his senior picture. Without the beard, but about fifteen years younger. It's got to be him."

"What makes you think the chief will go for this?"

"I'll give him the option of saying no. But if he does, I'll make it clear that the media will hear about his mistake in arresting my client, a poor, innocent man."

"That's blackmail."

"Not exactly. I'd prefer to think of it as the power of letting out the truth." He smiled. "Besides, if my little idea pans out, then I'll be sure he gets plenty of positive exposure for cooperating with us." He took back the college yearbook. "The key question is, if my client can help you solve the fraud case, will you see to it that the feds go light on him?"

"You'll still have to worry about the state officials. And there's always Chief Harris. I doubt he'll be agreeable to going easy on Andy for the hit-and-run. He might even try to go after him on assault charges."

"Assault?"

"He opened people with a knife, didn't he?"

"With their permission."

"But they wouldn't have given it if they'd known he didn't have the training. Harris isn't going to be easy on him."

"I'm going to have to make the chief realize it's in his own best interest. I'll have to make him look awfully good."

"How will you do that?"

"By giving him credit for solving the murder."

"I get it," Jim said nodding. "You help me sting Winters for fraud. You help the police by solving the murder." He sat down on a leather chair. "Where'd you learn to work out these deals?"

"From my brother."

"Your brother?"

Al smiled and pointed at a photo on the bookshelf beside his desk. "See that moose of a man standing next to me? That's Phil. He weighed three hundred and five pounds as a high school senior. He was an offensive lineman for the Nebraska Cornhuskers under Tom Osborne."

"So he could play football. How does that translate into learning to work out deals?"

"I couldn't outfight him. I had to outwit, out-negotiate, out-compromise him. Anything but fight."

Jim looked at the picture and laughed. "I wish he could go with us to see if Chief Harris will cooperate."

"He'd better."

"It's Andy Cunningham's only hope."

CHAPTER
25

CHIEF OF POLICE Samuel Harris was livid. Livid and loud. Livid, loud, and red-faced. "I can't believe you two would dare bring this kind of story into my office."

"But it's true," Jim said.

"And clearly documentable," Al added. "I can produce any number of people from Andy's past who will testify to his identity." He held up his hand and pointed to his fingers one by one as he counted off. "Past working associates, college and PA school classmates, an old girlfriend, a cousin or two. The truth has got to be accepted, Sam. Adam Tyson couldn't have murdered Dr. Crawford. Tyson was dead long before Crawford was."

"But I did arrest the right man, just for the wrong crimes. In fact, I think the list of forgeries, impersonations, fraud, and hit-and-run will have our state's attorney salivating over new ways to prosecute your client."

"I want you to release him."

"Release him?" Harris laughed.

"You heard me. You have no right to hold my client until you've gathered enough evidence for an arrest warrant."

"You said yourself that he'll confess to the hit-and-run."

Al held up his hands. "He will . . . in time. But for now we want him to continue to act as Dr. Adam Tyson."

"What?"

Agent Jim Manning leaned forward. "Just listen to our plan. I think it will be to your advantage to cooperate. You may even catch the real murderer of Mark Crawford."

"And how's that?"

"We think it's all tied together. Medicare fraud. OxyContin drug trade. The murder of Mark Crawford."

Serenity's police chief put his hand on his chin. "I don't understand. But I'm listening."

Al stood and paced as he explained his plan. Jim added details, citing the evidence he had gathered during his Medicare fraud investigation. Finally he summed up the scheme. "If the real killers think we're on to them, they may make a move that reveals themselves."

"You're asking me to let an impostor continue to operate on unsuspecting—"

"He won't be allowed to operate any longer."

"How do I explain letting him go?"

Jim looked at Al. "What do you think? Say he made bail?"

"Or just say he had a lock-tight alibi. The media will usually believe anything you say in a press release."

"How can I be sure he won't run?"

"It will be part of the deal. I'll promise he won't run if you'll go light on his sentence."

"I'll think about trying to get the judge to go light on his sentence if you help me solve the murder of Mark Crawford. But it's not just up to me. We'll have to talk to the state's attorney to see if he'll agree to this little bargain of yours." He paused. "And I doubt he'll want to go too easy on a man who has lied to so many. People could have been killed."

"But people were helped. He may not be licensed, but my client does excellent work. I'm sure I can line up a number of OR nurses and referring physicians who are willing to testify to that end."

"Talk to the prosecution. If they agree, I'll cooperate."

"We have to move fast. We think Dave Winters is involved in all this, and he's about to skip town with Gerri Fiori in his new yacht."

Sam raised his bushy eyebrows. "Gerri Fiori? The nurse?"

"The one and only. Do you have anything on her?"

"Nothing I can prove. One of the kids we busted for OxyContin possession claimed he heard kids talking about buying the drugs from a woman who rode a Harley. She's the only woman who drives a

Harley around here." He folded his hands on his desk. "We watched her for a while. She seems whistle-clean."

"Liz Winters overheard her husband talking to Gerri about an opportunity for OxyContin over in Durham. I'll bet Gerri's involved."

Al was starting to sweat. "We don't have much time. Will you let my client go?"

The chief leaned back in his chair. "Talk to the state's attorney. If he's willing to bargain, I'll bargain." He pointed to a phone on his desk. "Just push line 4. It will patch you right into Peter Brentwood's office."

Al ran his fingers through his thinning hair. "I hope this works. For Andy's sake, I sure hope so."

∽

That evening, just before supper, a knock came at the door of Beth Carlson. "Travis, will you get that?"

"It's Andy, it's Andy!"

Beth heard the door open and the commotion as Andy and Travis embraced in a bear hug.

Beth couldn't believe her eyes. "What's going on here?"

Andy smiled. "I busted out. I just had to see you guys."

She put her hands on her hips. "What!"

"Sit down. I was only kidding." He lifted his nose in the air. "What's that great smell?"

"It's a chicken and broccoli casserole."

Travis slapped Andy's back. "Can he stay, Mom?"

Beth studied her son for a moment. He seemed to have forgotten the lies Andy lived. "Uh—"

"I really didn't come to invite myself to dinner."

"We've got plenty," Travis offered.

Andy's eyes met Beth's. She held up her hands. "Sure, why not? Stay."

"How are you feeling since surgery?"

"I'm fine," she snapped. "Now will you tell me what you're doing out of jail?"

"I've got a great attorney." He paused. "He's a brother too. He's been praying for me."

Beth lifted her head and studied him before looking at Travis, who just shrugged his shoulders. "Slow down. A brother?"

Andy couldn't seem to keep a broad silly grin off his face. "You know, brother in Christ." He returned Beth's gaze. "I've never been in so much trouble in my life. And I've never been happier."

Just then Ike crept up the hall. "Sounds like someone's cheese has slid off his cracker."

Beth shook her head. "I don't think so, Daddy." Then, to Andy, she asked, "What's happened to you?"

"I'm a believer now, Beth." He held out his hands, palms up, and looked at Ike. "I guess all that stuff you've been feedin' me took root."

"When? How?"

"In jail," he said, slowly shaking his head. "I guess I should have been at my lowest. But what you did finally convinced me." He paused. "I prayed yesterday morning before going to turn myself in. It was nothing big. Basically just a cry for help." He started pacing, obviously too excited to sit. "And you know what happened. You showed up for surgery. And I guess that practically blew my mind. I thought after what I'd done you'd be the first in line to lock me up and throw away the key."

"Andy—" Beth started.

"But you didn't. You trusted me in spite of knowing who I really was." He turned to the back deck overlooking the ocean. "And it sparked a hope in me—a faith that God really can love unconditionally. I was sitting in a locked room at the police station. Alone for hours. But I started thinking about my prayer, and how you trusted me, and—I don't know how to explain it really. I— I—well, my heart just kind of melted," he said, looking back at the trio standing in the center of the den. "I was crying. I just knew I was different. Forgiven."

"All right!" Travis shouted. "All right!"

"It's crazy-sounding, I know. I should have been at my lowest, but suddenly I just knew that everything you'd been telling me about God's love was really true. I just believed it." He started chuckling. "The Chief of Police thought I'd gone bonkers. When he showed up with my attorney, I was a mess." He laughed. "It was the first time I'd cried since I could remember."

Ike walked over and placed his arms around Andy's shoulders. "Welcome."

Travis put his arms around them both. "I knew you'd come around."

Beth cleared her throat. "But that doesn't explain what you're doing here."

"I wanted to share the news."

Beth stood back. "Andy, how did you get out of jail?"

"Don't call me that," he said, walking over to a kitchen bar-stool. "It's part of my release deal. I still have to live my life as Adam Tyson for a few more days."

Now they were all confused. "What?"

Andy looked over his shoulder toward the oven. "Is that stuff about ready? I'm starved. Jail grub ain't much in Serenity, I'm tellin' ya."

Beth sighed. "Yes, it's about ready. But what about the story?"

"I'll tell you over dinner."

CHAPTER
26

AFTER SUPPER, TRAVIS twisted his mother's arm to let him go up to the Seagull Inn to look for sharks' teeth with Kristy. He ran most of the way up the beach, until he was winded and starting to sweat. At which point, in a moment of adolescent anxiety, he wondered if he'd remembered to put on any antiperspirant. He hadn't started to sweat much yet, at least not like his dad used to, but if anyone could bring out the sweat, it was Kristy. And being with her was not exactly the time he wanted to start smelling like a real man.

He put his nose under his arm and sniffed. Safe so far. But it didn't smell flowery like the deodorant his mother had bought him. He must have forgotten.

Andy's news had him busting at the seams. He knew he wasn't supposed to tell anyone, but he couldn't keep this from Kristy, could he? After all, she wouldn't tell. Her father was a pastor.

He found her hanging out just beyond the fishing pier, just like she'd said. She smiled and took his hand. "Hi, Trav."

"Hey."

"What's with the big grin?"

"Andy, uh, er, Adam Tyson became a Christian."

"Trav, that's so cool. Now he and your mom can get together."

"Maybe."

"What do you mean maybe?"

"Did you read the paper? He's in a lot of trouble."

"Do you think he killed that doctor?"

Travis shook his head. "Can you keep a real secret?"

She dropped his hand. "Of course."

He looked around. "You can't tell a soul, OK?"

"Travis!"

"Kristy, I'm serious. If word gets out that I told someone this, I could be in a ton of trouble."

She started walking down the beach. "I said I can keep a secret." She glanced over her shoulder. "Don't you trust me?"

"Ugh!" He jogged to catch up. "Of course I trust you, it's just— well, uh, this is just such incredible stuff that it's going to be really hard not to tell it, that's all."

"What could be so incredible? Dr. Tyson became a Christian. That's not the secret, is it? 'Cause if it is, it's a stupid one. You're not supposed to keep that sort of thing a secret."

"That's not the secret, OK?"

She turned and faced him, her hands on her hips. It was the first time he'd seen her mad, other than in small spats with her little sister. "Are you going to tell me, or am I going to have to strangle you?"

Travis put his index finger on his temple. "Hmmm. Strangle me, huh? That might be fun. But first you'll have to catch me."

He ran down the beach and had traveled thirty yards in record time before he realized she hadn't taken chase. And he was sweating again. And breathing hard. He sniffed at his underarm nonchalantly. Relieved not to be smelling too manly, he sauntered back toward Kristy, who had plopped down in the sand and was staring at the surf. "I've decided to let you strangle me."

"Trav, stop the games! It's not fair to tell me you have a secret and then not tell me."

He sat beside her in the sand. "Adam Tyson's been dead for six months."

"What?"

Travis looked around nervously. "Keep your voice down, would ya?"

She shrugged. "Sorry. But I don't understand."

"Just listen—"

"OK, but—"

He put a finger in her face. "And don't interrupt."

She nodded silently.

"The guy we all know as Adam Tyson is really Michael Cunningham, the driver of the car that hit my mom."

"What!"

He whispered, "Kristy, keep it down."

She winced. "Sorry."

"Michael Andrew Cunningham goes by the name Andy. He never liked his first name, I guess. Anyway, he learned a whole lot about operating from this Dr. Tyson. So when Tyson died, Andy looked for other jobs and finally ended up here, posing as a real surgeon, with all of Dr. Tyson's credentials."

"I'll bet your mom's ready to deck him."

Travis shook his head. "Not really. I think she likes him."

"But he operated on her. Twice! And he's not a real surgeon."

"Mom says he's a real surgeon, but not one who has any paper credentials."

"Then he's not a real surgeon, Trav."

"Whatever." He lifted up a handful of sand and let it slowly start to fall between his fingers. "Anyway, he finally confessed his scheme to Mom before her surgery. That's the part I'm not real sure about. Mom didn't just come right out and say it, but I think he must have told her he loved her and wanted to be honest with her about who he really was."

"How romantic."

"Whatever."

"Travis, how can you just say, 'whatever' to something like that. A man revealing his inmost secrets to the woman he loves just so he can be open with her—that's romantic." She smiled. "No wonder she likes him."

"I think she's pretty upset with him for foolin' us over who he was and all."

"But it is romantic to think he confessed it all to her because of love."

"Whatever. The part about him being a pitcher in college was true. I think that's pretty cool."

She imitated him. "Whatever."

"He still might be in deep trouble. 'Cause now even though he's kind of off the hook for murdering Dr. Crawford—"

"Slow down. How'd he get off the hook?"

"As Michael Cunningham, he has a ton of alibis because he was in Florida when Dr. Crawford was killed."

"Oh."

"Anyway, so now the police want him for mom's hit-and-run, impersonating a doctor or something like that, and some other stuff I don't even understand, stuff that's illegal for pretending to be something he wasn't or whatever."

"Wow."

"But his lawyer has worked out a deal to try to get him a softer sentence if he can help catch the real bad guys. Andy says the FBI has been investigating the hospital, and specifically a guy named Winters, and that woman who drives a Harley, Gerri Fiori. The feds think they are involved in Dr. Crawford's murder as well as some drug deals and some sort of insurance fraud."

"How's he going to catch them?"

"By continuing to pose as Dr. Tyson, I think. He's going to try to find out what's going on at the hospital from the inside." He dropped the remaining sand from his hand. "The thing is, this dude Winters and the Harley nurse are supposedly running off tonight on his yacht. The FBI thinks they are pulling out because they are getting too close to getting caught."

"That lady that drives the Harley lives right down from your place. I've seen her in her bikini waxing her cycle in her driveway."

"My neighbor Bart told me that his brother got some drug called OxyContin from some guy named Timmy that said a woman on a Harley sold it to him."

"It's got to be her," Kristy said, wrinkling her nose. "She looks evil. She gives me the creeps. It's like she thinks she's all that."

"I'm worried about Andy. If he can't help break this case open, he's going to be facing a lot of years in prison."

They sighed together and looked at the ocean. Travis looked down, and Kristy's hand was lying on the sand beside him, palm up. He kept looking straight ahead and slowly moved his hand toward hers. When they touched on the side, Kristy slid her hand under his and let their fingers intertwine. Travis was in heaven.

After a few minutes, Kristy looked over at him. "Trav? I think we should help Andy. My dad says it's better to act than sit on your butt worrying."

His eyes widened. "He said that?"

"Well, he didn't actually use the *b* word. He's way too proper for that. I think he said, 'backside.'" She giggled.

"My mom says 'booty.'"

That made Kristy laugh harder.

"She's always yelling at me after bedtime. 'You'd better get that booty in bed before I come up there.'"

Kristy snickered until a little white piece of spit hit Travis right on the nose. And that caused her to laugh all the more.

Travis wiped his nose with his one free hand and studied the girl who now had tears in her eyes.

"Oh, Travis," she laughed. "I'm so sorry."

He looked back at the ocean. "Forget it."

"I love your mother. She's so funny. My mother would never say 'booty.'"

"What does she say?"

"She says 'bottom' to my little sister and 'gluteus' to me."

Kristy sighed. "I'm serious about helping Andy. It sounds like time is running out for him."

"What can we do?"

"Maybe we can find out if the Harley lady is really selling drugs."

"Oh, right. Like we're just gonna go ask her or something?"

She raised her eyebrows. "Something like that."

"What do you have in mind?"

"Do you have a video camera?"

"Yeah." He squinted at her. "You're scarin' me."

"Oh, stop it, Travis. This is serious."

"OK, OK, I'm all ears."

"We can trap her selling drugs. We'll get it on tape. Then we'll give the tapes to Mr. Harris."

"How are we going to do that?"

She stood up. "I'll explain it to you later. The sun's going to set soon, so unless she's got a bright porch-light, we'd better try to do this before dark."

Travis followed as she started up the beach, heading for the Seagull Inn. "I'll go get the video camera."

"Cool," she said calmly. "Meet me on your bike at the Inn in ten minutes. We can plan the next step then."

∽

Dave Winters expected some negative reaction from Liz, but she wasn't giving him the satisfaction. At least he wanted her to appear sad or angry that he was leaving her, but she wouldn't let him have an ounce of gratification. Instead she listened quietly to his explanation that they'd grown apart, that they needed to go their separate ways so their individual growth wouldn't be stunted. Their marriage had been an empty form for some time, devoid of the love they used to share. He was thankful for the time they'd had. But now it was time to move on, walk their own paths. He would make sure she was taken care of.

With the last statement, he noticed a twitch of her left eye. Maybe she was listening after all. He paced back and forth and told her how he'd been the one to cause the marriage to fail, that he was incapable of dedication to work and the marriage. He wasn't worthy of her. He was stunting her growth. She was being smothered in his shadow. It was time for her bud to flower.

He studied her as she sat motionless on the side of the bed they'd shared. Maybe she was in shock. This may have been harder on her than he feared. She was evidently devastated, sitting there in silence. He'd heard of cases like this, where a state of catatonia overtakes a person who experiences an extreme trauma, a sort of post-traumatic stress syndrome or some such psychobabble.

She blinked once, twice; so he decided to continue. He'd stop if she clutched her chest or stopped breathing.

"I'm sure this will work out for the best. We can even still be friends. Remember the Hudsons? He still changes the oil on Doris's car even though they're divorced. And the Cooleys? They go out to eat together more now than when they were married. And the Thompsons even have sleepovers. But they're free to see others, and their professional and emotional lives aren't cramped by the needless boundaries of marriage."

"Are you finished yet? You don't have to convince me."

He looked up, surprised. She had been listening.

She lifted her purse from the nightstand and retrieved a business card. "This is my attorney. I'll accept communication only through him."

"Wh-what?" He looked at the card, recognizing the name of the law firm, reputed to be the most vicious and successful defenders of women in getting money out of rich husbands. "You've already retained an attorney?"

"Of course." She kept her voice steady and at a normal volume when she added, "And it will take a considerable sum to keep my mouth zipped about your extra income."

The words found their mark. A vise began to tighten around his chest, squeezing his breath into short gasps. "I don't know what you're talking about."

"A half-million dollars. Transferred from your secret account into a new account under my name."

"What?"

"That's what it will take to keep me from telling everything to the police."

"Telling what?"

"Don't make me enumerate your crimes. Don't think I haven't enjoyed all the gifts, but I know all about your little scheme with Ms. Fiori."

He squinted his eyes at his wife. He'd never expected a hard fight. He'd wanted a reaction, yes, but not this. He had no idea his wife knew anything. "Tell me what you know. Or what you think you know," he bluffed. "You don't know anything."

"Maybe I should call the police and just tell them while you're here, so you can hear just what I know."

"You wouldn't."

"Five hundred thousand dollars, Dave. And not a penny less."

"You're insane."

"You're a thief."

He shook his head. "This is too much. I don't have that kind of money."

"How much was your new yacht? Seven, eight million?" She

stood up to walk away. "And how much does it cost to spend the rest of your life lounging on the deck of your boat sailing the Caribbean?"

"How do you—" He put his hand on her shoulder and spun her around. "You won't get away with this. This is blackmail."

"Call it whatever you want."

"You won't make the call. You've loved the money too much."

She stepped toward the phone and lifted the receiver. "Shall I tell them about the OxyContin too?"

"What? How . . . ?"

"You can't hide from the law. If I don't see the money transferred into my account within twenty-four hours, I'll go to the police. And when they find out how much money you have, they will track you to the ends of the earth."

He couldn't control his anger. He lifted his hand.

"Do that and I won't settle for anything less than seven hundred and fifty thousand dollars."

He cursed her. "You can't get away with this."

"Get out."

"You—"

"I'll see you in court, Mr. Winters." She walked to the door, then turned to face him, her body silhouetted by the light in the hallway. "Or in jail, if I don't get my money in twenty-four hours." She looked at her watch. "I'll give you an hour to get out."

She left him alone and wounded on the bed. He felt like calling Gerri, but he didn't have the time. The nurse was right. Things were getting hot in Serenity. It was time to leave. He took a deep breath and blew it out through pursed lips before he looked at himself in the mirror. This was not on his radar screen. How did his wife know all this?

The phone chirped. He looked at it and muttered, "Probably Liz's attorney."

He lifted the phone from its cradle. "Dave Winters."

"Mr. Winters, this is Dr. Adam Tyson."

He jerked his head up. "Dr. Tyson?" he gasped. "Where are you?"

"I'm a free man."

"What?"

"I need to meet you. We need to talk."

"I—well, I'm kind of busy."

"It's to your advantage to talk to me. I can help you."

"Look, I have a very busy schedule. I—"

"I know all about it. And I know you're about to leave. But don't do it. If you think things were good with Crawford, they can be doubly good with me."

He felt his jaw slacken. He stared at the phone. How did he know this? "How did you get out of jail?"

"It's a long story. Bottom line is, the charges have been dropped. The Serenity Police force is pretty inept."

"Well, I—"

"And that's in our favor, because we can continue your little insurance scheme for a long time and they will never know."

He shook his head, incredulous. "What do you know?"

"Meet me in your office."

He sighed. "Look, I'm leaving town. I've resigned my position at the hospital."

"They will hire you back in a second. You know that. The hospital was in deep trouble before they hired you. Now they are profitable."

"I've got plans."

"Change them. Meet me in your office. I can make it worth your while."

"I don't have time."

"You need money? I can help."

He shook his head. This was too weird. "When?"

"Now."

∞

Liz Winters walked slowly down the hall, then hurried her pace to a near sprint, or as close to a sprint as she'd come in the last five years. She crossed the living room with its oriental rug, oil paintings, antiques, and her favorite vase, a nineteenth-century original. She scurried around a leather ottoman and stopped short of running into the front door. Then she quietly exited the house and dashed across the lawn and down the sidewalk to the corner where a blue Ford Taurus was parked.

She slowed, and the window opened as she approached. Jim Manning smiled. "Well done. Are you sure you haven't done this before?"

She smiled. "I acted in a play in junior high once."

"You were brilliant. I think he's worried. He might be scared enough to reveal what I need to know when he talks to Dr. Tyson."

She slipped off her light jacket and turned around to allow the agent to remove a small wire from the back of her blouse.

She turned around and winked, surprising herself. She hadn't done anything remotely flirtatious for years.

He smiled and thanked her again. "Go back to your house. And don't worry, you've done the right thing."

She walked slowly back toward the house she shared with her husband. She suddenly felt like crying, but at the same time strangely exhilarated. There would be time for tears later. Now she wanted to put a stone face forward to face Dave again. She could have a good cry later.

She pushed her shoulders back and lifted her head before pushing open the front door.

Yes, she would cry later. Now she needed to be strong.

∞

Forty-five minutes later Travis and Kristy crouched behind a short board-slat fence across the street from Gerri Fiori's place. The fence stood about six feet tall and was designed to hide the trash cans from view. Travis looked out between the slats at the front porch across the street and focused the video camera before looking back at Kristy. "You know, I think you look pretty good the way you're dressed."

"What do you mean, 'pretty good'?"

"You know—"

"Say it, Travis."

He blushed. "I can't."

"Say it," she said politely, "or I'll strangle you."

"That's what you said earlier and you didn't do it."

"Travis!"

"OK," he said quietly. "You look hot."

"I know. I'm supposed to look older this way."

Travis shook his head. "Did your mom see you?"

"Are you kidding? She'd probably fall down on her bottom if she saw me this way."

Travis snickered, then studied the innocent girl he thought he knew. She was wearing red lipstick, blue eye shadow, large hoop earrings, and a pair of short blue jeans.

"Are you ready?" she whispered.

"What if someone sees me down here?"

"There's no one home here. They are probably down at the beach."

"But what if they come back?"

"Look, do you want to help Andy out or not?"

"Sure, I do, but—"

She shushed him and started across the street, walking up the driveway and sidewalk slowly, swaying with attitude. She knocked on the door.

Behind her, Travis zoomed in. He hoped he could pick up the sounds on the tape.

The door opened. Gerri Fiori was standing there holding a grocery bag. "Can I help you?" Her voice was faint but plain.

"Timmy told me I might find you at home."

"I don't know anyone named Timmy."

Kristy put her hands on her hips and chewed her gum with her mouth open. "I think you do. You sold him some stuff I want."

Gerri squinted and leaned forward. "How old are you, kid?"

"Doesn't matter."

"It does to me."

"I don't want to use it. I want to sell it."

"Sell it?"

"OxyContin."

"You're too young. Get out of here."

"I'm perfect for this, Ms. Fiori," she said, smacking her lips. "The police never look at me twice. I've sold stuff right under their noses and they think I'm just a sweet little schoolgirl."

"You'll have to find someone else. I'm moving out."

The door started to close, but Kristy blocked it with her foot. "Come on! Just this once. I'll make it worth your while. I can get you ten bucks a tablet."

The door started to close again. "Twenty!"

The door slowly opened. "Twenty?"

Kristy nodded. "I can sell it for twenty-five or thirty and still make a profit."

"My stuff isn't here."

"I don't need much. I want to make the deal right now."

"Don't get snotty, kid." Gerri ran her hand through her hair. "I'll tell you what. Meet me at the Soundside Yacht Club at 10:30." She smiled thinly, right toward the camera.

For a moment Travis thought she must have seen him, because she appeared to be primping for the camera. His heart caught in his throat.

Gerri looked at Kristy. "Your mommy does let you out that late, doesn't she?"

"She won't care." Kristy hesitated. "Don't you have anything you can sell me here? I'm on my way to a party. I'm sure I can score a sale."

"You don't listen well, do you? I'll see you at the Soundside Yacht Club at 10:30, OK?"

Kristy took a step back. "OK."

"Go to a large white yacht parked in the second slip. It's called *Bliss*."

"How original."

Gerri didn't smile. Or say good-bye. The door simply shut in Kristy's face.

Travis turned off the camera and was about to straighten up when a car pulled in and stopped in the driveway right beside him. A tall, muscular man jumped out and stared in Travis's direction. "What's that you've got there?" he said, looking at Travis's hand. "Hey, that's a camera. What are you doing?"

"Uh, hello, sir," Travis said, pointing the camera in his direction. "I'm conducting a little research for a school project on Serenity's compliance with the new recycling regulations." He popped the lid off the nearest garbage can and swung the camera down to inspect its contents. "See these aluminum cans, sir? These are supposed to go in the blue recycling bin provided by the city. And these newspapers belong in the green one." He pointed the camera back at the man, who was now backing away from Travis. "A recent study revealed that the United States wastes enough aluminum to build an aircraft carrier. Could I have your name for my study, sir?"

The man covered his face. "I don't think so," he said, retreating into his garage and shutting the door.

Travis took a deep breath.

"Pssst!"

He looked over to see Kristy peering around the end of the fence. "Let's get out of here!"

They ran for their bikes, which they had abandoned at Travis's home several doors down. "That was close," he said, panting.

The stress erupted in laughter for both of them. Kristy covered her mouth. "I can't believe you told that guy you were doing research!"

"I panicked," he gasped, bending over and resting his hands on his knees.

"Aircraft carriers aren't made of aluminum."

They burst into laughter again.

In a few minutes they sat on the front steps and backed up the tape, watching it on a small screen pulled out from the side of the camera. "It will be clearer on the TV monitor. It's too grainy here."

"It doesn't matter, Trav. The police won't arrest her just for this. They need to see drugs exchanged for money. And it will be too late at 10:30 to get good film."

He sighed. "So now what?"

She thought for a moment before responding. "I'll go make the purchase. But we have to make sure the police will be there to see it."

"Like Mr. Harris will agree to let a fifteen-year-old buy drugs in a sting."

"He won't know. I won't tell him."

"How are you going to sneak out?"

"I'll think of something." She slipped her hand easily into his. "It'll be easy since my room is different than my parents'. They're boring. They're in bed every night by 10."

"Tonight they'd better get their booties in bed by 10!"

"Travis!"

They laughed again. "Hey, my mom says it, not me."

"But going to the Yacht Club is only part of the plan. We've got to find out how Mr. Winters plays into all this."

"How? You want to ask him for drugs?"

"Maybe. Or better yet, just tail him. If he is involved with Ms. Fiori in this drug stuff, she might go to the hospital to meet him."

"He's probably at home by now."

She shrugged. "Probably. So ride your bike around his subdivision. Try to follow him if he goes anywhere."

"Like I can follow him on my bike."

"He'll never suspect you're following him."

"He'll lose me."

"You'll be able to tell if he goes to the hospital. If he does, follow him in to see whether he meets with Ms. Fiori." She smiled. "Then you'd better get home and get your gluteus up to bed!"

"Stop it," he said, feigning a frown. "That sounds so gross."

"It's just medical talk."

"That's why it's gross. They talk Latin to make the rest of us feel stupid."

The porch-light went on. Kristy turned away from the light. "I'd better not let your mother see me like this. She won't let you hang out with me if I wear so much makeup."

"You'd better worry about your own mother." He walked over to his bike. "I'll ride with you to the Inn. Then I'll head to the hospital to see if I can find this Winters dude."

He followed behind her on the bike path beside the road. The sun was beginning to set, and her strawberry hair looked lovely in a mature sort of way. Not just pretty like a little girl. This one was a real catch. Lively. A woman with a plan. Travis liked that.

"You're going awful fast, Kristy."

"I need to get back before my mom comes up from the beach. She was going to watch the sunset with my dad."

Travis pedaled faster and smiled at his own thoughts. *She's a good catch all right. But a difficult one. I'm not sure I can keep up with her at this pace.*

∽

Greg hoisted another slice of pepperoni pizza from the box and looked at Dan. "Hey," he said, gesturing with his free hand, "as long as the boss is making us work late, I might as well enjoy it."

"I don't know how you do it. You must eat twenty-four hours a day. If I did that, I'd have to waddle to work."

Sam Harris burst through the door and poured a cup of black coffee without speaking.

Dan raised his eyebrows at Greg, then asked, "Is it true, boss? Did you let Dr. Tyson go? Did he make bail or something?"

Sam mumbled something under his breath about the feds. "I had to. The prosecuting attorney talked to Judge Bailey. I think they were afraid of being sued or something."

Greg inhaled the pizza. "Sued? We have a witness. He paid to have that body dumped! If he wasn't guilty, why'd he do that?"

The chief walked to his desk and sat down. "Boys, what I'm about to tell you doesn't leave this room."

The deputies looked at each other and shrugged. "Of course, boss. What's this all about?"

"Adam Tyson isn't who you think he is. The man who's been masquerading as a surgeon is no surgeon at all. It's Michael Cunningham, the PA who used to work for Dr. Tyson."

The deputies leaned forward. "What?"

"It's true. The real Adam Tyson is dead. Michael Cunningham just took his credentials and opened up his own shop."

"No way."

"It's true. I've seen all the identification papers. Cunningham isn't dumb. Evidently he learned enough as a PA to pass as a real surgeon. And he thought a small town like Serenity would be the perfect place to pull it off."

"Why'd you let him go?"

"Cunningham's attorney put the pressure on. He threatened to make the department regret they'd arrested his client for a crime someone else had committed. And he had too many alibis to make the accusation stick."

Greg moaned. "We'll end up looking like jerks."

"The FBI has agreed to go easy on him if he helps solve their fraud case."

Greg scoffed. "Go easy? That guy has been nothing but trouble since he got here."

Sam nodded. "Really. I don't care if the feds feel like going easy on this guy. He came in here acting so cocky, like he saved Ms. Carlson's life, and all along he's the guy that almost killed her."

"His whole life is a sham."

"They might want to plea-bargain, but I didn't give any written agreements to hand out any favors. Even if he isn't a murderer, I can nail his butt for practicing medicine without a license, forgery, and hit-and-run." He chuckled. "Heck, I'll bet the state's attorney and I can dig up half a dozen crimes he's guilty of."

Dan stood up and picked up a piece of pizza of his own. Diets to the wind. He always ate when he was excited. "I don't get it. He's probably still guilty. And not just hit-and-run, boss. He has even more of a reason to bump off Dr. Crawford to make an opening in the perfect small town to practice. A real surgeon wouldn't need to do that to get a job."

The wrinkles in Sam's forehead deepened. "Huh?"

"I'll bet he's been planning this ever since the real Dr. Tyson started to chill." Dan shoved a generous bite of pizza into his mouth and wiped his chin with the back of his hand. "Don't you get it, chief?" he mumbled between chews. "Michael Cunningham hired a drifter to dispose of the body when he was posing as Adam Tyson." Dan started pacing. "It's adding up, boss. He told Timmy he was Adam Tyson because it wouldn't make sense that anyone else would be needing a cadaver."

Greg nodded his head. "It was consistent with his story."

The chief ran his fingers through his thinning, gray hair. "Oh boy."

"Michael Cunningham probably stored the body away after doing a quick job, then left the city, suspecting the body would be discovered long before he turned up in town to assume his role as a surgeon."

Samuel Harris slammed his fist down on the desk, sending the pizza box to the floor. Greg hurriedly picked up the remaining piece of pepperoni pizza that flew from the box. He blew across the surface and shrugged before attacking the point of the triangle.

"I hadn't thought about it that way," Harris responded. "Cunningham's attorney just sat there like it was obvious I'd made the biggest blunder of my life in arresting a man who'd been dead for six months."

"I'll bet he's going to run," Dan said. "He'll be in the Caribbean before tomorrow morning."

"His attorney guaranteed he'd stay around."

Greg retrieved a long string of mozzarella from his chin. "I don't get it. You could have still held him for the hit-and-run."

"But the feds want to use him in a sting to settle some Medicare fraud case. They claim millions of government dollars have been paid out for procedures never performed right here at our hospital. They wanted him released with the agreement that we wouldn't reveal his true identity." He paused and started pacing behind Dan, following a path from coffeemaker to copy machine to the door, stepping over the pizza box and back to the desk. "I knew that FBI agent was trouble as soon as he came in here. He seems to think he can settle our little murder, solve his fraud case, and make a dent in the OxyContin problem at the same time."

Dan drained the last of the black coffee into a styrofoam cup. "What does the FBI know about Serenity? They need to stay out of our way and let us take care of our own crimes."

Greg nodded and swallowed, then thumped his chest with his fist until he belched. "Excuse me, boss. Thanks for the pizza. Dan's right, Sam. We know this community. We shouldn't let some fancy attorney and a federal agent run our investigation."

Dan tapped his foot. "Since when did anything helpful come out of the federal government?"

Sam sat back down and put his face in his hands. "I can't believe how messed up this is." He sighed. "I wish you two had been in on the discussions with Cunningham's attorney. To be honest with you, everything seemed a little bit different when he explained it to me."

Dan sipped his coffee. "That's his job, Sam. They spend all day sitting around figuring out how to twist words into meaning something other than what they really mean. Before they're done, there is so much smoke and mirrors that no one can see the truth."

"Now we really are going to look stupid. I've released Michael Cunningham back into society to continue his charade." He shook his head. "The media is going to have a fit."

"So what do we do?"

"We've got to solve this problem quickly so the public can maintain their confidence in us."

Samuel Harris stood up. "Dan, I want you to get over to Adam Tyson—er, Michael Cunningham's place. Tail him. But don't let him see you." He paused, picking up the pizza box. "Greg, head over to the hospital. Watch for Mr. Winters. The FBI is convinced he has something to do with the fraud at the hospital and that he's getting ready to flee Serenity with Gerri Fiori on his new yacht."

Greg's eyes lit up. "Gerri? How's an old guy like Winters get a babe like that?"

Dan slapped Greg's chest with the back of his hand. "Stop slobbering. It's all about money."

"Not on the beach," he said, puffing his chest out. "The women don't care how much money you have when you look like this."

"Do you do free weights?" Dan rubbed his own biceps and frowned.

Greg shook his head. "Bow Flex."

"Really? You ordered it from the TV ad?"

"Sure. Only twenty minutes three times a week."

"Did you get the free video?"

"Yep. It came with an abdominizer too. I want to get one of those electric ab stimulator jobs so I can hook it up when I'm on patrol."

"Really?"

"Guaranteed six-pack abs in eight weeks or your money—"

The chief stood up and screamed, "Would you guys focus? I don't care about Bow Flex, abdominizers, or six-packs!"

The duo winced. "Sorry."

Sam pointed at Dan. "Tail Cunningham. Make sure he doesn't run. If you see anything, and I mean *anything* suspicious, I want him arrested again. We still have our warrant for an arrest for murder."

"What about Winters? What if he tries to leave with Ms. Fiori?"

"See if you can look around his yacht. Try to detain him long enough to see what he's up to. Maybe you can bore him to death talking about Bow Flex."

Sam pointed to the door. "Get to it, men. We've got to work fast if we're going to save our department from looking like total idiots."

CHAPTER
27

TWENTY MINUTES LATER Samuel Harris took a damp washcloth and a can of Lysol and started cleaning his desk of pizza grease. Every time he splurged to feed the gang, he remembered why he didn't like to do it. The seat of one chair and, thanks to his own fit of frustration, half the floor was covered with a fine dusting of Parmesan cheese. He lifted the coffeepot and scowled. The handle was slippery with grease.

Just as he finished wiping it down, the phone jangled.

He cleared his throat and immediately slipped into his police voice, one notch lower and two notches louder than the one he used with his children. "Serenity Police. Chief Harris speaking."

After a hesitation, a timid voice cracked. It was female. Probably a teenager. The volume was low but grew as the first sentence came to an end. "Listen up, Mr. Harris. If you want to make a drug bust, you need to be at the Soundside Yacht Club at 10:30."

"Huh? What? Who is this?"

"Doesn't matter. Just come, and stay out of sight. A drug sale is going to happen on a boat named *Bliss*."

Sam looked at the caller ID. It was a pay phone. He strained to listen. The little voice was too flat to be spontaneous. It was like someone reading their lines in a play for the first time.

"This is for real."

"Come on, kid, I don't have time for this."

"Mr. Harris, please come. You have to be there."

He shook his head. Who was this? The voice was suddenly edging toward desperation. It reminded him of his own daughter when she was a middle schooler. Usually the desperate voice was followed by a bucket of tears.

"OK."

"Stay hidden or the deal won't happen."

Click.

The chief immediately sat down and started to write everything he remembered from the conversation. Then he called the phone company with the number from his caller ID. It was a pay phone across the street from the Seagull Inn.

Should he take this seriously? It might be a prank.

But if he didn't show up and it was real, he'd miss his chance to make a bust.

He decided to go. It would be worse to miss an arrest.

He checked his watch. He had thirty minutes. He'd better get going if he wanted to arrive unseen. But where would he put his vehicle?

He locked the station and walked to the parking lot. He decided to take his old Bronco. He still had a police radio in it, and it would be easier to be undercover in his four-wheel-drive.

But just as he was climbing in, he had another sobering thought. He touched his holster as the acid rose in the back of his throat. *What if it's a trap?* He shook his head. No one would use a little girl for a trap.

Would they?

⚭

Ike walked down the hall and touched Travis's door. It was locked. Middle schoolers like their privacy. He smiled to himself, remembering how excited Travis had been at the news about Andy Cunningham. He'd been worried about Travis's relationship with Adam. He knew Travis adored the man, and Ike had been concerned that Travis might be confused if a role model didn't believe as they did.

He walked softly down the stairs to see the dim light of the lamp beside Beth's favorite leather lounger. "Not sleepy?"

Beth smiled. "It's too early. Besides, I don't think I could sleep if I tried."

"Are you having pain from your surgery?"

"Not much." She laid her novel aside. "But it's not my surgery or the results that have me wide awake."

Ike grinned. "Andy Cunningham?"

She nodded. "Isn't it exciting?"

"Sure is. I thought he'd come around." He walked to the kitchen. "Want some hot chocolate?"

"I'm OK." She followed him and sat on a bar-stool. "Have you seen Travis?"

"I think he came in from being at Kristy's while I was in the bathroom. His door is locked. I think the poor boy is whipped."

"I guess the excitement had the opposite effect on him. It woke me up."

"Me too."

"Must have pooped him out." Beth's brow furrowed. "What do you think will happen to Andy?"

Ike set the teapot on the stove. "I don't know, baby. He could be in a lot of trouble."

"I've never seen him like he was tonight. All through supper he joked with Travis like he didn't have a care in the world. I've never seen him so peaceful."

Beth looked off toward the sound of the ocean, which penetrated the house through the screen-door at the back of the den.

Ike touched his daughter's hand. "You like him, don't you?"

She looked around until her eyes met his. "I guess I should hate him for what he did. He lied to me. Could I ever trust a man who did that?"

"But he didn't have to fake his feelings about you. They came as naturally as the sky is blue. Anyone could see that."

Beth looked down. "I know. He's the same man who rescued me, the same man who paid so much attention to Trav when he was floundering, the same gentle man who seemed to hang on every word I said . . ."

"But he did lie to you."

"I know."

"He's got some things to set right."

"He's a man, Daddy. He's ready to face the music for what he did. He's not afraid to admit his wrongs."

"Don't be so quick to trust him again. Give him some time to grow a little. See what change is lasting after all the dust settles."

"I'll be careful, Daddy."

"I'm not sure I understand something. Why, if you knew about his charade, did you let him operate on you again?"

Her jaw slackened. "I did this for you. I knew you didn't want to risk any more delays. I was all set to tell you what he'd told me the morning before my surgery, but when I saw you walking out, carrying my overnight bag, I just didn't think I could back out. I thought I'd upset you."

"Me?"

She nodded slowly and shrugged. "I knew from personal experience and from the OR staff that he was an excellent surgeon."

"Beth, you—"

"Don't worry about it now. He did a good job. I came through the surgery without any problems."

Ike yawned. "You should have been more worried about yourself than about your crazy old man."

She reached for his hand. "You're not crazy."

Beth watched as her father began to pace in silence around the room. "Are you as concerned about him as I am?"

He nodded.

Beth went on, "I'm uneasy about this deal his attorney worked out. With Winters and Fiori about to leave, it doesn't seem to give Andy enough time to help expose the fraud."

Ike put his hand over his heart. "I know. I have an uneasiness in my soul about his situation. It's like I'm overjoyed about his salvation, but as the evening has progressed, my heart is burdened for him."

"I feel it too."

"He's in danger. Or maybe it's just the legal problems he is confronting. I'm sure he'll be facing trouble."

Beth nodded as the teapot began to whistle. Ike poured the steaming water into a cup and emptied a packet of hot chocolate into it.

"I'm going to my room to pray. I haven't had a burden like this for a long time."

Greg sat in his police Jeep Cherokee and watched the employee parking lot. Winters had been inside for a while. Soon after he had arrived, Greg watched as Travis Carlson pulled up on his bicycle. He rode across the parking lot, then disappeared behind the hospital. Greg lifted his binoculars and stared at the spot where Travis disappeared, wondering if the hospital had a back entrance. After that, the surveillance action slowed. The only interesting thing that had happened since then was that Gerri Fiori sauntered by, and she wasn't dressed for the office. She wore a white halter top and shorts and carried a large gym bag. Boy, she was a looker.

He sighed and rolled down the window. The night was muggy, and the asphalt parking lot beneath him still radiated heat. He picked up a *Muscle* magazine from the passenger seat beside him. He flipped through the pages, looking at the ads for protein drinks and exercise equipment. Gerri Fiori would never go for a guy like him. He twisted his wedding band. *I shouldn't be thinking this way.*

He sipped a Styrofoam cup of lukewarm coffee. Watching Winters hadn't turned out to be much fun. He radioed Dan, who informed him that Cunningham was still at home.

A minute later he saw Jim Manning, the FBI agent, walking across the lot dressed in a pair of khaki shorts and a flowered shirt. Something was up. He wanted to appear like a tourist.

He pulled up his binoculars and studied the agent as he stood at the information desk. He appeared to have an earpiece. *He must be wired to listen to something. Or someone. Maybe he has Winters's office bugged.*

The FBI just comes in and take over. Well, the Serenity Police will show them who can solve a crime.

He kept his binoculars to his eyes as Gerri Fiori came back out the front entrance. Her gym bag was bulging. He followed her long legs across the parking lot, then lost her in the blur as she came too close. He was still looking around the front of the hospital through the binoculars when he felt a tap on the arm.

"On a stakeout, Greg?"

He jerked his head back and put down the binoculars. "Hi, Ms. Fiori."

"Ms. Fiori? Since when do we have to be so formal?"

He felt his cheeks flush. "I'm just being polite."

"Who are you waiting for?"

He clenched his jaw. "No one in particular," he lied.

"I'll bet you were waiting for me," she said, smiling.

"'fraid not." He tilted his head toward her gym bag. "What's in the bag?"

"Just some things I needed from work."

"You must have a lot of work to do."

"I can handle it."

"I'll bet you can."

He watched as her jaw dropped.

He followed her gaze. "What's up?"

"It—it's Dr. Tyson. I didn't expect to see him back here for a while."

"You didn't hear?"

Her free hand played with a small necklace above her halter top. "No."

"He was released this afternoon."

"Did he make bail?"

"Are you kidding? He's a free man."

Her mouth dropped open.

"That's right. The charges were dropped."

"Dropped?"

"Sure." He studied her for a moment. The news seemed to distress her. "Something about new evidence clearing him."

"I thought the newspaper article made it sound like you had a pretty solid case against him."

"Evidently not," he replied. "Are you OK? You look a little pale."

"I'll be OK. I guess I was just a little unnerved by seeing Dr. Tyson." She leaned over, resting her arm on the door, allowing her necklace to dangle onto Greg's arm. "He scares me. I think there is more to him than he lets on."

"Oh yeah?"

She nodded. "Just a feeling I get when I'm around him. That's why I wasn't surprised at all to hear he'd been arrested. Didn't surprise me a bit." She checked her watch. "I'd better get going. Nice to see you again."

She walked away from him, but not from his gaze. He enjoyed the view and twisted his wedding band again. He had to watch her. After all, it was part of his assignment.

∽

Kristy said good night to her parents at 10:10 and nervously waited until her sister Rachel's breathing turned deep and regular. Then she slipped from beneath the covers and stripped off her pajamas, already clothed for the night's adventure. She tiptoed into the bathroom and closed the door before turning on the light. There she tried to duplicate her makeup job from earlier that evening, adding bright red lipstick and mascara.

She primped before the mirror for a moment and found herself wondering what it would be like to kiss Travis. She leaned forward toward her own reflection until her nose gently brushed the cool glass surface. She backed off teasingly, imagining herself giggling a little. Her heart rate picked up just imagining such behavior. In actuality she thought she'd be so nervous, she might hurl. She approached the mirror again and whispered, "Oh, Travis" as she slowly and gently pressed her lips to the mirror. Her fantasy was fine until she opened her eyelids. The image of her own eyes so big and staring back at her snapped her back to reality. She pulled away quickly and looked at the red lip-print on the mirror. She imagined writing Travis a note to give him as she left at the end of the summer. That would be the perfect time to plant her first kiss on his lips. As long as her mom wasn't hovering around to watch. Or worse yet, Rachel would be wedging herself in between them.

She doubted she could ever bring herself to actually do it. But maybe she could write him a note and seal it with a red lip-print like the one in the middle of her mirror. She wiped it with a generous swath of toilet paper, smearing the print sideways and down until it looked like a large frown. The print was superimposed over her own image as she looked at herself in the mirror, making her look like a circus clown. She wrinkled her nose and continued wiping the stubborn lipstick. She winced as her vigorous wiping made rhythmic squeaking noises. The last thing she needed was to wake her little sister. She flushed the T.P., not wanting to leave the evidence around for her mother to see.

Then she turned off the light and slowly pulled open the door. She crept across the room and unlatched the door before she remembered that she needed money. She'd saved two hundred dollars for this summer at the beach and hadn't spent it on anything except a new beach towel. She wanted to buy Travis a shark-tooth necklace but hadn't found the right one. She retrieved her money from the bottom of her underwear drawer and shoved the wad of bills into her front pocket. It wasn't enough to make a real drug deal, but she hoped it would look like more if she kept it in a wad. Besides, if everything went as planned, she would take the drugs, hand her the cash, and run away as the police moved in.

The last thought gave her pause. What if the police didn't believe her? Would she be arrested for possession of drugs? That thought quickened her already-pounding heart more than her thoughts of Travis. She would be the disgrace of her family.

She slipped into the damp night air and peeked into her parents' room. A dim light burned. She clenched her teeth and checked her watch. Ten-fifteen. It was now or never. She'd just have to sneak away and hope her parents didn't have any excuse to go to her room.

She dropped to her knees and crawled below her parents' windows, then stood up and scampered to the stairway. She dusted off her knees and walked across the parking lot to her father's van. There she retrieved a beach-bag, which she emptied of its contents. She wanted to look ready to take whatever Ms. Fiori would give her. Then, jumping on her bike, she headed down the street toward the Soundside Yacht Club.

∞

Travis Carlson was thankful when he saw Mr. Winters pull his Mercedes into the hospital parking lot. It wasn't going to be too easy to follow him anywhere else. He pumped hard to keep up, cut diagonally across the front parking lot, and hid his bike in the bushes near the employee entrance. Unfortunately, it took him ten minutes to find the administration offices. He passed the only open door and to his delight, it turned out to be Winters's. He quickly passed the office and ducked into what appeared to be the old back entrance to the cafeteria kitchen before some sort of renovation. The main entrance to the food lines now came in from a parallel hallway in the front of the hospital. Travis had eaten there many times while his mother was in the hospital.

He rested with his back against the wall, wondering just what kind of ridiculous plan this was. Just what was he expecting to do? The best thing would be to march right in there and repeat Kristy's story. Ask him if he could buy drugs to sell. He leaned out from the small alcove, his heart beating fast. But how could he convince him? What if he knew him from seeing him around his mother's room?

Travis moved slowly back up the hall and knocked once on the outer door-frame just as sharp footfalls behind him caused him to turn around.

"That you, Gerri? Come on in, babe."

Travis whirled around. Someone was coming! He quickly crawled behind the receptionist's desk and tried to slow his breathing. A moment later he heard a female voice.

"Hey. Ready to go?"

"I've got to meet someone."

"I thought you quit your job."

"You know me. Always time for one more meeting."

Travis listened to what sounded like kissing noises and a soft, "Ooooh."

"You make me want to leave now."

"I have one more meeting too."

"What's up?"

"A final drug sale. I think I have a few Oxys left in my locker. I came to clean them out."

"I wish we'd never started that business. It's the one part of this I regret. I don't mind stickin' it to the government, but drugs, well—"

"Dave, these kids would just buy it from someone else. If they're going to party anyway, why shouldn't they buy it from me?"

"I guess."

"How's Liz?"

"She must have seen it coming. She's hired a pricey divorce firm to clean me out."

"Can they do that?"

"She can only get what she knows I have. I'll give most of that up with a perfunctory fight. She knows little about my offshore investments. They are in my name."

She raised her voice. "You don't think—"

His voice was stronger in response. "She can't get it." He sighed. "I'm sorry, babe." He paused. "How about you? Any regrets?"

"You know."

"Crawford?"

"He was a nice guy. Too bad he had to be so inquisitive."

"Accidents happen."

"I know it was an accident. But a jury wouldn't see it that way. You pushed him. You didn't mean for him to slip."

"Let's forget that, OK? Tonight should be the night we leave our troubles behind. I'll see you on the boat as soon as my business is over."

"OK," she responded softly.

More kissing noises. These guys acted like goofy teenagers.

"I'll see you in a little while."

Travis waited until her footfalls receded before slipping out from beneath the desk. Now what should he do? Andy was right. Dr. Crawford's death and the drug business were linked! He couldn't wait to get back and talk to Andy or call the police to tell them what he'd heard.

He moved to the hall, where he again heard footsteps. Hurriedly, he moved back to the alcove at the old back entrance to the cafeteria kitchen. When the sound was loud enough, he risked a glance around the corner to see. Andy!

What was he doing here?

He flattened himself against the wall. As long as Andy didn't come down the hall past the office, Travis wouldn't be seen. He snuck another peek and saw Andy enter the office.

Oh great, now what do I do? He slipped up the hall and stopped short of the door-frame. From there, he ought to be able to hear everything . . .

"Sit." It was Winters's voice. "Cigar?"

Travis listened to the two men talk, and terror gripped his heart. He couldn't believe his ears.

CHAPTER

28

TEST ONE TWO three four five." Adam Tyson spoke in a regular voice so Jim Manning could adjust the sound volume on his earpiece. He took the hospital elevator to the fourth floor, which housed the administrative offices. He checked his watch. Winters should be waiting for him.

He walked past the empty receptionist's desk through the open door leading to Winters's office, where he could see the administrator sitting behind a large teak desk. Winters was in casual clothes— a shirt open at the collar and a blue baseball cap emblazoned with *Bliss*. He was smoking a fat cigar and lifted a second out of a small desktop humidor for Adam.

Winters didn't say hello, only, "Sit." He pointed to the chair. "Cigar?"

Adam nodded. He rolled the tobacco stick between his fingers, then pulled on it sharply while Winters held up his lighter.

"It's Cuban."

Adam nodded, looking around the room. It was strictly Williamsburg decor. The pictures were all portraits of Civil War battles, and the sconces on the wall appeared to be wrought-iron candleholders. On the corner of his desk sat a long, white clay pipe, its bowl resting in a clay ashtray.

"This had better be worth my while," Winters said mechanically. "I'm leaving town within hours."

"Then I won't bore you with details." He leaned forward. "I was a friend of Mark Crawford."

He studied Winters for a response. There was none. Winters

seemed relaxed and leaned back to blow thin, blue smoke in the air above his head.

Adam continued, "We met at the American College of Surgeons conference in New Orleans. We used to compare notes, talk about the differences in our practices, his in Serenity, mine in Southern California."

Winters nodded. "So?"

"We continued our friendship over the years. He even invited me out to Serenity for a vacation, so I could see how his practice ran." Adam paused. "We complained together about insurance companies and getting the shaft by Medicare."

Winters's jaw clenched around his cigar.

"When I was injured in a skiing accident, I lost time on the job. I had rotator cuff surgery and had constant pain." He looked down. "That's when my problems with narcotic addiction began."

The administrator leaned forward. "Look, Tyson, I don't have time for rambling confessions here. We talked all about your record when we reviewed your application to join our staff. You assured me that was all in the past."

Adam held up his hand. "It is. Crawford reached out to me, offered to give me a place to recover. Then he opened up to me about what was going on in Serenity. Some of his patients had contacted him about bills for surgeries that hadn't been done." He paused. "It wasn't too hard to figure out what was happening. I contacted Medicare myself and found out he'd billed for over eight hundred procedures last year." He offered Winters a thin smile. "So I became very interested in Serenity. Crawford confided in me that his wife was clueless, but he needed a friend for advice. He told me he was going to approach you about the evidence he was gathering." He lifted the cigar to his mouth and pulled in the fragrant smoke. "And that's when my friend disappeared."

He watched as Winters's top lip quivered.

"I was in a bad way by then. I started padding my Medicare bills, adjusting codes here, adding another there, always careful to keep up the documentation in case of an audit. But my drugs ruined everything. I had my license suspended, lost my reputation and my practice in California. My drug habit had left me in financial straits. I'd spent everything. I needed a new start, a place where I could rebuild my retirement nest in a hurry." He pointed his cigar at Winters. "That's when I realized Serenity would be the perfect place for me." He stood and pretended to examine the oil painting of a Civil War battlefield. "Except that my experience with Medicare billing would make Serenity even more profitable." He turned to face Winters. "I'm sure that together we can easily double what you were turning with Crawford."

"You don't know anything."

"I know enough."

Winters shook his head. "Don't waste my time."

"With me in the loop, I can screen out the patients who have enough savvy to question their bills. We can concentrate on the ones with Medicare supplements who don't pay a dime for their care, so they won't question the amounts their carriers pay."

"I'm leaving Serenity, doctor. My game is over."

"Help me then."

"Help you?"

"Tell me how you did it. Help me refine the process."

"It will cost you."

"It will cost you if you don't cooperate." Adam chomped on his cigar. "I'd be glad to talk to Mr. Manning about what I know."

"You'd be cutting your own throat."

"Don't be so sure. I can win either way. Whistle-blowers can take in a lot of money when they uncover large government losses through fraud." He held up his hands. "Help me and I'll turn your operation into a gold mine. Refuse and I'll blow the whistle on this whole little haven of yours."

Winters sighed. He was a beaten man. First his wife's threats, now Adam's. He looked up and cursed Adam to his face. "There's a special place reserved for people like you."

"Make sure you tell them I'm coming."

The administrator clenched his teeth. "All we did was identify Medicare patients who had visited our ER during their vacations to Serenity. Then we duplicated the medical records, copying the histories and exams of legitimate patients from our past records, making a new file under the patients' names. We submitted bills for everything: hospital stay, anesthesia, surgery, even pharmaceuticals for the patients with prescription cards."

Adam smiled. "OxyContin, no doubt."

Winters nodded. "Someone else took care of that for me."

"Fiori."

At this point Winters didn't even flinch. His guard was down. Way down. "Yes. The pharmacy didn't know we weren't dealing with real patients. They filled the prescriptions and tubed the drugs up to the ambulatory surgery center, where they were quietly retrieved by Gerri. She took care of them from there."

"Nice setup. Insurance pays for them, you pocket the money, then sell them again on the street."

"I didn't like that part. I didn't mind squeezing what I could get out of the giants—the insurance companies and the government. They've been milking us out of every penny they could for years. But the drugs, well . . . that bothered me at first."

"But . . ."

"But Gerri showed me how much she was making. And she wanted to team up with me." He looked at Adam, their eyes meeting in a moment of trust between men. "Who could resist a woman like that?"

"I'm not blaming you. Take what you can get. Life's too short."

Winters almost laughed. "Really." Then, almost in a moment, his countenance changed, as if he suddenly realized how vulnerable he'd made himself. His face tightened. His gaze was steel. "Don't even think about double-crossing me, Tyson."

"Or?"

"You'll regret it, that's all."

"What? Say it. I'll end up like Crawford?"

"What, now you're accusing me of murder? Rather ironic considering what the police think of you."

"I'm accusing you of nothing. I just know my friend was on to you. And then he disappeared."

"I had nothing to do with that."

"I'm not accusing you. Crawford is probably sunning himself in the Caribbean right now."

"What are you talking about? They pulled his body out of the Atlantic!"

"That's what everybody thought." He sat back down and puffed on his cigar, waiting for Winters to respond.

"What? What do you know that everyone else doesn't?"

"How do you think I'm sitting here right now? The Serenity Police are idiots."

Winters shook his head. "How did you get out? You never told me."

"The charges were dropped. They jumped the gun on arresting me. It just so happens that they got the DNA report back on the body right after they brought me in. As it turns out, the body isn't Mark Crawford's after all."

"That's ridiculous! How—" Winters stopped.

"Don't ask me how. The working theory at the moment, according to their witness, is that the body was just a cadaver. Some body dumped by a local hospital or maybe even a medical school to avoid paying for an expensive disposal."

"That's bull! You're lying!" Winters stood and pointed at Adam.

"Easy, easy." Adam's face was an icy cool. "Why should you care?"

"I—I don't." He shook his head. "It—it's just that I wouldn't believe the police. They've messed this up so much—"

"You know something."

He didn't respond.

"Crawford knew too much, didn't he?"

The administrator clammed up. "Get out of here. I've told you what you wanted to know."

Tyson stood up, slowly retreating as Winters walked around his desk, pumping his fists.

"I don't want to see you again. And don't even think of crossing me. I'm done, you hear me? I'm done. I can't do this anymore!"

"I'll pick up where you left off."

Winters snapped. It was as if the regret, the anger, his embarrassment at being exposed, and his confession all boiled up in a volcano ready to erupt. He grabbed the back of the chair Tyson had occupied just moments before and hurled it against the wall. "Get out!"

Tyson backpedaled quickly into the reception area, slamming the heavy wooden door closed behind him. His heart was pounding as he turned and ran down the hall.

∞

Travis hurried back to the entrance to the kitchen when he heard the crash of furniture.

Great. Winters is going ballistic. Andy alias Adam is really a crook, and I'm stuck in the hall. If he sees me and knows I heard his secrets, I'm dead meat.

He took a deep breath. He needed to get to a phone, to call the police so they could pick up Winters before he took off. And he needed to talk to his mother about Andy. *Boy, have we misjudged him! What a snow job he's doing! I thought he was giving up surgery. All that talk to my mom was pure baloney.*

He snuck a look as Andy dashed down the hall. He stepped out into the hallway and paused, not wanting to follow too closely behind.

Inside the office, he heard Winters utter a curse, then the thump of furniture.

Then he heard Winters leaving his office. He jumped back into the recess at the back entrance to the kitchen.

He's coming this way! Travis tried the door behind him and breathed a sigh of relief as the knob turned. He slipped into the kitchen. The light from a streetlamp shone dimly through the window, illuminating a large room with empty counters and several large steel sinks. It appeared to be abandoned. There was a solitary door on his right.

The door behind him squeaked. Winters! Panic! There was no place to hide. The sink? He pulled open the door on his right, an old walk-in freezer of sorts. *Odd, it's still freezing in here.* It was now or never. The freezer was empty except for an old tarp on the floor.

He let the door close behind him. It was dark and cold. He felt for a handle on the inside of the door, tracing it with his fingers. He listened. He heard the door close, footsteps . . . then silence.

The handle began to move. Winters was on to him! He dove to the floor, groping in the dark for the tarp. Maybe if he covered up in it, Winters wouldn't see him. He heard the door open. He closed his eyes and began to pray.

∽

Winters picked up the overturned chair, then collapsed into it, his face falling into his hands. He cursed. *What is going on? I paid that jerk to dispose of Crawford's body. If the DNA test shows it's not Crawford, who is it? Where did he get it? And what did he do with Crawford? Maybe he didn't even do the job I asked him to do. I'd better check for the body and dispose of it myself.*

How could things get so messed up?

He rubbed his temples and stood up. He looked around his office, decided to leave his books, turned to leave, then lifted one photograph from his desktop, a picture of him and his son on a deep-sea fishing trip. He dropped the picture into his briefcase and closed the door behind him. Then he walked down the hall and into the old kitchen. He paused, letting his eyes adjust to the dim light. He slowly pulled open the freezer door, letting the light fall onto a rolled-up tarp on the floor. Crawford's body!

Winters cursed again. Just wait until he got his hands on that kid! The administrator weighed his options. He could leave the body there, then risk the suspicions that would come when some hospital employee found it. It wasn't too likely they could link the body to him—he looked at his hand on the door—unless they checked the place for prints and connected it to him that way. He cussed, this time loudly, before hoisting the body over his shoulder. Crawford was a little man, fortunate for Winters.

He would leave the back way, hide the body in the bushes, then go out front for his car.

∽

Manning unclipped the wire from the inside of Cunningham's shirt. "Good job. I think you and Ms. Winters ought to be in Hollywood."

Andy smiled.

"I've got to run. I want to see if Winters goes for the body. If he does, I can bust him right there." He paused. "Why don't you hang out at my car? I'm sure Winters will have a few choice words for you when I bring him down."

"Great."

The agent ran for the back stairwell. He ran two flights, slowed, and took the steps two at a time for the third and one at a time, even slower, on the fourth. He stopped at a right-angle bend in the hallway and glanced around the corner. His jaw dropped as he saw Winters pulling a tarp from the back entrance to the kitchen.

Incredulous, he pulled his head back and leaned against the wall. What should he do? Bust him? What was Winters dragging? A body? Does he think this is Crawford? He shook his head, trying to figure the possibilities. He didn't understand. What was going on around this crazy place?

Following the administrator unnoticed through the hospital was not hard. Winters made enough noise grunting and bumping the body around that for the most part, Manning just walked along, staying one corner behind him.

On the stairs it was nearly comical. The tarp slipped, landing on the stairs with a thud. At that point Winters was on the flight below him, and it sounded as if Winters had given up lifting his prize and had decided to drag it down the stairs. He pulled it through a back door, and just as Manning was reaching the door handle, the door swung back toward him. He backed against the wall and watched as Winters ran frantically up the hall, away from the agent, never pausing to look back. Something had spooked Winters big-time, and he wasn't wasting any time.

Manning smiled and gave chase. This was better than pushing papers any day.

∞

Beth rose from her chair and slowly ascended the stairs. She paused at her son's door and listened. Normally, she could hear his heavy breathing through the door. But not tonight. There was complete silence.

He wouldn't mind if she woke him. She was so excited about the change in Andy, and yet burdened at the same time about the future.

She hadn't had time to talk with Travis earlier, due to his insistence that he visit Kristy as soon as dinner was over. She tried the door. It was locked.

She knocked softly.

No response.

She knocked again, more forcefully this time.

No response.

"Trav?" She paused, pressing her ear against the door. "Travis? Wake up, honey. I want to talk to you."

She shook the doorknob, trying to suppress a rising dread. "Travis!"

Ike walked from his room into the hall. "He must be bushed."

Beth shook her head. "Something's wrong. He wakes easily. Maybe he's sick."

Her father shook his head. "I was a teenager once. He wasn't sick at supper. He's probably out with Kristy."

"He's never done that before." She walked to her room and returned holding a key. She looked at Ike. "If he's not sick, I'll kill him."

She opened the door and snapped on the light. No Travis, only his sleeping bag partially unrolled and placed under his bed blanket.

The window was half-open. She pushed it open and leaned out. Travis could easily walk onto the low roof line outside his window and climb down onto the back deck.

"He's dead meat," she whispered.

"Calm down," Ike responded. "I seem to remember you doing the same thing when you wanted to visit Amy Fowler."

"I did no—" She stopped. "You knew about that? Why didn't you punish me?"

"I called Mrs. Fowler. She told me you were practicing a skit to perform at my surprise birthday party." He shrugged. "I knew you were safe." He pointed at her. "But I did expect you to fess up at the party," he continued, his eyes narrowing. "But you never did. You just lived on, having no idea that I checked your room every night an hour after you went to bed for a year."

She smiled. "I'll call Cheryl Thomas," she said, checking her watch. "I hope 10:30 isn't too late."

She looked up the number for the Seagull Inn and dialed. "I need the room for Nick and Cheryl Thomas please."

The phone rang once, twice, three times before a male voice picked up. It was thick with sleep. "Nick Thomas."

"Nick, this is Beth Carlson, Travis's mother. I'm terribly sorry to call you at this hour, but I'm concerned about Travis. Is he with Kristy?"

"Kristy?" His voice was slow and dull.

"Your daughter."

"Oh yes, of course. She's sleeping. Travis can speak to her tomorrow."

She feared he was about to hang up. She raised her voice. "Nick!"

"Huh?"

"Travis isn't here. Can you check Kristy's room?"

"What? Umm . . ." She imagined him sitting up, stretching. "OK. Give me a minute."

She waited. And waited. She heard Cheryl's voice. Then Nick's. He was calling Kristy's name. She heard a door slam.

"She's not here. They must be together."

"Travis has never done this before."

"Well, neither has Kristy!"

"Oh my, I'm sorry—I didn't mean to imply that it was her fault, Nick. I'm just not accustomed to dealing with this."

"It's OK. Listen, I'm going over to the pier. I heard Travis talking about night fishing. Maybe they went there."

"I'll meet you there." She whispered to Ike while covering the phone, "Kristy is missing too. He thinks they are at the pier."

"OK, Beth. And relax. The children belong to the Lord. As soon as I hang up, I'll pray."

"Thanks."

She laid down the phone.

Ike was putting on his windbreaker.

"Where are you going?"

"I'm driving you. You just had surgery. You shouldn't be driving." His face was set, determined.

"Yes, Daddy," she said obediently. Then, as she descended the stairs, she muttered, "I'll kill him."

Then she began to pray.

∞

Greg Monroe picked up his radio. "Dan, Winters is on the move. Cunningham and Manning are in a vehicle together. I think they're following him."

"Why don't you follow too?"

"On my way. Everyone of interest seems to be leaving the hospital."

He followed Winters's Mercedes toward the back of the hospital. He slowed, headlights off, and pulled over to a stop beside a large metal dumpster. Winters had popped his trunk and was getting out.

Greg slipped from his Cherokee and peered from around the dumpster to witness the administrator dragging a rolled canvas of some sort out of the bushes beside the employee entrance. Then he hoisted it into the back trunk with a grunt.

The deputy's eyes widened. It sure looked like a body. He hustled back to the jeep and radioed his chief.

Sam replied with a whisper, "Harris here."

"I'm watching Dave Winters. It looks like he just hoisted a body bag of some sort into the trunk of his Mercedes."

"Follow him. Manning told me that Winters's wife informed him that Winters was leaving tonight on his yacht. I suspect that's where he's heading."

"10-4, boss. I think Manning is on him too. And he's got Cunningham with him."

"Showtime. I'm already at the yacht club. I got a tip about a drug sale. So far all I see is Gerri Fiori unloading groceries onto the boat." He paused. "Uh oh. Here comes a girl. Gotta go. Over."

CHAPTER
29

TRAVIS OPENED HIS EYES to complete blackness. *I'm blind! I can't see! Where am I? What happened?*

He wiggled, straining his arms and legs. He was wrapped in a cold blanket, and his head pounded. He tasted metal. He licked his lips. Blood. His own. His hands were cupped up to his face and he felt his own breath, hot and moist. The material restraining him wasn't tight. He worked his hand up behind his head and explored a lump the size of a peach. His finger felt a jagged cut. He moaned, and the sound reverberated in his head as if his ears were stopped up.

Slowly a memory returned. The hospital. Listening to Andy. Hiding in the cold place. Then he remembered hiding in the tarp, being carried. By Winters?

He listened to the gentle throbbing of an engine, smelled exhaust, and worked his right hand above his head and out the top of the tarp. He felt a short, matted carpet and realized he was in a trunk. Travis thought about the conversation he'd overheard between Winters and Andy. *Andy told Winters that the body wasn't even Crawford's. He must think I'm Dr. Crawford. He's going to ditch my body in the ocean!*

He tried to focus, tried to discern the speed of the car or their direction. It was hopeless. He had no idea how long he'd been out. He could be in Georgia for all he knew.

He took inventory. His head was cut, his hair matted with blood. His neck and elbow were sore, either from the position he'd been in or from whatever had busted his head. *He must have dropped me.* He wiggled his toes and ankles, but the tarp prevented much movement of his knees and hips. The car swayed gently, stopped, and started again. The motion made him sick. His stomach was empty, and the taste of blood and the knot of fear in his gut didn't help. He felt a little like he'd just ridden a roller coaster at the state fair.

He concentrated on making a plan. He would have to stay in the tarp until Winters opened the trunk. Hopefully he would be left alone long enough to unroll and escape. If all else failed, he would make moaning noises to freak them out. Lazarus returns!

There was another noise, faint music—the car radio or a CD. He strained his ear, hoping to hear the time. He hadn't worn a watch all summer and only now regretted it. If he knew what time it was, he could figure out how long they had been traveling, and roughly how far they had gone.

He listened again. The engine noise revved and slowed. Unless Winters was a goofball, this wasn't an interstate.

He wished he had a weapon. *Maybe I can get the tire iron!*

The car slowed again and lurched like they went over a speed bump.

He began to pray.

⟨⟩

Kristy turned into the Soundside Yacht Club entrance and slowed her pace to ease her pounding heart. But exercise had little to do with the thumping in her chest. She stood, lifting her leg until both feet were balanced on one side of the bike for a few feet before she jumped to the sidewalk and steered her bicycle into the bushes where she paused to question her sanity. *What if the police don't come? I'd better get the drugs before I give her my money.*

She crawled from the bushes and wiped the freshly cut grass from her knees. The Soundside Yacht Club property was well-groomed, including a manicured median on the main drive to the piers. Richly mulched groupings of azalea bushes and a few weather-beaten palms dotted the roadside and median. Kristy stood and listened to the high-pitched symphony of frogs and cicadas. Although the night was cool, she wiped drops of sweat from her forehead.

She walked along, adopting an attitude of teenage cool. She chewed her gum, nervously snapping it by blowing little bubbles, the sound insignificant in the night noise at the water's edge. Feeling her wad of bills for the third time, she rehearsed her lines. "You got the stuff?" She imagined she'd look more convincing if she was smoking. She'd never tried it. She didn't want to. But if she ever went undercover and it was part of the job, she thought she might do it, but not inhale.

In her nervousness, she began to hum, squinting at every bush and tree to see if she was being watched by the police. There certainly weren't any vehicles nearby.

She came to the end of the pavement, a cul-de-sac with a small parking lot to the right and a bulkhead with wooden pilings to the left. In front of her, three piers extended into the water. The one on the right was covered by a high overhead copper roof that connected with a boat repair and tackle shop. Yachts, mostly sailboats, were located in the slips to the right and left of each pier.

She passed a set of gas pumps and hummed the theme song for *Gilligan's Island*. She had just gotten to the part about a three-hour cruise when she heard the squawk of a group of seagulls, fighting over the remains of someone's fish cleaning. The noise raised the hair on the back of her neck and seemed in a weird way to predict trouble. She imagined it to be the screams of adults busted in a drug raid. *Freeze! Police! We're busted! Ahh! Ahh! Ahhhh!*

Suddenly a wave of nausea hit. She couldn't do this. She took a deep breath, a mistake, it turned out, because the air close to the first pier was thick with the smell of fish guts. She grabbed a piling and lost her supper into the dark water below.

Oh, God, what am I doing?

She prayed a simple prayer. A prayer for strength and the grace to do what she thought was right. She felt better after barfing and stronger after praying; so she resolved to find the right boat and get this over with. Near the second pier was an S.U.V. with the back hatch open. It was then that she saw Gerri Fiori.

She nodded her resolve and resumed the casual attitude of a druggie.

It was time for action.

∞

After talking to his deputy on the radio, Samuel Harris raised his binoculars and studied the young girl walking toward the pier. It was then, for the first time, that he wondered if he should have had backup. He hadn't taken the threat too seriously, thinking it may have been a prank of some preadolescent with mischief on the brain. But now, studying the girl, a young teen trying to appear old, he wondered if a real drug deal might be going down. Maybe another girl was ratting on a schoolmate she detested. He felt his Glock semiautomatic and trained his ears on the conversation about to unfold.

The young girl spoke first. "Did you get the stuff?"

Gerri Fiori nodded. "You can come up here."

The girl obeyed, stepping over several portable gas tanks and onto the side of the pristine sailing vessel.

Fiori was drinking beer from a green bottle. The teen stopped on the back deck of the boat and put her hands on her hips. "Well?"

"It's in here," Fiori said, motioning for the girl to follow her through a door.

The girl shook her head. "Out here."

Fiori appeared to be upset. She shook her head and disappeared.

The girl paced and turned around with her hands up mouthing, "Don't shoot me." She repeated this in several directions.

Sam wasn't sure what to make of this. Maybe she knew he was there. He thought about standing up, revealing his position from behind a Jet-Ski. But he didn't want to risk being seen by Gerri. He'd been wanting to bust up the Oxy traffic on the beach for a long time. This might just be the break he'd been waiting for.

Gerri came out holding two pill bottles. She held them up.

The girl looked surprised. "That's all?"

"One hundred pills. Fifty each. That's two thousand dollars," she said, holding out her hand.

The girl reached into her pocket and cast a glance over her shoulder. A car was coming up the road, slowing at the cul-de-sac.

"Don't worry. He's with me."

The girl nodded. "Here it is," she said, holding up a wad of bills."

Gerri motioned. "Here. In my hand. I want to count it."

"Not before I have the Oxys."

"You'll run."

"Do you want to do this or not?"

"I want the money." She grabbed the girl's arm, scattering the money onto the deck. The two women dropped to their hands and knees in a scramble for the bills.

"You little tramp! This isn't enough."

"Take it or leave it," the girl screamed, standing to her feet.

Gerri's attention was drawn to the parking lot.

The girl turned to follow her gaze.

Sam did the same, daring to crouch in order to see.

It was Winters! Sam watched as the trunk lid opened and Winters grunted to hoist a rolled tarp into his arms, then knelt to position it over his shoulder. Greg was right. It sure looked like a body bag. Sam hoped Greg was close behind. He might need a hand real soon.

∞

"He's stopping." Andy took his own pulse. Without time to get an accurate count, he estimated his rate easily over one hundred.

Jim Manning nodded. "You'd better go with me." He pulled off the road a hundred yards from the piers and stopped behind an azalea grouping.

They ran, crouching below a line of bushes in the median.

Andy jogged behind the agent, wishing for the first time in his life that he knew how to handle a weapon. The last thing he'd shot was a Super-Soaker water gun when he visited his nephew back in California.

They stopped behind the gas pumps and watched as Winters unloaded the trunk.

Andy whispered, "I'd sure like to see what's in that tarp."

"It sure looks like a body. But this is too freaky. What is he thinking?"

"He must think it's Crawford."

"Why didn't he look?"

"He's not thinking. He was in a complete panic when he left the hospital. He's probably freaked out over the failure of his little plan." Andy squinted at the tarp to get a closer look. "I wonder what is in there."

"Whatever it is, he dragged it out of the freezer."

"Maybe it's a bunch of frozen chicken wings." Andy laughed nervously.

"Let's see if we can get a closer look." Jim scrambled to a new position behind a palm.

Andy crawled beyond him to kneel behind a pier piling.

Jim called for Andy's attention and pointed. "Pssst."

Andy looked behind them to see Greg Monroe dashing from tree to tree, then nodded back at Jim. "We've got company," he whispered.

He turned his attention back to the yacht where Gerri Fiori stood. It looked as if she was upset with a young girl. The girl looked familiar. Maybe he'd seen her at the beach. He watched as Gerri walked to the back of the boat to see Winters. The girl then retreated away from Gerri and knelt behind a cushioned chair. Winters stumbled forward across the deck and out onto the pier with the tarp. Then, with one final grunt, he dropped it onto the back of his sailboat.

Gerri looked distressed. "What are you doing? What is that?"

"What do you think it is? The little druggie you recommended for our last job didn't do what he was paid for!"

"You're crazy."

"The police did the DNA studies on the body that was found. It wasn't Crawford." Winters jerked his head in the direction of the young woman crouching behind the chair. "Who's she?"

Gerri smirked. "Nobody."

The girl stepped out from her hiding spot. "Give me the Oxys. I couldn't quite get all the money. I'll pay you the rest when I make my sales."

"I'm not running a charity." Gerri held up a single bottle. "You can have one."

Jim told Andy, "Time to move."

Andy followed Jim into full exposure on the pier and smiled as Gerri shoved the drugs into her pocket.

Jim Manning opened his wallet to expose his badge. "Good evening. I believe we've all met before," he said as if he were starting a board meeting at a corporate headquarters.

Winters's mouth opened, and he moved to the far side of the yacht as Jim and Andy took their positions on the pier beside the boat slip.

Andy nodded. "What's in the tarp, Dave?"

"Just a sail cover."

"Really? Mind if I take a look?"

Winters stepped forward. "Stay where you are." He pointed at the FBI agent. "You need a search warrant."

From the shadows, Samuel Harris appeared.

"Mr. Harris," Jim responded. "What brings you out on a night like tonight?"

"I was about to make a drug bust until you interfered."

"Sorry about that, but we were just talking to Mr. Winters about his cargo here. It seems he's found himself a body."

Winters straddled the tarp. "Ridiculous."

Samuel Harris stepped aboard the vessel.

Winters's eyes were wild, darting between the FBI agent and the police chief and Gerri and back to Andy. "Get back, Sam," Winters yelled. "You need a search warrant to look at anything here!"

Andy hitched his thumb in his belt. "You think you've found Dr. Crawford, Dave?"

The chief snorted and spat in the water over the back of the boat. "What's up with you, Tyson? Mark Crawford's body is in the morgue."

Andy smiled. "Why do you call me Tyson? Adam Tyson has been dead for six months. My name is Michael Cunningham. I'm just here with the FBI to figure out how Mr. Winters makes so much money."

Winters looked at Gerri and backed away, edging closer to the edge of the boat. "What are you talking about?"

Harris reached for the tarp. "It seems no one knows who anyone is." He pointed at Andy. "First he's Dr. Tyson. Then he's not. Someone thinks this is Dr. Crawford, but this can't be him." He yanked at the edge of the tarp, unrolling a body onto the floor of the sailboat.

The young girl screamed. Andy jumped onto the boat and knelt over the apparently lifeless body of Travis Carlson. "Travis!" He placed fingers on his neck. Feeling a pulse, he knelt closer and whispered, "Trav?" He watched as Travis quickly opened and shut his left eye. It was a wink, a sign saying, "I'm OK." Andy looked around. No one else had seen the subtle message. He straightened up and stared at Winters. "Wasn't Crawford enough? Is this your latest victim?"

The young girl slumped to the floor, knocking the remainder of a six-pack of imported bottled beer off a glass tabletop. Beer and glass exploded in a fizzy mess at Gerri's feet.

Gerri Fiori screamed, "Get off the boat!"

Andy lifted his eyes from the girl to see Gerri leveling a pistol at Samuel Harris's chest. She cautiously stepped forward until she was almost standing over Travis.

Andy started backing away, when Fiori screamed again. "Start the boat," she commanded, glancing at Dave. Then, looking at Andy, she added, "Take the girl with you."

Andy nodded, praying under his breath. He started to walk up the pier beside the boat to get the girl. *I've got to do something quick.*

At that moment Travis let out a ghastly moan, something deep and mournful, increasing in volume and pitch to a piercing scream. His eyes were open, and his hand darted to Gerri's left ankle, yanking it forward.

Gerri gasped with shock and lost her balance as she pulled her foot away from the resurrected corpse. She slipped on the beer and threw her hands in the air, losing her grip on the pistol.

The gun hit the deck as Travis and Mr. Winters scrambled to claim it.

Mr. Winters won and pointed the gun back at the police chief, who struggled to free his gun from its holster.

Andy watched as Winters's hand trembled, his fingers white around the pistol grip. Winters screamed, "Leave it alone, Sam. I'll shoot."

Sam lifted his hands in the air.

Andy traded glances with Jim, who had retreated in the confusion behind a pier piling where he was hidden from Winters's view. Jim lifted his gun to show Andy and signaled him silently toward the back of the yacht. Andy moved slowly toward the sheriff, keeping his head down and his eyes on Winters, whose total focus was on the police officer.

Suddenly Winters jerked his gun toward Andy. "Hey, hold still!" He pointed the gun toward Travis who was crawling away from him on the deck of the yacht. "That's right, boy. Get off this boat and everyone will be OK."

With Winters's focus on Travis, Sam Harris dropped his hands toward his holster again. Unfortunately, the leather cover pulled free with a snap, which attracted Winters's attention.

Winters's eyes widened like a caged animal, darting first right and then left, evidently in search of the FBI agent. He lifted his lip in a snarl as Fiori struggled to her feet. He pointed the pistol at Sam. "Drop it!"

"Shoot him!" Fiori screamed.

Winters's index finger started to close as Andy dove toward Harris, taking him down to the deck behind a small dinghy. The crack of gunfire filled the air. One shot, then a second, and then silence.

Andy felt a rush of warmth in his abdomen and slid his hand onto an expanding sticky red circle on his white shirt.

He looked up as Winters's body snapped back, over the railing, into the water, blasted in the chest by a bullet from Manning's gun.

Jim Manning rushed Gerri, ordering her to the ground, his revolver pointed at her head.

Andy felt faint. The chaos of activity around him seemed surreal. Travis knelt over the girl, calling her by name. "Kristy, Kristy."

Gerri Fiori cursed as Jim pulled her hands behind her and snapped the handcuffs in place. She pointed at Andy with her head. "You fake!"

Sam Harris grunted and pushed himself out from under Andy. "Cunningham's been shot," the chief said. "Someone call 911!"

I've been shot? He felt cold and was suddenly aware that his throat was parched.

Andy struggled to press his hand against the entrance wound in his abdomen. Strangely, he sensed no pain. He squinted at Sam, Travis, and Jim and thought about his life. His surroundings blurred.

Travis's voice sounded distant. "Andy!"

Andy felt an overwhelming need to sleep. The last thing he remembered later was thinking, *I wonder if this is what it feels like to die.*

⬯

Beth Carlson's stomach tightened in a knot of anxiety. Kristy and Travis weren't in the motel lobby, the fishing pier, the public beach, or the Dairy Freeze.

Ike lifted his head. "Did you hear that?"

Nick Thomas nodded. "Probably some kids shootin' off fire-crackers."

"Where could they be?" Beth shoved her hands into her pockets and yawned.

"Let's check back at the motel. They could be back there for all we know."

"I can't help thinking that they're in some kind of trouble. I think we should call the police."

Ike protested, "They won't even pay attention until they've been missing for at least a day."

"I want to call home. Maybe they're at our house."

Nick nodded. "Let's call from the motel. It's closer."

The trio left Ike's truck parked at the fishing pier and rode in the van back to the Seagull Inn.

Then, as they were climbing out of the van, the distant wail of sirens began. It was faint at first, then unmistakable.

"Listen," Beth said.

A moment later a rescue squad raced by on the beach road.

Beth's eyes met Nick's. "I've got a bad feeling about this. Let's follow the ambulance."

Nick glanced at Ike, who nodded his agreement. Nick shrugged. "Let's do it."

They jumped in the van and followed without speaking, each in thought. Beth prayed for the son she feared was in trouble.

Nick drove the speed limit, then five miles per hour over, then ten, but the rescue squad pulled ahead into the night.

Beth breathed a sigh of relief when she saw the brake lights go on. The squad turned left toward the sound.

"He's heading into the Yacht Club," Ike said. "Serenity's wealthiest."

Soon the squad came to a stop next to a Mercedes parked with its rear to the pier, trunk lid open. Beth strained her eyes to see a group of people on a yacht. "It's Travis. I see Travis!"

Nick skidded to a stop, and the trio jumped out and ran toward the boat. Nick was in front, jogging quickly to Travis and Kristy. Beth and Ike weren't far behind. Nick raised his voice, looking at his daughter. "Kristy?"

"Daddy!" she said, collapsing in his arms.

Beth's eyes went from Travis to the body lying on the deck of the boat, surrounded by paramedics. She moved around to see and then collapsed to her knees beside Andy. Blood, too much blood, was on his clothing and the boat around him. A male paramedic managed an oxygen mask, and a female started two large-bore IVs.

"What happened?" She leaned close to his face. "Andy . . . Andy—can you hear me?"

His eyelids fluttered. Recognition?

She shook his shoulder. "Hang on, Andy, help's here."

The beeper on Andy's belt sounded. Beth unclipped the pager, which was sticky with blood. She looked at the number. It was a code for an emergency in the ER.

"BP's sixty," the male paramedic shouted. "Did you get the ER?"

"I told them to page the surgeon. They said they'd have him meet us there."

Beth shook her head. "Don't you know who this is?"

The paramedics continued the resuscitation without speaking.

"This is the surgeon! Don't take him to Broward County. They don't have another surgeon."

"W-what?" the paramedic shouted. "Radio Duke or Greenville. Tell them to send a chopper to pick him up right here at the scene."

Jim walked forward with Samuel Harris and the deputy, Greg Monroe. He touched her shoulder and helped her to her feet.

"What happened?" she asked.

"We confronted Winters and Fiori. She freaked and pulled a gun. Travis there knocked the gun from her hand. Winters got to it first and tried to shoot the police chief."

Greg Monroe spoke up. "I arrived right at the end. I saw Winters pointing his gun at Sam here," he said, nodding to his left. "Then Dr. Tyson tackles the chief just as Winters squeezed off a shot." He nodded his head. "He took the bullet for the chief."

Suddenly Beth felt very weak. Travis slipped next to her and put his arm around her waist.

"You've got a lot of explaining to do, boy," she said before taking his face in her hands and kissing his cheek.

They watched as the paramedics squeezed in IV fluids and covered Andy with warm blankets. It was twenty minutes before he began to come to. By then the second liter of IV fluid was in, and the sound of helicopter blades grew from the western sky.

Beth stayed back while the paramedics worked, clutching the neck of her blouse, pacing on the pier.

When they loaded Andy on a stretcher and started to carry him to the air-evac chopper, she pushed through the rescue workers to grasp his bloody hand.

He opened his eyes, his lips twitching at the corners as a quick smile. "I love you, Beth Carlson," he whispered. Then his eyes were shut, and the team pulled him away and loaded him into the helicopter.

"Where are you taking him?"

A paramedic in a blue jumpsuit who looked too young to drive lifted his head. "Duke University Medical Center."

She watched him disappear, first the white and blue of the Sikorsky chopper in view, then a silhouette, then a flashing red light that dimmed to an orange star and then vanished.

It was only then that the dam was released. She stood in the cul-de-sac of the road clutching her son and began to cry. She was confused. She felt the confliction of love, anger, and hurt. This was the man who had saved her life and brought joy back into her family. This was the man who had lived a lie behind a false identity, and now she was just supposed to receive him back because he confessed that he loved her?

Deep sobs overtook her, cleaving her soul, as she turned to her father and collapsed in his aging arms.

CHAPTER
30

TWENTY MINUTES LATER Beth, Ike, Travis, Kristy, and Nick joined Cheryl, Nick's wife, in the parking lot of the Seagull Inn. It was midnight, an hour befitting a hearty snooze, but for this gang, sleep was the farthest thing from their minds.

Beth looked at her watch. "I want to go to Duke."

Ike added. "Not alone you don't."

Travis rubbed his head. "I'm going."

Beth lifted her hand to his matted hair. "I want to check out this wound first. You've had a concussion. I'm not sure you should go."

Ike disagreed. "If he goes home to sleep, someone will have to wake him every hour to check on him. He might as well go along."

Kristy stepped forward. "I want to go too."

Cheryl frowned. "Don't you think you've caused enough trouble for one night?"

Beth smiled. "I don't mind. Really. We'd love to have her. She can help keep me and Travis awake."

"Can you drive that far so soon after your surgery?"

Beth nodded. "Ike can do the driving. And I'm only a little sore. I can help out if I'm needed."

Nick laid his hands on the shoulders of Travis and Kristy. "We'll deal with the consequences of your actions later. Just because Mr. Cunningham may need our support right now doesn't mean we've forgotten what you did."

Kristy looked at Travis, then at her father. "Yes, sir."

"OK," said Beth, "let's get cleaned up. I'll make sure this one doesn't need stitches," she said, putting her arm around Travis. "Can we be ready in half an hour?"

The group nodded.

Cheryl offered, "I'll make a thermos of coffee."

"Better take a few things in case we need to stay a day or two."

Nick took Ike, Travis, and Beth back to her van.

During the ride back to the house, Ike and the Carlsons were silent. Beth tried balancing her relief that Travis was OK with her disappointment and growing fury at her son's stupidity.

Five minutes later, with Travis sitting on a chair in the bathroom, Beth cleaned his matted hair with hydrogen peroxide and a long black comb. Progress was slow going.

"You've got a bad cut." She leaned closer. "Kind of a little cross, really. But it's flapped back together, and it's not bleeding, so I think you'll survive without stitches."

"Ow! Don't pull so hard!"

"I have to. Your hair is caked with blood." She teased at a tangle.

Ike stuck his head in the doorway. "You could always buzz it."

"Yeah, shaved heads are in."

"Mom!"

"OK, OK, hold still. We're getting it."

Ten minutes later Beth stood back. "There. Now go change your shirt and get your toothbrush. I want to pack some snacks."

The van pulled back into the Seagull parking lot ten minutes late. It was now nearing 1 A.M. After a short prayer for safety, Nick sent them on their way, remaining behind with Cheryl and Rachel.

On the trip, Ike and Beth heard the unedited version of "teenagers undercover."

Beth shook her head. "Weren't you scared you'd be arrested?"

"It was all supposed to be on video. But then Ms. Fiori insisted that Kristy come to the boat at night." Travis beamed. "Hey, we've still got the video of Kristy on Ms. Fiori's porch." He looked over at Kristy. "I'll bet your dad will enjoy seeing it."

"I'll be grounded for a year. I'll be lucky if he brings me back to Serenity next summer if he sees that." She stuck out her tongue. "I think your mom would like to know about your recycling documentary!"

Beth sipped her coffee. "OK, smart boy, time to come clean."

Travis squirmed. "Well, you see, I was taping the video from across the street behind a fence that hid the garbage cans. When the owner pulled in and asked me what I was doing, I told him I was doing a school project on recycling."

"Travis! You lied!"

Kristy imitated him. "A recent study revealed that the United States wastes enough aluminum to build an aircraft carrier. Could I have your name for my study, sir?" She giggled. "You should have seen that guy run for the house."

"Did you guys ever stop to think how much danger you could have been in?"

"I never thought it would end up like this," Kristy responded.

"Me neither." Travis said. "Boy," he added, shaking his head, "I was so mad at Mr. Cunningham when I heard what he told Mr. Winters. I thought he was really interested in scamming the insurance companies. I thought what he'd said to you was a big fat lie."

Beth smiled. "He must have done a good job of acting."

Travis laughed. "I'll say. It wasn't until Mr. Winters threw me down on his yacht and I heard Andy tell his real name that I realized he must have just been yankin' Mr. Winters's chain."

Ike glanced over from the driver's seat. "I was sure taken in by Andy's Adam Tyson charade. I never suspected he wasn't legit."

"We all were." Beth looked back at Travis. "You'd better let me give that video to Mr. Manning or Mr. Harris. It might be important evidence to convict Ms. Fiori."

"See," Travis responded, "it wasn't so stupid after all."

"It was stupid," Ike said. "But it just might be helpful stupidity."

They stopped at Rocky Mount for gas and snacks. Kristy was on the verge of sleep.

"Maybe we should stop somewhere to sleep," Ike said.

Beth offered to drive. "I want to keep going."

"What's the rush? You know he'll be in surgery a long time. And after that, he'll be so sleepy that he won't be able to talk."

"I know."

"Then why don't we stop?"

Beth pulled the van back out onto the highway. "I want to be there, that's all."

"It won't do him any good if we're a bunch of zombies."

"I want to see him alive. Then we can get a motel and sleep. Why don't you lay your seat back and catch a few winks?"

"Can you stay awake?"

"I bought more coffee."

"Why don't we call ahead and find out how he's doing? Then we can all rest."

"I'd rather just keep going," Beth insisted.

Her father threw up his hands. "OK, OK. You just want to see him."

"Yes," she responded, casting him a sideways glance.

Beth set the cruise control and flipped on the high beams, unwilling to explain her desire to press on. She thought about the words Andy had spoken before falling unconscious again. *I want to be the first thing he sees when he opens his eyes.*

∞

Pain. He tried to open his eyes, but things were blurry. He tried to take a deep breath, but a knifelike agony prevented him. He tried to speak, to call for help, but air would come to him only in shallow gasps. A vise tightened around his chest. The searing anguish turned every breath into a struggle of marathon proportion. It would be so easy to stop breathing and die. There was noise, loud noise, drowning his weak attempts to speak.

"His pressure's down again. I can barely feel a pulse."

"No breath sounds on the right. The bullet must have passed his diaphragm into his lung."

"Give me a chest tube."

"Betadine."

Cold fluid poured across his chest, chilling him.

"Knife."

"What about lidocaine?"

"He won't feel a thing. He's unconscious."

Torment, a sharp, stabbing pang in his right chest. He tried to pull away.

"Hold him down."

I'm being killed. Someone is killing me. He tried to remember. *Winters?*

Another sharp pain in the chest, followed by a gradual easing of the vise. He inhaled, slowly, more deeply than before. *Someone must have cut the band from around my chest.*

"Mr. Cunningham?" The voice was female, screaming into his ear.

He opened his eyes. A nurse perhaps. "Where am I?"

"You're in a helicopter, on your way to Duke University Medical Center."

"What happened?"

"You were shot."

Andy tried to lift his head to see.

"Don't try to move," she yelled above the noise. "You were struck in the abdomen, but the bullet traveled through your lung as well. You have a chest tube in place."

"Chest . . . tube," he repeated slowly, starting to understand what he was sensing. He'd put dozens of them in others but had never been on the receiving end.

He looked up at a tangle of IVs and a plastic bag of blood. Over his head to the right was a cardiac monitor. His rate was 140.

"His abdomen is getting bigger."

"Give more blood."

"Give the trauma team an alert. We're on the ground in ten."

Andy closed his eyes and searched his memory. He'd been talking to Jim Manning. Travis was dead. Maybe he was shot. No, he was in a tarp.

Travis scared Gerri. Winters shot Police Chief Harris.

He looked at the flight nurse, a woman about thirty with beautiful auburn hair sticking out from under a headset. "How's the police officer?"

"Fine. You jumped in the path of the bullet."

"I don't . . . remember."

"You're a hero."

"Not . . . me." He felt sleepy; his eyelids were lead. "Did they catch Winters?"

"The FBI agent shot him. He won't be bothering anyone anymore."

Andy understood. He yielded to his fatigue and closed his eyes.

I should be afraid. But for the first time, I'm not afraid to die. Jesus, I'm ready.

Peace. Unconsciousness.

∽

Beth flipped the pages of the magazine without inspecting the colorful images. Instead, the words and pictures blurred as she stared at the pages unseeing. Her mind was far from the articles in her hand. She cared only for the patient beyond the double swinging doors, the doors that proclaimed "No Admittance" to anyone even thinking about entering the operating rooms beyond. Michael Andrew Cunningham had been under anesthesia for two hours now, supported by the efforts of the operating team and their prayers.

Ike sat across from her in the crowded waiting room, his head bobbing as he surrendered to sleep.

Travis and Kristy were the only ones fully alert. They had walked the halls exploring the areas of the University Hospital open to visitors and now sat playing a game of chess on a small magnetic board. "You took your hand off. It's a move!"

Kristy protested, "I was just thinking."

"A move's a move."

Beth caught her son's eye and gave him a subtle shake of the head and a wink.

"Uh, but I guess it would be OK for you to take it back if you were just thinking," he added.

Beth smiled and twisted in her chair, feeling the tug of the incision under her left arm. She hadn't taken any pain medication since leaving Serenity, and she was beginning to regret it. But if she took it now, the drowsiness from the medication might send her over the edge into sleep, and for now she wanted to be alert, so she could be the first to see Andy after surgery.

After another hour a surgeon wearing a long white coat over a pair of blue scrubs approached the edge of the room. "Anyone waiting for word about a Michael Cunningham?"

Beth quickly stood and tapped Ike. "Daddy, the surgeon's here."

She tried to read the man's face. Pleased? Upset? She wasn't sure. He looked more tired and perhaps hungry.

He held out his hand. "I'm Dr. Slater. You must be Ms. Cunningham."

His hand was smooth, soft. "Just a good friend."

"He lost a lot of blood. The bullet passed through the upper part of his liver, passing first through his lung. The good news is, he'll have a full recovery."

Relief flowed over her like refreshing water. She took a deep breath and felt the tension in her back and neck begin to evaporate. She hugged Ike and Travis and thanked the doctor. "When can I see him?"

"He'll be in the intensive care unit. Give the nurses some time to get him settled in. Someone will be out to lead you in when it's appropriate."

Thirty minutes passed with agonizing leisure. Beth filled it with pacing around the room and drinking a cup of lukewarm coffee from a vending machine.

Finally Beth was led to his room, a well-lit suite with high-tech monitors displaying vital signs and light blue walls and a bed with high metal rails. Andy appeared to be the hub of a large wheel, the spokes made up of IV tubing, oxygen tubing, cardiac monitor lines, a nasogastric tube, a urinary drainage tube, a chest tube, and tubing leading to inflatable bladders to squeeze the venous blood in his legs. He was swollen, his eyelids looking like those of a fat drunk. His color seemed good to her, better than when she'd last seen him in Serenity.

She had been ready for a thousand other bad scenarios she'd grown to expect from her nursing training. She'd envisioned paralysis, a colostomy, feeding tubes, or worse. So in spite of his swelling, he looked much better than she'd feared. She approached his bed and took his hand. "Andy?"

His eyelids fluttered.

"Andy, it's me, Beth." She paused, squeezing his hand again. "You're at Duke University Hospital. You were shot in the belly. You had surgery." Another squeeze and a trickle of a tear down her cheek. "You're going to be OK."

Andy's breathing was regular, like someone in a deep sleep. She looked over her shoulder at his nurse.

"He hasn't responded yet. The anesthesia is still wearing off."

Beth understood and slid a chair closer to the edge of the bed, so she could sit and hold his hand. She watched his chest rise and fall and listened to the blipping of his heart monitor. In a few minutes she stood and wiped his forehead. "Andy."

His eyes opened into shiny slits between his puffy lids. He squinted.

"Andy, you're in the hospital. You had an operation. You're going to be all right."

"Beth," he whispered.

She brushed his cheek. "Don't try to talk. Just nod. Do you remember being shot?"

A single nod. He understood.

She put her face close to his. "Do you remember what you told me before they took you away in the helicopter?"

His eyes closed a moment. Then two. Then he opened them and nodded. "I . . . love . . . you."

"You passed out, and they took you away." She sniffed and wiped her eyes with the back of her hand. "I was afraid you would die."

His voice was thick and slow. He shook his head. "For the first time in my life . . . I was at peace with that . . . I wasn't afraid to die."

Beth squeezed his hand. "I'm glad you didn't."

She listened as the constant blipping of his heart monitor quickened. She looked at him. "Does it happen like they say? Did you see your life pass before your eyes?"

"Something like that." He paused. "My biggest regret was the fool I've been." He searched her eyes. "I'm so sorry for the way I misled you."

She held her finger up to her lips. "Don't."

"I need you to know. The best part of my life has been meeting you. I know you didn't know my real name, but I never faked the way I acted or felt around you."

She nodded silently.

"Can you ever forgive me?"

She dabbed the corner of her eyes. "I think so."

"What are you doing?" His nurse approached, carrying a clipboard. "His heart rate is up." She looked at him. "Andy, are you in pain?"

He shook his head. "No."

Beth watched as the nurse checked his urine output and adjusted his IV.

The nurse frowned and studied his cardiac monitor. "Tachycardia could be a sign of bleeding," she said, pushing a button that inflated an automatic blood pressure cuff.

The blood pressure reading was normal, yet his heart rate stayed above 110.

"I'll have to notify your surgeon. We will probably need to check your hematocrit." She nodded decisively and left the room.

For the next few minutes Beth sat beside his bed, her hands folded in her lap. She watched as his heart rate slowed again into the eighties.

Then she leaned over him again, this time watching the monitor. She touched his hand and whispered, her lips grazing his earlobe as she spoke, "I'll give you one more chance."

His heart rate spiked to 120.

"I've never had this effect on a man before."

"Oh, I bet you have," he said. "But they were never on a cardiac monitor."

She smiled. "Neat. Now what should I try?"

"I'm going to report you to the state board. You've used me as a guinea pig in your experiment."

She folded her hands across her chest. "Report me and I'll never whisper in your ear again."

Andy's nurse returned and cast a worried glance at the monitor. "I need to draw your blood," she said, stepping in front of Beth. "You'll have to wait in the waiting room while we work."

"Do you have to do that?" Beth asked.

"The surgeon said I should if his heart rate stayed up."

Beth raised her eyebrows. "I tell you what, why don't I leave for a while, and if his heart rate isn't normal in five minutes, then draw the blood."

The nurse's eyes narrowed. "Why?"

Beth shrugged. "He's smitten."

∞

That evening Ike took Beth, Travis, and Kristy out for Mexican food before they crashed at their motel. With two double beds, Grandpa

Ike and Travis took the one closest to the bathroom, and Kristy and Travis's mom had the other.

Within minutes of lying down, the adults surrendered to the bliss of sleep, and for Grandpa Ike, the regular, deep, sonorous snoring. In the darkness, Travis squinted toward the other bed.

"Pssst."

Kristy's eyes opened, her pale baby-blues glistening in the dim light streaming around the nearly closed bathroom door.

This was new, fun, and exciting. Travis had never slept in the same room with a girl besides his mother. And though he was exhausted from missing sleep the night before, his heart quickened with the drama of the moment.

Their eyes met across the narrow divide between the beds, each resting with their heads upon their pillows.

Travis winked.

She responded in kind.

Wink the right eye. Wink the left eye.

Kristy followed his lead.

Two winks with the left, then one with the right.

She imitated exactly.

They played their silent game as a smile crept over Kristy's face.

Travis thought he had never seen anyone so beautiful.

She closed her eyes.

Don't sleep, Kristy. He yearned to see her wink at him again.

Her eyes remained shut, the smile receding from the corners of her lips.

"Psst."

She didn't respond.

Travis sighed quietly. Kristy was going to sleep. The only time he'd had a chance to gaze into her eyes until dawn, and she was going to sleep.

And then, across the space separating them, she stirred. The edges of her blanket wrinkled and rose as her fingers appeared and wiggled to celebrate their freedom. A wave perhaps?

Her movements froze for a minute, then, barely perceptibly, her whole hand emerged, then her wrist, forearm, and elbow, and then her upper arm. He watched as her hand extended in the dim light toward his bed. She held it in the air over the abyss between them.

She wasn't asleep.

He slipped his hand from beneath the warmth of the covers and out into the air toward Kristy's.

They bumped, touched again, and then her index finger traced a serpentine pattern on his palm and wrist, finally coming to rest as their fingers intertwined.

His heart leapt. Her eyes remained closed, her face a vision of peacefulness.

For a long time, they lingered, hand in hand.

Some time later Travis awoke to realize he had drifted into a deep sleep with dreams of holding her hand. He opened his eyes, felt the cool air on his arm and hand, still clasped in hers. He moved his fingers, awaking new sensations of her smooth skin against his.

He gently squeezed her hand.

She answered in kind.

Then they slowly wiggled free, withdrawing their hands across each other's until only their fingertips touched. Then, one by one, they separated until only their index fingers touched.

Then she withdrew her hand, placing it against her lips, her eyes never opening. He did the same.

Heaven. Serenity.

Travis slept unmoving until morning.

CHAPTER
31

AL BELL SPENT THE coming weeks in and out of the state's attorney's office, in and out of the Serenity Police building, and on and off the phone to Jim Manning and his superiors. Plea-bargaining. Negotiating. Compromising. Offering a new deal.

The most fun was tracking down the small multitude of patients Andy Cunningham had operated on during his tenure as Adam Tyson, M.D. The scenario repeated itself over and over on the porches, back decks, and kitchen tables of Serenity.

"I'm Al Bell, the attorney representing Andy Cunningham."

"Who?"

"Michael Andrew Cunningham. You knew him as Adam Tyson. Certainly you've been reading about his situation in *The Outer Banks Daily.*"

"Dr. Tyson was the best doctor I've ever been to," Ms. Shifflett said, folding her hands across her ample waist. "I used to get sick ever' time I ate fried oysters. I'd vomik ol' bile juice ever' time." She lifted her T-shirt to point at her little scars. "Dr. Tyson took my gallbladder out, and now I can eat anything I want."

"That's nice, Ms. Shifflett. But you understand, he wasn't really a qualified surgeon. Mr. Cunningham was only pretending to be a surgeon."

"He was the nicest doctor I've ever met. He sat down and talked with me like he really cared."

"That's nice. I have some papers I'd like to show you. Would you be willing to sign a paper giving up your right to sue Mr. Cunningham for treating you without a medical license if I can arrange to have the money you spent for surgery returned to you?"

"Sue?"

"That's right. I'm suggesting that I get your money back and you in turn will agree not to sue Dr. Tyson, uh, Michael Cunningham, my client."

"I would never sue him."

"Do you understand he didn't have a medical license to practice medicine?"

Ms. Shifflett took a deep breath and closed her eyes for a moment, concentrating real hard. Then she pushed herself back from the table and pointed at a pile of breakfast dishes. "You know how long it's been since I could eat bacon?"

Al tried not to smile. "No, ma'am."

"I'd get that ol' green gall up in my throat. I'd be sick for hours over one little slice of bacon." She nodded her head and laid her finger against a mole on her cheek.

Al had been trying not to focus on it, but now with Ms. Shifflett playing absentmindedly with the hairs sprouting from its surface, he had to turn away.

Ms. Shifflett continued, "And sausage? My goodness, I'd be sick for a day if I tried to eat sausage."

"Ms. Shifflett, I understand you are very grateful for what my client did for you. Can I have your signature promising not to sue Mr. Cunningham or the hospital if I can get you your money back?"

"My husband's Ford needs a new muffler."

"Maybe I can help."

"I'd never sue Dr. Tyson. I took him a nice plate of brownies after he took my gallbladder out. Back in Weyers Cave, Virginia, I won a contest for my brownies."

"I'm sure." He slid the paper across the table and pointed. "Right here. I just need your signature."

"My first name is Donnalynn, all one word. I don't have a middle name, only two first names all run together like. My father made it up. He always just called me Donna."

"Right here, Donnalynn. Just sign the paper, and I'll be on my way."

She concentrated on each letter. "I want it to be neat."

"It's just fine. I'll try to get you a refund for your expenses."

"My grocery bills have gone up since my surgery, 'cause now I can eat fried foods again. Used to be I'd vomik bile and—"

The image of Donnalynn bending over a porcelain commode brought a queasy feeling to Al's stomach. He snatched the paper away and shoved it in his briefcase. "Thanks for your time. I'll let myself out."

"Say hi to Dr. Tyson for me. Tell him I'm gettin' along just fine."

Al retreated onto the porch and into the salt air, pausing to take a deep breath and look at his "To Do" list. It was time for a visit to Samuel Harris.

∾

Serenity's police chief was a harder sell than most of Cunningham's surgery patients.

"I need you to talk to the prosecuting attorney. The state office is willing to plea-bargain, but I'll need you behind me."

"The way I see it, we have an obligation to protect the public from the likes of con men like Cunningham."

"No doubt. No argument here. The issue is just what punishment is needed." He paused. "I've collected signatures from all his patients, except a few from out of town, and I'm contacting them by mail. Everyone is willing to let this go quietly into the past. And Beth Carlson isn't willing to press charges either. Without an upset public, it will be difficult to convince anyone that he needs a stiff penalty."

Harris pushed back from his desk. "How's your client doing?"

"He's recovering. He still has pain, and he tires easily, but he's thankful to be alive. Thankful for another shot at life."

The chief sighed. "My wife had been talking about seeing him to have her moles checked." He lifted his fingers up, indicating a small gap between his thumb and index finger. "She was that close to making an appointment, even though I told her I thought he was shady."

"Jim Manning said he took a bullet for you."

The chief ignored him. "If he'd have laid a finger on my wife, I would have arrested him for assault so fast—"

"He saved your life, Mr. Harris."

"I was about to blow that Winters away when your client tackled me."

"Winters was this close," he said, mimicking the chief's gesture, "to putting a bullet in your chest. Your deputy told me as much."

"Another moment, and Winters would have been down because of my gun, not Jim Manning's."

"Would you like a jury to hear how Mr. Cunningham saved your life?"

The chief glared at him.

Just then Deputy Greg Monroe appeared at the doorway. "Oh, hi, Mr. Bell. How's Michael Cunningham? I still can't believe that guy. He saw a gun pointed at the chief there and didn't hesitate. It was all instinct, I tell ya. That guy ought to be a cop."

Sam Harris huffed.

"Come on, Sam. Just talk to the prosecuting attorney. The feds are going to drop the fraud charges against him since he helped deliver Winters and Fiori. Two private insurance companies have agreed to do the same as long as all their costs are reimbursed by Mr. Cunningham and the hospital. And the administration has agreed to that and more. They are willing to pay interest charges as long as the insurance companies will agree not to sue."

"I don't know—"

Al leaned over the chief's desk and lowered his voice. "What my client did was wrong, Mr. Harris. But no one got hurt. In fact, a lot of people were helped. And with the reimbursements, a lot of people are getting free surgeries. And you, whether you'll admit it or not, are sitting here alive and well while my client is at home recovering from major surgery for a wound he took on your behalf."

When Harris started to object, Al continued, "Not to mention, he helped pin down the OxyContin flow in Serenity. And you got all the credit for that."

"Ms. Fiori confessed to everything."

"All on your promise to try to get the prosecution to lighten up. You're willing to cut a deal for Timmy Stevens, a druggie, and Gerri Fiori, a pusher and a thief, but not for my client?"

"OK, I'll talk to the prosecution."

"Tell them you want to preserve Serenity's image of a family place."

"I said I'll talk to them."

"Do a good job, Sam. I wouldn't want to have to explain all of this to the media. I'd hate to see those two kids getting the credit for busting up Serenity's drug problems."

Sam held up his hands. "I'll do what you want. But tell Mr. Cunningham that I won't take too kindly to any other funny business. I don't care if he jaywalks, I'll see to it that he pays for it."

Al kept from smiling. "Thank you, sir."

∽

Andy looked up from his lounge chair where he'd been reading. Beth struggled with six plastic bags of groceries and plopped them onto Andy's kitchen table. "What's with all the food?" He struggled to his feet and examined the assortment of frozen dinners, cereals, and soups.

"You need to eat. I didn't think you'd be up for much in the way of preparation."

"Does this mean you're not making me dinner any longer?"

She continued stacking the dinners in his freezer. "Not as much."

He sat on a bar-stool and slowly straightened his torso until a pain in his incision convinced him to stop. "Are you starting work?"

"No. The hospital has given me indefinite leave."

"Before you even started?"

She smiled. "Basically, yes." She sat at the table and looked up at him. "I have to leave Serenity for a while. I need to start radiation therapy soon. I've decided to go back to Richmond."

His throat tightened. "Move away?"

"Not forever. Just for my therapy. I checked out the closer places, but all of them are too far for Ike to take me every day. Cheryl Thomas invited me to stay at their place while they are here. Dr. Warren Harper can look after me, and I can get my radiation and come back here on weekends."

"What about Trav?"

"He'll stay and look after Ike. Besides, the J.V. baseball team has summer camp, and he wants to attend. And Cheryl promised to check in on him."

"I'm sure Kristy will too."

She smiled. "I'm sure. Should I worry?"

"Can I stop you?"

"Probably not."

"He's a good kid, Beth. I don't need to tell you that. I'd be awfully proud if he were my boy."

"I am." She stood and opened the pantry to put away the soup she'd purchased. "What about you? Will you stay in Serenity?"

"I'd like to stay around."

"What will you do?"

"Depends on what kind of deal my attorney can work out."

She turned to face him. "What's the next step?"

"I have to meet with the state's attorney, some key witnesses, the feds, and the local authorities before a judge. Mr. Bell has worked out a deal for me to make restitution and get probation and some community service. Then I have a hearing before the state board of medicine to see if they will let me keep my license to be a physician's assistant."

"I'll be praying."

"Me too." He leaned forward to release the tension on his scar. "When do you leave?"

"Tomorrow morning."

"Will you need chemotherapy?"

"Only Tamoxifen." She frowned. "Here comes menopause."

He nodded. He wasn't sure he could relate to what she faced. Treat the cancer and face early menopause, or not treat it and face cancer recurrence.

She opened a can of chicken soup and set a pot on the burner. "After my accident and my surgery, I found myself taking inventory a lot."

"Inventory?"

"Sure. You know, soul-searching, asking 'Why am I here?' Setting priorities."

"What'd you see?"

She stirred the soup. "I guess I took the bad with the good. I believed God allowed the bad in order to do something He couldn't accomplish any other way." She lowered her voice. "I started thinking that maybe we would never have gotten acquainted otherwise. I saw Travis, how my accident affected him, how I saw him starting to change into a little man instead of a boy." She sniffed at the soup. "I came to Serenity because I thought I was losing him. Without his father, he'd started to drift. I know he blamed God. He refused to love Him because of what He'd allowed to happen to his father."

"Did you find what you were looking for?"

Her eyes met his. "I think so. What about you? What were you looking for, Andy?"

"Identity. I wasn't satisfied with who I was. I decided I could be who I wanted to be. It was a crazy idea."

"Not so crazy. Everybody dreams of that."

"I came to be Adam Tyson. I wanted respect. I wanted to be the boss, the one others looked to for answers."

"You had it. Why'd you give it up?"

"You know."

"Tell me again."

"I realized that I couldn't allow you to love who you thought I was. I knew I had to take a chance that you would hate me. And the small chance that you would love me as I really am prodded me to tell the truth."

"What would you have done if I rejected you?"

He shrugged. "I don't really know."

They stayed quiet for a moment before he continued. "I know I would have been very low. As it was, with you knowing the truth, you still wanted me to do your surgery. It was that crazy trust that convinced me that everything you and Ike had been telling me about the unconditional love of God must really exist." He lifted his hand and accepted a soup bowl. "Then, in jail, it was like I just knew. I realized that my heart had changed. I was no longer a skeptic. I knew God loved me, and I wanted to love Him in return."

"So you found the new identity you were looking for after all."

"What was that verse Nick quoted? 'If any man is in Christ . . .'"

"He is a new creation."

He nodded.

He'd found his new identity.

CHAPTER
32

Two months later Andy sat across from Beth in an exclusive restaurant on the sound. He lifted his glass. "Here's to the completion of your radiation treatments."

She lifted her glass. "Hear, hear."

Andy watched as Beth scooted the lettuce around her salad plate. "Travis's coach wants you to come back and do a pitching clinic as soon as you're able."

"I'd like that. When will you start work?"

"Next week."

"You've been through so much since coming to Serenity. Any regrets?"

She shook her head. "No."

They dined on fresh fish and shrimp, potatoes and hot bread. When the peanut butter pie arrived, Beth sipped hot coffee and looked out over the sound. "When do you have to start your payback?"

"I already have. The judge has allowed me to do some work in some boys' clubs."

She raised her eyebrows. "Like what? Aren't you too sore?"

"I'm healing fast. But I'm not doing any heavy work. Mostly just doing some anti-drug presentations. When school starts again in the fall, I can do school assemblies again, like I did in Florida."

"Do you think you'll miss being in medicine?"

"Maybe." He shrugged. "The board said I can reapply for a new PA license next year." He lifted a forkload of creamy peanut butter pie slathered in whipped topping. "Nick introduced me to a contractor at the beach church. He said he can give me work painting as soon as I'm ready to lift."

"From surgeon to painter."

"It's fine with me. For now I'm just enjoying not having so much of my identity wrapped up in my job."

"This pie is too rich." She pushed it away. "You'd better let me pick up the tab. At least I'm going to be starting work next week."

"No way. This is my treat. I'm the one who asked you to celebrate."

"How can you afford this? I thought the judge made you give everything back."

"He did. But I sold my vehicle."

"Not your truck!" She frowned. "It had such character."

"Not the truck. I might need it for my new job, you know?" He smiled. "I sold the white Cadillac."

"Sam Harris finally released it to you?"

"Yep."

Andy paused and stared across the table at the most beautiful woman he'd ever seen. She returned his gaze, unflinching. "What?" she asked. "You're staring. Didn't your mother teach you that's impolite?"

He didn't feel like answering. Instead, he dared to ask a question of his own, seeking an answer he desperately needed, an answer that he knew could crush or heal.

"Is there a chance for us?"

"Us?"

He sighed. "You know. Us together."

She broke eye contact and looked away. "One time I told you that I was falling in love, but I knew it wasn't right to give my heart to someone who didn't believe like I do." She paused.

"I believe now. With all my heart."

She looked back. "Part of me would like nothing more than to fall back into your arms, to give you my love willingly, fully . . ."

He felt his chest tighten. *She's going to say, "But . . ."*

"And believe me, I want to do that, but part of me is hesitant. I want to give it time. I have to think of Travis." She smiled. "He's crazy about you. He asks me every day to ask you to marry me."

Andy chuckled. "Smart boy."

"I don't want to risk being hurt again. I know you were an excellent surgeon, even when you didn't have the paper credentials, and as stupid as it seems to me now, I wasn't afraid to trust you with my life . . ."

"But—"

"But trusting you with my son and with my heart is a different matter." She seemed to be searching his face for understanding.

He lowered his eyes to the table. He didn't want to hear the rest.

"I need to go slow, Andy. I know how you feel, and believe me, I don't want to hurt you, but I'm going to need time. I thought I knew who you were. I thought I was falling in love. I thought about you all the time." She touched his hand. "But I didn't really know you."

He nodded silently.

"I didn't answer your question, did I?"

He shrugged.

"You asked if there was a chance for us."

"So?"

She cupped her hand over his. "Yes. A good chance, Andy."

He felt the knot of anxiety begin to loosen. "So where do we start?"

"The beginning. I want to get to know the real you." She sat up straight and folded her hands in her lap. "I'll need to ask you some questions." She winked.

He straightened. "OK." He could do this.

"Who are you?"

He ate the last bite of his pie before pointing his fork at Beth. "Have you been talking to Ike?"

She nodded. "Of course. Now answer the question."

He spoke in a monotone. "Michael Andrew Cunningham."

"True, but that's your name, not who you are. Who are you? What defines you?"

He rolled his eyes at her.

"Come on, Cunningham, this is important. Shall I repeat the question? Who are you?"

He took a deep breath and smiled. It felt grand to know the answer. He'd found his real identity. "I've only recently started to understand . . ."